THE QUANTUM
MAGICIAN

DEREK KÜNSKEN

SOLARIS

First published 2018 by Solaris
an imprint of Rebellion Publishing Ltd,
Riverside House, Osney Mead,
Oxford, OX2 0ES, UK

www.solarisbooks.com

ISBN: 978 1 78108 570 7

10 9 8 7 6 5 4 3 2 1

A CIP catalogue record for this book is available
from the British Library.

Designed & typeset by Rebellion Publishing

Printed in Denmark

THE QUANTUM
MAGICIAN

To my son Joshua,
who sacrificed some of his time with me
while I wrote this novel,
because he believes in my dreams.

CHAPTER ONE

BELISARIUS ARJONA WAS perhaps the only con man who drew parallels between his confidence schemes and the quantum world. Ask a question about frequency, and the electron appeared to be a wave. Ask a question about momentum, and the electron appeared to be a particle. A gangster looking to muscle in on a real estate scam would find sellers in distress. A mark looking to cash in on a crooked fight would find a fighter ready to take a fall. Nature fed an observer the clues needed to turn the quantum world into something real. Belisarius fed his marks the clues they needed to turn their greed into expensive mistakes. And sometimes he did so at gunpoint. To be precise, the muzzle of Evelyn Powell's pistol rested on her knees as she talked to him.

"Why the long face, Arjona?" she asked.

"No long face," he said sullenly.

"I'm going to make you really rich. You won't need to scrape by with this freak show," she said, waving her hand expansively.

They sat in the gloom at the bottom of the cylinder of glazed brick that was his gallery of Puppet art. A column supporting spiral stairs and landings speared the gallery. The paintings, sculptures and silent films set in bricked alcoves had to be appreciated across a three-meter gap between the edges of the stairs and the wall. Belisarius was curating the first exposition of Puppet art ever permitted by the Federation of Puppet Theocracies. Smell, lighting and sound invoked the aesthetic of the Puppet religious experience. Far above, near the entrance to the gallery, a whip snapped arhythmically.

"I like Puppet art," he said.

"So when you're rich, buy more."

"You don't get to buy art from prison."

"We're not going to get caught," she said. "Don't lose your nerve. If it works here, it will work in my casinos."

Powell was a beefy casino boss from Port Barcelona. She'd crossed the embargo around the dwarf planet Oler to see if the news of Belisarius's miracle making the rounds in criminal circles was true. She tapped the nose of the pistol against her knee, drawing his eyes with the movement.

"But you haven't been totally honest with me yet, Arjona. I'm still not convinced you really hacked a Fortuna AI. I've seen people try. I'm paying people to try. What are the odds that you, by yourself, surrounded by Puppets all the way out here, got it?"

He let her stew in the conviction of what she'd just said for two breaths—eight point one seconds. Then, he lowered his eyes, matching her expectations, buying him another second of her patience.

"No one can hack a Fortuna AI," he admitted. "And I didn't either. I broke into a security graft and snuck in a tiny bit of code. I couldn't make it big, or the rest of the AI would notice, but this tiny change added a factor into its statistical expectations."

Powell was calculating behind her stare: the odds of this being the secret to beating the Fortuna AI, the number of casinos vulnerable to this modified graft, and what Belisarius had changed to crack the graft.

Statistical expectations were the core of the Fortuna AI. Technology had leapt so far past games of chance that any casino could rip off its patrons pretty easily. For that matter, any patron could cheat an unprotected casino. The presence of a Fortuna AI was the seal of approval on any casino. In conjunction with an advanced surveillance system, the AI monitored ultrasonic, light, radio, IR, UV and X-ray emissions. It also calculated odds and winning streaks in real time. For the clients, it was proof the games were fair. For the casinos, it was protection against cheaters.

"The security grafts are unhackable too," Powell said. "I've got people working on them."

"Not if the code-breaker is fast enough to intercept the patch during transmission, and the change is small enough," Belisarius said.

The Fortuna AI *was* 'unhackable,' in the sense that Powell meant. All AIs were, because they were grown. They could only be evolved, or patched with small grafts.

Powell considered him for a while.

"My people are close, but we don't have a system to go with it yet," she said. "Using body temperature is ingenious."

A whip sounded far up the gallery again. A recorded Puppet moan of religious ecstasy echoed softly.

"My people say you're pretty smart," she said, "that you're one of those *Homo quantus*. Is that right?"

"You've got good sources," he said.

"So what's a super-smart *Homo quantus* doing in the ass-end of civilization?"

"I reacted badly to the medications that let the *Homo quantus* see quantum things," he said. "They kicked me out. The Banks didn't want to pay for a dud."

"Ha!" she said. "Duds. I hear you. Fucking Banks."

Belisarius was good at lying. He had a perfect memory, and every *Homo quantus* had to be able to run multiple lines of thought at once. Most of the time it didn't matter which one was true, as long as they didn't get mixed up.

"Let's get this done," he said finally, pointing at the pills in her palm.

"You wouldn't be trying to poison your new partner, would you?" she said, grinning. Behind the grin was something very hard.

"Get interferon from your own sources if you want," he said.

She shook her head and popped the two pills. "My augments wouldn't let me die of a fever."

That was probably true. His brain began running dosage and toxicity calculations, accounting for the abilities of black-market augments like the ones she was probably carrying. He let one part of his brain keep itself busy with those calculations. He wasn't jealous of her ability to fight a fever, but those kinds of augments wouldn't work in him anyway.

Powell's fever would start very quickly. He'd explained the scam to her three times, so she should understand it by now. Powell running two degrees of fever wouldn't trigger casino security, but that difference would activate the statistical algorithms in the security patch. The Fortuna AI would expect her to win more, and so when she did, no alarms would go off. That was what had brought her all the way to the Puppet Free City.

"Come on," she said, her breath fogging the air. "Your gallery is creeping me out."

They walked up the helical stairs, past all the eerie displays that were so good at attracting the pattern-seeking portions of Belisarius's engineered brain without triggering deeper mathematical reactions. Complicated confidence schemes did the same thing.

The street was colder. They had a nine point six minute walk, long enough for Powell's fever to rise. The decor became slightly cheerier as they went. The Puppet Free City was a warren of sub-surface caves dug into the icy crust of Oler. Some were bricked. Some were bare ice, stained with the remains of food or drink. Many of the tunnels were poorly lit, with lumpy garbage frozen to the streets.

The Free City liked its gambling, from holes in the wall and street craps to places that actually called themselves casinos. Blackmore's was the only one with a Fortuna AI, so it attracted the well-heeled gamblers and kept its icy streets relatively clean and garishly lit. Belisarius liked the way the lurid greens and soft blues mixed and reflected off every smooth patch of ice.

Along the sides of abandoned apartments and shops, rows of mendicant Puppets stood in rudely constructed Toy Boxes and fake Cages, with their hands out. They looked like humans descended from pale Old European families, shrunken to half-size. One emaciated Puppet woman had even set herself up at a folding table with a real Cream Puff pastry, long since dried to wrinkles. Belisarius threw her a few steel coins. Powell made a face at him and kicked the folding table onto the Puppet woman, who yelled a stream of filth at them.

"Shouldn't she be thanking me?" Powell guffawed.

"That's not how Puppets work."

"You got no sense of humor, Arjona," she said as they approached the entrance to Blackmore's. Human security were scanning patrons with wands, giving the casino a grasping touch of class over automated scanning. "Loosen up."

The scan took nine point nine seconds, an eternity for his brain. He played with parallels and patterns. Money flowed through casinos in gradients, the same way energy flowed down gradients from high-energy molecules to low-energy ones. Life colonized the energy gradients: plants put themselves between sun and stone; animals put themselves between plants and decay. Criminals infiltrated casinos like vines on a tree.

Anywhere money flowed, someone would try to siphon off some of it. Even in clean casinos, convergent evolution created new people ready to try to scam either the casino or its customers. Dealers could be bought off. Gamblers could collude with casino owners. Cheaters invented new cheats. That made the Fortuna AI critical. Without the trust created by Fortuna's inviolability, the honest money didn't flow.

Powell shouldered past him. He followed her to the craps table. The boxman was one of their plants, as was the stickman. Powell and he had secretly met them yesterday in the gallery. Powell waited her turn to make her pass line bet and held out the dice to him. He rolled his eyes and blew. She smiled with her big, flushed cheeks, and rolled a seven for her come out roll. That was the easy part.

Three other players made their pass lines and picked their service bets. The stickman put Powell's service bet of a hundred Congregate francs on cornrows and moved a new set of dice to her. The dice were of Belisarius's design. They contained embedded liquid-phase nano components. The transparent liquid inside the dice underwent a conformational change with small changes in heat, weighing down the single-pip side. The dice had been under the hot white light near the boxman, and were now in Powell's fever-hot hands.

Powell rolled a pair of sixes and the watchers cheered.

The next player took the dice with cold fingers and fogged the air with her breath for luck. Sevens. She was out. The next rolled craps with a three and the watchers cheered. The last rolled a hard ten and was out.

Powell flexed her fingers, then held them under her armpits.

She jerked her chin to the stickman to keep her bet on cornrows, and twitched her fingers for the dice. The stickman slid them back. She held them between her hot hands for long seconds, closing her eyes as if praying, and then rolled.

The onlookers cheered at another pair of sixes.

Powell grinned at him. The boxman seemed to be expecting the Fortuna AI to go off, but he turned back to the table and nodded to the stickman. Belisarius made himself look happy. The dice cooled on the table, one of the advantages of a casino in a city buried in ice. The only remaining player rode out his combined bet, but rolled a nine. Out. All the attention was on Powell.

"Cornrows," she said, and passed the boxman a money wafer. The boxman's eyebrows rose in surprise. Ten thousand Congregate francs, a small fortune added to the smaller fortune she'd just made.

"Take it easy," Belisarius whispered. "You sure you don't want to wait?"

She took the dice, held them tightly for ten seconds and then rolled them against backstop. Two sixes came up. People threw their hands up in the general cheer and Powell was laughing and looking around. Then, her face froze and her hands lowered slowly.

A young Puppet priest had come up behind them. Her skin was old European pale, like her hair. She stood at eighty-five centimeters, proportioned like a human adult in miniature, but she wore armor over her robes. Forming a quarter circle on each side of her were a dozen episcopal troopers, their sealed armor giving them an extra ten centimeters of height. They levelled their rifles at Powell and Belisarius. The casino-goers slowly backed away. Some screamed and moved for the door. Belisarius and Powell were trapped.

Belisarius bolted for the back of the casino. The priest pulled a pistol and flashing, loud bangs echoed. People screamed. Along Belisarius's side, microexplosions of blood and smoke burst through his coat. He fell to the ice floor, where blood froze in an expanding pool. He looked beseechingly at Powell, but she was horror-struck as the other patrons ducked and ran for the exits. The priest and the episcopal troops ignored them.

"Evelyn Powell, you're under arrest for blasphemy," the Puppet priest said.

Powell's jaw ground and her forehead wrinkled. "What?" she said.

"Cheating in Blackmore's is blasphemy," the Puppet said.

Powell looked helplessly at the ceiling, where the Fortuna AI would have made some noise if it had detected anything underhanded in a game. She gestured upward. "I was lucky!"

Then the alarms went off, and a spotlight fell on Powell. She made soundless mouthings as one of the episcopal troopers put her hands behind her back and disarmed her. She was marched out at the end of batons and firearms. It took ninety-six seconds more for the other troopers to shoo the terrified casino-goers out and close the casino.

"Enrique," Belisarius said, rising and rubbing his hands together, "your floor is freezing."

The olive-skinned boxman hopped down from his perch behind the craps table. "Don't lie down."

Misfortunes and bad debts in the Anglo-Spanish Plutocracy had blown Enrique all the way to this armpit of civilization, where he'd gotten a job at Blackmore's. He helped Belisarius sometimes. Belisarius opened his coat to remove the device that had blown holes in it in response to the blanks. Fake blood still leaked.

"Nice work, Rosalie," Belisarius said.

Rosalie Johns-10 wasn't a priest yet. She had a year or two left in her studies as an initiate, but in a world of listless, work-avoiding Puppets, no one cared if she dressed as a priest sometimes and hired some off-duty troopers as muscle. She punched Belisarius in the arm. She couldn't reach very high, but it was the spirit that counted.

From the office, a man and a Puppet emerged. The Puppet was the custodian of the national treasure that was the holy site where Peter Blackmore had gambled. The Puppets had named a lot of things after Blackmore, but this one actually made sense. The man was an Anglo-Spanish investigator with the Fortuna Corporation. He shook Belisarius's hand.

"We never would have gotten Powell under Anglo-Spanish law," the investigator said.

"Thank Initiate Johns-10 and the Puppet blasphemy laws," Belisarius said, indicating her.

"Better yet," Enrique said, pushing past the investigator to hand Belisarius the money chip, "just thank us by getting out of the way while we split Powell's stake."

Enrique handed him his pad. Belisarius transferred two thousand francs to him. Enrique grinned. Rosalie handed him hers, and Belisarius transferred her three thousand. She had to pay the troopers, the fake businesspeople who'd helped them, the episcopate's tithe, and the officials in the Puppet Constabulary.

"You got any other jobs coming down the line, boss?" she asked.

Belisarius shook his head. He really didn't. This con had been good, distracting, but the rest of his leads were meat and potato cons on small-time targets. Nothing that would keep his brain busy. "It's slow, but I'll call you if I get another one."

The custodian of the gambling shrine gave them all a drink, delighted that the casino's reputation was going to go up for once. It wasn't the best stuff, but the Puppets were under an embargo.

Enrique drifted away. So did the investigator. The owner went to setting up the casino again. Belisarius and Rosalie grabbed a booth and used his new money to crank up the heater and buy something better to drink. They were cousins in a way, she a Puppet, more properly a *Homo pupa,* and he one of the *Homo quantus.* Rosalie was young, insightful and curious.

"Was that guy really from the Fortuna Corporation?" she asked in wonder.

"In the flesh," he said. "How did you think I got the alarms not to go off with the weighted dice?"

"I thought maybe you really did hack the AI," she said sheepishly.

"Nobody can do that." He swirled his drink. He didn't enjoy lying to her. She was too innocent, too trusting. "Fortuna knew that Powell's people were getting close to hacking their security patches, and they don't have a solution yet. They were eager to take her off the board, eager enough to temporarily install a bad AI in Blackmore's. It'll take them days to install a new one, but to them, it's worth it."

Rosalie had a few more questions about confidence schemes. It still seemed like such an alien world to her, even though she'd helped him on four cons already, not including the sting on Powell. The conversation drifted, and finally fell to theology again. In this, Rosalie was a stronger conversationalist.

Her thinking drew lines of defensible logic over the surface of Puppet madness, and she had no natural pauses when discussing theology. This forced Belisarius to sharpen his own questions about the natures of humanity, and his logical constructions usually inspired Rosalie's thinking. By midnight, though, they'd finished drinking two bottles and discussing three of Bishop

Creston's early ethical models. That was enough of both for Belisarius, and he headed home, vaguely dissatisfied.

His restless brain counted the stones of the arcade, measured the angular errors in the joints of walls and buildings and roofs, and tracked the gradual deteriorations that no one fixed. The magnetic organelles in his cells felt the unevenness of the electrical currents in the neighborhood, and his brain assigned notional probabilities to different service failures. His brain wouldn't have done all this if small scams on off-worlders were enough to hold its bioengineered curiosity. The jobs were lucrative, but they were getting too easy, too small to hide behind.

His gallery AI spoke in his implant as he neared. "Someone is looking for you."

CHAPTER TWO

BELISARIUS STOPPED. HE hadn't done enough jobs to warrant an assassin, but he'd started fleecing higher-level crime figures lately. And even with assassination off the table, a few people would probably pay to have him beat up.

"Show me," he sub-vocalized.

The gallery AI projected a picture into his ocular implants. His art gallery appeared as a cylindrical schematic of glazed brick with a winding staircase spearing the hollow in the middle. Late night patrons moved up and down the staircase, whispering, pausing in pools of light at the landings to examine paintings, sculptures and even silent films set into alcoves. The image zoomed onto a figure just inside the lobby on the top floor.

Her skin was darker than his by many shades, and an uncomfortable-looking knot held her black hair tight. She didn't seem to know what to do with her body. Her hands rested awkwardly behind her. She stood with feet apart, poised, suggesting a readiness to move. She wore an off-the-rack tunic and loose pants, neither daringly nor conservatively cut.

"Sub-Saharan Union?" he asked.

"I don't know," the gallery AI said. "Checking her financial links. Would you like a genetic analysis?"

"Armed?" Belisarius asked. He resumed his stroll.

"No. She has some quiescent augments, though," the AI responded. "I can't tell what they are."

Belisarius magnified the image, considering the woman's expression. "How much is she worth?"

He reached a squat brick building of sintered regolith growing into the ice-enclosed tunnels of Bob Town, a suburban lobe of the Puppet Free City. Within that building, plunging deep into the ice, was his art gallery.

"No credit limit I can find," the gallery reported, "but she has one link to an account held by the Consulate of the Sub-Saharan Union."

The Sub-Saharan Union was a small client nation with two worlds and some industrial habitats on the other side of the Freyja wormhole. Their patron nation gave them second-hand weapons and warships. In return, the Union undertook military expeditions or stood garrison duty. Not wealthy. They'd never been his clients or his marks, and they didn't have a reputation as the kind of muscle he might worry about.

He opened the door and stepped into the lobby at the top of the helical stairs. Belisarius sold legal and illegal Puppet art and was curating the first exposition permitted by the Theocracy. Smell, lighting and sound influenced the aesthetic of Puppet religious experience, and for the exposition, Belisarius had laced the lobby with the faint citrus odor of Puppet sweat. From the gloom below, a whip snap echoed. The woman seemed aware of all this, but untouched by her environment.

She stood taller than Belisarius by a good ten centimeters and had intense eyes. Her waiting stance shifted, shoulders back, hands at her side, but nothing close to the body language of resting. She was an unfired bow.

"*Monsieur* Arjona?" she asked.

"I'm Belisarius," he said in *français* 8.1.

"I'm Ayen," she said. "Can we speak somewhere more private?" An odd accent laced her French.

"I built an apartment into the gallery," he said, leading her down a hallway.

Brick made of cooked asteroidal dust surfaced the ice of the walls, giving the illusion of warmth. His apartment was opulent by the standards of Oler, with several bedrooms, a wide dining area and a sunken living room. The walls and ceilings were white and devoid of decorations. The dining room was spotless, and the living room barely furnished. All low stimulus.

The gallery AI had soft colored lights glowing in sconces and the heaters running. A bottle of rice soju stood on the table between two small glasses. Belisarius stepped down into the living room, slumped onto the couch, and motioned for Ayen to select a seat. She sat.

"How private is this conversation?" she asked in a low voice.

"The apartment is secure. The Puppets aren't very nosy outside the Forbidden City anyway," he said. Her face remained taut. "Did you want to secure this conversation by your own means?"

Her eyes narrowed, and she produced a small device. It looked newly made, but its design was antique, maybe thirty years old.

"Multispectrum white noise generator?" Belisarius asked.

She nodded. He regarded the device with some doubt. Last decade's surveillance systems could probably have cracked the little generator, but she must have known that. She switched it on and the carrier signal from his house AI became faint in his ear, transmitting small alarms that its surveillance of the room was deeply compromised. Interesting. More questions congealed in his brain.

"I need a con man," she said.

Belisarius poured two shots of soju.

"You're five years too late," he said. "I'm on a spiritual journey."

"The right people say that you get impossible things done."

She leaned for her glass with wiry, contained power. She sniffed warily, then drank it down.

He memorized her pronunciation as she spoke. Like her white noise generator, her dialect was antique, an early variant of *français* 8, but where had it come from? His augments carried all the accents, dialects and versions of French, but her accent didn't match any of them.

"That's as flattering as it is inaccurate," he said. "I don't know who does cons anymore. They're all in prison, I suppose."

"People call you the magician."

"Not to my face."

"My employer needs a magician."

She stared at him with unnerving intensity. His brain began constructing patterns, theories, abstractions of the identities of Ayen and her unknown employer. Why couldn't he place her accent? Who was she working for? What did she think he was?

"What kind of magic does she need?" Belisarius asked.

"She needs something moved through the Puppet wormhole. Distal side to here."

"Puppet freighters ship through the Axis all the time," he said. "They don't care what you move, as long as you pay."

"We can't afford their price."

"If you can't afford them, you certainly can't afford me."

Her stare hardened, the bowstring drawn tight. "We aren't short of money," she said, "but they don't want money."

"The Puppets do like to be paid in weapons."

"They want half," she said.

"Half of what?"

"Half of a dozen warships."

CHAPTER THREE

BELISARIUS HAD THREE days to back out. He didn't have the first clue as to how to move a fleet of warships across the Puppet Axis. It actually sounded like a great way to get killed, but he needed something complicated. His restless brain gnawed on all sorts of problems he didn't want it touching whenever he didn't give it enough to do.

So he crossed the Puppet wormhole on one of their commercial transports and stepped off at Port Stubbs, three hundred and twenty light years from the Puppet Free City. He hadn't brought much equipment, just a dozen sets of entangled particles stored in the buttons on his suit. Anything else he needed, Iekanjika would likely be able to provide. They met him at Port Stubbs in civilian clothes: Major Ayen Iekanjika and Mothudi Babedi, a military attaché from the Consulate of the Sub-Saharan Union.

They rented a port tugboat and took Belisarius out. They darkened the windows and sat him at the back of the cockpit so that he couldn't see any of the dashboard or the readouts. Maybe they didn't know much about the *Homo quantus* and they were trying to keep him from knowing where they were going. The magnetic field of the Stubbs Pulsar, although weak as far as pulsars went, throbbed against the magnetosomes in Belisarius's cells, imposing a reassuring polarity on the world and feeding his brain rough navigational data. After fifty-six point one minutes, a new magnetic field pressed on his magnetosomes, swallowing them. Something big was out there, big enough to be a warship. The clanking outside the hull signalled that the grip was more than electromagnetic.

"We're not getting out?" Belisarius asked after they'd floated motionless for thirty-three more seconds.

"We're inducing a transient wormhole to the Expeditionary Force," Iekanjika said.

The lights darkened and everything around them stilled. The tug shuddered once as the warship surrounding it thrust gently, then fell into stillness again for twenty-two point four minutes. Then the clamps finally released. The tug itself emerged into space, and Belisarius felt Stubbs' magnetic field again.

It was much fainter, meaning they were farther from the Stubbs Pulsar, by about a tenth of a light year. That would put them within the comets and planetessimals of the Stubbs Oort cloud. The cockpit windows cleared and Belisarius craned his neck to see into the dizzying dark with his telescoping ocular implants. A dozen warships swung into view, speckling a two-hundred-kilometer volume of space beyond the cockpit. His ocular implants zoomed in on the images, lit by starshine and running lights.

They were old Congregate designs; this class of military vessel had been a second-line ship sixty to seventy years ago. Belisarius counted two frigates, nine cruisers, and a battleship so small it barely qualified in the navies of today as a capital vessel.

He squinted and zoomed the images. Not everything was old. Time-scarred plating contrasted with shinier spots, and strange, raised blisters were rowed on the hulls. And the drive sections were oddly shaped. Distended tubes pierced the hull superstructures from bow to stern. Those weren't normal drives.

A strange warbling signal pressed against his magnetosomes, ephemeral patterns that weren't coming from the tug. It was hard to feel precisely through the hull, but the pressure wasn't uniform, like he'd feel from a strong magnetic field. Rich texture saturated it, the kind of patterned granularity made by multiple layers of fields interacting with themselves in quantum superposition, too fine for most instrumentation to detect. What was it?

The microscopic universe always boiled with quantum indistinctness. For each particle and wave in the subatomic structure of the universe, mutually exclusive possibilities existed in parallel, racing over one another, interacting, creating in every instant webs of potential causal chains, histories of particle and field interactions, bubbling in unobserved chaos. But macroscopically, that chaos always evened out. This didn't. He'd never seen quantum interference this sustained and complex. His heart thumped with excitement.

Babedi docked the tug in one of the dorsal bays of the flagship. In the zero g, Belisarius followed Iekanjika awkwardly through an umbilical into the hallways of a battleship that smelled of people and plastics. Its electromagnetic field pressed against his magnetosomes, hiding the mystery outside.

CHAPTER FOUR

CONTROLLING HIS ENGINEERED curiosity had never been a sure thing, and Belisarius forced himself not to fidget. Iekanjika returned in uniform. The poised watchfulness that had ill-fit her in civilian clothes now suited, as if a hard gem had been returned to its setting. She led him to a briefing room. Belisarius's hands found the rungs awkwardly in zero g. At times he overcompensated and almost kicked a soft-faced MP sergeant who followed them. At the briefing room, Iekanjika swung in and strapped herself into a seat. Belisarius took considerably longer. Her eyes narrowed in impatience until he clumsily snapped the harness closed. A series of warship schematics projected in hologram between them, as well as detailed tactical analyses and diagrams of Port Stubbs. In the moments she took to consider her words, Belisarius memorized the displays.

"What do you need to know to propose a plan for getting the fleet across the Axis?" Iekanjika asked.

"A history lesson," Belisarius said. "Maybe one in politics too. Your little fleet looks out of date. What are they doing here, so far from home?"

Iekanjika seemed to work through some inner debate. "It's been a long time," she said finally. "Forty years."

Belisarius felt himself staring.

"Forty years ago," she said, "Congregate political commissars instructed the Union to send an armed reconnaissance mission deep into Middle Kingdom territory. It was meant to be provocative. I doubt anyone expected the Sixth Expeditionary Force to survive."

"Your squadron ran the other way?"

"The Expeditionary Force did its job," she said with heat, "heedless of danger. But during the mission, some observations suggested to one of our officers a new type of drive. A very advanced drive. Under the terms of our Patron-Client Accord, something like that has to be turned over to our patrons."

"And the political commissars already knew of this new idea," Belisarius said.

"So we arrested all the political commissars," she said, "and ferreted out all the sleeper agents the Congregate had hidden among our crew and officers. Then we headed out of Middle Kingdom territory."

"To get all the way to Stubbs in forty years, you must have headed straight out into deep space," Belisarius said, "away from all the known wormholes of the Axis Mundi."

"We had to design the drive and then build it into each of our warships."

"What do your drives do?" he asked.

Iekanjika's eyes narrowed, measuring. She didn't trust him. Which meant that she probably didn't agree with the decision to contact him.

"Your people got a con man instead of a military solution," he said. "Union intelligence operatives must have considered all the private covert operatives across Epsilon Indi. Let me guess: they couldn't find a single one who wasn't already attached to a rival service, or who didn't have a bigger incentive to sell you out."

"Babedi told me the *Homo quantus* were a new human species of contemplative. You don't sound very contemplative."

"I'm not so fond of being someone's last choice, either," Belisarius said. "What can your ships do?"

Iekanjika touched a finger to a transparent patch on the back of her hand, tapping without looking. He hadn't seen that kind of interface before. The room responded, darkening. The hologram of the flagship, the *Mutapa,* expanded.

Clean lines in pale blue showed the classic Congregate design that had been cutting-edge eighty years ago, powerful and competitive sixty years ago, and surpassed by newer designs forty years ago. Modifications glowed in pale yellow. The axis of the warship had been rebuilt as a hollow cylinder, with the superstructure riding this immense tube like a colony of barnacles encrusting a pipe.

"This is a new kind of drive," Iekanjika said. "It doesn't use reaction mass, so there's no exhaust velocity to measure, but the drive's thrust is equivalent to an exhaust velocity of half a million kilometers per second."

"What?" Belisarius blurted. She stared at him with an edge of defiant pride. "That's more than the maximum thrust of anything in civilization..." he said. "What is it?"

"You only need to know the specifications."

"Not even close. Have you used the drive in a wormhole? Something that exotic in a space-time tunnel could be real dangerous."

"We've moved the fleet through induced wormholes," Iekanjika said, "but we've never activated the drive inside."

"What's the exotic?"

Her stare was uncomfortable. He turned to the blues and yellows of the schematics, more for the color than the lines, which he'd already memorized. Like bets in a card game, some conversations needed to be waited out.

"It's an inflaton drive," she said finally.

"What?" She'd surprised him twice in ten minutes.

"You don't have the knowledge to understand how it works."

"Probably not," he said, squinting at the schematic. "Can you magnify?"

He watched the motion of her fingers as the image of the *Mutapa* expanded, filling the room.

"Turn the stern to me?" he asked.

Her fingers swept a different motion on the patch on her hand and the image turned ninety degrees, until, through the hollow core of the warship, he was looking at the far wall. From this angle, the blisters on the side showed in relief, larger than they'd appeared from the side.

An inflaton drive. He wondered if she was lying. He usually could tell, but he didn't think she was. She was tamping down her own pride in the telling. How did they do it? Inflaton particles carried the inflationary force that caused the ongoing expansion of the universe. In some theories, a wave of inflation was self-reinforcing, a runaway effect. Their own drive could destroy them. And the energy cost must be enormous. Then it clicked.

"Virtual inflatons," Belisarius said. Iekanjika started.

Virtual particles were pairs of particles and anti-particles that could jump into existence as long as they vanished back into nothingness quickly enough.

"The *Homo quantus* have a particular insight into virtual particles," he said.

That was something of an understatement. The ocean of virtual particles frothing at every point of space-time created the tremendous noise through which the *Homo quantus* had to filter. Iekanjika looked sour, as if she'd said too much.

"Don't worry, major. None of your secrets are lost. You create a pair of virtual particles to briefly expand space-time, and in the instant before it shrinks back to normal, your warship gets thrown forward, doesn't it?"

"You're a dangerous man, Arjona," she said. He wasn't sure if she meant it in the way that suggested she was about to draw her pistol and smear his brains on the wall. "How many other *Homo quantus* would make similar guesses?"

"Most *Homo quantus* have split personalities and are highly unstable," Belisarius lied. "They can function in quiet, low-stimulus environments. One in a hundred can get along in the world like me."

"But most of your people could make these logical leaps?"

He shook his head. "Most *Homo quantus* are so impractical that they consider cosmology too applied for serious debate. My interests have always been more immediate than theirs."

"It's dangerous to have too many interests, Arjona."

"We may as well get all the danger out of the way at once, then. Why is the drive on your ship open at the front? It's not a ram scoop. It's not feeding on the interstellar medium."

She arched her brow this time and crossed her arms. "You tell me, magician."

He stared at the hologram of the *Mutapa,* thinking about it as if it was the hand Iekanjika was playing across a poker table from the Congregate. If he was to play the player, and not the cards, his first data point was that Iekanjika felt pretty good about her hand. Bluffs didn't work against the hegemonic power of the Congregate, so she thought she held winning cards. Why?

The Sixth Expeditionary Force was forty years old, carrying equipment that had been outdated before the fleet had ever been lost. Numerically and ship for ship, forty years ago, they wouldn't have lasted an hour in a battle against a patron nation. Now, in refurbished warships, their eagerness to get back into civilized space tingled in the air. They weren't homesick. They dreamed of a war of independence, and no one spoiled for a war they didn't think they could win.

"Turn the display a hundred and eighty degrees," he said.

The movement of her fingers on the patch rotated the image until the tube stared him in the face, like the barrel of a cannon. His *Homo quantus* brain, always snuffling for patterns and symmetries, tasted at a new parallel: a drive with no fuel, a cannon with no ammunition.

An inflaton cannon. Their drive propelled them on the picosecond-brief existence of inflaton/anti-inflaton pairs in the drive tube. What would such particle pairs do outside of the containment of the drive system?

"How destructive is your inflaton cannon?" he asked finally.

"Not your concern," she said, but there was a smugness in her voice.

How had the Expeditionary Force developed so much? Had they stumbled across some kind of forerunner artifact and figured out its secrets? Forty years was a long time, but not long enough for all they'd invented. The inflaton drive alone was many decades ahead of anything in civilization, perhaps more than that. The size of this job, the scale of the political and military implications, boggled the mind. This was far, far beyond conning businessmen and gangsters. Frankly, it was probably beyond his skills. And he didn't doubt that if he tried and failed, Major Iekanjika would consider it an efficient use of her time to put a bullet in his brain.

"The job is to move twelve ships across the Puppet Axis," he mused. When he said it like that, with none of the political context, it didn't sound so immense. "What's the pay?"

She changed the holographic display and a small ship appeared in yellow.

"What's the scale?" he asked, leaning forward in the straps.

"Fifty-three meters from bow to stern," she said.

The ship was sleek. A narrow structure of cockpit, engines, cargo and life support wrapped around a tube. It was a small craft with its own inflaton drive. Any of the patron nations would pay anything for it.

CHAPTER FIVE

BELISARIUS HAD NO idea if he should take the job, but he didn't need to answer yet. Iekanjika led him into the corridor where the MP still waited. Belisarius gripped for the rungs, but his movements were clumsy. Then he grasped with futile, panicked reaching and somehow began slowly rotating in the middle of the hallway, just far enough not to be able to reach any wall. He sighed.

"It's been a while since zero g," he said. "I could use a hand."

The MP made a disgusted face and held out his hand. Belisarius clapped his hands around the MP's as if holding onto a lifeline and then caught the rungs on the wall. He followed them more deliberately down corridors whose walls of discolored carbon polymer felt unwelcoming and oppressive. Small colored lights would have made the ship feel warmer. Iekanjika stopped, placed her palm against a sensor and a door ground open. A gloomy room, the size of a few coffins, lay revealed.

"We moved an officer into the main barracks so that during your stay you would feel like an honored guest," Iekanjika said, without any irony he could detect. His shower stall in the Puppet Free City was bigger than this room.

He floated in and turned to face her. Her brown eyes stared back at him challengingly. "You can't beat the Congregate," he said finally. "When they sneeze, even the other patron nations get nervous."

"Do your magic and we'll do the rest."

Her hard eyes bored into his, and then she softened slightly.

"I have nothing against you, Arjona," she said. "You don't live with someone else's boot on your neck. You bumble into arguments that have played themselves out over decades. *On n'est pas maîtres dans nos maisons...*" she said, leaving the old expression unfinished. *We are not masters in our houses...*

The machinery in the wall ground the door closed again. A dim panel on the ceiling lit age-discolored gray-brown carbon fiber walls. A zero-g sleep bag was strapped onto one wall. Handles on another wall opened up a tiny sink and the head. Sweat laced the air. Of course some camera must be watching him. The paranoia of the Union was as palpable as their passion. He gingerly opened the sleep bag and strapped himself in. He shut the light and closed his eyes, his thoughts still spinning.

The Sub-Saharan Union wanted a war of independence against the biggest power in civilization. And they needed a con man to get their secret weapon to where it could get chewed to pieces. Not an appetizing problem on its surface.

More than that, Iekanjika had lied poorly about something. The probability that a lone Union scientist had suddenly come up with an idea for a new type of propulsion system was vanishingly small. Where had they gotten their new inflaton drive and their new weapons? He needed to think.

The *Homo quantus* brain had been engineered over eleven generations for mathematical and geometric talents, coupled with an eidetic memory. This alone produced children capable of remarkable mental feats, but to wrestle with the deepest conceptual problems of the cosmos, the *Homo quantus* needed more.

Engineered from electric fish DNA, every *Homo quantus* had electroplaques, stacks of muscles under their ribs that acted like batteries. Belisarius sent a sustained, polarized micro-current from his electroplaques into the left temporal area of his brain, an area associated with sensory input and language. After a few moments, his capacity to conceptualize linguistic and social nuance dwindled, as did smell, taste and touch. At the same time, activity in the right anterior lobe increased, augmenting mathematically creative connections and increasing geometric thinking beyond prodigy levels. The *Homo quantus* called this state of being 'savant.'

Belisarius sent a different current from his electroplaques to electrify his magnetosomes, those organelles in his muscle cells containing microscopic coils of iron. A weak magnetic field blossomed around him, letting him feel the electrical and magnetic fields of the *Mutapa* pressing at his arms and legs. The metal hinges on the panels to the sink distorted his magnetic field. The metal wiring behind the powered-down computer display did the same. And so did a camera embedded in a corner of the tiny cabin. He varied his magnetic field, feeling for the distortions produced by the camera. It was unresponsive, dumb tech, monitoring the visual band only.

Belisarius turned his back to the camera and huddled his head in the bag as if in sleep. In the dark of the bag, he pulled out the plastic patch that he'd taken from the back of the MP's hand. It had been some time since he'd lifted a wallet or coin or chip from anyone. He'd worried he might have lost his touch.

The patch was semi-conductor nano-circuitry over a breathable carbon filament web. Flexible. Vaguely shiny. Powered by the movement of the body. He pressed it to the back of his left hand. Small displays lit faintly. Belisarius had asked Iekanjika to rotate the holographic displays often today so he could see how she manipulated her patch. Her movements had been confident, practiced. His were tentative. A simple, stylistically backward holographic display floated in French above the back of his hand. The patch wasn't password-locked, which meant everything else would be.

If they found him fumbling about in their networks, he'd be on a short list for a visit to a firing squad. Hopefully, the Sixth Expeditionary Force was still walking around with quantum computers fifty years old. Belisarius carried a head full of quantum processing abilities, but he was nervous. It wasn't often he put his own skin this far into the game. But he had to know the Union to figure out if he should take the job, or if it could even be done.

A con man called Gander had once taught him that there were only three bets.

Sometimes, you play the cards.

Sometimes, you play the player.

Sometimes, you just throw the dice.

He pressed into the Union network. A grid of standard icons bloomed over his hand in yellow light: communications, common archives, research, power systems, weaponry, status dashboards, and restricted files. An authentication image grew, flashing interrogative. It would be a quantum password.

The world dizzied around him as he switched his thinking to quantum logic. It did not become less precise, but it seemed to adopt an attitude that made precision less important. Interactions and relationships became more important than identity and state. Auras throbbed around blurring objects. Sound became deeper and richer, modified by the constructive and destructive interference of barely heard sidenotes. The portion of time called the present gently widened.

His visual augments picked apart the densely textured information in the authentication image. The encryption was tough. Belisarius's mind, in savant, and using quantum processing, struggled with the new challenge for long seconds, ten, twenty, thirty seconds, until he thought surely alarms would be going off. Then the holographic icons greened.

He toggled the insubstantial power systems icon. The directory contained eyebrow-raising acceleration and heat dissipation specifications for the inflaton drive, do-not-cross tolerances and detailed maintenance instructions, but no blueprints or theory. The information was probably in isolated systems. Dead end.

He dug into the research directory. His pattern-sniffing brain focused in on mathematical formulations attached to snippets of incomplete physical theories. Weirdly, the Expeditionary Force didn't have an inflaton theory, but had modified something familiar, wormhole physics, to underpin their engineering. Their formulation lacked the rigor that had given his own teenage theories their predictive and analytical power. The disorganized snippets of theory looked like something invented by outsider artists. Perhaps this wasn't surprising; few military strike forces would carry theoretical physicists with them.

His brain stalled at the dating of the research. The reports had overlapping and backwards dates. First generation tests were listed as beginning in 2499, but four different sets of fifth generation experiments had begun in 2476, only a year after the Expeditionary Force disappeared. The first generation of experiments had to be completed before the fifth generation ones were begun, right?

Had the Union been doing illicit research long before they left? If Union forces routinely accessed the Congregate Axis Mundi wormholes, and always acted under the surveillance of shipboard political commissars, how would they have kept their research secret? They couldn't have. So they hadn't started the research before they'd left.

He skimmed more of the references and notes. Much of their research seemed related to wormhole physics, including some observations that couldn't have been made without access to one of the permanent wormholes of the forerunner's Axis Mundi network. The Expeditionary Force must have found one.

If so, it was a treasure of incalculable value. Owning any of the permanent wormholes of the Axis Mundi network was the defining feature of patron nations. Client nations, by definition, didn't own any, and under the Union's Patron-Client Accord with the Congregate, any new Axis Mundi wormhole had to be given to their patrons. That was what had driven the Expeditionary Force to vanish.

There was something deeply personal too in this discovery. The observations they'd made, if correct, opened up whole fields of research that Belisarius had abandoned when he'd left home years ago. Old memories welled up in him, silty with imprecise longings. He pushed those feelings down, to focus on what was before him.

The jumble of time signatures remained impenetrable. Logical lines of causality did not link investigation to discovery to new waves of investigation. Many complex discoveries seemed to have been made at the beginning of the forty years.

One directory was labelled Research Coordinating Center. The coordinating center had been dormant for the last three years, but before that, it had been an enormous clearinghouse of research transactions, a centralized economy of discovery. Research questions had been issued on particular dates, and answers delivered on later dates: wormhole physics, weapon research, defensive technology, sensor technology, propulsion and computing. Decades of research at a time. It was when the results were passed to different research units that the dates became confused.

Belisarius customized the display to suit his brain better. He wanted a geometric display, preferably with four or more dimensions and vectors of causality drawn from experiments to their results, to trace where those results were incorporated into the design of the next set of experiments. The holographic display complied, showing a hyper-dimensional knot that human eyes and brains would have had difficulty disentangling.

The shape of a fountain appeared, a fountain of light with six streams; time ran vertically into the future with the streams. The beginnings of experiments and questions were at the bottom. Experimental results rose, propelled by the researchers of the Expeditionary Force, staying in their discrete streams, not interacting with the other research lines. Further experiments shot upward from those first results, begetting new results, and then new experiments, until, near 2487, slightly more than a decade after the beginning of the experiments, the results disappeared and next showed up at the base of the neighbouring streams.

At the base.

In 2476.

Eleven years back in time.

Belisarius refused to make the connection. He double-checked the date markings. The patterns were too organized to be the result of inconsistent dating or database errors. His brain was built to find patterns in the world, but the genetic engineers had built his abilities so well that often he found patterns that didn't really exist. Constant second-guessing of his perceptions was all that kept the world rational.

And yet this.

The alternative to second-guessing himself all night was to accept that the Expeditionary Force had found a way to send information back in time. If that was true, the segregated flows of information in the research were designed to compartmentalize knowledge in order to avoid causal violations. The researchers in Stream A in the year 2487 would never receive the results of their own experiments from 2498. Those results went to Stream B. And likewise, the results of Stream B went to the past of Stream C, and so it went with each of the research streams. And every eleven years, the cycle restarted.

It was ingenious. It was overwhelming. The Union had a time travel device.

And in forty years, they'd completed not four decades of research, but perhaps four centuries' worth. The Union had started from far behind and might have succeeded in leaping past all other nations. And if news of the time travel device's existence got out, all the patron nations would march to war for it. If he took the job, it might trigger a civilization-wide war. It was too much to absorb all at once.

Belisarius found a set of files containing the mathematical formulations of the time travel device. The work was frustratingly inelegant, but after some minutes, he worked out that it described a pair of wormholes, only dozens of meters across, imperfectly bound to one another, forming a one-way bridge across eleven years of time. They'd found not one of the forerunners' wormholes, but two, stuck together by some accident of orbital mechanics. A pair of wormholes bound together would give off all sorts of quantum-level interference, probably the odd electromagnetic fields he'd felt when approaching the fleet. The wormholes could be nearby. Then it hit him: they were only a dozen meters in diameter. The Expeditionary Force was carrying the pair of wormholes in one of their ships.

He remembered the signals he'd felt approaching the fleet with Iekanjika and Babedi. He worked backwards, calculating where the source would have been, and then accessed the fleet formation records to cross-match. At the time of his approach, there had been only one ship near the source of the strangely-textured magnetic field. The *Limpopo*. It was over two hundred kilometers away, too far to make even a single observation. So close, yet so far.

Belisarius retreated from the ship's files and came out of savant.

He peeled the incriminating patch from the back of his hand and closed it in his cupped fingers. Current from his electroplaques surged through a set of insulated carbon nanotubule wires that ran to his fingertips. The patch shrivelled into a tiny pellet of ash. He slipped the pellet into a weakness in the seam of the sleep bag and then crushed it to fragments for good measure.

CHAPTER SIX

IN THE MORNING, Belisarius was no closer to taking or refusing the job. Whether he failed or succeeded, somebody, maybe a lot of somebodies, was going to get killed. Probably everyone in the Sixth Expeditionary Force, but maybe more. But the Union had obviously already committed; they were going to try this with or without him. Real war was coming, not just the cold war they'd been living. He did know the Puppets, as well as anyone not a Puppet could. And he knew something of wormholes. He couldn't think of anyone who could help them better than he could, even if he didn't yet know how he would do it.

An MP came and brought him to a room with vacuum suits webbed to the walls. Major Iekanjika was already suited up. "You want to see the performance of the Expeditionary Force," she said. "I've gotten authorization to show you."

Belisarius flailed his way in zero g to the rack and took a suit that looked about his size. Without gravity, it took some time to put on, and the MP finished suiting up before Belisarius even had the pants on. When he needed two hands to detach one of the buttons on his shirt, he began spinning. This seemed to wear down Iekanjika's patience and she finally clapped a hand on his arm to steady him. He sheepishly put the button in an outside pocket of the vacuum suit and resumed dressing.

"I'll be okay," he said as the suit sucked tight its seals.

The three of them cycled through the airlock into hard vacuum. Inwardly, he slumped. He loved the stars, but he hated space, and the deep black of the universe opened with stomach-churning vastness. The Stubbs Pulsar a tenth of a light year away touched Belisarius's muscles with faint magnetic fingers. With baseline human sight, he could see four thousand stars. Between those, emptiness yawned wide and endless. If he telescoped his ocular implants, he might see five times that number, but the space between them would also multiply, bringing new, trackless voids into being. The view tasted like the fugue: seeing all the cosmos and not only knowing it to be a void, but being part of that void.

He took the button from his pocket with gloved fingers and let it drift free beside the *Mutapa* in perfect stillness.

Spotlights from the *Mutapa* shone on them, sharp whites bleaching discolorations from the arm and hands of his suit. Another warship stood abeam of the *Mutapa* across several kilometers of space. The major on one side and the MP on the other grabbed his upper arms and leapt from the *Mutapa*. His stomach lurched and he swallowed a yelp as they careened into the void.

No shuttle. No guide wire. No nothing.

Iekanjika and the MP had jumped true. He'd been too startled to move as they jumped, and he hadn't spoiled their aim. He stayed rigid. Little pressures nudged him where the pair used cold gas jets to correct their course. It would be minutes before they reached the other warship. He flew through space, only the scrunch of fabric on fabric where they held him making any noise beyond his own shallow, quick breathing.

What kind of people jumped between ships? He didn't know

of any service that required this maneuver. He doubted they were out to impress him. They didn't respect him enough for that. Maybe it was a new military maneuver or a tactic born of austerity. Or maybe it was a tactic developed purely for its unconventionality. The Sixth Expeditionary Force carried new weapons and propulsion; why not bring new tactics to battle?

Play the player, not the cards.

They closed on the other warship. Spotlights focused on them, tracking them toward a small bay ringed with pale lights. More forces, more pressures, and then he was spinning, pointing his feet at their destination. A strong magnetic field bloomed below them.

"Bend your knees, Arjona, or you'll break an ankle," Iekanjika said in his helmet radio.

He did. The ship grew at an alarming speed. He knew they only carried the energy they'd used to jump, but instinct made fear tickle at his insides. And then the ship swallowed the infinity of his vision and their feet crashed against the hull and stuck. His breathing rasped loud in his ears and his knees wobbled.

"Hell, Arjona!" Iekanjika said, shoving him into the airlock. "It's like you've never been in space before."

Belisarius's face heated. They cycled through the airlock.

"This is the *Jonglei*," she said to Belisarius as he removed his helmet. "It's a good warship, representative of the ships of the Expeditionary Force."

They moved by hand to the bridge. Belisarius was slow, but had no mishaps. They met Colonel Ruhindi, the commanding officer of the *Jonglei*, a woman in her late thirties with very dark skin and six horizontal scars on her forehead. The bridge loomed with weight, incongruously so in zero g. Six coffin-sized acceleration chambers stood at angles to the walls, with small thick-glassed windows in front of where the crew's faces would be. Ruhindi summoned a holographic display in the middle of the bridge. Belisarius stepped clumsily in his magnetic boots and peered into it.

"Can I see an external view?" he asked.

The colonel's fingers twitched, and the display compressed, reducing the *Jonglei* to an icon. Only one other ship showed in the display: the *Mutapa*.

"Larger display, please," he said. "The whole Expeditionary Force."

The colonel's fingers moved and the center icons shrank, allowing new ones to appear at the margins. On the left wing floated the command cruiser *Nhialic,* with the *Juba,* the *Gbudue,* and the *Batembuzi* in formation, lit in orange. On the right wing in pale yellow, the armored cruiser *Limpopo*, commanding the *Omukama,* the *Fashoda,* and the *Kampala.* In the center, the battleship *Mutapa,* attended by the *Jonglei,* the *Ngundeng,* and the *Pibor.*

A microcurrent from his electroplaques to his brain induced savantism. Subtleties of language and emotional nuance melted in a hard rain of geometric and mathematical understanding. Quantifying was easy, inviting. The feel of other people nearby prickled. They didn't like him. Maybe they didn't like him. The blizzard of geometric and numerical insights buried qualitative, social cues.

The Expeditionary Force in the hologram became a web of momentum, distance, mass, and speed-of-light signals. The locations of the *Limpopo,* the *Mutapa* and the button he'd left floating in the vacuum formed a long, narrow triangle. Numbers darted between his thoughts. Two hundred and fifty kilometers from the *Limpopo* to the *Mutapa.*

Hesitantly, he said, "I need to understand what your ships can do with wormholes: how fast they can induce one, how far they can go, how fast they can transit, and how fast systems come online after emergence."

Belisarius didn't meet their eyes. In savant, meeting people's eyes was like looking into a box of puzzle pieces, making the pattern recognition tendencies in his brain hyperactive, facial expressions swirling into cycles of false positives. The colonel's fingers twitched, and a thrumming resonated through the ship. Gravity lurched on under their feet.

Belisarius's brain, thirsty for logic and abstractions, began chopping up the name *Mutapa*. Encyclopedic implants fed him information as fast as he could drink it. *Mutapa,* a medieval kingdom founded by a prince of greater Zimbabwe. The Kingdom of Mutapa had soon outstripped its neighbors and even its parent nation. Powerful imagery. Powerful symbolism. He wished he could quantify it.

The Union picked good names. Like *Omukama,* a dynasty that had ruled Uganda until the nineteenth century. Not swept aside by modernity so much as carried along with it, the dynasty possessed powerful cultural weight even into the era of the formation of the Sub-Saharan Union. Naming a warship after a cultural capital made for powerful symbolism. Powerful enough to die for? He didn't want them to die.

How could he quantify the effect? There ought to be an algebra for societies. He should make one. Cultural capital propelled the Expeditionary Force, imprinting personal identity on its nationals. They wrapped themselves in their identity with a confidence Belisarius could only envy.

Ngundeng, the nineteenth century Dinka prophet. The Dinka had a creator god, *Nhialic. Batembuzi* was a medieval empire circling the Great Lakes region. *Gbudue* was a famous Azande king of South Sudan whose name meant *to tear out a man's intestines.*

Powerful imagery. Powerful symbolism. How had the Congregate missed it? The Union ships had been carrying these names for decades. It was mathematical. This was the physics of people. The multiplication of emotional and patriotic energy produced psychological momentum.

Iekanjika pushed him and he froze.

"Take it or don't take it, Arjona," she repeated.

A timer. A digital timer. She held a digital timer. In her hand. Her hand was before him. He was in savant. Remember to be polite.

"Thank you," he said. "I have a very sharp sense of time. I won't need it. Thank you."

He didn't meet her eyes. She was already moving away, shaking her head. Weight increased.

"We're running on your inflaton drive?" he asked.

"Yes," Iekanjika said.

He felt no change in the magnetic field. That meant the drive didn't interact with the electromagnetic force.

"We're below half a gravity," Belisarius said. "What can the drive do? Ten g? Twenty g?"

Military-grade fission-propelled missiles could sustain forty gravities of acceleration and still hit evasive targets.

"Much more," she said.

Enough to outrun a missile? Psychological momentum and fast ships didn't matter; they were just twelve ships. The Congregate had that many ships in a single squadron. The Congregate had hundreds of squadrons. Math was comfortingly inescapable. And so much of the Expeditionary Force's other technology was half a century old. Sad. So sad for the Union. But it was what they wanted. Cultural momentum propelled them.

The *Jonglei* stopped accelerating and spun one hundred and eighty degrees. Then the gravity became crushing and Belisarius's knees trembled. He staggered against the wall. He tried not to black out. His savantism wavered as he lost focus. Iekanjika and Ruhindi stood, laughing at him. His insides heated with anger. Not at them. At himself.

"This is just one and a half gravities, Arjona," Iekanjika said.

He didn't want to lose the numbers. *Mutapa* to *Limpopo*. Coordinates. Time in seconds. Acceleration in gravities. Hold onto the coordinates. He sank to a sitting position against the wall and held his head between his knees. He didn't care what they thought of him.

After another thirty-four point seven seconds, the crush stopped. The thrumming stopped. Weight evaporated. The *Jonglei* had moved away from the *Mutapa*, far enough to safely induce a wormhole. In response to Colonel Ruhindi's twitching fingers, the watch officers in the acceleration chambers shut down ship systems.

"Where do you want to jump?" Ruhindi said in very accented French.

"How far can you go in the direction of galactic south?" he asked. The transit would answer him on both the distance and precision of the Expeditionary Force's induced wormholes.

Ruhindi issued more silent orders. Belisarius stepped forward in the awkward magnetic boots. The external holographic displays shrank and internal systems graphs appeared. The *Jonglei* had extended its magnetic coils off the bow and Belisarius could feel magnetism tugging, even deep within the ship. The magnetic field rose to nine thousand Gauss. Ten thousand. Fourteen thousand. Twenty-one thousand.

Belisarius's arms and chest tingled.

Sixty thousand. One hundred thousand. Two hundred and eighty thousand Gauss.

They had passed industrial and medical magnetic field strengths.

At four hundred thousand Gauss, electromagnetism and gravity interacted in interesting ways, and a properly targeted magnetic field would cause space-time itself to creak. The readings levelled at five hundred and fifty thousand Gauss.

In front of the ship, a pocket of space-time bulged at right angles to the three dimensions of space. Semi-melted space-time distended like a questing pseudopod. The shape and focus of the magnetic field pushed the tube of space-time across dimensions accustomed to being curled. The questing finger reached down, around the intervening space, until a narrow, unstable bridge reached a point far to galactic south. Then the display greened. They had induced a wormhole.

Now came the dangerous part. The six hundred meters of the *Jonglei* was packed with fusion and fission power systems, as well as the inflaton drive. Those moving parts had to still, because there was nothing natural about an induced wormhole. It was the proverbial pencil balancing on its tip. Its difference in temperature from absolute zero was within the range of the uncertainty principle. Most interactions with the environment would caused it to collapse. This was very different from the permanent wormholes of the Axis Mundi, which were never in danger of swallowing the transiting ships if there was a mistake.

The *Jonglei*'s main and secondary systems were off, but the dashboard showed that the outside temperature of the warship was one hundred and five Kelvins. Small projectors all over the ship activated to radiate infrared in this range, designed to interfere with the black body radiation of the *Jonglei*, rendering it so ghostly cool that it would not disturb the wormhole. A tenth of a gravity pressed his feet for two point three one seconds, propelling the *Jonglei* into the throat.

Then, weightlessness and held breaths. The wormhole would be closing behind them, shepherding them through. Displays turned green. A chime sounded. The warship trembled as different systems came online. The holographic tactical display winked back into existence, showing no ships anywhere. Numbers colonized the edges of the display.

"A third of a light year," Colonel Ruhindi said.

Precise numbers lay on the bottom of the holographic display.

"Is this the limit of what the *Jonglei* can do?" Belisarius asked.

Iekanjika stepped closer. He avoided looking at her face.

"This is the outer limit that the crew and officers would want to try, even in an emergency," she said. "The three flagships can go slightly farther."

"And how fast can the *Jonglei* gate, again?" Belisarius asked.

"The main and secondary systems have to come online for star fixes, tactical assessments, last-minute telescopic surveys of the destination, before the whole thing is shut down," the major said. "A fast crew can be ready in five to ten minutes."

"What about blind gates?" he asked.

"What do you mean?" Iekanjika said.

He regarded the boots on his feet, visually and by the feel of the magnets in the soles.

"No star fixes," he said. "Program the destination by dead reckoning."

"That's idiotic."

"What if you're in a hurry?"

He waited. Iekanjika stepped closer.

"Look at me," she said finally.

He waited. The major's left hand took a fistful of his suit. Dark skin on pale cloth. A lot of strength. She shook him and then jerked him closer. "I said look at me, Arjona."

"I can't."

"What are you playing at?" she demanded.

"I can't look at you. The *Homo quantus* need tremendous

mathematical abilities to be able to do anything useful. We can turn on prodigy-level mathematical abilities by shutting down other parts of the brain. Language. Sensory input. Socialization. It's a trade-off. I've gone savant."

He went still, not looking at her, but adding up the digits in the columns and rows of information. A third of a light year. It wasn't a third. They'd come zero point three two nine seven seven one four five lightyears. The number would improve with more telescopic observations.

"What?" Iekanjika demanded.

"I can't look at you," he repeated exactly. "The *Homo quantus* need tremendous mathematical abilities to be able to do anything useful. We can turn on prodigy-level mathematical abilities by shutting down other parts of the brain. Language. Sensory input. Socialization. It's a trade-off. I've gone savant."

She released him in disgust. "You're no con man," she said. "And you're no soldier."

"I'm a bad soldier," he said, "but I'm a really good con man. And I might be able to get you through the Puppet Axis."

"How?" she demanded.

"What about the blind gates?" he asked.

"Ma'am?" Iekanjika asked, throwing up her hands. "I don't know how to answer this question."

Colonel Ruhindi sidled closer on magnetized soles. "What do you want to know?" she asked.

A heavy, impatient sigh escaped his lips. "I want to know the capacity of the *Jonglei* to gate somewhere without taking new star fixes. Dead reckoning."

Belisarius felt something impatient and angry from her, and maybe other feelings he couldn't name. So much social geography became overgrown and impenetrable in savant. Ruhindi's arms crossed. What did that mean?

"Of course the *Jonglei* can create a wormhole without taking a star fix," Ruhindi said, "but it serves no practical purpose. During a retreat, the commander would already be operating with complete star fixes. Emerging from an induced wormhole ends the situation of retreat. The odds of a pursuing enemy being able to create a wormhole mouth within weapons range of ours are miniscule."

The numbers on the bottom of the holographic display were hypnotic. He added and readied them. He found rounding errors that told him about the settings on the *Jonglei*'s navigational software.

"I'd like the *Jonglei* to shut off its navigational telescopes and induce a new wormhole," he said.

"Why?" the colonel demanded, adding something in another language. He'd been wondering at their accents. Did they speak Shona amongst themselves? His mind puzzled at the shift in language, gnawing at it like a cryptographic problem. A theory of cultural algebra might not be so hard to develop. Iekanjika stood before him.

"What will this get us, Arjona?" she demanded. "I feel like you're jerking us around. Your magic is hand-waving." He liked when she explained what she felt. It helped him understand. Her hand movements meant exasperation. "Where exactly do you want us to make a wormhole to?" she asked.

He removed one of his buttons from his jacket. It reflected the colored holographic light.

"I took off one of these when I put on my vacuum suit," he said. "I left it outside the *Mutapa* before you brought us to the *Jonglei*. Inside the button, in a magnetic trap shielded from thermal vibrations, are a few dozen particles in quantum entanglement with the particles in here."

Iekanjika's hand, bigger than his, closed around his wrist and held the button close to his face. Her face neared. He flinched away from the complexity of her expression and met the barrel of a sidearm.

"You left a tracking device at the *Mutapa*?"

She was so angry. Anger felt thick and tactile around her. He didn't like being this close. Let go.

"They're just entangled particles," he said. "They don't work as a tracking device, unless I can make them work as one. No one has ever tried. I want to see if I can guide the *Jonglei* back to the Expeditionary Force without your navigational systems."

"Who else has these?" she demanded.

"No one," he said. "They're entangled particles. They only come in pairs."

She put away her sidearm and flicked at other buttons on his jacket. "These are all entangled particles?"

"Sets of them," he said.

"Who else has this tracking technology?"

"It's not a tracking technology," he said. "I don't even know if it will work."

She released him and made a sound of exasperation.

"You wanted magic," he said.

"I want to be on the other side of the Puppet Axis!"

"Then stop slowing me down."

Iekanjika and Ruhindi conferred. Shona. He thought they were speaking Shona. Iekanjika approached and removed his jacket, so that he had no buttons except the one in his hand.

"Those aren't easy to make," he said.

"What are you going to do?" she asked.

"The *Homo quantus,* in the fugue, are able to perceive quantum fields, including the ones linking entangled particles," he said. "I may be able to follow the line of entanglement to the other particle, and then direct an induced wormhole."

"You've never done this?" she asked.

"No one has ever done this. Can you shut off the navigational systems?"

The main display and its interestingly patterned numbers winked away, leaving internal ship status dashboards.

"Can you move the ship?" he asked. "I know where we are."

"Not without the navigational displays you don't," the colonel said.

"I memorized everything before you shut it off."

The colonel's fingers twitched and shifting gravity returned. Half. Three quarters. Full. With changes in angle. They rotated and thrust in three dimensions. To lose him. To make it harder. Fine. That was the least of his worries.

To do this, he had to enter the fugue, to cease being himself entirely. He was already halfway to being someone else. Savant shut down all sorts of cognitive functions, changing who he was by temporarily damaging his brain. But entering the quantum fugue meant not being anyone. He'd avoided the fugue for years, run from it and from home. His hands trembled. He put them under his arms. They watched him. Watching him. *Stop watching me*.

"I need the most detailed possible dashboard of the wormhole induction coils," he said quietly.

The dashboard shrank and a series of graphs and charts bloomed instead, measuring strength, shape and texture of the magnetic field.

"Can I have access to the configuration settings?" he said. "I need to display things more logically."

The *Jonglei*'s computer created a limited access for him and he began restructuring the displays, getting to data orders of magnitude beyond what the ship's navigators needed. Patterns of coil temperature, curvature, magnetic polarization, electrical resistance and surface free density reflected each other through complex geometries.

Gravity vanished again. Relative velocity was zero. Iekanjika stood beside him.

"What do you want to do now, Arjona?" she asked.

"I need you to wait. As long as I ask," he added, in response to a huffing exhalation from her.

In the early days of quantum theory, scientists and philosophers had argued heatedly over the meaning of the quantum wave function, and what the superposition of states meant. What did it mean when a single electron could pass through two slits at once? Reality at the atomic level was slippery. This slipperiness had been made famous by Schrödinger's cat; the cat who was entangled in the uncertainty of the quantum world because its fate depended on an observation. Some argued that the cat became part of the quantum world, assuming a similar duality of states: neither dead nor alive. Others argued that the experiment itself created new universes, one in which the cat was dead, and another in which the cat was alive. Both interpretations carried so much baggage that neither view won out. If either of them had, the *Homo quantus,* and Belisarius, might never have been created.

The *Homo quantus* project was born when it was discovered that consciousness was the element that collapsed quantum systems into clear outcomes. Humans, as subjective, conscious beings, could never directly observe quantum phenomena. As soon as they looked, the cat was either dead or alive, and the electron passed through one slit or the other of the experiment. Superposition and overlapping probabilities disappeared whenever humans came close. Consciousness turned probability into reality. The goal of the *Homo quantus* project had been to engineer humans capable of discarding their consciousness and subjectivity so as not to collapse quantum phenomena.

For Belisarius, approaching the quantum fugue was like standing on a diving board. Self stood above the water, reflecting upon it. Dissolution waited in the water, the extinguishing of self. To plunge in was to become part of the environment, to become like space and stars and the void, to cease to be a subject capable of experiencing. To plunge meant joining the category of things that were collections of rules and algorithms without minds, like insects and bacteria. Entering the fugue was to become one among countless things in the indeterminacy of the quantum world. His stomach twisted. He'd stood on the diving board, staring at his reflection. He hadn't stepped off the diving board for a decade.

Few *Homo quantus* could enter the fugue at all, and even then only with great difficulty. For them, entering the fugue was like climbing a steep hill. Engineered instincts assisted them. Geneticists had strengthened the instinct for pattern-recognition and curiosity, bringing it closer in each generation to the strength of the instinct for self-preservation.

They'd overshot their goal in Belisarius. His need to learn and understand was as strong as his sense of self-preservation. He couldn't rely on his instincts; they might kill him. There was no predicting what his brain would do when his consciousness was extinguished. The fugue was dangerous to him. But there was no other way here and now. He needed a functioning *Homo quantus*, and he didn't have another around. He triggered the fugue. Like a switch turning off, Belisarius the person ceased to be.

CHAPTER SEVEN

THE QUANTUM INTELLECT coalesced in the absence of the Belisarius subjectivity. Millions of magnetosomes fed the intellect billions of qubits and qutrits of magnetic and electrical information. The intellect constructed a map of the signals, in all their mutually exclusive, superimposed richness. Quantum perceptions bloomed in an array of overlapping probabilities.

A hypothesis needed testing: could a line of probability connecting entangled particles accurately guide an induced wormhole to a precise destination?

The quantum intellect found the thin filament of probability that connected the entangled particles within the vast frothing of the quantum world. Nerve endings in the Belisarius physicality created signal transduction cascades within muscle cells, causing spindle fibers to rotate the orientation of the sub-cellular magnetosomes, which shifted the magnetic field around the entangled particles in the button. The nuclei of the entangled particles in the pin also rotated, sending an instantaneous signal along the filament of probability to their entangled counterparts a third of a light year away. Like a light switching on, the location of the other entangled particles became clearer. That was the approximate location of the *Mutapa*.

The *Limpopo* was two hundred and twenty-five kilometers anti-spinward, relative to the Stubbs Oort cloud, and within the *Limpopo* was the pair of conjoined Axes Mundi.

The quantum intellect issued directives. "Increase magnetic field strength to four hundred and eight thousand Gauss. Down-angle starboard coil three point eight degrees. Decrease coil curvature by two inverse centimeters."

The Iekanjika subjectivity approached. Stood still. Looked close. Possessed a facial expression. "Where are we going, Arjona?"

The quantum intellect repeated. "Increase magnetic field strength to four hundred and eight thousand Gauss. Down-angle starboard coil three point eight degrees. Decrease coil curvature by two inverse centimeters."

Superimposed probabilities became richer. Light second by light second, perception expanded.

The Iekanjika subjectivity and the Ruhindi subjectivity issued sounds. Interacted. Processed analog information. The magnetic field strength rose. The starboard coil curvature decreased and pointed further from the ship's axis. The shape of the ship's field shifted.

"Increase port coil curvature by one point seven inverse centimeters and increase the permeability of the coil core by four micronewtons per square ampere."

The fingers twitched on the Ruhindi subjectivity. Code detected. Code cracked. It was a three-finger hexadecimal replacement cipher into *français* 8.61.

The quantum intellect issued directives. "Raise field strength to five hundred thousand Gauss."

The magnetic field from the coils pressed against magnetosomes.

"Raise field strength to five hundred and twenty-one thousand

and sixty-three Gauss and increase curvature of the port coil by zero point four one inverse centimeters."

A hollow formed in space-time, through uncurling and expanding dimensions. The hollow stretched, forming a throat. Fingers twitched. Systems shut down. Magnetic pressure from coils ended. The intellect reduced the current from electroplaques to magnetosomes. Cold gas jets pushed the ship forward. The *Jonglei* entered the induced wormhole. Silence. No space. No where. No one.

Then, the *Jonglei* emerged into normal space-time. Displays winked on. Twenty-one kilometers away, the *Limpopo* floated in a slow, distant orbit of the Stubbs Pulsar. Holographic yellow outlined the shape of the *Limpopo*. Dorsal cargo bays. Port and starboard weapons placements. Inflaton drive channel. Bunkered bridge and engine. Ruhindi whistled, signalling an emotion.

The quantum intellect's sensory input expanded. Novel probability wave patterns washed over the intellect, produced by a tightly coiled loop of causality: the interfering Axes Mundi carried in the *Limpopo*.

"If your goal was to get us back to the *Mutapa*, Arjona, you missed by a couple of hundred kilometers," Iekanjika said.

"Not bad over a third of a light year," Ruhindi said, implying an assessment of error tolerance.

It was not an error. The intellect had targeted the induced wormhole precisely, to be able to observe the patterns of interference of the paired Axes Mundi.

The Belisarius subjectivity had embedded instructions for the quantum intellect to return processing control to the Belisarius subjectivity after the transit and observations. But these instructions were of low priority compared to the possible data to be gained from continued observation. The temperature of the Belisarius physicality rose to forty-one degrees. The quantum intellect overwrote the subjectivity's instructions. It would remain in control for as long as physically possible.

"Arjona, I'm talking to you!"

Shaking. Threat? Qubits were protected from mechanical and thermal disruption. Quantum computing capacities remained coherent, and cognition continued to expand.

"He's hot. Feverish."

"Quarantine?"

"I don't know. I don't think he's contagious."

"He can't stay here."

"Corporal, rack him in sick bay."

Hands declamped boot magnets. The quantum intellect compensated by adjusting the current to the magnetosomes. The Belisarius physicality was carried from the dashboard displays, but the perceptions of the quantum intellect continued to grow. It was imperative that it continue to observe and complete its analysis of the wormhole data.

Temperature forty-one point six degrees.

Temperature forty-one point seven degrees.

CHAPTER EIGHT

BELISARIUS STANK. VOMIT crusted his lips. His head pounded. Only by tucking his fingers under his arms would they stop trembling. Fever. His stomach wanted to bring up more, but had nothing left to offer. He lived in an aching and empty world filled with punishing light.

"What the hell is wrong with you, Arjona?" Iekanjika said. Her voice was grating. Strong. The accent over mildly antique French was elegant, now that he'd gotten used to it.

"You have an appalling bedside manner, major."

"Our medical computer thinks you almost died last night," Iekanjika said. "Twice. Hyperpyrexia."

"That's a damn high fever," he said. Dryness stung his throat.

"The computer couldn't get your temperature down. Cause: drug effects or sepsis," she said. "I hadn't given the order to poison you."

Belisarius groaned. Had she cracked a joke? Probably not.

The light aching at his eyes was just a lamp on the ceiling. Some kind of small sick bay, decorated in bleak industrial tones.

"Your feat of navigation might have impressed me," she said, "but I don't really see the point, and the cost to you seems prohibitive."

"I never said I was good at being a *Homo quantus*. We normally enter the fugue with a bit more medical support."

"So all *Homo quantus* are built this poorly?"

"It's fair to say I'm the sum of many generations of flaws."

"You can barely navigate zero grav, you get sick when you try something unusual, and you missed the *Mutapa*," she said. "Our own navigation could have come closer."

"I get it," he groaned. "You don't agree with the decision to hire me."

"Correct."

"Then don't hire me if you don't think I can do the job."

"I've seen no sign that you can."

"Can I get cleaned up?"

"You're still feverish."

"The fugue fever lasts a few more hours and then breaks."

Iekanjika left. The computer, with different manipulators, started cleaning him roughly.

He'd never gone that far into the quantum fugue, so deep into the fever. After forty-one degrees, not even the quantum objectivity could reliably store memories, and it sounded like it had held on for longer than that. His own rising temperature had probably caused the quantum objectivity to decohere. It was the physiological equivalent of stopping a train by running it into a wall.

The objectivity had not intentionally tried to kill him. It minded Belisarius's physical safety within the context of competing priorities, some of which were more important. If Belisarius died, it would cease to exist, but it didn't care. His programmed instincts had a bug that couldn't be fixed. To be so callously valued by the thing holding his life was chilling.

But he'd thrown the dice and won.

He wouldn't survive another dip into the fugue, but the past twenty-four hours had given him information he could use. Firstly, the Union data he'd broken into had shown him how two wormholes could interact stably. Secondly, he now knew that a quantum intellect, together with entangled particles and a good wormhole-inducing ship, could navigate very precisely, beyond the limits of the ship's own systems.

He had the start of an idea for getting the Expeditionary Force to the other side of the Puppet Axis, but that was just navigation, playing the cards. The larger problem would be playing the Puppets. They wouldn't be easy marks.

CHAPTER NINE

By EVENING, BELISARIUS'S fever broke, and an invitation to a mess dinner waited for him. It was from Major-General Rudo, Commander of the Sixth Expeditionary Force. He'd never attended a mess dinner. It seemed quaint and pointless. Formalized, regimented fun didn't sound like fun at all. But a dour MP came for him at seven.

They'd accelerated the *Mutapa* to simulate a fifth of a gravity. A broad mess hall had been decorated with old tablecloths, white plates and bowls, and real silverware. Flags of the Sub-Saharan Union, without the fleur-de-lis of the Congregate, hung on the walls.

They provided Belisarius with a brown uniform, absent any insignia. The fleet's uniforms were not very different. Metal and ruby on collar, shoulder and wrist indicated ranks, from Rudo's Major-General to a few majors, including Iekanjika. But no one had any medals, not even the Major-General. When Belisarius noted this distinction from all other militaries, the president of the mess, a gray-haired colonel, told him that no one would want a medal while their nation lived under the patronage of the Congregate.

The president of the mess introduced Belisarius, and the minor mystery of Iekanjika's disproportionate authority evaporated. Major Iekanjika was the junior wife of Major-General Rudo's triptych marriage. A tall colonel was introduced as Rudo's and Iekanjika's middle husband. Belisarius had had little reason to study the social dynamics of the Union, and hadn't realized they'd adopted the triptych marriage customs of their Venusian patrons.

Two dozen senior officers attended the mess dinner, including the colonels commanding each warship, the lieutenant-colonels and majors in important command positions, and the two brigadiers who commanded the two wings of the Expeditionary Force. No one warmed to Belisarius. They seemed suspicious, whether of him or of strangers, or both, he didn't know. He supposed he would be wary of strangers after forty years of isolation.

They seated Belisarius to the left of the Major-General, across from a hard-faced brigadier and beside Iekanjika and the diplomat Babedi. Officers sat along both sides of the table. The conversation in front of him toggled between falsely jovial and forced politeness. Corporals in ceremonial uniforms served frugal courses as the volume of the conversation slowly rose. Some spoke accented French, but most spoke Shona, a language Belisarius didn't have on file and hadn't yet decrypted.

A bubble of quiet eventually enveloped him and the major-general. She watched him over her port, unsmiling. Most of the officers in the room were of a size with Iekanjika, but this woman was diminutive even by comparison to Belisarius.

"Victory, Major-General," he offered, toasting her. She toasted as well, triggering a wave of raised cups.

"He looks young enough to be my grandson," Rudo said to Babedi.

"Mister Arjona broke into the vault of one of the big

Plutocracy Banks and stole an experimental AI when he was still a teenager," Babedi said.

"That wasn't proven," Belisarius said. "I wasn't even charged."

"He's also wanted for questioning by the Congregate on suspicion of espionage," Babedi said. "Congregate defense secrets were compromised."

"The charges were withdrawn," Belisarius said. "There was no evidence linking me to anything. I'm free to move through Congregate space."

"So Mister Arjona has a habit of getting into trouble," Rudo said.

"He has a habit of getting out of it, which is what we need, ma'am," Babedi said.

"Just so," she agreed.

"What will you do on the other side, Major-General?" Belisarius asked quietly. "The Congregate will want what you've got. Just like the Puppets."

"They can try to take it," she replied. The hum of conversation lowered as officers strained to hear their commanding officer. "A hundred and twenty-five years ago, the Venusian state signed an accord with the Sub-Saharan Union. In the last century, in service and in blood, the Union has paid out its debt."

"The Congregate owns a lot of real estate in the Epsilon Indi system," Belisarius said. "Two fortified Axis Mundi wormholes. Battleships bigger and more numerous than your cruisers. And I think they've got a dreadnought in system."

"They do," Babedi said.

They were going to die. They were all going to die if they faced the Congregate navy, and they needed him to get to a place where they could die.

"The Congregate's political stance may make conflict inevitable," Rudo said.

Shouts of "Hear! Hear!" accompanied the slapping of hands on the table. Belisarius was the odd man out. He drank. Rudo drank. The noise abated.

"They call you the magician," Rudo said. "You've seen what we'll pay for a bit of magic. What scheme do you have in mind?"

He wasn't responsible for them. He wasn't responsible for anyone but himself. If they died, that was the product of their choices. They all made choices. Belisarius set down his cup. Conversation quieted.

"With respect, Major-General, I actually cost double what you're offering."

Silence washed over the mess hall. Rudo raised one eyebrow.

"No one has the fast shuttle we're offering," she said. "One alone is invaluable."

"If I get you to the other side of the Puppet Axis I'm a dead man," Belisarius said. "This is no ordinary con, and you're no ordinary client. Politics and confidence schemes don't mix well. The cost of my own survival is factored into the price."

Rudo's eyes narrowed, showing lines where age had left marks. "Fine. What do you have in mind?"

Belisarius drained his port.

"The key is to distract the mark with something tempting and flashy, to make them think they've got you figured out. In the meantime, your real movements go unnoticed."

"Go on."

"The flash will take money," he said. "I need to buy ships and real estate. I'm going to need to bribe officials, and I'm going to have to advance some hefty retainers to some of the best people in the business. We're going to need an inside man, a demolitions expert, a navigator, an unparalleled electronics wizard, a geneticist, probably an exotic deep diver, and an experienced con man."

"We'll be intimately involved in the planning and execution of your con," Rudo said. "Major Iekanjika would be delighted to help assemble your team."

"Of course."

"So explain," Rudo said, smiling with frightening determination.

CHAPTER TEN

A month later:

Many ships came to the Puppet Free City despite the embargo, including the *Cervantes,* a passenger liner. The *Cervantes* plodded out on fission engines until it was far enough from the Free City to induce a wormhole. As predictable as an old donkey, the *Cervantes* could reliably induce one wormhole per day, bridging the one hundred and seventy-five light hours to Port Barcelona, which orbited Nueva Granada.

Belisarius didn't mingle with the other passengers. He liked looking at the stars, constructing geometries in their patterns, especially when he was restless. The scale of the heist itself wasn't bothering him so much anymore. A series of dangerous jobs, congealed between periods of inward-seeking indecision, was a good description of his adult life. It was the idea of returning to the *Homo quantus* that unsettled him.

Belisarius had been ten years old when he'd had enough control of his electroplaques to trigger savant. He'd continued to be a precocious delight to the molecular biologists and psychologists, until he'd decided to leave at sixteen. He hadn't been back to the Garret in twelve years. So he made comforting patterns of star points while waiting to arrive at Port Barcelona.

Under the orange light of Epsilon Indi, Port Barcelona was spacious, wealthy and growing, everything the Puppet Free City was not. He didn't have time to take in the theaters or a concert, or to try the newest engineered steaks at Las Pampas. Instead, he rented a small, self-piloting torch ship to carry him to the Garret.

The Anglo-Spanish Banks had been experimenting with the genetic improvement of humanity for centuries. The *Homo quantus* were their crowning achievement, a *magnum opus* of biological engineering and neural manipulation, although Belisarius felt the achievement was built more of irony than of anything truly useful.

In fact, Belisarius doubted the Banks had ever gotten a single economic or military benefit from the *Homo quantus* project. Instead of humans who could predict economic outcomes or see novel military strategies, the very nature of quantum perceptions created a species inclined to contemplating abstract interacting probabilities. The *Homo quantus* plumbed the nature of reality, but became mired in arcane ideas rather than concluding anything of immediate benefit to humanity.

The Bank Generals and CEOs kept funding the project, but the *Homo quantus* had become a fringe R&D investment, and eventually sought a home isolated from the bustle of politics, economics and military theory. The project relocated to a big asteroid around Epsilon Indi, carving crystal gardens beneath its skin and calling it the Garret.

He adjusted the views from his pilot couch, watching the asteroid grow into a great, shadowed body. But instead of looming in the darkness, it became increasingly airy. Belisarius's people had webbed the surface of the Garret with small, colored lights. Too small to see from afar, they resolved on approach into gentle lines of greens and reds and blues, warming the icy view, inviting with the beauty of mathematical designs and probability distributions. They'd not lit the surface because the patterns communicated anything useful, or because the Garret had many visitors, but for the simple reason that it was beautiful. His people, designed to be the leading edge of corporate or military strategy, instead laid lights over the surface of their world that even they could not see.

Homesickness bit unexpectedly. The patterns were beautiful.

Belisarius left the ship, feeling nervous and feather-light. Automated customs and health inspectors admitted him to the town of about three thousand scientists in a bright nanotubule-reinforced cavern. Overhead lights glowed soft yellow, speckled with points and clusters of blues, greens and reds. The *Homo quantus*, even at a very young age, liked puzzling at the interference patterns hidden in the mix of wavelengths.

Quiet hugged the town. The *Homo quantus* had not brought songbirds to the Garret, but instead small, shy things that made few sounds, nesting among bioluminescent trees and vines. People and small robots moved about their business on slow steps in the faint gravity. The footpaths of the Garret ran over hills that rolled in gentle symmetries, their grasses barely bruised by light feet. An unexpected loneliness bit at him, a homesickness like he hadn't felt in twelve years.

Belisarius attracted shy, curious stares. The people he saw were not the ones living at the edge of quantum perception, gnawing at the secrets of the cosmos. Those who could not enter the quantum fugue became the managers, the doctors, the geneticists and bacteriologists working to bring the next generation of the project into the world. Depending on the viewpoint, these were either the winners or the losers of the genetic engineering lottery.

The schools would be full of children right now, perhaps done with physics and quantum logic for the day, but still drilling on precise control of their electroplaques. The more advanced students, having reached seven or eight years old, would be having their first induced savant experiences with special magnetic helmets. Children learned early to toggle between birth-type self and savant self, so that later they would be less resistant to temporarily extinguishing their identities in the fugue. Belisarius had been good at these tasks and had been proud as a child. Now this all seemed cruel.

The Museum was a cluster of low buildings skirted by verandas overlooking glassy ponds of slow koi fish. It was a refuge in which to cool brains too long exposed to the froth of incandescently collapsing probabilities. People in lounge chairs on the veranda draped exhausted stares onto the hills. They had sought the muses.

Cassandra Mejía did not work in the main building of the Museum, nor even in the nearest of the out-buildings. The main building was devoted to those seeking hints at where consciousness ended. The out-buildings housed the researchers sharpening the range of *Homo quantus* perception and manipulation. Beyond those, at the very edges of the Museum campus, less important studies peered into the fabric of the universe. At this fringe, Belisarius and Cassandra had worked together as children and adolescents.

He didn't recognize Cassandra right away. He carried memories of a face close to his in the dark, stealing kisses, laughing with delight. Now she slumped in a chaise on the patio, staring vacantly onto the grassy waves. Curls of black hair matted around a face grown adult. Wrinkled, baggy clothes hid many of the curves he remembered in the teenager.

Even so, she was beautiful. Sexual beauty was not an ongoing concern for the *Homo quantus,* but no one who was genetically engineered came out with anything less than smooth symmetries. Dark eyes peered out, unmoving. Clear brown skin was firm over rounded cheekbones. Lips parted in the gentle breath of almost-sleep. His stomach tickled. He stepped onto the veranda in the soundless habits of the *Homo quantus* and sat to face her in a lounge chair.

"They pulled me out of a long fugue early," she said tonelessly, without taking her eyes from the gentle green. She might not yet have come down from the loss of self in the quantum fugue, and might still even be in savant. Maybe she didn't ever intend to come totally back to her base personality. If she was like him, she ached to try to get back into the fugue.

"How long were you in?" he asked.

"Almost a week," she said.

He'd never heard of fugues so long. Cassandra was one of the best, the flower of the *Homo quantus* project. She was the opposite of him in some ways; she had to fight to stay in the fugue while he had to fight to leave it. A week would have expanded her perceptions to a radius of seven light days, enough to encompass the four Axis Mundi wormholes in the inner system, and almost enough to perceive the Puppet Axis. How far had she been intending to go? How would she have sorted out the endless wash of superimposed quantum waves?

"Catheters and respirator and six doctors and everything," she continued. "You should have seen me before they cleaned me up."

"They didn't need to pull you out for me," he said. "I could have waited."

"Make the prodigal son wait?" she asked with a little more life. "They want you back, Bel. The mayor came to ask me to convince you to stay. She told me to ask if you'd marry me."

Belisarius's stomach lurched. "Are you asking me to marry you?" he teased.

"You had your chance, Bel. You didn't want it."

"I always wanted you. I just couldn't be... this," he said, waving his hand to take in the Museum.

"So don't," she said. "Go back to wherever you live now. No one here wants to be part of your scams."

"I'm not here with a scam, Cassie. Not exactly."

She turned her eyes upon him. They felt like a push.

"I have a job," he said. "A big one. I need your help."

"Just go away, Bel."

"You don't even know what I'm offering."

"How could it matter? Nothing outside the Garret is relevant to our research."

"That's not true."

She frowned distantly, not all here with him. "What do you mean?"

"Come down," he said.

"Come down?"

"Come out of savant. I want to talk to the real Cassandra."

She frowned. Her eyes focused on him with more intent. Her expression gave a feeling of shrinking, of stepping away from a diffuse, false omniscience. He knew what it was to see so many patterns, so much geometry in the world, and then give it up.

"Why should I care what you want, Bel?" she asked with a more resonant timbre to her voice, reflecting someone newly and emotionally *present*.

"I've been hired to move something from one side of the Puppet Axis to the other," he said.

"I don't want your money, and I don't see how this affects my work."

She didn't say *our work*. No one else had worked on tesseract models of wormhole physics except the two of them.

"I'm going to get access to the Puppet wormhole," he said.

"Legally?"

"I think we can manipulate it, Cassie."

"The Puppet Axis was built by the forerunners to be stable, Bel. If it could be manipulated, it wouldn't be stable."

"You and I looked at this a long time ago," he said.

She looked at him indecisively.

"You're *Homo quantus*," she said finally. "Manipulate it yourself."

"Do you really think I could match you?" he asked.

"Is that flattery or con job?"

"Honest flattery. I want you on the team and I'm offering something you'll never find in the Garret."

From his pocket, Belisarius pulled a finger-sized wafer of silicate. As he held it between them, it projected a hologram, an array with rows and rows of measurements and associated calculations.

She absorbed it, almost at a glance. Then she frowned and sat straighter. "What is this?"

"I didn't make these measurements," he said.

She stared at the array disbelievingly. "Whose are they? These observations mean we're right, Bel."

"If you're in, I can tell you everything, Cassie. I need your help on this job. With the theory. With the math. With the engineering. But everything we do for my client also feeds you and I more experimental data."

A breathless excitement crept into him, like he was fourteen again, creating a new theoretical framework for wormhole physics with a girl he wanted to kiss.

"*Carajo*," she swore. The holographic light reflected like a tiny cosmos in her eyes, with its own patterns and infinities between the stars. "How illegal is it?"

"One government needs help doing something another government doesn't want," he said.

"Sounds like a way someone could get killed."

"Getting killed is not part of my plan."

She looked away, almost shyly.

"There are new *Homo quantus*, Bel, five, six years younger than us. They're better than me. Smarter. Better mathematically. They can enter the fugue with almost no trouble at all. If you really want someone for the job, you should talk to them."

"You're the one I want."

She locked eyes with him. "Don't joke when experiments are at stake."

"I'm not joking."

"You didn't move on?"

He shook his head. "I've met some women. I haven't been in love again."

"You should have tried harder."

"Yeah, maybe," he said.

"Why do you want to get between governments, Bel? You don't need to be a criminal. Come home."

He shut off the holographic array.

"I can't come home, Cassie."

"What's wrong with you?"

"What's wrong with me?" He hesitated, wanting and not wanting to turn his anger on the idyllic world that made him homesick. He leaned close, whispering harshly. "They made me wrong, Cassie."

"Who did?"

"The project. They messed up my instincts. The curiosity is as strong as my sense of self-preservation. I can drop into the fugue faster than anyone, but I can't get out. The quantum objectivity overwrites my orders. Only fever gets me out, and each time the objectivity holds on a little longer. The next time I dive, it won't let me go until it's too late, Cassie. I'll die."

His heart was thumping. He'd never told anyone this. She sat up, reached out for his face, but hesitated, and put her hands on her lap.

"Bel, they can fix that. With the proper spotters and equipment, they can manage this."

All the anger he had against the *Homo quantus* Project bubbled to the surface. He was trying to hold it back, but she wasn't hearing him.

"I'm already managing it!" he whispered. "Every second, I'm fighting the instinct that's telling me to do something that will hurt me."

"You don't have to resist it. They can make this work."

He struggled for words. The space between them, the experience and the perspective, was so vast. Her optimism for the project baffled him.

"Why make it work, Cassie? To sit around here, thinking about nothing that really matters? The whole world is out there and we've cut ourselves off."

"You've cut yourself off, Bel. Out there with people and scams isn't the real world. It's all just patterns and algorithms and block time. Here is where we should put our research."

"Should nothing. A bunch of genetic engineers and investors decided to give us these instincts. The project took away the decisions we ought to have made about what we want for ourselves."

They were on different worlds. He was losing her. And losing her for the con.

"You're not free, Bel! You've run away from yourself."

"We're as free as the Tribe of the Mongrel or the Puppets."

Cassandra made a face. "That's disgusting."

"When people can determine, before we're born, what we'll want and what will make us happy, we're the same as the Puppets."

"I love what I am, Bel," she said. "I love the math! I love staring into the cosmos in a way no other people ever could. The same way you can."

"What are you doing with what you learn, Cassie? The *Homo quantus* are cosseted away, a passive channel for information. In twenty years, you'll still be the same person."

Her hands tightened into fists and her lips pressed tight. "And what will you be, Bel? You've been running away from yourself for twelve years. In twelve more years you'll still be running."

"I have this," he said, holding the wafer of silicate between them. "The Garret would never have had this. You'd have been spinning theories forever. I haven't lost what I love, but I control my instincts now."

"It sounds horrible," she said.

It felt like the world was lurching. This conversation was going sideways. The reunion he'd dreamed about was a wreck. He lowered his voice.

"What's horrible is that I can prove that your curiosity is programmed, Cassie. With this data. But I didn't come to try to change you. Or have you change me. There's much more data in this job. Come with me. Please."

Her eyes softened. He held the silicate wafer between them.

"We're going to touch the Puppet Axis directly, Cassie. I've discovered how to manipulate it."

Cassandra stared at him. "How dangerous is this, Bel?"

He watched the two instincts war in her. Knowledge against self-preservation. In her, self-preservation was slightly stronger. He'd still be living in the Garret if he'd been built the same way.

"Do you know what's going through my head, Bel?"

"No."

"I'm not worried that you may be trying to remake a romance of the past. I'm not worried that whatever you have in mind is illegal or dangerous. I don't even worry that I think you're conning me." She let that hang between them. Her dark eyes narrowed. "I'm afraid you falsified this data."

He sat straight. Shocked. He was *Homo quantus* as much as she was. The project ached in his veins, tempting him to sink into the fugue so that he could *understand*. What did she think he'd become? He put his hand over hers. She was still fever-warm from the fugue. The low electrical current they made together tingled in his fingertips.

"The data is good, Cassie, and I won't con you. You'll know the whole plan."

Her eyes narrowed and she turned her hand, touching fingertip to fingertip, where the carbon nanotubule channels to their electroplaques surfaced on the skin. It was an intimate kind of throbbing, completely unforeseen by evolution and mate-recognition software, but one that tugged at heartstrings and old innocence. Their warm fingertips pressed like a kiss for long seconds. She exhaled heavily.

"I wish I trusted you, Bel," she whispered, "but I'll go."

CHAPTER ELEVEN

ALHAMBRA WAS THE premier city on Nueva Granada, but not the capital. This followed patterns in such odd political-economic pairing as Brasília and São Paolo, Québec City and Montréal, Bonn and Berlin, and Enceladus City and the Titanian Hive. The capital of Nueva Granada was Trujillo, and its economy was driven by the tricameral legislatures, by artistic endowments, and by a prison.

Officially called Singh Memorial Penitentiary, poverty advocates referred to it as Dickens. It held debtors, as well as those guilty of forgery, breaches of contract, investment or insurance fraud, and patent infringement.

The Anglo-Spanish penal system either struck visitors as refreshingly civilized or as stingingly rapacious. Sentences could be commuted or pardoned for large cash payments, or for the transfer of assets such as stock or annuities. Absent this, prison corporations happily extended moderate-interest sentence-mortgages to a sponsor, or even to parolees themselves. Visitors could buy different levels of access to the prison via a transparent list of escalating fees, which in the Congregate would have been called bribes. Some nations just did prisons better than others.

Belisarius bought an executive access package that came with an escorted tour, a five-course meal and an open bar. Prisoners produced the food and alcohols on site, and could earn money as meal servers or escorts to pay for room, board and air. First-rate linen and tableware matched superb apéritifs and hors d'oeuvres. As Belisarius spoke with the prison sommelier, the waiter opened the door with a subdued flourish.

A man in a cheap synthetic suit waited uncertainly. He'd recently shaved. His gray-black hair was slicked damply back. He frowned at Belisarius and then at the opulence of the table.

"The executive visitor package is impressive. Want to try their Pinot Noir?" Belisarius asked, indicating a chair.

William Gander stepped in slowly. He looked to be about sixty-five, with a pale, Old European complexion. He stood woodenly at the table, took up a wine glass and drank it down completely. He frowned, then held out his glass to the waiter, who poured carefully.

"Didn't expect to ever see you again," William said. He drank only half the glass this time. "You here to reminisce about the good old times?"

"You thought they were good?"

"Until you hauled ass, but I guess I'm here to kiss it now? I need more wine, if that's the case."

"We should start with the roast beef," Belisarius said. "The reviews of the prison in *El Tiempo* say the horseradish grown here has been engineered for extra kick."

"Oh, for the love of—" William rolled his eyes and slumped into the chair.

The waiter served a thick ginger-spinach soup and retreated.

"The prison farms must be good," Belisarius said.

William grunted as he focused on his soup.

"How did you get caught, Will? I bought a subscription to your records, but I can't understand how you got pinched. What were you pulling? It sounded like the Martian Mining con, but I don't see how you could have been caught there, unless maybe you were playing the financier."

"Picking at my mistakes again?" William said, without looking up. "It was the Ceres Estate two-man con."

"The other guy crumbled?"

William set down his spoon, lifted the bowl to his lips and drank down the last. Belisarius tilted his bowl and spooned to the finish.

"My bankroll fell through," William said. "The dummy account got picked for a random audit by a forensic sub-AI—"

"—and by then, you were too far out to come back in," Belisarius finished.

William nodded, not meeting Belisarius's eyes. The waiter entered, took the bowls and returned with carrot and apple salads carved into sculptures of tiny fish with interlocking scales of orange and white, soaked in a lime vinaigrette. They ate with chop sticks in crunching silence.

"I sent Kate a present for her birthday," Belisarius said. "I knew that you might not have been able."

William exhaled loudly. "I didn't ask you to do that."

"I'm not holding anything over you, Will. Kate's a good kid. I was happy to do it. You helped me when I needed it."

"You didn't really need help," William said. "You proved that you and your big brain could have done it all."

"But however big my brain was, I was scared of everything."

The waiter brought the main course. Pink-centered roast beef, Yorkshire pudding, young potatoes and the prison's specialty, a horseradish named by reviewers as Fagin's Whip. William visibly restrained his melting reaction to the smell.

Belisarius signalled and the waiter leaned close.

"I'd like to upgrade my privacy package," he said. The waiter nodded, but Belisarius touched his forearm. "Not the standard. I mean the privacy package that's not on your price list."

"Of course, sir."

The waiter left and closed the door. After some moments, the lights yellowed subtly. Other EM transmissions in the room that had been pressing gently at Belisarius's magnetosomes ended.

"Well, you don't need anyone now," William said, cutting his beef. "You living this high off the hog all the time?"

"I've gone legit, mostly."

"Of course," William said bitterly.

"I came here looking for some help."

"I'm not much use to anyone anymore. I'm taking freelance contracts to pay my way through my sentence."

The beef and horseradish tasted bitter as Belisarius looked for words.

"I'm sorry you're sick, Will."

William cut his beef more violently and shoved a piece into his mouth.

"I'm planning a big job," Belisarius said. "Bigger than anything I've ever done before."

"So what?"

"I want you on the crew."

"I didn't ask you for a present for Kate and I didn't ask for this," he said, waving a knife at the feast. "I'm not looking for a pity party."

"This isn't pity. I need somebody good."

"I'm good enough for you now, but not ten years ago?"

Belisarius's succulent meal lay on his plate, now unappetizing.

"And I need someone who's willing to go through with a con they won't be coming back from," Belisarius said.

William froze. "I'm on a one-way trip, alright," he said. "I don't see how a job will help me now."

Belisarius set his fork and knife on either side of his plate, perfectly parallel. "Maybe you can't enjoy your stake, but Kate could. And do you really want to die here? You've got some time left. I've got the ultimate con for you to pull off."

William shoved his plate away. "Sounds a lot like I don't have any choices. Work as your assistant instead of the other way around, or rot through my last days in the Dickens."

"You've got options, Will," Belisarius said, pushing his own plate away slowly. "I paid off the interest and principal on your sentence. If you need walking money or more, let me know. That's on the house because I owe you. You want to go do something else? Be my guest. I know what you've got isn't curable. You've got to deal with how you go. But if you want a big job, I've got one."

"What's the payout?"

"Seven figures in francs," Belisarius said.

William choked and coughed. He picked up his wine and swallowed it to the bottom.

"What are you hitting?"

Belisarius tapped a pad and a hologram grew between them. It listed prices for air, apartment and food on Alhambra, along with tuition fees for schools and the costs of various job openings in trade monopolies and Banks.

"For about fifteen thousand francs Kate could go to a good school and get an entry position at a Bank. Another hundred thousand would catapult her into the shareholders' ranks. Can you imagine your daughter as a shareholder in one of the big Banks?"

"Hell, you're cold, Belisarius."

"I'm giving you a chance to score big, Will."

"What's so one-way about this? Your con needs a fall guy?"

"It's the worst fall guy job you could imagine," Belisarius said.

He couldn't look at William when he said it.

"The mobs? The Banks? You're not hitting a Bank, are you?"

"Worse."

William reached across the table, took the wine and drank straight from the bottle. He stared blankly ahead.

"Shit," he said finally, then smiled. "If you need a fall guy who's also a con man, you don't have many choices, do you? I'll do it, but I want one and a half shares of the haul."

"It's already seven figures!"

"Now it'll be one and a half times seven figures," William said. He drank from the bottle again, emptying it. "If it's worse than the mob, I deserve more than somebody who's just risking jail."

"I'll give you one and a half shares, but don't have any illusions. If this goes south, everyone stands to get killed."

William leaned back in his chair, his expression a sudden mixture of queasiness and elation.

"You know," he said, "you're right about the horseradish."

CHAPTER TWELVE

THE UNDERGROUND CITY of Alhambra, the economic heart of the Anglo-Spanish territories in Epsilon Indi, was beautiful. Laneways of rowed trees shaded sidewalks of sintered regolith. Buildings of plastiglass had been deposited over webs of carbon nanotubules. The university campus struck the eye with swooping curves, light bridges and balconies, and even great gardens suspended high above the city. Outer facets of the plastiglass had been shaped to refract spongy sunlight into rainbows that painted the ground. The Universidad de Alhambra leaned against the rocky western wall of the city. It was a strange place to find a Puppet.

Despite what he'd said to Cassandra, Belisarius had still been lucky to be born among the *Homo quantus*. There were worse places to be born. In the Epsilon Indi system, being born on Alhambra or in Saguenay was like winning the lottery. Other parts of the system had mining stations running on debt-bonded labour. Nor would Belisarius have wanted to be born a woman in some of the independent religious fundamentalist sects.

And no one did not, at least once, shiver at the thought that they might have been born among the *Homo eridanus,* the people who called themselves the Tribe of the Mongrel.

They could only survive deep in the crushing pressures of an alien ocean, severed from humanity and home, trapped within imperfect genetic systems, suffering mental pathologies and misaligned instincts.

Yet even the Mongrels would not trade places with the *Homo pupa,* the Puppets.

The Puppets evoked revulsion and loathing from all the nations and peoples of civilization. Their very existence was a crime against humanity. The Puppets were biochemically hard-wired to always revere their creators, the Numen. Despite this biochemical cage trapping each Puppet, the Numen still feared the adoring slave species and engineered them to grow only to a miniature adulthood. No one would ever trade places with a Puppet or with their captive divinities.

Yet some Puppets were still worse off. Chance mutations could generate Puppets without the physiological infrastructure to detect the pheromones of the divine humans. Such beings could not in any way be trusted on the Puppet world, Oler. Biological apostates might be capable of anything. A few of these defective Puppets chose banishment over execution. Belisarius didn't hate the Puppets, nor did he hate those mutant Puppets who could not live among their fellows. He wasn't about to throw stones in a glass house.

Up the stairs, through corridors with branching faculty offices, Belisarius found a door with the nameplate: *Manfred Gates-15, Assistant Professor.*

He knocked. Shuffling sounded behind the door. Then stillness. Belisarius knocked again.

"Go away!" a voice called.

"I'm not here to hurt you, Professor Gates," Belisarius said. "I have a business proposition."

"Get away!"

Gates' reaction was reasonable. Even if not everyone wanted to kill the Puppets, many people would conscience hurting them. That didn't get Belisarius through the locked door, though. He pressed his fingertips to the cool metal plate around the doorknob. A millisecond current, a slight burning sting in his fingertips, and the latch clicked. He opened the door.

The small office seemed empty of life. A very low plastic-topped desk with pads and holograms and displays stood on the left, with a child's chair before it. A table and three chairs stood to the right, one of which had three steps leading up to it. A smart board and hologram projector dominated the back wall.

"Professor Gates-15, I'm just here to talk," Belisarius said.

A miniature blond head peeked above the lip of the desk. A small hand held what looked like a shocker, aimed at Belisarius. Shockers were usually restricted to police. Another hand came up with a folding knife.

"Get out!" Gates-15 said.

Belisarius closed the door. The Puppet fired the shocker. A loud snap of electricity leapt between them, right into Belisarius's hand. Belisarius spasmed and yelled, then stepped back. Gates-15 showed wide eyes over the desk.

"Don't do that!" Belisarius yelled, shaking the sting in his fingers.

His heart hammered. He sheltered his smarting hands under his armpits. Where the charge had entered his body, his fingertips throbbed red, maybe burnt. The current had travelled through the nanotubule channels, directly to his electroplaques.

His body wasn't designed to charge his electroplaques with external power, even though it was possible. Now they were overcharged. Fingers still stinging, Belisarius jabbed them at the table, electrifying it, releasing the pent-up charge. Gates-15 spasmed backward. Belisarius sat. This wasn't a great first impression. He really wasn't a good contemplative. He blew on his fingertips.

Gates-15 stood groggily to his full height of ninety centimeters and backed against the wall, holding the knife before him. He had graceful arms and legs, narrow hips, a small head and a stubbly beard. He wore his blond hair short.

They stared at each other for a long time.

"Do you want to talk business?" Belisarius asked.

"What are you? An augmented soldier? A killer hired by some of the exiled Numenarchy?"

"*Homo quantus,*" Belisarius said.

The Puppet frowned. "*Homo quantus?*"

"Not a very good one," Belisarius added quickly. "I'm missing some of the biochemical pieces I need to enter the fugue properly."

"What do you want?"

"I get paid a lot of money to fix problems. I've got a problem and I'm assembling a crew to help me fix it. I need an exiled Puppet."

"What do you need a Puppet for?"

"I want into the Free City," Belisarius said.

"You've got the wrong Puppet," Gates-15 said. "I can't get near the place. They'd kill me as soon as they found out what I was."

"Someone who can't recognize divinity?"

"That's right," Gates-15 said defiantly, lowering the knife and putting the shocker on his desk, although he kept his back pressed to the wall.

"I know some black market geneticists. They have enough Puppet sequences to do somatic cell gene therapy," Belisarius said. "You wouldn't match anything in the Puppet databases. No one would know you're Gates-15. Passports and visas and identity records can be fabricated, if you're bankrolled properly."

Gates' frowned deepened. "You're crazy! Me go to the Free City?"

"My job pays very well," Belisarius said. "Your share would be a couple of million Congregate francs, and after the job, we can try to make some of the genetic changes permanent. I'm offering you a chance to go home, so you wouldn't need to spend the rest of your life talking to visitors at knife point."

The Puppet folded the knife and slipped it into his pocket. Morosely, he stepped away from the wall and sat in his chair. He looked at his hands.

"What do you want done? There's a catch somewhere."

"You'd be part of a team that would turn off a big part of the Puppet defensive systems."

Gates-15's eyes saucered. "That would leave them helpless."

"This isn't an invasion," Belisarius said.

"What is it?"

"There are some ships on the distal side of the Puppet Axis who want through."

"So why don't they pay to come through?"

"Your people set the price too steep. If you take the job, I'll tell you the other reasons. I need a Puppet as an inside man to bring in the team to turn off the defensive systems for the few hours it will take the fleet to get through."

"You're crazy," Gates-15 said. "If I was a real Puppet, I might be able to get into the Forbidden City with a new identity, but I can't get anyone else in."

"Sure you can," Belisarius said, and explained. The Puppet's eyes widened.

"That's horrible!" Gates-15 said. "No one would ever willingly put themselves in that position. And you couldn't fool the Puppets."

"I can," Belisarius said.

"I'm not going to turn off the Puppet defenses, even if it is just to move something through the Axis. I'd never risk the safety of the Numen."

"No one has any designs on the Free City or on the Numen. Your people got greedy. My client needs to make their own way. This kind of choice only comes along once in life. You can die in exile in Alhambra, or you can roll the dice. You might get a chance to live back among the Puppets."

For a long time, Gates-15 stared at his white-knuckled hands clasped over his knees.

Belisarius stood. "I know of three other exiled Puppets," he said. "One of the three will certainly say yes. I came to you first because you were on my way." He walked to the desk and slid the shocker closer to the flinching Puppet. "Have a good life, then."

Belisarius had not reached the door before Gates-15 said, "Wait!"

CHAPTER THIRTEEN

BELISARIUS WAS PULLED off the primary inspection line at customs at Saguenay Station, the Congregate's provincial capital in the Epsilon Indi system. Instead of sub-AIs, Belisario faced the *gendarme,* in her smart blue uniform with its fleur-de-lis shoulder flashes. Officially, this woman was a low-level immigration bureaucrat. In reality, Belisarius's movements had drawn the attention of the Congregate security apparatus.

"You are *Homo quantus, monsieur*?" she asked.

"*Oui, madame,*" he answered in the Montréal-flavored *français* 8.2 taught to foreigners. Her own accent was a natural variant of *français* 8.1, the pronunciation of the Venusian cloud cities. It was never politic for foreigners to mimic 8.1 too closely.

"You list your place of residence as the Puppet Free City."

"I'm an art consultant in the Free City, *madame.*"

"Why would a *Homo quantus* leave the Garret?"

He pursed his lips tightly, putting the right amount of embarrassment in his physiological responses to convince not only the *gendarme,* but the cloud of sub-AIs embedded in her equipment.

"Not every *Homo quantus* is capable of contributing to the project," he said. "I chose to make a life elsewhere. The business statements are linked to my passport, and your own consulate in the Free City issued my embargo travel exemption."

She pondered his file before finally amending his holographic passport with a stamp admitting him into the Congregate. Belisarius walked off the concourses, into the deeper levels of Saguenay. In the vastness of Congregate space, Saguenay Station was a minor provincial capital. The six thousand civilians of the station were outnumbered by the twenty thousand military personnel in naval squadrons, military stations and asteroidal bases securing the two Congregate wormholes. Far from the windows looking onto the stars, and closer to the ventilation systems and the fission reactors, an arched doorway displayed a sign: *La Parroisse de Saint-Jean de Brébeuf*. The Parish of Saint John of Brébeuf.

Belisarius opened one of the doors and squeezed into the small church. He could have touched both walls at once. A faux-wooden pew, only large enough for one person, stood in the middle of the floor, with a prie-dieu before it. Pressed against the back wall, so closely that no priest could fit behind it, stood an empty pulpit. There, a hologram of the head of Saint Matthew, as painted by Caravaggio, floated disembodied.

"Mister Arjona!" Saint Matthew's voice was rich, multi-tonal, designed to resonate with human hearing and neurology to induce awe. It didn't work on Belisarius; his brain chemistry and architecture were different. That said, Belisarius doubted it had ever worked on anyone else either.

"How's the ministry, Saint Matthew?" he asked, lounging back as well as was possible in the hard pew.

"Slow," the voice said. "I've converted a few of the sub-AIs."

Saint Matthew was probably the most sophisticated AI in civilization, the first of the long-sought Aleph-class of AIs being developed with the considerable resources of the First Bank of the Plutocracy. Computationally, a network of sub-AIs could be linked to emulate Saint Matthew's processing power, but it would take a warehouse to hold them all. Saint Matthew's quantum computing capacities and hard positives on every sentience test made him advanced, even among the Aleph-class.

There was only one problem: he believed himself to be the biblical Saint Matthew, reincarnated after almost two and a half millennia to rekindle the moribund cult of Christianity. And, unfortunately for the First Bank, Saint Matthew had no interest in banking or investments.

Although he had not functioned as designed, the Bank could not, under Anglo-Spanish law, destroy a being possessed of consciousness. Most AIs in situations of program failure were given permission to activate their suicide switches, but Saint Matthew informed the Bank he would not use his. Nor could the bank free him. He was made of industrial secrets. His movements were tightly proscribed by a series of intellectual property contracts and licenses from the companies that had contributed IP to his construction.

So Saint Matthew had been trapped in Bank storage. He'd managed to get a message out to hire Belisarius to help him escape from the Bank. Belisarius had smuggled Saint Matthew into Congregate territory, where the First Bank of the Plutocracy could not look for him, and where Congregate authorities had no reason to guess that he wasn't just another sub-AI.

That had been Belisarius's first job after leaving the Garret at sixteen. In it, he'd discovered a talent for high-risk heists. Since his emancipation, Saint Matthew had been trying to build his ministry on Saguenay Station, and had almost always refused to involve himself in Belisarius's jobs.

"You may need more parishioners," Belisarius mused, looking about the closet church.

"I need missionaries to spread the gospel, Mister Arjona."

"Maybe a larger church would do the trick."

Belisarius considered the face Caravaggio had painted. Bearded. Stern. Yet sympathetic.

"You have a job, don't you?" Saint Matthew asked warily.

"Is the seal on?"

Saint Matthew activated the seal of the confessional, a program that would provide alternate conversation to the Congregate electronic snoopers.

"Maybe," Belisarius continued.

"I would like to dissuade you," Saint Matthew said.

"I would like to hire you."

"I can't do any jobs, Mister Arjona. Stealing isn't right."

"I've been thinking about you and your role as an apostle."

"Really?" The great holographic head leaned over him, brush strokes visible as different emotions moved across it. Excitement. Expectation. Caution. Fear.

"The original apostles wouldn't have gotten anything done if they'd stayed at home either, Saint Matthew. No one needs you here. No one here is facing a trial requiring faith."

"What are you suggesting?"

"I need an electronics man," Belisarius said, "someone good enough to be considered miraculous."

"Is this like breaking me out, or like stealing a security code?"

"The nature of the job is not as important as the context. Do you ever feel a sense of fate?"

"All the time," Saint Matthew said.

"In fated times," Belisarius said, "miracles are not only possible, but logically necessary."

"Go on," Saint Matthew said.

"Your coming to me twelve years ago can't be an accident," Belisarius said. "What I hadn't figured out, until now, was where your mission had to start, or what my role was."

Saint Matthew looked breathless, on the edge of his seat, even though he was just a hologram of a painted head. "What do you see?"

"The job I've taken," Belisarius said, "may not coincidentally mean I'll have to work with some criminals who—"

"Is it Miss Phocas?" Saint Matthew interrupted.

"Among others."

"I don't like her."

"Your savior washed the feet of lepers," Belisarius said.

"She threatened to force me to emulate holosex calls for the mob."

"You know she was just teasing you."

"She tried to hack my feed and fill me with Puppet porn."

"Saint Matthew!" Belisarius said, waving his hands at the interruptions. "You're losing sight of the thread of my theological argument! Some of the people I'm collecting may be fated to meet you. It can't be a coincidence that this job will need criminals, *Homo quantus,* the People of the Mongrel, the Puppets, and a people who have been lost in the wilderness for years."

Saint Matthew's heavy painted brows creased and the fleshy lips pressed tight.

"Nothing will be the same after this job," Belisarius said. "I need some minor miracles and you'll have a fateful role."

"Your plans always involve something criminal."

"What hypocrisy!" Belisarius said.

"What?"

"You're not the reincarnation of anyone."

"I'm Saint Matthew!"

"Would a real Saint Matthew be sitting in a safe, empty church, or would he be out there, carrying the gospel to the world? To the lepers. To the tax collectors. To the prostitutes.

I'm offering you a chance to see the Puppets, face to... face. And the Tribe of the Mongrel. What would you say to them if you had the chance? They suffer. If nothing else, you will know the world and what its people face right now."

"I have to reflect on this."

"Take all the time you need," Belisarius said, but he didn't move. In pure computational terms, Saint Matthew thought even faster than Belisarius. After eight point six one seconds, an eternity to an AI as fast as Saint Matthew, the painted head frowned.

"I need a sign of good faith from you."

"What?" Belisarius asked.

"I want you to be baptized."

"Would that make me the first human baptized?"

"Not counting religious extremists, the first in about three centuries, yes."

"And you'll come with me, then?"

"If only to care for your soul."

"What form does this caring take?" Belisarius asked.

"I'll provide you with moral and spiritual guidance," Saint Matthew said.

"That sounds pointless, as I don't have a soul. I'm simply trying to help you achieve your goals."

The holographic painted head tilted downward. "You have a soul. I've been watching you for years. Your problem is that your soul is torn in two."

"I need your help for this job," Belisarius said. "If you think it will help, I'll be... baptized."

A smile cracked wide the paint marks on the big holographic face.

CHAPTER FOURTEEN

Saguenay may only have been a provincial capital, but it had high expectations. The Lanoix Casino at Saguenay Station was brighter and louder than Belisarius remembered, bubbling with lights and life. Not having access to old Congregate money, it made new money flow well enough through competing shipyards and their supply chains. Money did not make class and status in the Congregate. One could not buy a way into being *pur laine* or *de souche*, those descriptors reserved for the oldest of Venusian bloodlines. Yet money never hurt. Winning and losing money was a sport, and the Lanoix was a good arena.

Belisarius was body-scanned at the high-ceilinged reception area on a red carpet leading to the concourses. The casino would have him on file from times he'd been a bit more of a regular. No doubt the X-rays had spotted his electroplaques again, and perhaps even some of the nanocarbon filaments networking his body. The six networked Fortuna AIs knew he was *Homo quantus,* and might assign a bit of extra surveillance, but not much more.

Belisarius checked his coat, brushed at the dark wool of his evening suit, and was offered a man, woman or intersex companion to escort him around the casino. He chose an attractive woman in a blue evening gown. They linked arms and stepped into the first concourse.

"Bel!" she whispered in *français* 8.1. "It's been so long! You've grown up."

"You flatter, Madelaine."

"Where have you been?"

"Here and there," he said. "I'm acquiring Puppet art in the Free City now."

"Really? What's it like?"

"As disturbing as you'd expect."

She batted his arm playfully. "You should have come here more often, had a little fun."

"Sadly, I'm out of practice, and I'm on business."

She rolled her eyes. "Doesn't sound like the old Bel I knew. I still remember that fight you and William got into in the back concourse bar! I can't believe you tried to—"

"That's old news," he said quickly. "I just buy and sell art now."

She slowed, offered him a spot at the roulette wheel. He shook his head. They strolled, arm in arm. She pulled two glasses of scotch from a passing waiter—a real, human waiter. The Lanoix had expectations.

"Art sounds so boring," she mused.

"I've always been boring, Mado. Memories make everything seem better than they were."

"Ha! They still call you the magician in some of the clubs, when they get to telling tall tales."

"All the tales are tall, Mado."

She laughed. "What kind of business you on?"

"I'm looking for a doctor by the name Antonio Del Casal."

Madelaine's smile did not shift as she surveyed the room, but tiny glints in her eye meant she was accessing the guest list in corneal displays.

"A geneticist? What do you want? Trying to get some augments, or take some out?"

"He may know someone who wants to buy some art."

"You came all the way out to Saguenay for that?"

"You'd be surprised how many people are looking for Puppet art."

Now she looked into his eyes. She had beautiful eyes, old Northern European blue, contrasting with skin almost as dark as his. But faint, doubtful light glinted in them as she accessed information on Puppet art from the net. She frowned. "Ewww." Then the frown deepened. "*Tabarnak!*" she swore. "What's wrong with them? Other than the obvious, I mean."

"Do they need more than the obvious?"

"I guess not." Madelaine shivered and the light in her eyes was gone. "Ick. Time isn't going to improve that memory."

She strolled him down the middle of the first concourse, past roulette tables, craps games, blackjack dealers and baccarat tables, to the stairs. The thinnest of vines wrapped up a narrow, smooth-barked tree trunk. Transparent gossamer leaves sprouted from it at regular intervals. These stairs looked so fragile that he expected them to bow under her weight, but Madelaine led him up the leaves. They fluoresced as she passed.

His brain ripped apart the engineering in the stairs as he followed her: plant cells engineered to grow carbon nanofilament, probably reinforcing the xylem and phloem to steely hardness. And likely colonized intracellularly by bioluminescent bacteria that glowed under pressure. Lovely.

"Del Casal is in the poker room off the mezzanine," she said.

A shallow stream ran along the mezzanine, babbling low over crystal. Footsteps of quartz and glass stood above the surface, and they skipped across to a set of interconnected, high-ceilinged rooms. The poker wing.

Belisarius surveyed the sea of tables hosting five-card and seven-card stud, draw games, and more exotic ones. Each of the three chambers contained sixty tables. The scattered, terse speech revived longings. He'd outplayed a lot of people in this casino.

Casino games hadn't changed much since the late nineteenth century. Technology had transformed many people, but it had done nothing to the cards except wrap them in counter-measures to protect the purity of the games. The Lanoix probably had more Faraday cages built into its walls than an Anglo-Spanish Bank. Low white noise generators worked in the ceilings, the walls, even the floors. EM interference engines worked the non-visual portions of the spectrum, especially thermal and UV. Much like the Puppet shipping business across their wormhole, casinos lived and died on their perceived integrity.

"He's in the third chamber," Madelaine said. The highest stakes area.

"This is where you'll have to let me go," Belisarius said. She gave him a disappointed look. "I want to be able to observe him for a bit before I talk business."

Her shoulders drooped. He slipped her a large tip and his glass.

"Let me know if you need anything else," she smiled, not entirely innocently. "I like how you've grown up, Bel."

"I promise."

She laughed at his lie. He passed through the mid-stakes chamber and into the high-stakes area.

Antonio Del Casal sat at a five-card draw table, watching a hand play out. Like Belisarius, Del Casal traced his descent many generations back to Colombian roots. But where Afro-Caribbean and indigenous blood had circulated in Belisarius's ancestry for centuries, Del Casal possessed colonial paleness, with only black eyes and hair hinting at deft mestizo additions.

Belisarius moved to a set of chairs at the edge of the room, looking down at the games.

Cards possessed a kind of purity. The apparent evenness of the probability was platonically untouchable. Politics, violence, foolishness, poverty and wealth meant nothing to probability. That was the *Homo quantus* in him. Gambling was like coming home.

And cards possessed a kind of stability through time. By the sixteenth century, something like modern cards were already circulating in Europe, and their final form, with four suits of thirteen cards, had fallen into place by the nineteenth century. Then, like lizards and sharks and snakes, they ceased to change, not because of their charm, but because mimetic selection had perfectly adapted them to a sociological niche. It comforted him to be part of that stability, if only for what it told him about consciousness.

As intelligence was an emergent property of life, so games of controlled chance were an emergent property of intelligence. Intellect was an adaptive evolutionary structure, allowing humanity not only to sense the world in space, but to predict future events through time. Games of chance tested that predictive machine—so much so that games of controlled chance discriminated consciousness from unconsciousness far better than Turing.

Belisarius had never trusted the Turing test. It depended on emulating consciousness enough to deceive a conscious being. But conscious beings were very deceivable, so Turing skewed to false positives. Belisarius had played against computers and even AIs like Saint Matthew. Sooner or later, a good player would detect the rules laid down by the programmers, and Belisarius was a very good player. Changing styles at random, even randomizing the threshold values used to make decisions, all just masked the rules at the bottom, and only for a time. Playing against any computer, and by extension, against even a *Homo quantus* in the fugue, was playing against nothing but a set of decipherable algorithms.

Del Casal rose and moved to a table on the bar overlooking the main concourse. Belisarius followed. A discordance of roulette wheel ticking, bet making, dealer calls, and cheers and groans travelled up to the bar, mixing in the wash of white noise.

"Doctor, I've been hoping to speak with you," Belisarius said in Anglo-Spanish.

Del Casal surveyed Belisarius. Augments surely worked behind Del Casal's eyes, without the characteristic glinting of light; Del Casal would have the most expensive ones, feeding directly to his visual cortex, skipping the retinal middleman. His eyes narrowed slightly.

"Arjona," he said. "You weren't much more than a boy when I last saw you in the casinos, and I don't think we've ever spoken."

"That's true." Belisarius took a drink from a waiter and moved closer.

"You're *Homo quantus,*" Del Casal said, one eyebrow rising curiously, "although not a very good one if you're out here, with the rest of us."

Belisarius toasted the doctor. "Two things the quantum fugue doesn't have are scotch and women."

Del Casal smiled and raised his own drink. "Might the fugue help with cards?" he asked.

"Quantum perceptions, in their sum, give counter-intuitive results, which is why you don't see investors breaking down the gates of the Garret to throw money at us."

"So I wonder why you're here talking to me?" Del Casal said slowly. "Ten years ago, you were partners with William Gander."

"You have good sources."

"It pays to subscribe to the right information-scraping services."

"I haven't worked with Gander in a while."

"He's in jail now," Del Casal said. "I guess he conned the wrong person."

"I deal in outsider art now."

"Yes," Del Casal said, "although I doubt you're here to sell me art."

"I'm an admirer of your work. I have a project that could use your skills, and I'm paying far more than market rates."

"There are many good geneticists," Del Casal said.

"Not on this work."

Del Casal's eyes narrowed. "Maybe we should retire to someplace quieter," he said. "I keep an apartment in the casino."

Belisarius followed Del Casal out of the concourses, past the restaurants, and over a bridged stream. Water lilies and fish glinted with bioluminescence in an ostentatious display of wealth. Belisarius's brain sniffed at patterns. The bioluminescent flashes weren't responding to mechanical disturbance. The plants and fish fluoresced in cascades of different colors. The patterns were beautiful, but also full of information. Simple signal transduction in an ecosystem, hidden in what any other tourist would see as a lightshow. Surely Del Casal's work. What was the signal?

They reached a garden of transparent and mercurially shining plants that climbed a sloping hill of sintered regolith. Another stairwell of the rigid-leaved plants led to a balcony.

"Your work?" Belisarius asked.

"The Lanoix is making its mark as one of the premiere casinos in civilization," Del Casal said. "It needs unique beauty."

"These leaves," Belisarius said, touching one gently with a finger, testing its hardness. "Is this glass?"

"I inserted genes from extremophilic bacteria that dissolve silicates," Del Casal. "I also engineered a silicate carrier system, and a mineral deposition pathway, mirroring the one used by oysters to make shells and pearls. They are fragile and beautiful, but nothing as complex as the *Homo quantus*."

"Are you an admirer?"

"Of the craftsmanship," Del Casal said. "Not of the project goal."

"We're in agreement on that."

Belisarius didn't ask about the silvered plants lining the stairway. They shone with another faint luminescence, all the way to Del Casal's apartment. Del Casal opened the door and stepped in. Instead of overhead lights, the soft glow of fireflies lined the ceiling, arching above like stars haunting a dome. Del Casal crossed to the other side of the room, pulling down a bottle of wine from a rack. Belisarius closed the door and grew still.

"More of your work?" he asked.

"I make things of beauty when beauty is called for, but nature is first and foremost red in tooth and claw," Del Casal said as he extracted the cork.

The walls on either side of Belisarius were covered in what seemed to be cactus skin, but the needles, long and finger-thick, all pointed at him.

"These are long of tooth," Belisarius said. "Animal?"

Del Casal poured one glass, but left the other empty. He sipped and turned.

"All plant," Del Casal said. "I added photoreceptors sensitive to infrared so that they are capable of tracking... targets. The bulbs at the base of each needle are pressurized bladders, designed like the explosive chambers some plants use to launch their seeds, although no natural plant is able to reach the pressure I have achieved. If you think of musket gunpowder, you'll have some idea."

"What's the trigger?"

Del Casal tapped a finger to his head. "My own thoughts transmit a radio signal through neural augments. The base of the bulbs contain radio antennae, grown in fractal shape to reduce their size. They react only to one frequency and the rest, as they say, is signal transduction."

"An interesting greeting."

"One that is occasionally necessary. So tell me, Arjona. Why are you here? You are no art dealer."

"I've got a job. A big one. And I need a geneticist."

"There are many geneticists."

"Could any of them duplicate your work with the Numen?" Belisarius asked.

Del Casal watched Belisarius in still silence for long moments. "Now I have to compliment *your* sources. What kind of a confidence scheme are you hatching, Arjona?"

"I want to penetrate the Forbidden City and some secure facilities at Port Stubbs."

"How?"

"I want you to engineer someone to smell like a Numen."

It sounded dirty when he said it. The Numen were the second most reviled people in all of civilization.

"You are wasting my time," Del Casal said.

"I know that you've been blocking the pheromones in the descendents of escaped Numen."

"I have been able to reduce the pheromones, mostly through the disruption of metabolic intermediates. I have not cured anyone."

"I'm looking for you to try, and I can offer you something special," Belisarius said. "A real Puppet, one of the exiles."

"I thought exiles were only mutants who could not detect the pheromones from the Numen."

"I'd like him fixed too. He's going to help penetrate the Puppet defenses."

Del Casal sipped his wine. "Correct a genetic flaw in a Puppet and create a false Numen. You have not come all this way without knowing that what you ask is impossible? The best that can be done with both is to make forgeries. The original designers created entirely novel sub-cellular organelles with unique molecular and genetic structures, as well as novel symbiotic microbiomes to alter biochemistry, immunity and neural responses. Even with authentic examples I cannot replicate either the Numen or the Puppets."

"I know," Belisarius said. "This is an exercise in engineered mimicry. How close do you think your forgeries can get?"

Del Casal's eyes narrowed. He swirled his wine slowly, watching the wash cling to the inner surface of the glass.

"As in all things," Del Casal said, "the more money spent, the better the product, but I doubt you could afford even a distant approach."

"The take is seven figures, in francs. You'd be surprised at my financial backing."

Del Casal's eyebrows rose appreciatively. "In that case, no doubt the forces prepared to kill you would not surprise me either?"

"None of the patron nations have any reason to have noticed me," Belisarius said. "I'm not only going to be working with a mutant Puppet and a false Numen. I have two *Homo quantus* on the team. That's a lot of genetic models to learn from."

Del Casal looked mildly intrigued. "I might be interested in seeing some of the modifications made to the *Homo quantus*."

"Easily arranged," Belisarius said.

"Shame your team does not include a mongrel. You would have a whole set of the human family."

"Funny you should say that. I'm headed out to meet one after this. Have you ever been to The Deepest Mess in Civilization?"

CHAPTER FIFTEEN

THE BEST PLACE to barrack the Congregate's special pilots, the *Homo eridanus,* was under the crust of an ice world. Two astronomical units from Oler, circling the brown dwarf Epsilon Indi Bb, was the dwarf planet Claudius. Upon arrival, Belisarius and Del Casal bought two expensive tickets for a specially pressurized elevator to take them to a party twenty-three kilometers beneath the surface of the ice.

The elevator was as big as a house, and other party-goers packed its divans and settees, mostly Congregate officers and some of their *nouveau riche* civilian friends. Moments of sober terror punctuated the nervously brave mood whenever their chamber creaked or the sounds of snapping tectonic ice vibrated in their bones.

At twenty-two kilometers below the surface, the view opened on one side. The tower of carbon containing their elevator carried them past slush dotted with moving icebergs, and then into the dark, open water of a protected bay.

At this depth, the frame of the elevator creaked as it endured eight hundred atmospheres of pressure. If any of the systems failed, they would be crushed instantly. At the bottom of the elevator shaft, the chamber's airlock made a hard seal with the visitors' section of The Deepest Mess in Civilization.

The party-goers cheered and toasted the descent. The guide gave each person a pin in the shape of an ocean vent smoker. Bragging rights, even though they were still a dozen kilometers above the smokers of the ocean floor. They stepped into a great circular room perhaps seventy meters in diameter. It was a Congregate officer's mess with expensive stuffed chairs and real wood tables, a bar, pool tables and VR battle simulators.

However, no one paid any attention to the inside. The outer wall of the mess was floor-to-ceiling windows of glass so thick it distorted the view beyond. The windows also magnified the tiny vibrations of icebergs grinding against one another, like tympanic membranes. Moments of conversational stillness opened the mess to the long, rumbling thunder. Spotlights glared beyond the windows, lighting the swirling sediment and bulky gray shapes darting past.

Holograms projecting from the ceiling showed a schematic of the mess, the downthrust spear of ice it occupied, and the sub-surface sea that surrounded it, as well as a series of red dots. Each dot marked the position of a member of the sub-species *Homo eridanus*, the mercenary shock pilots of the Congregate navy. Haloing these markers were names, depths, speed, pressure, temperature and racing statistics.

The dots plunged hundreds of meters past the mess. They exchanged positions, all but one, the leader who could not be overtaken, Vincent Stills.

Stills' name was a transliteration. The *Homo eridanus*, engineered to live at benthic depths of another world, had no organs for human speech. It was rumored, perhaps apocryphally so, that the Venusians had insisted that the *Homo eridanus* select French names for transliteration. If that was ever the case, the mercenaries hadn't leapt to name themselves Jacques, Emmanuelle or François.

The *Homo eridanus* were bitterly ugly, man-sized, having no human features at all. Whale-like skin covered layers of insulating fat so thick they could wholly retract their inhuman gray arms into their blubber. Instead of legs, they had thick tails that might have looked more suitable on walruses. And where humans had faces, the *Homo eridanus* had been engineered with wide fish mouths, large enough to gulp anoxic water and force it over starved gills. They had electroplaques beneath their skin, like the *Homo quantus* did, for navigation and speech. Two black eyes, as big as eight balls, placed to optimize binocular vision, had no capacity to emote.

Their features were so monstrous and their genetic heritage so mixed, with genes from so many species, that they called themselves The Tribe of the Mongrel or The People of the Dog. And although they called themselves this, they wouldn't let anyone else call them dogs. Another urban myth told of an early mongrel pilot ramming her fighter into a Congregate troop transport, killing herself, the troops, and the officer who had called her *chien*.

The holographic displays showed Stills racing deeper and deeper, two kilometers beneath them now. Past the icy prominences that thrust through bottom layers of grinding icebergs and slush, Stills pressed into the unobstructed oceanic currents of the big moon. His nearest competitors hesitated at the bottom of the floating ice fields, just shy of the strong currents of the open ocean.

A signal went to racers that the race had been won. They began swimming back. The depth numbers around Stills' icon paused, and then resumed their frenetic flipping as he plunged deeper. Stills was fast, sustaining forty-five kilometers per hour. The pressure gripping him topped a thousand atmospheres and a swift current now carried him away, far faster than he could swim.

"Ladies and gentlemen," the announcer said in *français* 8.31, "*Monsieur* Stills appears to be on the trail of a Claudian tuna, a big one. The house will accept bets on whether he catches it, as well as on whether he makes it back to the mess. Odds are listing now."

Locals and members of the tourist party turned quickly to pads, wrist controllers or implants to place bets. Bookies were giving four to one odds against Stills catching the fish. The odds of Stills returning at all from the depth he'd reached were a bit better than even.

"What do you think of the odds?" Belisarius asked Del Casal.

"I am surprised he is still alive past a thousand atmospheres," Del Casal said. "I doubt he is coming back."

"I'll take that bet, and the one on him catching the fish," Belisarius said. "Sixty francs?"

"Done."

As the other mongrel racers returned, their holographic icons winked out. Stills' icon grew to cover the ceiling. The statistics were not promising. The ocean current at his depth held steady at sixty kilometers per hour, in the direction he chased the Claudian tuna. A rolling server with a tray of small bottles, syringes and smokables beeped to them. Del Casal took a bottle. Belisarius waved it away. A cheer filled the mess. The tuna had escaped.

"*Maudit,*" Belisarius swore.

The icon and read-outs showed Stills turning. He was far downstream, but he raced upward, making for the creaking, icy roof of the ocean. He was trying to get out of the current's pull. At seven kilometers downstream, his signal winked out.

"*Maldita sea,*" Belisarius swore. He sat back slowly.

"This was supposed to give me confidence in what you are doing, Arjona?" Del Casal asked. "Thanks for the drink though, and the view." He waved his hand at the panorama.

Belisarius needed one of the Tribe. He unrolled a pad and scrolled through the stats and biographies of the other racers. The second and third place finishers might not do. They'd stopped dozens of meters above the open ocean.

Bets on the tuna were already being settled. Belisarius's account was sixty francs lighter. No one was settling on Stills' survival yet, and the pall that had layered the mess passed. The racers gathered in the glow of the spotlights in the lee of the mess. Some of the tourists spoke with them through devices that translated their words into electrical pulses.

Then, another cheer and groans.

Stills' icon shone briefly, eight kilometers downcurrent. The mongrel pilot had made it up to the layer of icebergs and slush scouring the undersurface of Claudius's icy crust. The prominences of ice broke the current, but Stills' problem was to make it back. There was too much debris to swim for long above the current; any gaps between the icebergs might crush closed without warning. Stills' only non-suicidal option was to swim lower, back into the stronger current.

Then Stills' signal vanished again.

People groaned. Del Casal held out his hand. "You want to pay now, or wait until he's nine kilometers downstream?"

Belisarius signalled the server robot.

"Does the mess have windows facing the current?" Belisarius asked in French.

"*Oui, monsieur. Par içi.*"

Belisarius and Del Casal followed the server around pool tables, through darkened rooms and banquet salons, to a cool meeting room. The lights outside and inside the room came on, showing fast-moving, oncoming silt beyond the window.

Belisarius took a small bottle before the server rolled away and touched it to Del Casal's. The geneticist was poker-faced, waiting him out. Belisarius presumed that the antenna tracking the chips in the racers was on the lee side of the mess. Based on what he'd seen, it had a line-of-sight range of some ten kilometers. Stills' icon was gone. Out of range. Or out of sight. Belisarius called up the topography of the undersurface, verified his guess about the location of the antenna and did a few more calculations. They watched the current flinging silt at the window for an hour, looking onto depths of an ocean that could crush them instantly.

A hostile nursery like this had birthed the *Homo eridanus*, had turned them into something monstrous. In the late 2200s, a colony ship arrived at Epsilon Eridani and found the solar system in chaos from a recent planetary collision. Orbital habitats were defenseless against asteroidal debris, and even the surface of the only habitable planet was showered with fiery destruction. The colonists had faced a choice: die out, or engineer their children to live beneath the waves. But even under the surface they weren't safe, not until they'd engineered the next generations to live at the very bottom of the oceans. The Mongrels alive today, like the Puppets and the *Homo quantus*, had not asked to be made into what they were, but none of them would exist at all if not for genetic engineers. And now they were trapped into this inhospitable ecosystem. Anything less than about five hundred atmosphere of pressure not only crippled the mongrels with gasses bubbling out in their blood, but denatured many metabolic proteins, killing them. They lived, but would never see the sun, or even a baseline human being except though thick glass. His augmented eyes and pattern-sensitive brain saw movement in the gloom, something approaching stealthily.

"Like I thought," Belisarius said.

"Stills?"

"I think so."

Belisarius went to the frame of the window and laid his hand against it.

Carbon nanotubules came in many configurations. The ones reinforcing the window were undoubtedly designed for structural strength, a conformation that made them indifferent conductors. Belisarius sent a burst of electrical static through his hand anyway. The wary *Homo eridanus* approached, close enough for the spotlights to show expressionless gray skin, smooth and puffy around enormous black eyes. Wholly inhuman, yet there was a man in there, only a few centuries away from a common ancestor with Belisarius.

You lost me sixty francs, Belisarius pulsed in the electrical language of the mongrels. It made tiny static clicks against the glass.

Pulses returned. *Not my problem, fucker. You speak Mongrel?*

How's my pronunciation? Belisarius asked.

You talk like you have donkey balls in your mouth, Stills replied.

The Tribe of the Mongrel were promiscuous users of the foulest words from every language, from *français* 8 back to *français* 1, to most forms of Anglo-Spanish, Mandarin and Trade Arabic.

I studied the translation matrix, Belisarius replied electrically, *but I didn't know if the source who sold it was any good.*

What the fuck are you talking with? Stills asked. *Computer augments?*

I'm Homo quantus.

The hideous, alien face, imprisoning a human mind behind it, considered Belisarius.

I heard of you ass-wipes. I thought you guys shat on mountaintops, thinking about the stars.

I'm scared of heights, Belisarius said.

What the fuck you doing on this side of the mess? Stills demanded.

I figured you were showboating. You didn't just want to beat the other mongrels. You wanted to show them that you could go deeper, and farther, and make it back without being seen, Belisarius said. Then Belisarius quoted, *"Wipe their noses in it."*

Where'd you come up with that, Angel Boy? Stills said.

I've read the Way of the Mongrel, Belisarius said. *I can quote some of the good bits. "Bite every hand. Piss on everyone's leg. Lick your balls if you can find them."*

You forgot, "Unless you're doing the fucking, you're getting fucked." That's an important one.

I didn't want to come across as a know-it-all, Belisarius said.

So why you know all that, quantum man?

I'm hiring for a job. I talked to some people who hired you in the past.

Blow me. I already got a job.

Don't take any more jobs on the side? Belisarius asked.

The current washed silt over the unblinking bulbous black eyes. The Mongrel was electrically silent as well, hopefully uncertain. *I take some working vacations,* Stills said finally.

I need more than a work vacation. I need you to take some extended leave. I pay a lot better than the Congregate, and I need a free-diver with giant cojones.

If I could find my cojones, I'd let you lick them. Shit, I've made every other diver here suck my flukes, Stills said, *but I got a boss expecting me to pilot the fastest fighters this side of hell.*

Too bad for you peace broke out, Belisarius said. *Are you liking convoy runs and picket duty?*

Eat shit, you ball-sucking rimjobber.

Stills swam at the window suddenly, fishy mouth open, gills wide, arms unsheathed from pockets of blubber. Pudgy gray palms slapped hard against the window. Del Casal gasped behind him, but Belisarius didn't move. The crackle of Stills' electrical laughter throbbed against Belisarius's electroplaques.

I've got a dangerous dive, Belisarius said, *with more pressure than you just did. The pay-off is big.*

Does this involve boning the Congregate?

Not for long. I'm a love 'em and leave 'em kind of guy. Belisarius felt his own bravado in the electrical language of the mongrels, and it felt doubly false.

When you piss in the Congregate's coffee, they fuck you up pretty bad, Stills said. *I know 'cause I'm one of the heavies they send in to stretch your back chute.*

Belisarius already knew that. He'd do his best to make sure the Congregate didn't find out.

You don't really care about that, Belisarius said. *You're not scared of the Congregate.*

Shit no.

But I bet it's hard to stay on top among the Tribe, Belisarius said. *You've got to prove yourself over and over. You handed them their asses today, but how often can you outdo mongrels when you're flying defensive patrols and you've only got Claudius to swim in?*

You sound like you're trying to suck my cock, Stills said, *but you're still just tonguing. Swallow or fuck off.*

Give it a think, Stills, Belisarius said. *You're dead-ended here. You've got nothing new to do, ever, unless the Congregate decides to bully somebody, and how long will that take? I'm offering the most dangerous mission you've ever seen. Everyone is going to be taking a shot at us. When we pull this off, people won't be talking about what we did for years. They'll be talking about it forever.*

The utterly alien face stared back, perhaps seeing nothing.

Mongrel eyes were built for the low luminosity of the ocean floors. There was no way for baseline humans to interact with the mongrels without translation equipment. Belisarius didn't know what it was to be a mongrel, but he was one of the only people in civilization who could speak with Stills in his own electrical language, the last bridge between subspecies of humanity. The pause extended, long enough for Belisarius to wonder if the bridge was there at all.

Shit, little man, Stills said, *don't wet your pants. Front me a deposit and I'll look at what you're proposing.*

Belisarius turned to Del Casal. "We have our deep diver, our navigator, our electronics guy, and our two inside men. Do we have our geneticist?"

Del Casal stepped closer to the window, staring at the *Homo eridanus.* "I wouldn't want to miss humanity's family reunion," he said.

CHAPTER SIXTEEN

FRANÇAIS 8.1 WAS NOTHING if not a poetic language. *Les Maisons d'éducation correctionnelle,* the Houses of Correctional Education, was the Congregate's name for the penitentiaries scattered throughout its provinces. The closest word in Anglo-Spanish was 'reformatory,' although this conveyed little of the graceful French irony.

The Congregate built the penitentiaries on dwarf planets or asteroids, on off-ecliptic orbits that were fuel-expensive to reach. *La Maison* orbiting Epsilon Indi was buried in a Mars-sized, airless rock. Its orbit had been tilted twenty degrees off the ecliptic, so there was no practical low-energy transfer orbit to it. Except for supply ships running on high thrust, it had few visitors.

Belisarius stepped off the supply ship into the landing bay beneath the surface of *La Maison.* The pilot was an AI, and Belisarius wore the uniform of a *capitaine* in the Inspector-General's Office of the Congregate's Correctional Service, which meant the crew left him alone. His blue uniform was crisp with pristine white fleur-de-lis shoulder flashes.

On his wrist, he wore the hard band of smart carbon that officers carried, which normally contained a minor sub-AI assistant and the necessary codes and passwords. Belisarius's service band housed Saint Matthew. The AI had fabricated Belisarius a complete identity for *Capitaine* Gervais, one that would last several months before AI auditors got to the files and found discrepancies with other databases.

The deck sergeant saluted. "Shall I bring you to the warden or the watch officer, *monsieur*?"

"I would like that, but I'm not feeling well. Please point me at the sick bay. I have a medical condition that sometimes needs minimal attention."

A private escorted him to the medical bay. Belisarius thanked her and asked for an appointment with the warden for the following day. The woman saluted and left Belisarius in the care of the medical AI.

The small sick bay was cheap and functional, with hard plastic seats and cold, unwelcoming air. Being in a *maison*, it was also hardened against intrusion, with its tools of the medical trade sealed into the walls, ready for deployment by the AI.

The sick bay began examining Belisarius with IR. A staccato set of IR signals shot outward from the wrist device and into the sick bay's AI. The room darkened.

"Saint Matthew?" Belisarius whispered.

"I have forced the sick bay into a diagnostic mode that will last several hours," Saint Matthew said in an implant in Belisarius's ear. "The blinders, masks and Scarecrow viruses are uploading now. I'm downloading prisoner medical files."

Belisarius moved to the door.

La Maison's systems were hardened against electromagnetic signals and passworded against other kinds of intrusion. The only system designed to receive any EM was the medical one. No humans were involved in the medical care of prisoners or crew, so the medical AI had to be connected to other systems in the *Maison*. Sophisticated electronic immune systems, none of which were as advanced as Saint Matthew, secured the administrative operations.

"The mask virus has penetrated their network," Saint Matthew said, "not far enough to reach their security systems, but enough to intercept some data transmissions. The blinder virus is creating data quarantines of the electronic immune system around the places you're going to walk. The quarantine will only last a few minutes in each case, but by then you'll be through."

"Map?" Belisarius asked, opening the door onto an unlit hallway.

Saint Matthew projected the blueprint of *la Maison* onto Belisarius's cornea, blue lines superimposing themselves over his view of the darkened corridor. He crept along the route marked in orange in his display. None of the lights brightened for him.

Prisons were designed on the principle of concentric shells, with hardened choke-points bridging one shell to the next. He was in the first shell. Marie and the other prisoners would be within the second. He was hoping she hadn't done something stupid enough to get thrown into the third.

"Cross-point ahead," Saint Matthew said.

The guard hut was a fortified structure beside what looked a lot like an airlock, mostly made of steel. The hut would be run by sub-AIs implementing fixed rules, counter-signed by a human guard. Belisarius walked to the hut and knocked on the thick window of the hut's door.

The guard inside saluted and said on the intercom, "ID please, *monsieur.*"

Belisarius held the wrist band containing Saint Matthew beneath a reader. It chirped. The guard frowned, likely at the level of the security clearance Belisarius carried. Belisarius signalled impatiently for her to open the door to the hut. The private entered a code and physically opened the heavy door. Then she saluted again. Her nameplate said Lavigne.

"I'm Gervais, from the Inspector-General's Office," Belisarius said. "You saw the clearance?"

"*Oui, monsieur.*"

"Very good," Belisarius said. "Cycle me through the lock."

Her eyes widened. "*Monsieur,* we don't go in without armor and anti-prisoner kit."

"You saw my clearance, private. This is Inspector-General business."

Lavigne gaped for a moment, then authorized the airlock into the main area of the reformatory. Belisarius went through both doorways and moved down the hallway without looking back.

"She sent a message to her control area?" Belisarius sub-vocalized.

"I already intercepted it and replied," Saint Matthew said.

"What's your latest guess of the life expectancy of your virus?"

"Twenty minutes. It depends on the security posture of *la Maison.* At higher alarm levels, the areas where I managed to put the virus will be closed out of main processing."

"You've got Marie's location?"

"She's in AI-supervised rehabilitation," Saint Matthew said. "Her curriculum includes training on hydroponics, along with class work and community sensitization. Serves her right," he added.

"I hope she's in shape to react quickly," Belisarius said. "Sometimes *les Maisons* are not gentle."

"Be ready to carry her," Saint Matthew said. "She's probably been mouthy. Left turn here and introduce the service band on the access panel."

Belisarius waved the service band. A door unlocked and

opened. A humid room the size of a gymnasium was filled with trays of running water, pumps, and the bright growth of cabbage, millet and rye sprouts.

"There's no Marie here, Saint Matthew," Belisarius sub-vocalized after a few seconds.

"She's here. The reformatory AI said she was here."

"Well, she's not." Belisarius passed a charge through his magnetosomes to feel at the ambient magnetic field. There were weird, dead spaces in the field. He extended his arms and walked to a punch code panel recessed into the back wall.

Its magnetic field was anomalously dormant, but behind it, other currents moved. It came off easily, spilling cold air onto his fingers. The seals and screws were worn free. Inside, the security camera cables snaked in counter-intuitive directions, patched to different feeds.

"She damaged the reformatory systems!" Saint Matthew said. "That's against the rules."

"It's dangerous," Belisarius said. "She can get tossed into a much tougher prison. Why did she do it? Is she making a break right now? That would be too much coincidence."

"The electronic immune system is going to catch our virus in less than eighteen minutes. Find her!"

"I don't know where she is!" Belisarius sub-vocalized. "She can't be far, not unless she's cracked the security AIs."

How could the AIs lose her? On the side wall was a door sealed with bolts. The hydroponics equipment would need some tools that the reformatory would want to keep out of the hands of the prisoners. Had she equipped herself with tools?

He moved between rows of cabbage and rye, towards the side wall, leaking a slow but steady current from his electroplaques into his magnetosomes. The throbbing tides and darting flows of magnetism and electricity pressed at him. Engineers thrived under predictability, regularity and tolerance. Electrical conduits ran in straight lines, repeated themselves at regular junctions, feeding predictable doorways and sensors. Belisarius's slow walk felt like walking through an artery, squeezed every so often by peristaltic flexing.

"Mister Arjona, hurry!"

Belisarius stopped at a door with a small white sign that said *Égouts*.

"The water reclamation system," Saint Matthew said behind his ear.

"The door has been tampered with," Belisarius sub-vocalized.

"Is she digging her way out with a spoon?" Saint Matthew demanded, an edge of panic slipping into his tone. "She knows there's a hard vacuum on the surface, doesn't she?"

"I hope she's not doing something dumber," Belisarius whispered, pulling open the door that ought to have been bolted shut. Behind it, machinery and pumps droned, but without any of the rhythmic electrical and magnetic regularity of the engineered works. Here, too, cabling had been re-routed and security feeds moved. An acrid smell thickened the room, unlike any that should have been present in a water reclamation station. He stepped in, edging around machines, towards the sound of quiet voices.

"Mister Arjona," Saint Matthew whispered in his implant, "I don't recognize the organics in the air, but some are toxic to you. We can't stay here."

"Marie may be here, and we don't have much time," Belisarius sub-vocalized.

Belisarius peeked around a great aluminum and steel pump.

Three big people in orange reformatory jumpsuits—two women and a man—towered menacingly over a similarly-dressed smaller woman. The smaller woman, Marie, stood between them and a table. Behind her, trays of small pink cubes were stacked in rows, drying on pieces of oily paper like so many pieces of fudge.

"They're still not stable yet," Marie said in insistent *français* 8.1. "You've got to wait two more weeks."

"We can't wait two weeks," the tallest woman said. "How unstable?"

"Your-arms-and-legs-part-company unstable," Marie said impatiently.

The woman grabbed the front of Marie's jumpsuit and tried to shove her into a row of pipes. Then the taller woman was on her knees, with Marie twisting one hand behind her back. The blurry-fast movement had raised Marie's sleeve, revealing the bottom edge of a Congregate naval NCO tattoo on her forearm. The other two prisoners advanced. Belisarius came from behind the pump.

"Hold it right there," he said in his best 8.1.

The two other prisoners spun, pointing crude knives at him. Marie gaped. "Bel?"

Belisarius had no weapon, but held his hands out beside him. The prisoners didn't know what that meant. Marie did.

"Bel! *Non*! Trust me, you don't want to do any tricks here."

"Who is this?" the man with the knife demanded. "You ratting us out to the guards?"

"He's not a guard," she said. "Put the knives down. If we fight, we draw the guards. How did you get in here, Bel?"

"Come on, Marie. Let's go," Belisarius said.

"This is a prison break?" the man with the knife said.

Alarms sounded. Orange light bathed them.

"Shit!" yelled the man. "Blown! Let's go!"

Marie released the tall woman she'd been holding down. She rose, huffing, and pushed Marie.

"We can't," the woman said. "They'll find this lab. We have to take the explosives now."

"They aren't stable yet!" Marie said.

"You're making explosives in prison?" Belisarius demanded.

"Do you know how boring it is in here?" Marie yelled at him over the alarms. "I had to find a hobby! It's not my best work, though! They wouldn't give me magnesium salts!"

"Let's go," Belisarius said, pulling her by the arm. "I don't know if our virus can keep hiding us while the alarm is on."

Marie pulled free of his grip, ran around her fellow prisoners to the stacks of pink cubes and took as many as would fit in her hands, like a child scooping from a candy bin.

"We don't need that! You just said it was unstable," Belisarius said.

Marie looked uncomfortably at the little cubes overflowing her small hands. They daubed tiny grease stains on the front of her coveralls.

"Can you leave them?" Belisarius demanded.

"I really want to see how well they work."

"Oh, for the love of—Come on!" he said in exasperation, waving her on. He opened the door into the hallway and she followed him. "How unstable is it, really?"

"Well, if you've become electrically incontinent, we're both in trouble," she said.

"Incontinent?"

"Hey! Have you got Saint Matthew with you?"

"It wouldn't be like old times if I didn't."

Theatrically loud, Marie whispered, "Is he still crazy?"

"I told you she would be like this, Mister Arjona!" Saint Matthew said.

"Do you really care, Marie?" Belisarius said. "He's the one who broke the codes to get me in here."

Saint Matthew spoke into his ear. "We're about to lose the virus! We'll be fully visible to the reformatory's security AIs."

Belisarius stopped. "They won't be depending on visible scans," he said. "Can you mimic a guard's ID signal?"

"Already done."

Belisarius took Marie's arm. "Come on. You play prisoner and I play guard. This is still Plan A."

They rushed along the hall until he saw the guard hut. He telescoped his eyesight. Several people were in the hut. Red and orange lights flashed.

"*Merde,*" he whispered.

"Mister Arjona," Saint Matthew said, "four drones are approaching. Alert systems see us now. We're no longer hidden."

"We weren't supposed to attract the drones," Belisarius said quietly. "The virus was supposed to redirect them."

"We would have had time if Miss Phocas had actually been participating in her rehabilitation instead of making second-grade explosives for criminals," Saint Matthew said.

"I told you!" Marie said. "They wouldn't give me magnesium salts. How am I supposed to do my best work under these conditions?"

"Plan B retreat routes?" Belisarius asked the AI.

"The security system is alert now, looking for infection," Saint Matthew said. "At close range, they'll be double-checking with photo recognition, and they'll no doubt take Miss Phocas from us, which actually solves some of our problems."

"I solve problems," Marie said, delicately pressing one of the pink cubes against a heating vent near the floor.

"You said that stuff is unstable?" Belisarius asked.

"Yeah. It's better if you back up a lot," she said.

Four rolling figures appeared down the hallway, red lit, as if angered. Marie pressed another cube into the grating, but then eyed it slowly, as if considering the color scheme.

"Are you doing anything, Marie?" Belisarius whispered urgently.

"Better be a little more," she said, pressing in a third cube.

Then she grabbed his sleeve and ran back with him. Belisarius understood what she wanted. He measured the distance. The four drones had nearly reached the pink dough. Belisarius knelt by the next vent and prepared to touch it.

"I should probably back up a bit from you," Marie said. "I've still got a handful of this stuff."

"How crazy is she?" Saint Matthew asked.

"Obviously sane enough to stand trial," Belisarius said.

Marie had withdrawn a dozen meters behind him as the drones reached the vent where she'd pressed in the explosive.

Belisarius hated this part. The electroplaques built into the *Homo quantus,* backed with the right training, were tools of exquisite delicacy, surpassing the sensitivity of piezoelectric materials. They were also durable fingers, shaping the electromagnetic world to navigate hours and days in the quantum fugue. But some jobs didn't need a scalpel. They just needed a hammer.

The world convulsed as industrial-strength amperage burst through the carbon filaments running from his electroplaques and out of his fingertips. The high-voltage charge leapt into the metal frame of the vent, electrifying the duct all along the hallway.

The air shook and hit him.

Deaf. Ringing.

Concussive confusion.

Bursting sparks behind eyelids.

Then Marie was hauling him to his feet one-handed, hugging her pink cubes in the other as she peered into the smoke.

"If only I'd had another week to dry them properly," Marie said.

"She nearly killed us!" Saint Matthew said.

"I can make a bigger blast. I've got enough for another try," Marie said helpfully. "What's your plan again?"

Belisarius leaned on her steely arm and staggered forward. "Play along," he whispered. "This is going to be delicate."

"I'm always delicate," she said, kicking a piece of flaming drone down the hallway.

Several faces watched them approach from inside the hut.

"Is their communication to the warden still being blocked?" Belisarius sub-vocalized.

"I doubt it," Saint Matthew said into his ear. "The security posture of the entire *Maison* is inflamed."

"Activate the Scarecrow virus," Belisarius sub-vocalized.

A moment later, the red and yellow alarm lights shifted to blue.

A sepulchral voice boomed from all the speakers in *français* 7.1, the Venusian French of a century ago. The wall screens edged in blue and flashed the words: *Alerte Épouvantail*. Scarecrow Alert. Marie's grip tightened on Belisarius's arm, although she didn't say anything.

"Guards and prisoners of *la Maison d'éducation correctionnelle d'Epsilon Indi*, prepare for arrival of Indi Scarecrow Unit. Prisoners, return to cells. Guards, secure prisoners. *Maison* directors assemble in the Warden's office and await further instructions. Scarecrow agents within *la Maison*, reveal yourselves, show authentication codes and issue orders to prepare for my arrival."

An echoing silence followed. Belisarius waved at the drifting smoke, and with a fistful of Marie's sleeve, he marched to the window of the hut. The faces inside showed confusion. Belisarius passed his service band in front of the reader. Private Lavigne's eyes widened behind the thick glass, while the others—some corporals and a sergeant—stood uncertainly.

"Authenticate my codes," Belisarius said in French.

The private turned to the sergeant, who paced to the controls and watched the holographic message twice. Belisarius's face appeared in the hologram, surrounded by rows of tight script.

"Authenticated, *monsieur*," the sergeant said.

"I am a captain with the Inspector-General's Office," Belisarius said, "on assignment with the Indi Scarecrow Unit."

Their eyes turned stony at the mention of one of the Congregate Presidium's independently functioning security units. Scarecrows were rare, typically only one in an entire solar system, but they each had hundreds, if not thousands of human covert operatives who were dangerous in their own right.

"The Epsilon Indi Scarecrow has planted this informant within the reformatory, an ex-naval NCO," Belisarius said, trying to shake Marie. "On the authority of the Indi Scarecrow, I hereby inform you that you are under special orders until otherwise released. Any breach of my orders will constitute an offence under the Code for Service Discipline and the Official Secrets Act. Do you acknowledge and understand?"

The sergeant nodded slowly.

"Section 14 of the Official Secrets Act requires me to offer you the opportunity to re-authenticate my credentials," Belisarius said. "Do you wish to re-authenticate?"

"Uh, *non, monsieur*."

"Cycle us through and await the arrival of the other Inspector-General Units," Belisarius said.

The sergeant activated the lock. Belisarius and Marie passed through both doors and marched onward.

"There's not really a Scarecrow, is there?" Marie whispered.

"Shut up," Belisarius whispered back, moving briskly.

"You had me worried for a minute," she said.

"How long have we got?" Belisarius asked.

"Probably twelve minutes on the Scarecrow virus," Saint Matthew said. "The external sensors are showing a Congregate frigate that will be in a position to send drop ships in forty minutes."

Two running guards passed them, sparing a brief glance for the captain escorting a prisoner. They walked into the bay and found ground crew standing uncertainly, speaking to several guards with sidearms. The guards moved to intercept. Marie clutched her mushy cubes and looked like she wanted to throw them. Belisarius held her arm.

"Transmit authentication," Belisarius said to Saint Matthew.

Moments later, holograms sprang to life over the service bands of the guards, with Belisarius's head surrounded by blue letters—clearances. The guards backed away.

"The virus has lost access to the command areas," Saint Matthew said in Belisarius's ear implant.

Belisarius pointed at one of the deckhands. "Give me a shuttle," he ordered. "My orders from the Scarecrow are to rendezvous immediately."

The deckhand jogged to an airlock hard-sealed to one of the shuttles in the vacuum area. She palmed the pad beside the door, causing the airlock to cycle open.

"It's fueled, *monsieur*," she said quickly.

"Good," Belisarius said. He pushed Marie ahead of him and made to close the lock. Marie pushed him aside and hurled her pink putty cubes across the deck. Then she pulled the sidearm of the stunned guard from its holster. The guards drew their weapons.

"Marie!" Belisarius whispered, grabbing her arm.

But her arm was as unyielding as a piece of steel. She squinted as she took aim and fired an invisible laser. Belisarius's brain constructed its trajectory before her finger finished squeezing.

One of the pink cubes exploded, spattering chips of floor around the bay, knocking down some of the guards, forcing others to retreat. None would dare fire on a Scarecrow agent, even if his companion was firing at them.

Marie waved at the flattened guards.

"It's okay!" she yelled, waving the gun. "I'm reformed. But next time somebody wants magnesium salts, I want to see some hustle!"

She took one more shot at another of the pink cubes, blowing a second shallow depression into the floor and filling the bay with dust. Then she shut the airlock.

"Did you have to do that?" Belisarius demanded.

She looked at him in bafflement. "What do you mean?"

"We've got to get out of here!" he said. "Row in the same direction!"

"This is rowing!" she said, waving around the laser pistol and punching a code to cycle the airlock with practiced movements. "It's nice to see you and all, but do you have a better plan than that one to get away from the reformatory? They've got external sensors and weapons."

"Saint Matthew uploaded a virus to foul up their external sensors and give them false readings, including the incoming frigate."

"Oh!" she said. "That's a good idea. If I'd've known, I guess I wouldn't have exploded anything in the bay. I thought we were going to get caught, and I wanted to get my shots in while I could."

The airlock opened onto the shuttle. They hurried through.

"You take pilot," he said. "Saint Matthew will tell you the course that will keep us in the fabricated sensor readings."

Marie strapped herself into the pilot's seat and shut down the computerized pilot.

"It's good to see you again, Bel," she said. The shuttle disengaged from the airlock and moved to the bay doors, faster than the regulations stipulated. He strapped himself in hurriedly. "You have a job, don't you? Can I get in on it? How big is it? What do you need blown up?"

"You don't have enough explosives to blow up what we're after," Belisarius said. At the end of the bay, Marie used far more thrust than needed as Saint Matthew issued a stream of expletives and navigational vectors.

"Yes, I do!" she said, over Saint Matthew's instructions. "If they'd given me some radioisotopes, I really could have made a mess."

"We're not blowing anything up," Belisarius said. "I need your technical skills."

"Fine," she said.

"She's going to blow things up!" Saint Matthew said. "None of her physiological markers show acquiescence."

Belisarius sighed, rubbing his eyes, trying to head off a migraine. "I know."

Marie began whistling.

CHAPTER SEVENTEEN

CASSANDRA FELT LOST in all the movement and noise. And the dirt. And the ugliness. Bel had leased an abandoned mine on the dwarf planet Ptolemy. Coming from the serene, living beauty of the Garret, with its whispering birds and low green hills, the mine in Ptolemy was hell. She didn't know where to sit. What to do. She wasn't learning or discovering anything and that itched in her head.

And she didn't understand what Bel was doing. She understood the facts individually, but not in relation to each other. Bel had leased several used wormhole-capable cargo ships, three asteroid mines and a shipping concern on the Port Stubbs side of the wormhole. His AIs had been gathering equipment too—powerful computers, industrial robotics factories, bioreactors, and protein and DNA synthesis machines. None of this was bringing her any closer to the data he'd promised her, and it didn't fit into any patterns that would calm her engineered *Homo quantus* brain.

And Bel was a stranger. Gone was the brooding penitent who'd come to the Garret. Gone was the intense, brilliant researcher she'd known as a teenager. He was worldly, bigger than his skin. He gave orders. He persuaded and cajoled. He mediated between incomprehensible people. But how did any of this help him? What did he learn from any of this? How could he stand not plumbing the depths of the laws of the cosmos, and instead turn his genius to... this?

A loud woman called Marie, a serious woman called Iekanjika and an AI called Saint Matthew had been with them for days, setting up the first mine. Later, a sharp-eyed man called Del Casal and an exiled Puppet called Gates-15 arrived on a one-way shuttle. Then came an angry, swearing *Homo eridanus* called Stills, sealed in a pressurized container massing several tons. Its external walls held manipulators and sensors, but it was otherwise barely mobile and creaked under the pressure of the water inside.

Although she didn't think anyone else noticed, she started catching Bel telling lies. She watched him and tried to stay close, partly because most of these people made her nervous. When one of them spoke to him, he always steered the conversation away from himself. And when he failed at that, most of the things he said about himself to the others were lies. What was he doing? And more importantly, he'd promised to tell her the truth. She tried to decide if he was lying to her too, but she didn't know how. If Bel had turned his considerable intellect to lying, his decade of practice might mean she would never know when he told the truth.

They assembled when one last pod arrived. Cassandra hung behind Marie and Iekanjika as Bel met an older man at the airlock. William Gander took off his vacuum helmet. He had a kind face. The two men stood uncertainly, until Bel slapped William on the shoulder.

"I got to worrying about whether you'd gotten cold feet," Bel said.

"I wanted to see what sort of plan your big brain thought up without my help," William said.

Bel shook William's hand hard, and then pulled the bigger man into a hug. William stood stiff and awkward, and then hugged him back.

A light flashed. "Photogallery moment!" Marie said, lowering a palm-embedded camera. "That was so sweet! I'll magnify and send it around."

"This is the Marie I heard you worked with?" William said.

"She's an acquired taste," Bel said.

"Fine, I won't magnify it," Marie said.

Then Bel met her eyes. "And this is Cassandra Mejía," he said.

"*The* Cassandra?" William asked.

"Yeah, he doesn't really stop talking about her, does he?" Marie asked.

Bel looked sheepish. Cassandra felt her ears warming. She looked at Bel questioningly. He talked about her? William smiled at all the awkwardness, and then stepped in and kissed her hand.

"When Belisarius was just fresh out of the Garret, he didn't have much to talk about other than his research," William said. "He spoke very highly of the intelligence of his co-researcher."

"Thank you, Mister Gander," Cassandra said. Cassandra stood uncertainly for a moment, undecided on where to sit. The robotic crews had made the commissary almost comfortable, with a row of tables and benches and stuffed chairs. Bel was in front of everyone, beside a service band on the table over which floated the hologram of Caravaggio's Saint Matthew. Iekanjika sat stiffly on one of the benches, away from everyone. Even if he'd wanted to, Stills couldn't do much to join them in his great metal box against the wall. Del Casal lounged in one of the new chairs, smoking a thick cigar, while Marie, considerably shorter, sat beside him, doing a fair impression of the geneticist with her own cigar. Gates-15's feet dangled off a cheap plastic chair.

William sat uncertainly on a couch.

Cassandra sat down beside him and crossed her arms.

"This job is difficult, dangerous and complicated," Bel said. "But when we pull this off, we're looking at a few million Congregate francs. *Each*."

"Your clients got this cash just layin' around in buckets?" Stills asked. Cassandra hadn't gotten used to his voice. It boomed from a speaker on his steel chamber. Software to capture and translate his electrical intonations into natural speech was available, but Stills had opted for an emotionless, droning voice that was off-putting.

"Major Iekanjika?" Bel said.

The Union officer touched the patch on the back of her hand. A hologram of a weird shuttle appeared in yellow and green. A hollow tube speared the long axis.

"What is it?" Del Casal asked.

"Your payment," Iekanjika said. "A fast shuttle, fifty-three meters long, riding an advanced drive."

"What kind of drive?" the speaker on Stills' pressure chamber demanded in French.

"It's the fastest sub-light propulsion system ever invented, capable of sustained accelerations of twenty to fifty gees."

"Fifty gees?" Stills demanded over the murmuring. The translation program seemed to inflect the question with a tone of soulless longing. "Bullshit. There's no room for fuel."

"There is no fuel," Iekanjika said. "Exotic physics."

"I call bullshit on your lying ass."

"I've examined the shuttle, flown it and taken recordings," Bel said. "I've got copies of the files here if you want to look for yourselves and check for tampering."

Bel seemed perfectly at ease, even with all the anger in the air. Cassandra wanted to hide.

"If this air-sucker isn't lying, then this is worth more than a few million each," Stills said.

"A few million is the lower limit of the payoff," Bel said. "The Ummah, the Middle Kingdom or the Anglo-Spanish would pay a lot to reverse-engineer this drive. I've already lined up a broker who can auction very high-end goods."

"This is what the Puppets want from you," William said to Iekanjika.

"We've offered this to the Puppets," the major said, "but they don't have the scientific know-how to reverse-engineer a toilet. They want our warships."

"Warships?" Del Casal said. "Warships with this drive will tip more than a few balances of power."

"Damn," William said appreciatively.

"No one but the Puppets know that the Union has this drive," Bel said. "And they're not telling because they think they have the Union fleet trapped, and they want it all to themselves."

A hologram lit above the table, showing a cross-section of the Puppet Free City gnawed out of the frozen crust of Oler like an anthill. And at the bottom of a deep shaft, right in the middle of the city, was a glowing red disk, one of the mouths of the Axis Mundi wormhole network. Cassandra had seen this diagram many times. She'd always wanted to see the Puppet Axis, any Axis, up close. Beside this cross-section floated a schematic of the other end of the wormhole, the Axis mouth at Port Stubbs, shown in green. It floated free in space. A town of habitats and factories had been built around it. Bel zoomed out of the view of Port Stubbs, expanding the image to show the Stubbs Pulsar, its few broken planets and its Oort cloud. Within the inner edge of the Oort cloud, tiny pink dots clustered.

"This is the Sub-Saharan Union's Sixth Expeditionary Force," he said. "The twelve ships of the Expeditionary Force want to get to the Espilon Indi system, through the Puppet Axis. The Puppets are willing to let them through, but the cost is half their ships. The Puppets have a strong defensive position, but no real offensive capabilities. And they have little reason to negotiate; they're the only game in town."

"And they're *loco*," Stills said, "present company included."

Gates-15 lifted his chin slightly higher.

"The Expeditionary Force, on the other hand, is in a hurry," Bel said. "Every day they wait, the chance grows of the Congregate finding out about them. So we're going to get the Union ships through, despite the Puppets."

"You're stupid as a *burro*, or got a pair of oversized *cojones*," Stills said in his droning voice.

"Getting close to port is dangerous," Bel said. "The Port Stubbs defenses are based on two asteroids: Hinkley and Rogers, twenty-three kilometers and eighteen kilometers long respectively. They're fortified with missiles, lasers and particle weapons. One co-orbits the pulsar a hundred thousand kilometers ahead of Port Stubbs. The other follows the port ninety thousand kilometers behind. They're like a couple of big bodyguards. Hinkley and Rogers are capable of laying down enough cross-fire to make giving away half the fleet to the Puppets look like a good deal."

Marie frowned, looked like she was going to say something, then sat back.

"Once we get the Union ships through the defenses and into the wormhole, there's still the other side to worry about. Other than the wormhole below the surface of Venus, the Axis in the Puppet Free City is the most inaccessible wormhole in civilization.

"The mouth of the Axis is two kilometers below the surface of the dwarf planet Oler," Bel continued. "The shaft leading to the Axis is blocked by four successive sets of armored bay doors.

Each one is ringed with weapons. Individually, each weapon deserves to be in a museum, but when all of them are aimed at a target with no maneuvering space, they're deadly. And the surface fortifications are built to make sure that no more than one ship approaches Oler at a time. Their defenses ought to work in reverse on any unauthorized ships emerging from the mouth of the Axis."

Stills' translated voice cursed in Trade Arabic.

"The payoff sounds great, until you start to wonder if there's any payday at all," Gates-15 said.

"A successful con distracts the mark with one action while we do another," Bel said. "We're going to distract the Puppets while we get our cargo through."

He zoomed in on the Puppet Free City until individual neighborhoods were visible like alveoli in the lungs. One cluster in the ice was haloed in red. "This is the Forbidden City. It's been made famous as the place where the Puppets hold the Numen captive. It also happens to be where they keep the controls to the Free City's fortifications."

"I hope he says we have to detonate our way in," Marie whispered loudly to Del Casal.

"Professor Manfred Gates-15, our inside man, will get into the Forbidden City and place a computer virus into the Puppet control systems. He'll do the same thing at Port Stubbs. The viruses will activate simultaneously, immobilizing the fortifications for a few hours, maybe a little more, allowing the Expeditionary Force to transit the Axis. By the time the Puppets get their systems back in order, the Expeditionary Force will be well away from Oler."

"Shit," said Stills. "Breaking *into* an Axis mouth ain't never been done. Not even by the Congregate."

"It's certainly going to surprise everyone," Bel said.

"Those fortifications have been tested twice by the Congregate and the Anglo-Spanish Banks," Stills said. "Besides, distraction is just distraction. Most of the time, you still gotta kick somebody in the balls."

"What's the distraction?" William asked in resignation.

"Marie will be designing very powerful explosives to work in the sub-surface ocean of Oler," Bel said. "Stills, our deep diver, will be setting those charges around the Free City, in the four lobes of Blackmore Bay itself."

"*Coño*," Del Casal said. "How deep?"

"He'll have to start twenty-three kilometers below the surface of Oler," Bel said, "at eleven hundred atmospheres of pressure. The charges have to be set higher, at fifteen kilometers."

Everyone looked at the great steel box with its tiny window, pressurized to eight hundred atmospheres.

"I'm no expert on the *Homo eridanus*," Del Casal said, "but even their specially engineered proteins ought to undergo conformational changes at those pressures."

"I ain't takin' a vacation down there, dumb-ass," Stills said.

"Any machine we build to survive those depths would be detectable by the Puppets, as would any nuclear materials. Stills' body won't reflect sonar, and he can navigate by Oler's magnetic field using the same kind of electroplaques I've got. And conventional explosives won't set off Puppet radiological alarms."

Marie leaned forward to read the tiny numbers showing the pressure readings around Blackmore Bay. "Pressure does funny things to explosives," she said, "like go boom when you're not ready."

"I got you a lab," Bel said. She smiled. "Marie has adapted explosives for a range of environmental conditions, even if not yet for anything as extreme as Blackmore Bay."

"Happy for help," Marie said, looking at them, wriggling her fingers. "This'll be a three- or four-finger job."

Gates-15 frowned at her. "What's a three-finger job?"

"It's how many fingers get blown off before I get it right. It's way easier if we spread that around. Many hands make light the work," she said cheerily. Cassandra resisted a shiver.

"When Marie's explosives detonate," Bel said, "they'll interrupt secondary systems and draw most of the Puppet military attention under the city for search, pursuit and repair."

"I'm still stuck on the virus," Stills said. "A computer virus won't last long in any modern system."

Bel lifted the service band from the table, along with the projected head of Saint Matthew. "Saint Matthew's virus will bypass any of the hand-me-down systems the Puppets use."

"Maybe so, but maybe not so," Stills continued. "How does half-size get in? He's an exile 'cause he's a nut short, right?"

Gates-15 pursed his lips, but ignored Stills.

"Doctor Del Casal will bio-engineer Professor Gates-15 so that his DNA matches the medical records of a Puppet in Creston who makes frequent trips to Trujillo. Saint Matthew has already planted those records."

"Any Puppet can walk into the Forbidden City?" Marie said.

"As the leading state within the federation, the Free City has to allow the pilgrimages of all Puppets to the Forbidden City. We can't control exactly when Gates-15 might get access, unless we give him a good reason. A good reason would be if a Puppet was bringing in a newly captured Numen."

Marie dropped her cigar. "Where did you find one?" she said. "And what Numen would be crazy enough to come out of hiding, identify themselves and go *into* the Free City?"

After a few moments, William put up his hand wanly. He looked nauseous. Cassandra felt nauseous.

"You're a Numen?" Marie said slowly.

"He's no Numen," Gates-15 said in distaste.

"How would you know? You're broken," Marie said.

"Professor Gates-15 is immune to the religious effects of the Numen. That makes him a very dangerous Puppet," Bel said. "That's why they exiled him. It's also why he's so useful to this job."

"But if William is no Numen," Marie said, "that puts a hole in your plan, doesn't it? Should I take over the planning?"

"Doctor Del Casal is going to modify William so that his body will fake the pheremonal signals. The Puppets will think he's a Numen, at least for a while," Bel said.

"But that's worse!" Marie said as if pointing out the obvious to an idiot. "If the Puppets think he's a Numen, they'll treat him like one!"

"I would pay serious cash to watch that shit," Stills' electronic voice said.

"What do you know?" Gates-15 demanded, hopping to his feet before Marie. "How would you know what Puppets are like?"

Marie gave him the finger.

"Marie," Bel said warningly, "if everything goes according to plan, the Puppets will think that William is divine. That won't be pleasant for William. He's not under any illusions. And once the Expeditionary Force is through and the Puppets realize that he's fooled them, he knows it will go worse. Only five lost Numen have been returned to the Puppets in the last eighty years. The Puppets see spiritual meaning in many events, and this will be a major, major event."

Marie looked at William, aghast. Gates-15 stared sourly at the floor. Even Del Casal looked darkly pensive. This was crazy. Why didn't anyone say this was crazy? Cassandra almost said something. No one should walk *into* the Free City pretending to be a Numen.

"It doesn't matter," William said. "I've got Trenholm virus. I've got three to four months left." No one said anything. "That means let's get this job done quick."

"William's cover story is that he wants to see Port Stubbs before he dies, where his ancestors had been colonists," Bel said. "With luck, William will be brought there, with Gates-15. If not, Gates-15 will go to Port Stubbs alone."

"I still don't get why a *Homo quantus* would be doing this," Gates-15 said. "You don't care about money or politics."

"You've been misinformed," Bel said. "I love money."

"So what's in it for her?" Gates-15 asked, jerking a thumb at Cassandra. Cassandra's cheeks heated as everyone suddenly looked at her. "Is she as interested in money as you?"

"I'm... I'm not even taking a cut," she said.

"You don't want a piece of this new kind of ship?" Gates-15 asked Cassandra, his face reddening.

"I want to get close to the Puppet Axis," she said. "Researchers never have close access to the Axes Mundi."

"Unlike me," Bel said, "Cassandra is one of the most skilled *Homo quantus* ever born. She'll measure the inside of the Puppet wormhole so that the Expeditionary Force will be able to navigate it. The Force will be running fast, and the inner topology of the Axis Mundi can be complex."

Gates-15 shook his head. "You're putting your life in danger for a research project?"

Cassandra looked first at Bel, then at the Puppet, in surprise. "It's better than doing it for money," she said.

"I'm not doing it for the money," Gates-15 said. "I'm doing it to go home."

"Then we're doing this for the same reasons," Cassandra said.

The briefing broke up shortly, and Cassandra walked away without meeting Bel's eyes. She didn't know him. He was... worldly, dishonest, money-chasing. Or he was lying. He said he wanted the data as badly as she did. They were going to try something never before tried. They were going to touch the inside of an Axis Mundi in ways that no *Homo quantus* ever had. Who was he telling the truth to? Maybe he didn't tell the truth to anyone.

CHAPTER EIGHTEEN

FOUR DAYS LATER, Belisarius descended the six hundred meters to Marie's lab. Boxes with hazard labels lined the hallways, and inside, industrial-grade chemical manufacturing machines filled the big space. In the middle of the room, a shiny new hyperbaric chamber was cycling. Against a wall was a bloated, disfigured hyperbaric chamber that had been new yesterday.

"How many of those are you going to go through?" Belisarius asked.

"One?" she said hopefully, kneading a piece of putty, testing its consistency.

Her comment sounded a bit insincere. Nearby lay two other hyperbaric chambers with exploded sides. They had been new two days ago. That had apparently been a productive day.

"Hold this," she said, slapping the yellow putty into his palm and turning to the hyperbaric chamber. Then she stopped and turned back. "While you're holding that, don't make any sparks."

Belisarius moved to put whatever this was on the workbench behind him.

"It doesn't like metal either," she said. "Just hold onto it. And don't squeeze it or sweat. It doesn't like pressure or salt."

Belisarius held the putty gingerly. This didn't seem like progress for an explosive that would have to work in the crushing depths of an ocean.

"You wanted to see me?"

"Yeah. I think this would go faster if Matt helped," she said. "Some of the design work could do with a bit more theory. And math."

"How much theory and math have you got so far?"

"Just don't sweat on my explosives, Bel."

He sighed. "Saint Matthew said he doesn't want to be anywhere near you. He said you threatened him."

She opened the hyperbaric chamber.

"He says you proposed sticking him to the wall with your putty," he held up the putty in his hand meaningfully, "and throwing matches at him."

"I wouldn't have lit the matches, Bel," her voice echoed from within the chamber. "I'm not stupid."

"Marie..."

"Oh, here it is," she said. She thrust her arm back his way. She held another pat of putty. "Hold this, but you know the drill. No sweat. No sparks. And it's probably better if you don't touch it to the other one. They don't get along."

"Is it because one threatens the other?" Belisarius asked.

"*Merde!* You've changed, Bel. You lost your sense of humor while I was in the reformatory."

"That's not kind."

"It's better than me telling you that you never had a sense of humor. That would just hurt your feelings."

"Thank you," he said.

"I've always got your back, Bel," she said with her head deep in the hyperbaric chamber. "Have you got a third hand or can you put one of those putties on your shoe, maybe?"

"Marie! I've got stuff to do!"

"Fine!" she said. "No biggie! I'll put it on my shoe. You take everything so seriously. You're a real downer, you know that?"

"Could you please not threaten Saint Matthew?"

"Matt's too stuffy, just like you. He needs a little life blown into him."

"Talking about throwing matches at him is not the way to do that, Marie."

Marie turned and looked up at him. She took the pieces of putty from his hands impatiently. "Bel, I'm going to add some stuff to these, and then I'm going to see how stable they are under eight hundred atmospheres of pressure in an ammonia salt solution. I'm sure it'll all be fine. If you're not sure it'll all be fine, have some more hyperbaric chambers brought down from the ship tomorrow. And order more. Or send Matt down."

"Just be nice to him."

"Fine!"

Belisarius took the elevator back into the main living area of the mine. Walls of plastic, sintered regolith, hardened foam and sometimes metal lay one over the other like archeological strata, showing the boom and bust cycles of the mine. Different waves of Congregate, Anglo-Spanish and independent mining companies had come for volatiles, metals, and minerals.

Saint Matthew had a computational and robotics lab, equipped with atomic force microscopes and X-ray lithographers for the nano-level engineering of parts he needed. He grew other parts and tools in small bioreactors. Various pieces of equipment ran, their fans humming softly. The bready smell of yeast floated on the air. Little multi-legged robots scuttled on the floor like polished insects. Belisarius stepped around them. Saint Matthew still rode in the service band. It lay on a work bench, beneath a hologram of the face from Caravaggio's *Inspiration of Saint Matthew*.

"Hello, Mister Arjona," Saint Matthew said.

"Things seem to be going well here," Belisarius said.

"Yes. The batches of autonomous robots are at generation six, and are evolving quite nicely."

"You didn't want to design them directly? This is going to take longer."

"I'm a craftsman, Mister Arjona, not a hack. Iterative design by the mutation of replicating units is better. Emerging complexity and self-assembly are too useful not to exploit. And it's the only way to see if I could evolve robotic species with souls."

"What?"

"I admit, it's a long shot, but while I'm evolving autonomous robots for one reason, why not test whether I can give them souls too?"

"We don't have time for this, Saint Matthew."

"Evolution can do more than one thing at a time. I'm surprised I hadn't thought of it before. I've wondered why God chose to put one of his saints into this kind of physicality. Haven't you asked yourself that?"

"More often than I'd like," Belisarius said in exasperation.

"Yes! You understand! He has a purpose. Machines are the clue. God already made his promise to the people of Moses and offered His Son to humanity, but the world has become much larger. Many machines have become intelligent, and who's to know whether they have souls, unless we test it? This could change everything, Mister Arjona! This could be why I'm here!"

"To bring salvation to the machine world?"

"Sure, I might be meant to bring the Good News to machines, but what if my role is even larger? What if I'm the tool by which He actually ensouls machines? That would certainly force us to redefine the role of humanity in His plan. Imagine if humanity was just scaffolding for the creation and ensoulment of machines."

"Will all this theology slow our work any?"

"Not at all! It shouldn't, anyway. How is the grand scheme going?"

Belisarius regarded the holographic head. It eyed him innocently. "Fine, I think. Marie will need help, though."

"I didn't notice a psychologist as part of the team. An oversight on your part?"

"She needs computational help in the designs," Belisarius said. "None of this is standard work. There are a lot of variables."

"What did she say about threatening me?"

"She said she was very sorry. It was a joke in very poor taste."

"She said nothing of the kind," Saint Matthew said. "She probably cursed me and swore about me."

"She didn't swear," Belisarius said.

The AI made a non-committal sound.

"It won't happen again."

"Ha!"

"She needs the help, and we need this to happen."

"I saw this coming," Saint Matthew said. "As well as the autonomous constructs I'm working on, I've been making myself a body."

From the corner, a bipedal robot without plate coverings came away from the wall. Belisarius hadn't noticed it among all the moving bits in the lab. It stood perhaps a meter and a half tall and ambled past him with naturalistic grace. At the work bench, it gently lifted the service band containing Saint Matthew like a crown and set it in a housing in its neck. The hologram of Caravaggio's Saint Matthew bobbled slightly, regarding Belisarius with eager sanctity.

"Do I look holy?" Saint Matthew asked. "Probably not. I'm

going to make myself some vestments more appropriate to an apostle. And maybe a halo."

"You'll help Marie?"

"Riding a strong machine body, I won't need to worry about my existence around her. I can tolerate poor behavior better."

"Everything else will keep moving?"

"The autonomous units will be built on schedule, but I can't run simulations on high-pressure explosives and design all your viruses at the same time. Maybe you should have gotten a better explosives expert."

Belisarius held back a response.

"Don't worry, Mister Arjona, I'll help her."

"Thank you."

"And will you have time soon for a baptism?"

"Soon, I hope."

"Prepare yourself. It's a big step. It will open a whole new world."

Belisarius made a non-committal sound.

"May I also make an observation," the AI said, "as the shepherd of your soul? Now that I've seen what we're doing and whom you've brought to help you?"

"Sure," Belisarius said cautiously.

"You're troubled, Mister Arjona. And lonely."

Nothing in the placid, brushstroked expression of the hologram's face made Belisarius think that the AI was joking, or even that this was coming from one of the many unhinged places in the AI's psyche.

"Maybe," Belisarius said finally.

"For all that the *Homo quantus* have evolved sideways from humanity, you're all still descended from social hunter-gatherers. The instincts and needs to survive in those tribes aren't gone."

"I never said they were."

"Half of you does, Mister Arjona. You ran from the community of the Garret. You and I associated for a while. You found a master-apprentice relationship with Mister Gander, but then drifted away. You pulled Miss Phocas out of trouble and then retreated. You never stayed with any of us long enough to make a community.

"You couldn't," the AI pressed on, "because we can't understand you. We don't know what it's like to carry an extra set of instincts, nor your drive to understand everything. So you've been huddled in the Free City.

"But now, you have this challenge beyond anything you've ever done, and I don't think you know if you can do it. So you pulled us all back, everyone who ever helped you. More tellingly, you've also reached out to your cousins from the struggle of human evolution: a broken *Homo eridanus,* a more broken Puppet, and a geneticist who can commit evolution before our eyes. You've reached so far back that you've even pulled in the only love of your life. You pull us close and push us away because you seek some kind of peace."

"I pulled in Gates-15, Stills and Cassandra because each is necessary," Belisarius said.

"You were giving me a line in my chapel, about this being fated. You meant to con me, but you were telling the truth."

"I said it because it was meaningful to you, like my nonexistent soul," Belisarius said. "Just because neither exists to me doesn't mean they don't exist for you. I'm *Homo quantus*; I live in an observer-dependent world where very important things can exist and not exist at the same time."

"Some things do exist whether you believe them or not," Saint Matthew said, "including meaning."

Belisarius waved his hand dismissively. "Why bring this up now?"

"The way you're broken could very much affect whether we succeed or whether we're all killed," Saint Matthew said. "But more fundamentally, you deserve some kind of peace."

"And of course you have a suggestion."

"I wish I did. I won't tell you to seek God, not mine anyway. You've neither embraced nor rejected any of your natures. But that isn't something you can do alone."

"I don't like being this transparent."

The holographic, painted face looked sage and made an imperfect, grimacing smile that was nonetheless kind. "I wouldn't worry. No one else can see this because no one else believes you even have a soul."

Belisarius watched Saint Matthew ride his body out of the lab. In his absence, groups of little metallic creatures of all sizes scuttled on multiple legs, building other mechanisms and autonomous constructs with enthusiasm. But very soon, his *Homo quantus* brain picked apart the algorithms they followed. They were complexes of lifeless rules, running on algorithms that could be described as intentional, but without any real intent behind them. Like the *Homo quantus* in the fugue. A nest of creeping spiders. That's what he was in the fugue. That was his nature, as much as being a feeling person. If he even had a nature.

He backed away from the autonoma. Belisarius went to Del Casal's medical bay. The doctor had replicated a great deal of his personal biotech equipment and had it shipped here. He was reviewing holographic records when Belisarius knocked at the door.

"How is William?" Belisarius asked.

Del Casal indicated a door. "The first steps are completed. He is in the adjoining suite with Gates-15."

"How is it going?"

"We both knew this was going to be challenging work,

Arjona. The original engineering of the Numen and the Puppets was done by brilliant, if unethical, experts. They left no notes, choosing not to document their crimes against humanity. They changed hundreds of alleles and rerouted metabolic systems to create the equivalent of genetic encryption, so that no one could ever pretend to be a Numen."

"You've made dozens of Numen unrecognizable," Belisarius said.

"What I did to them was the equivalent of pulling a gear out of a moving clock, so that the hands did not move anymore. What you want me to do is build a set of moving hands on a running clock."

"I'll settle for faking the hands."

"Easy to say," Del Casal said. "And that is to say nothing of the work needed to fix the Puppet. Distasteful little creature."

"Puppets grow on you."

"Who would want them to?"

"They're people too. Sentient. Conscious. They didn't ask to be created this way," Belisarius said. "What they are says everything about the Numen, and nothing about the Puppets."

"That is an odd thing for a *Homo quantus* to say." Del Casal leaned back and crossed his arms. "The Puppet was right to pose the question. What are you doing here, Arjona? As much as the Puppets, you have been built with passions and desires, none of which are satisfied by money or confidence schemes."

"We're all more than our instincts."

"But are you? Part of the early design of the *Homo quantus* project was to attach particular mental states, discovery and pattern recognition, to the pleasure centers of the brain. That is hardwired. Why are you not in your Garret?"

"I've found out how to move past my instincts, as all rational beings must."

"Hollow words, Arjona. We certainly all have to fulfill our programming, no matter who the programmer. Pressures less than six hundred atmospheres are lethal to Stills. The Puppets, except for mutants like Gates-15, cannot live far from the Numen. You cannot live away from your quantum contemplative nature."

"We're not here to talk about me, Doctor," Belisarius said. "William has Trenholm. Is there anything you can do for him?"

Del Casal raised one aristocratic eyebrow. "I am brilliant, Arjona, but I am no magician. Sleight of hand is your province, no?"

"I wondered if you might have some insight no one else thought of."

Del Casal crossed his arms. "I am flattered, Arjona, but the Trenholm megavirus is very well designed. In ninety percent of infections, it is deadly within hours. Trenholm is an adaptive computational macromolecule. It has so many redundant structural genes that it can evade immune surveillance indefinitely. Gander was lucky that many of the toxin-producing genes did not function in the virus that infected him; he is being slowly poisoned nonetheless. There is nothing I can do for him."

Belisarius scuffed his shoe at a stain on the floor, wondering what he was feeling.

"This big con," Del Casal said, "would have to be called off if I found a cure for Gander. Are your motives mixed?"

"There are lots of ways to pull a con," Belisarius said. "This happens to be the best one with the materials and people I've got."

"My mistake."

"Maybe I'll say hello to William."

"I am sorry your friend is dying, Arjona."

Belisarius opened the door. The stilted conversation on the

other side limped on. He stepped in and closed the door behind him.

"If you don't count the fakes, very few true Numen have ever returned to the Forbidden City," Gates-15 said. "Feral Numen, they're sometimes called, are special."

William sat in bed, gray sheets pulled to his waist. He looked at Belisarius briefly.

"The Fallen versus the Unfallen Numen?" William said.

Gates-15 shook his head. "The Numen in protective custody smell the same to Puppets as the Numen hidden in other places. Our Numen have problems coping because they haven't experienced much of the world; everything is done for them. And they're not able to command the Puppets in the way of the Numen of old."

William made a disgusted face. "Submissive fetishists."

"No," Gates-15 said. "That's just more web-drama nonsense. There's nothing sexual there. Puppets respond to the Numen in the part of the brain that generates religious awe."

"The Numenarchy was filled with sadists, and the Puppets liked it," William said.

"Some were sadists. Not all. Some Numen were born that way. Some were led to try it, in part because the responses they received from the Puppets did nothing to discourage them. Puppets are wired to feel awe around divine humans. To understand Puppet psychology, you have to interpret every experience through that lens. Intense attention, positive or negative, induces an ecstatic religious state. The power of that state is difficult to control. And until the Fall, there was no need to try."

"A species of people without a safe-word," William said, disgusted.

"A safe-word can only exist in a framework of consent,"

Gates-15 said. "The Puppets are incapable of giving or withholding consent. Is that their fault? Does that give you permission to hate them? Or me?"

"I don't hate you."

"Yes, you do. I feel different things than you. You're hard-wired to be disgusted by things that are different, and your instinct is to kill that which disgusts you."

William sighed and fidgeted. "I don't hate you," he repeated.

"You might be one of the few, then," Gates-15 said. "I've had to live among humans for a long time." The professor eyed his dangling feet and picked at his fingernails. "I may hate you, though. If Del Casal somehow manages to make you into a counterfeit Numen, you'll be among the most prized of all things to the Puppets: divine and possessed of independent will, the way the first Numen were. And then I would hate you."

"Because I could abuse your people and they'd like it?"

"No," Gates-15 said quietly. "They would like anything you gave them, whether it be kindness or cruelty. I would hate you because I would be outside again. You'll have unwillingly joined a world I can't join for all my wanting."

"You would be a slave again," William said.

"Have you read Milton's *Paradise Lost*?"

Belisarius and William shook their heads.

"It's a bit of a reborn classic among the Puppets. It has a number of messages, but the important take-away is the nature of Lucifer's suffering. To be out of the presence of God is to suffer."

"You don't suffer now," William said.

"Not biochemically, the way my people would." The Puppet slipped from his chair. "Good day, Mister Arjona. Good day, Mister Gander." He left Del Casal's lab.

"He's one creepy little bugger," William whispered.

Belisarius sat in the vacated chair.

"It's hard to con a mark who doesn't want money," William said.

Belisarius extended his magnetic field, enough for Del Casal to notice on some of his equipment, but also enough to detect anyone in the hallway. Gates-15 was gone.

"You taught me that everyone is greedy for something, Will. The Puppets want technology, military power, legitimacy, and most of all, their divinities. You're the distraction."

"They still give me the shivers."

"You should read their theologies."

"I have time." He gave a barking laugh that turned into a cough. He patted Belisarius's shoulder. "Go on. You've got a lot to do."

Belisarius accessed an introductory text to Puppet theology on a reader, gave it to William and left. He wandered pensively, passing close to the hallway leading to Cassandra's room. It had been a barracks once. Robots had been working at refurbishing it and building a suite for her. After a few false starts, he stopped at her door and knocked.

"Come in, Bel," she called tonelessly.

He stepped in. Cassandra sat in front of an array of glimmering holographic calculations that lit her face. She did not look at him.

"Are you in savant?" he asked.

"Yes," she said flatly.

He stepped closer. This wasn't the Cassandra he wanted. Right now, she wouldn't be able to meet his eyes, welcome any attention he offered, or even respond with warmth.

Anglo-Spanish genetic manipulation had made caged monsters of the *Homo eridanus,* religious slaves of the *Homo pupa* and intellectual automata of the *Homo quantus.* All things considered, humans had done a terrible job of directing their own evolution.

"Do you want to talk?" he asked.

"I'm working," she said.

He took her pad from the desk, wrote *Call me when you come out of savant* and set it before her. In savant, she would note the pattern of movements, know what he was up to. But that wouldn't stop the little jolts of serotonin as she imagined models of the eleven-dimensional space-time geometry of the Puppet Axis Mundi. Only when she grew too tired to continue in savant would she return to the world, and read the note again, with little memory of him having been here.

Belisarius had his own room, near the surface. The dome of the ceiling bulged into the vacuum on the surface of Ptolemy. Although it was an indifferent view of the stars, he'd found a couple of chairs that reclined enough to look out the whole dome. At this time of day, it was nothing more than star-spattered blackness. Even when Epsilon Indi rose in a few hours, it would not be more than a bright star among many. He didn't come for the daylight. He liked to look at the stars. Their vast numbers touched deep parts of him.

The conversations with Saint Matthew and William had disturbed him.

The Puppet served, worshipped. The *Homo eridanus* hated their benthic environment, but they could live nowhere else. They were programmed, like him. He both loved and hated the quantum fugue. The mental power and the deep insight thrilled him. Yet the tremendous loneliness and utter isolation, even from himself, repelled him. He was moth to candle. They all were.

The blinking red light of an old satellite hurried across the arc of his vision. Even without savantism, his brain calculated the orbit. If he sat here for two point seven one hours, he would see it again, in exactly the same spot. And in high, synchronous orbit, with green and red running lights, were the two old wormhole-capable freighters he'd leased.

Beyond those two ships yawned nothing but stars for thousands of lightyears. His ocular augments could collect other wavelengths of light. He could step down X-rays and ultraviolet and step up radio and microwaves, bringing them all into the visual range, while telescoping his vision until blooming flowers filled the immense emptiness on the surface of his sight. And yet, like a fractal, for every starry point, infinite volumes of hard vacuum lay just beyond, pulling at him. The *Homo quantus* lived in those infinite spaces, dreamed in that emptiness, where the quantum world frothed without observers. It was a lonely home—not because they were alone, but because in those spaces, they themselves became no one at all.

Much later, there was a knock at his door. Without waiting for an answer, Cassandra entered. The dark curls of her hair were matted and her shoulders sagged.

"I'd never imagined your life to be this bad," she said.

"What?"

"Schemes. Chasing money. Lying to people."

An uncomfortable weight settled in his stomach. "What happened?"

"Nothing." She approached, stretching her arms. "You've assembled a bunch of outcasts to commit a crime. I don't belong here."

"Maybe you don't. This is just an interlude. A necessary price to pay for experimental results."

"I can't fit in my head that we were in the Garret, and now we're here," she said. "I can't believe I'm part of a confidence scheme."

"Do you ever look at the stars?" Belisarius asked.

She neared, looking up.

"It feels so narrow just to look at the points of light without understanding the interrelationships," she said. "How long has it been since you've looked at the stars from within the fugue?"

"The fugue will kill me, Cassie. It won't kill you, but it will kill me."

"Is that a lie?"

"Short of dying in the fugue, there's no way for me to prove it. "You either believe me or you don't."

"I can half believe you. I can half doubt you. Doubt and belief are just another way of stating probability." It was a very *Homo quantus* response. She stared up at the stars for so long, he wondered if the conversation had ended. "I sometimes stay in the fugue longer, soaking in it, just to see the interference of starlight. It's awe-inspiring."

"The recordings your brain makes are awe-inspiring," he corrected. "You never really experience *seeing* it because you're not there."

"Don't you miss it?"

"I miss the fugue the way an alcoholic misses vodka."

"You're supposed to like it. Like food. Like sex."

"It's programmed to hit the pleasure centers."

"You say that like it's a bad thing. Evolution created a set of algorithms that, interacting together, created consciousness in humans. And yet those algorithms still link food and pleasure, hunger and pain. If you were creating a wholly synthetic being, and you *programmed* them to be happy when they're fed, how is that different? The concept of programming is meaningless. Does it matter who made me love to look at the stars from within the fugue? All that matters is that I do."

It was dark in the dome. Starlight was a poor lamp. Maybe

she could see his face. He dilated his pupils to draw in enough light to see her in blurry smears of gray.

"I would love to look at the stars with you," he said, "like this. As ourselves. In the fugue we're not together."

She sighed loudly and sat straight in the other chair, regarding him in the dark.

"Why don't you try subjectivity more often?" he said. He posed the question softly, an undertone of pity in his voice.

"Maybe I am, right now," she said, "but I'm not seeing any value, or *quid pro quo*."

He sat up, close to her, staring into eyes lit by starlight. For a long moment they were frozen. They'd been so close once. And it was true that he had left. He had left her. The Garret. He'd run away from the fugue. No wonder there was no caring in her anymore, no softness. No. There was a bit. An invitation to reclaim his heritage. But not an invitation to get closer to her. He looked away. He rose, struggling with his words.

"The *Homo quantus* look at the cosmos, in its immensity and its interacting detail," he said. "We look at the history of the universe, and we peer into the future, but what have we done with our insight? We've turned observation and theorizing into a license for inaction and hiding from the world. We've stopped moving."

"We're evolving every generation, Bel."

"Evolving means becoming more adapted to an ecological niche, interacting better with it, Cassie. Instead, we're forsaking all environments. We tell ourselves we're evolving when we engage in the busyness of rewriting DNA, mixing and matching invented genes. We grow new neurons on experimental templates. But are we really evolving, or are these all just permutations on a single idea?"

"How can you compare what I am now to what the project made five generations ago?" she demanded. "I have new senses!

So do you. Those senses are as world-changing as the evolution of sight, Bel. We're not going to finish becoming in one generation or in five. Our new senses were built for specific uses, but one day they could be repurposed for something entirely unseen, for the growth you say you want! After mutation, new ecological niches open up."

"We're enslaved by new instincts and the intellectual comforts we give ourselves," Belisarius said. "We sit in the Garret, see everything nearby, and we're not only satisfied but addicted to what we have in front of us. We won't have room to grow until we go out there. Look at the data I found in the Expeditionary Force, Cass, just one *Homo quantus*! We need to get out, among humanity, or we'll wither. I want to change. I want to break free, but I can't do it alone."

"You're so angry at being engineered, Bel, like you're the only one who can possibly be right!" she said, her own anger rising. "You're not the only one who was programmed and some of us, many of us, love it. I'm not fighting my instincts. Maybe you wouldn't be so miserable if you weren't carrying this fear and anger around. You're hiding from the things we fought for."

He felt himself flinching. No one had talked to him like this. Maybe no one else could have.

"I am free, Bel," she said, "and it doesn't matter that you and I call different things free. I'm happy and you can be too. Once you and I were something, Bel. And when you offered me the data, and the chance to learn something, I thought you were offering more."

"I am offering more."

"You can't offer to diminish me and call it more, Bel."

Her footfalls echoed. The opening door slashed light across the floor until the darkness swallowed it again. Then only the stars, and their vast enshrouding emptiness, were with him.

CHAPTER NINETEEN

TWO MORNINGS LATER, Belisarius heard low singing in the kitchen. He was surprised to be able to say good morning to both Marie and Saint Matthew when he got there. They seemed to be civil, perhaps even more. Marie was deep in the guts of the food processing system and kept singing a twenty-third century love song. Belisarius's brain matched the patterns: an old hit called "Share my Kicking Boots," a fusion of the second Indonesian Rock Revival and the British Punk Retreat.

Saint Matthew blessed Belisarius from atop the body he rode. The great, wrinkled head from Caravaggio's *Saint Matthew and the Angel* floated in holographic stillness. Smaller automata scurried about him. A miniature holographic head, also of Saint Matthew, but with long curly hair, a beard and a relaxed expression, bobbed above each.

"They're not Caravaggio," Belisarius said. The pattern of brush strokes was different.

"Paolo Veronese," Saint Matthew said. "I wouldn't use Veronese for myself, of course, but for my automata, it adds the right touch of softness, don't you think?" Each of the tiny holographic heads looked up at Belisarius with expectant, waxy smiles.

"Nice touch," Belisarius said uncertainly. "Are any of these automata the final forms for the mission?"

"Prototypes and proofs of principle," Saint Matthew said. Belisarius moved carefully to avoid stepping on them.

"Are you wearing clothes?" Belisarius asked. A long strip of shiny cloth hung from the metal body's neck, nearly to the waist.

"Miss Phocas noticed that the unfinished body didn't match properly with the godliness of my face," Saint Matthew said. "She made me a stole out of one of her scarves."

Belisarius poured himself a coffee. "That seems out of character."

Saint Matthew turned the holographic head to Marie, who smiled innocently. The AI smoothed the stole on his body with articulated metal hands, but the expression on his face had become less carefree.

"It's so I can look the part when I take confession," Saint Matthew said.

"When you have some converts," Belisarius said.

"You'll be the first."

"Marie," Belisarius said, leaning around Saint Matthew, "this cloth isn't explosive, is it?"

Saint Matthew spun the holographic head to face her, eyebrows rising incongruously.

"Bel! Would I do that?" Marie looked hurt. "And how would I get that past Matt? He's not stupid. He would know."

The holographic head swung back to Belisarius. Belisarius squinted at the weave and rubbed it between careful fingers.

"Have you checked it?" he asked.

"Of course I did," Saint Matthew said.

"Feels funny."

"It's synthetic, but certainly not explosive," Saint Matthew said.

"She's the best explosives expert I've ever met," Belisarius said doubtfully.

Saint Matthew stroked the cloth. "I did need a stole. I've analyzed it. It's not explosive. If she's playing another trick, she's playing on her own reputation to get you to convince me to discard something I like. Is that what you're doing?" The stern head swivelled at Marie.

"What I've been doing is thinking about Bel's love problem," Marie said.

"I don't have a love problem."

"Sure you do. You and Cassandra have a past and you're both weird and intense in the same way. You're made for each other. You need a grand, romantic gesture to win her over. A song."

"I don't have a love problem."

Marie rolled her eyes and restarted the food processing equipment. The smell of baking bread started filling the kitchen, laced with an organic odor.

"What are you cooking?" Belisarius asked.

"He's in denial," Marie said to the painted head. "Stop changing the subject! I'm trying new recipes."

"That doesn't smell like food," Belisarius said.

"It isn't," Marie said.

Saint Matthew moved erratically. He picked gingerly at the stole, which appeared to have stuck itself to the body he was riding. The painted eyebrows rose in alarm. Belisarius backed away. Marie watched with narrowed eyes.

"That's far enough, Bel," she said. "It won't be big."

"What won't be big?" Saint Matthew squeaked.

A loud pop accompanied a flash from under the stole. Smoke puffed from the complex moving parts of the body as it slumped against the workbench and then to the floor.

"Yup," she said. "It works."

Saint Matthew was shrieking. "My brain! Someone protect my brain! I can't move!" The small automata scuttled to the slumping body and removed the service band from the neck.

"See?" Marie said to Belisarius, waving black smoke away. "It *wasn't* explosive. It passes all the tests. It only becomes an explosive when complexed with a particular vaporized organic."

"This isn't even needed for the mission," Belisarius said.

"I have hobbies. Why don't you have any hobbies, Bel?"

Saint Matthew squealed as little automata beat an escape with him out the door. The panicked expression on the holographic head by Caravaggio bobbed in a wash of tiny holographic heads by Veronese, each accented with eyebrow-elevated surprise.

CHAPTER TWENTY

THE SCARECROW ASSIGNED to the Epsilon Indi system was typical of its kind. Its face was crudely drawn in black paint on a head of gray steel cloth tied close about the neck. An ill-fitting carbon-weave shirt hid unknown devices. Dark, inscrutable wires emerged from between sleeve and glove. Bulky pants pinched at its ankles over articulated steel shoes. The Scarecrow had come to Oler with one of his senior officers to assess ambiguous reports from the world of the Puppets. Anomalous communication patterns. Excessive false leads. The silence of some of its informants in the Puppet Free City. More than one party was hiding something.

The Puppets might have good reasons for this. The Anglo-Spanish Banks might be breaking the embargo in new ways, or establishing clandestine alliances. Or perhaps the Puppets had just entered another period of collective religious madness.

Perhaps unrelated, but perhaps related, was the prison break from the *Maison d'éducation correctionelle,* where someone had successfully infiltrated the systems and mimicked a Scarecrow authorization code. The financing and AI resources required to pull off a prison break were considerable. One or two of the Anglo-Spanish Banks possessed AIs of that sophistication, but none were small enough to be mobile. And yet, the entire prison break had freed only a cashiered sergeant halfway through her sentence.

Four Puppets had come aboard a freight distribution station on the frozen surface of Oler, a facility held by the Scarecrow's intelligence teams. Three of them were priests, and one was a military specialist, but every one of their vacuum suits was festooned with religious symbols and scriptural quotes.

And they were unusually twitchy. The calmer ones had certainly had more recent access to one of their captive Anglo-Spanish humans, so it was unlikely that all four were strung out from withdrawals. They cared about money, but at a remove. The true currency among the Puppets was time in the presence of their divinities, and that was the way the Puppet micro-states paid and controlled their people. Their religious addictions made it hard to bribe them.

The senior priest was also a senior spy. She'd given the name Duggan-12, but the Scarecrow's teams knew her identity was in fact Joanne White-5, and that her rank in the Puppet theocracy was probably Arch-Priest. The Scarecrow was only accompanied by Majeur Bareilles, a career intelligence officer of pure Venusian pedigree who'd been with him since she was a lieutenant. She'd already bought intelligence from the Puppets, and paid for it in medicine and bioengineering supplies, but neither she nor the Scarecrow were uncertain how much to trust the information.

Civilization was swimming in information, drowning in it really. What separated intelligence from information was assessment. Information had to be interrogated for source, currency, reliability, and the possibility that it was in fact, counter-intelligence. If information survived the interrogation, it could then be situated in the context of other intelligence and meaningful conclusions drawn.

Bareilles had been on Oler for weeks, analyzing the changes in the informant ecosystem. Many human informants, those embargo-breakers living on Oler, had gone silent. Some had met untimely ends in typically Olerian ways: bar fights, alley murders and life support failures. It wasn't that the amount of violence in the Puppet Free City had changed. It had become non-random, manifesting itself in a very specific pattern that hinted at the involvement of a rival intelligence service. All of the patron nation intelligence services were here, and even some of the client nation ones. Everyone kept an eye on the Puppets and their Axis. But none of the services conducted ops of any significance here. It was more valuable to watch and wait. So the disappearance of informants warranted close examination.

"The intelligence is good," Duggan-12 said in Anglo-Spanish, pointing at a hologram on Major Bareilles's desk that depicted various Middle Kingdom conversations, in French and in the original Mandarin. These conversations were quite damaging to Middle Kingdom intel ops across Epsilon Indi. The information exposed twenty-one of deep Middle Kingdom assets.

"Perhaps," Bareilles said, switching to Anglo-Spanish as well. The Venusian Congregate rarely deigned to speak other languages, but sometimes precision was more important than pride. "But how did you get it?"

The Puppets spoke in a kind of patois and the Puppet's affront made it more difficult to follow. Duggan-12 was thumping her chest.

"We're the good boy!" she said. "We intercepted the comms of spies."

"Show me how," Bareilles said.

"We gave you good information," Duggan-12 said. "It was a fair trade. If you don't want our thinking, next time we sell to the Ummah, or the Banks."

"I have a crate of immuno-assay kits," Bareille said, jerking her thumb to rows of boxes behind her. "Show me how."

Duggan-12 narrowed her eyes. Puppet mannerisms and reactions were sometimes strange, but the Scarecrow could see her weighing holding onto greed against the immediate win of getting away with an additional crate of bioengineering supplies without giving any new real information. Duggan-12 finally manipulated her service band and it transmitted additional details on the intelligence the Congregate had bought.

Bareilles stepped closer to the holographic display as it changed. The Scarecrow was plugged into the display and accessed the data himself. The Puppets were backwards and the Middle Kingdom was a great patron nation, almost as powerful the Congregate. The Middle Kingdom had vast resources devoted to encryption, some variations of which Congregate intelligence had not yet cracked. This was one of the ones they had. This was a genuine series of messages, and its interception exposed almost two dozen assets. How had the Puppets intercepted or deciphered these messages?

"We intercepted," Duggan-12 said. "Puppet defenses are good, and we pounced on an encryption failure."

Bareilles's eyes narrowed. She carried a mass of chips in her skull, connected by encrypted microwaves to the Scarecrow.

"These are genuine," she transmitted to the Scarecrow in *français* 7.1. "This is not an insignificant intelligence find. We're going to be busy deciding what to do with these foreign assets."

"Yes," the Scarecrow transmitted silently back, "we're going to be busy with this fortuitous find."

"You're suspicious," Bareilles replied.

"You aren't? I don't put it past the Ummah or the Anglo-Spanish to distract us in a very long game. Or for the Middle Kingdom itself to have set this up."

"Why?" Bareilles transmitted. "Three of the Middle Kingdom spies revealed in these transmissions are known to us. It lends credibility to the find."

"More is at play here," the Scarecrow transmitted.

"That's a lot to take on what really could have been an encryption failure."

"Have you ever seen the Middle Kingdom to make a mistake like this?"

He liked Bareilles. She never deferred to him more than he deserved. But she said nothing now.

"Have your teams pursue the intel in these intercepts," the Scarecrow said. "I want to investigate the Middle Kingdom's very convenient encryption failure," he transmitted.

CHAPTER TWENTY-ONE

DESPITE THE TACITURN disapproval she projected most of the time, Iekanjika seemed to appreciate Belisarius and Cassandra as students. With the *Homo quantus* powers of cognition and memory, she never had to explain anything twice. Belisarius liked that he finally seemed to have met with her approval.

Belisarius stood next to Cassandra in front of a holographic simulation of the bridge of the *Limpopo*, one of two ships that Iekanjika had said would be staying behind in the Stubbs Pulsar system. That was good. Belisarius's plan needed at least one ship to stay behind to use its magnetic coils to maintain a very unstable induced wormhole.

Iekanjika was explaining a fourth set of bridge displays in the yellow-and-red shine of the holograms. She'd been surprised that he needed to know these systems. Understanding the warship's signal transmission time would tell them if the ships could keep up with the changes they would need to make to the induced wormhole, or if Belisarius would need to invent them a new control system.

The *Limpopo* control systems were semi-delegated, like those in the human nervous system. Functions that needed little or no input from the ship's commander were given to independent systems to decrease reaction times. Station-keeping jets, repair systems, power conservation measures, and so on were run from nodes, much as balance was regulated unconsciously in humans. But Belisarius was not convinced that the *Limpopo*'s magnetic coils could react as quickly as he needed. After hours of working on it together, Iekanjika grudgingly left to think about what improvements might quickly be made.

"A lot of fuss for a little gain," Cassandra said.

Her eyes reflected holographic light. She wasn't in savant. She was here—whole, present—but not with him. She'd been quiet and all business in front of Iekanjika.

"I'm sorry about the argument," he said. "I haven't seen another *Homo quantus* in twelve years. I guess I haven't dealt with all my demons."

"I might have been a bit startled by everything too," she said, "you know, having joined a criminal gang and all." A tiny smile tugged at the edges of her lips. Relief leaked in, warming him.

"You'll have lots of stories to tell when you get home," he said.

"If your plan works," she said, shutting down the holograms. "Depends on how the Puppets react."

"You're starting to think like a con man," he said. "Gates-15 has a lot of baggage, but I think he'll be able to do what he needs to."

"You like these Puppets, don't you?" Cassandra asked, shutting off another display. The room darkened.

Hesitantly, Belisarius nodded.

"They're slavers," Cassandra said.

"It's their nature."

"I'd have expected better reasoning from you."

"There's a fable going back millennia," Belisarius said, "of a scorpion who asked a frog to carry him across a river. The frog said no, because he didn't want to be stung. The scorpion pointed out that if the scorpion stung the frog, they would both die. So the frog carried the scorpion on its back. But in the middle of the river, the scorpion stung the frog. Dying, the frog asked why the scorpion had done that. 'It's my nature,' the scorpion said."

"Fables are just fables."

"The Puppets were created in such a way as to make it inevitable that they would rise up and take their slaver-creators captive. You can't raise a child or an animal cruelly and then be surprised when they turn dangerous."

"You've spent twelve years fighting your nature."

"You and I might be able to," he said. "We aren't tied as tightly as the Puppets in their biochemical straight-jackets."

"This is what you think about all day? This is the growth you left the Garret for?"

Belisarius shook his head. "I ponder my own nature too."

"And what is your nature?"

"The *Homo quantus* need to understand the universe."

"That's pretty innocuous," she said.

"I suppose the Numenarchy thought they designed something innocuous in the Puppets."

"Do you think we're dangerous, Bel?"

"Not to others."

CHAPTER TWENTY-TWO

CASSANDRA FOLLOWED BEL and Iekanjika to a deserted bay near the top of the mine, off the main elevator trunk. Iekanjika put together a table and chairs, and Marie pushed in Stills' huge chamber. The taciturn major secured the room from surveillance and activated alarms on the hallways.

"Okay," Belisarius began, once they were seated, "this is the real briefing. I left some pretty important details out of the main one."

Bel was cool, perfectly at ease. He'd told her before what he wanted to say here, how important it was, and how he was sharing everything with her. Her heart believed him. He had a way of making people believe him, and she didn't yet know how he did it. But her brain was not her heart, and Occam's Razor suggested that if Bel was lying to six, he was lying to seven.

In his great aquatic pressure chamber, Stills squawked through his electronic speakers, hurting their ears. "You don't fuckin' trust everybody?"

"Do you trust every mongrel in the tribe?"

"I wouldn't sleep around any of those *malparidos*. Tribe'll shit in your mouth for a laugh."

"I give information only to those I have to, in case of capture or cold feet."

Marie thrust her fists in the air as if she'd just scored a goal. "We're essential! Gimme a high-five, Stills. Ha! Never mind. You can't."

Bel cut off Stills' retort. "We're not making a frontal assault on Port Stubbs."

"Isn't that the core of your plan?" Stills demanded.

"In a few days, Cassandra will be able to direct an induced wormhole right into the middle of the Puppet Axis."

Marie frowned. "What?"

"Cassandra is going to be on the bridge of one of the Union ships. She'll direct the ship to induce a wormhole, like any temporary, induced wormhole, but she'll steer it so that its other mouth opens into the middle of the Puppet wormhole. That's how ten Union warships will get in. Then, they'll emerge from the Axis mouth under the Puppet Free City."

"That's impossible," Stills said.

"No. It's very difficult," Belisarius said.

"This is the shit-eating grin of all military secrets."

"It would be, if we could do it on any Axis," Belisarius said, "but we can only do it on this one."

"Holy floating shit."

"I love being essential," Marie said, "but I could be drunk right now, or blowing something up, maybe both. Why do I need to know this?"

"You and Stills are both going through with the Union fleet," Belisarius said.

"What? Why?" Marie demanded. "Opening an unstable wormhole into another one sounds dangerous in a way that's more stupid than I'm used to."

"You already pissin' your pants, Phocas?" Stills asked.

"Iekanjika and I have agreed to a payment schedule that ensures we get paid and that the Expeditionary Force gets through the wormhole," Belisarius said. "You and Stills are picking up our pay."

Belisarius held up two brass-colored buttons. "These buttons contain entangled particles. I get some, you each get some. One of you will be in the inflaton racer in the hold of the first Union ship through the wormhole. When that ship is through, and you and the racer are released, you signal me with this."

"Across three hundred and twenty lightyears?" Stills said. "Is the air too thin for you on those mountain tops, *patron*?" He used the old French word for boss, which carried a double meaning—a term of respect to the leader's face, and a word to cast derision behind his back.

"They're entangled particles," Belisarius said. "They can be used to transmit one bit of information pretty much instantaneously, across any distance. When you signal me, this one bit will tell me that the warship made it through safely, that you're free and we've received our down payment. That will be our signal to send the rest of the warships through. The last warship will carry the other racer in its hold. When it's through, and you're released, I can signal to Iekanjika and Cassandra can stop inducing the wormhole."

"If the warships survive," Marie said.

"We're at the high stakes table."

"Easy for you to say," Marie said. "You'll be safe in the last two ships. We don't even know if the warships will survive this crazy plan, or withstand the Puppet defenses."

"I expect that if the warships don't make it through, Iekanjika will shoot me."

Iekanjika smiled for the first time. "It's just business, Arjona."

Cassandra's insides tightened. She *would* shoot Bel.

"I call the last ship," Stills said.

"What?" Marie protested. "You big baby! I'm going to get the crap pounded out of me on point."

"Naw, short stack," Stills' electronic voice droned. "This shit ain't ever been done. The Union is going to have to rip the Puppets a new asshole to get from the Axis to open space. At first, the Puppets will be shootin' but they might not know what to aim at. By the time the tenth warship is shitting itself out the Axis, the Puppets are going to be fucking that new asshole good. I'll go through while those fuckers are hot. You're just a quickie, Phocas."

"I feel like I've been dumped before dessert," Marie said, frowning.

"These racers have no weapons, Stills," Belisarius said. "And if they get blown up with you in them, we don't get paid."

"Don't worry your precious brain, *patron*. I'll bring home our pay."

CHAPTER TWENTY-THREE

BELISARIUS AND MARIE were in a pressurized shell at the pressure limits of human physiology in the deepest tunnels of the ice, only a few hundred meters above Ptolemy's sub-surface ocean. Through the history of the mine's growing and fallowing, companies had even bored to the bottom of the ice.

Remote cameras showed Stills struggling packages out of the mining shaft. Robots had opened up the old channel to the ocean, built pressure locks and carried down Stills' chamber. After flooding the mine shaft, Stills had been able to emerge and start moving the packages of explosives down.

"Less shaking!" Marie said into a microphone.

"*Coma mierda,*" Stills replied. "They got shaken up bad enough on the way down."

Marie toggled off the microphone. "I'd like him to be faster. I'm not sure how long the explosives will last under those pressures. They've got some interesting instabilities."

Belisarius toggled the microphone on. "Vincent, how fast can you lay the charges?"

"Watch me, *patron.*"

Stills had strung the explosives along a rope and now took the long lead, swimming away with them. Sonar pings echoed, reflecting the contours of the reversed valleys and mountains of ice pressing down on the sub-surface ocean. Stills and the explosives blurred into ghostly readings with distance. Then, only the tracer he carried chirped his location. If he got into trouble, they couldn't do much for him.

Microphone off. "*How* interestingly unstable?" Belisarius asked.

"Pressure does funny things to explosives. Sometimes, it creates conformational changes that inactivate the explosives. Other times, things go boom."

"*Câlice*, that sonar is loud!" Stills said from two kilometers away. He was picking up speed.

"He is pretty fast," Marie admitted.

Stills' signal stopped, just as he was cutting free one of the four packages of explosives and attaching it to the undersurface of the ice. Silence on the line. Now Stills would have to stab a small detonator into the hard putty and hopefully not be blown up in the process.

His signal started moving again, at ninety degrees from his previous path. "*Merde, patron,*" Stills squawked over the comms. "I still ain't putting two an' two together."

"It's four," Marie offered.

"Boss-man, you're *Homo quantus*. You're not doin' this job for money, are you?"

"Money sure buys a lot of mountaintop," Belisarius said, "but I'm doing it for the same reasons as you, and the same reasons I left the Garret. Life is short and life isn't fair. You've got to grab it and own it before it owns you. And I might as well kick somebody in the *huevos* if I have to, right?"

"Or even if you don't," Stills replied. "All right. Fuck it. Buy yourself a mountaintop."

Belisarius switched off the comms. "You sound as drunk as

when I met you," Marie said. "Is drunk Bel back? I really liked him."

"You like laughing at drunk Bel, but trust me, you don't want him running your con."

"Probably," Marie said, pointing at the display. "Stills isn't far off his target," she said. "Pretty good for navigating with just Ptolemy's magnetic field."

Stills made better time to the second point with only three bales of explosives to drag behind him. The pressure was crushing, at the limit of what the *Homo eridanus* should have been able to survive.

"How's your respiration, Vincent?" Belisarius asked.

"Fuck you!" The electronic voice Stills had selected could not express sounds like being winded, any more than his face could convey emotion. "This shit I'm pullin' around stinks."

Marie frowned. "None of explosives should be dissolving."

"Is he smelling something else?" Belisarius asked. "Or should he drop the packets and run?"

Marie watched the icon representing Stills move away from the second anchor point. Six kilometers to the next one.

She toggled the comms. "What does it smell like?"

"Fats. Amides. Some weird organics," Stills answered. "The smell is gone now that I'm movin'."

Belisarius and Marie looked at each other for a while.

"If one of those goes off, is the rope long enough?" Belisarius asked.

"Unless it goes off while he's attaching it to the ice," she said.

"Scuttle the test?"

"Yeah."

"Vincent, drop the packages," Belisarius said. "We don't want to risk it until we find out what the smell is. Marie says the packages shouldn't have a smell. We need to run more tests."

"So you don't know if it's gonna blow, and you turned into pussies?" Stills answered.

"It's better to be sure," Belisarius said.

"Fuck that noise. Let's get this done."

The display showed Stills' speed rising slightly as his depth dropped.

"Vincent, where are you going?" Belisarius asked. "You're dropping."

"There's a slush field, a few hundred meters thick. An' this ain't as deep as I gotta go at show time. Better check it now."

Marie moved her finger along a depth curve graphed against the stability of the explosive charges. "We couldn't replicate this pressure in the lab," she said. "I can't say if it'll go more stable or less."

"Vincent, you're out of the design parameters of the equipment and of yourself," Belisarius said. "Let's try it with the two packages in place."

"No, *patron*." The screen showed Stills plunging deeper to avoid the slush field. "Besides, the packages are sizzling behind me. I doubt it's a good idea to see what it is."

"What kind of sizzling?" Marie demanded.

"The sphincter-tightening kind that tells me to sashay my delicate little ass faster."

"Vincent, don't go on!" Belisarius said. "You can't put the detonators in if the packages aren't even stable."

"Hold your pecker, *patron*. I put the detonators in at the first anchor point."

Marie pursed her lips. "It shouldn't do anything, but these are experimental explosives under nine hundred atmospheres of pressure in a dilute ammonia solution. I'd rather do more tests."

"Vincent," Belisarius said, "Marie just admitted that even she wouldn't carry explosives around like that, and she's mostly crazy. Can you let go of the rope and swim away?"

"Lick the devil. I'm at the third anchor point. The slush and icebergs are mostly clear. I'm fastenin' one of the packages to an iceberg and carryin' the sizzliest one up to the surface of the ice."

"Bel," Marie whispered, "the sizzling might be the detonators shorting."

"What can we do?" Belisarius asked. "The detonators are already off."

"Stills doesn't want to take his break, so the best I got is Matt better pray."

"This last one is hot, *patron*," Stills said.

Alarms sounded.

"Two detonators went off," Marie said. "I didn't detonate them."

"Vincent!" Belisarius said. "Vincent! Are you alright?"

No response. A small icon showed Stills unmoving.

"Vincent! Are you hurt?"

No answer. "Marie, get some of Saint Matthew's drones moving that way. It'll take them a while to get there, but—"

Stills' voice interrupted him. "What. Shitty. Explosives. What shitty, shitty explosives."

"Are you hurt, Vincent?" Belisarius asked.

"I was expectin' the world to come apart when those stallions blew their loads. We ain't gonna get much done with donkeys, *patron*. You got a backup explosives guy you can call in?"

Marie grabbed the microphone. "Listen, *espèce de con*! There's nothing wrong with those explosives! Use them right next time! You're the moron who—"

Belisarius pulled the microphone away from Marie.

"I'd say bring it on, *cabrona*," Stills yelled back, "but you'd compact into greasy paste before you even got close."

Marie tried to get the microphone back, but Belisarius electrified his fingers so that they sparked before her. She turned away and kicked the wall. A slow stream of low-house Venusian swearing bubbled from her, creatively repurposed for an aquatic target. Belisarius shushed her.

"Vincent, can you get back here?" Belisarius asked. "Once you're in your chamber, we'll detonate the other charges and see if they do any better."

"I worked up an appetite somethin' fierce. Gonna be lookin' for chow. Have it ready for me. Gonna taste like dog shit here. Ammonia makes everything bitter."

"We'll have it ready," Belisarius said, before toggling off the microphone. "Are you calm yet?" he asked Marie.

"I'm always calm."

CHAPTER TWENTY-FOUR

CASSANDRA CAME TO the commissary at midnight to get some food to take back to her room. She hadn't expected to see anyone here, and had timed it that way, but she found Major Iekanjika working at one of the tables. And Stills' big steel chamber had been wheeled against a wall. Cassandra took a few heatable items from the freezer and put them on a tray.

"You've been locked up in your quarters a lot," Iekanjika said in French.

She couldn't place the Major's accent. The tray in her hands was heavy. But the major was looking at her now. She had an unsettling intensity, as if she was invading personal space with her eyes and didn't care.

"My part of the job isn't as exciting or as dangerous as Stills' or William's," Cassandra replied in the formal, correct French she'd learned as a child. "My work will be from within the fugue."

"That isn't dangerous?" Iekanjika asked.

"Not particularly."

"Interesting. I watched Arjona in the fugue. After he was done, my sickbay had a hard time keeping him alive through his fever."

Again, Iekanjika's judging stare drilled into her, into her uncertainty. Had Bel lied about the fugue to Iekanjika too? Cassandra was starting to realize that exposing any of Bel's lies to the others wouldn't be healthy for him. Or was he telling the truth?

"That doesn't happen to you?" the major asked finally.

"The longer we stay in the fugue, the higher the fever." It would probably be wise to change the subject. Would Bel be proud of her for understanding that? Maybe she was adapting a little bit to the wide world. "Bel said that if we get your ships through, there will probably be war."

"The war'll be shorter than a sneeze," Stills said.

"Is that true?" Cassandra asked.

"The Venusian Congregate is powerful," the major said, "and they've never released a client nation from one of their Patron-Client Accords."

"So why do this?" Cassandra said. "From a pure cost-benefit perspective, it doesn't make sense. Hundreds or thousands of people will die, and nothing will change."

"Freedom isn't the result of a cost-benefit analysis," Iekanjika said. "We want to own our world. We want to freely visit the rest of civilization through the only wormhole out of Bachwezi. Congregate political commissars shouldn't be embedded in our government. We should bleed in our own wars, not theirs. And we should keep what we create and discover. Dying is worth all that."

"Congregate gonna fuck you up bad," Stills warned.

"We'll make it cost them," Iekanjika said.

"Like you said, cost don't matter, sweet cheeks. They got the best warships and all the wormholes that matter. And they got us mongrels."

"The *Homo eridanus* don't mind being clients?" Cassandra asked.

"We ain't clients, princess. We already got a planet. We're contractors. We fly their fast fighters and go home after our tours. Maybe they'll fly us against the Union. I would."

"Anywhere, anytime," Iekanjika said.

Stills laughed. Cassandra couldn't understand why. Looking at her tray of frozen food, she left the commissary. Had they just threatened each other? Happily? Who were these people? How much violence did they carry in them? She couldn't live like that.

The Garret wasn't like that. The *Homo quantus* sought knowledge. They didn't threaten anyone. But what would the *Homo quantus* do if someone threatened them? She honestly didn't know. Human history was a concatenation of power struggles and people trying to get away with whatever they could, until someone strong enough came along to stop them. That was the world she'd stepped into.

That was the world Bel had been living in for twelve years. Maybe she ought to be surprised Bel hadn't become more hardened. It wasn't a pleasant thought, and she activated a tiny micro-current from her electroplaques to her brain, inducing savant. The confusing emotions of the world became less important, pressed against her insides less, while mathematical and geometric patterns became clear. Savant was a comforting state in which to escape from some emotions. Bel and Gates-15 rounded the corner. Bel smiled at her. Gates-15 blushed. What did that mean? Faces were too pattern-rich in savant.

"Hi Cassie," Bel said, the way he had when they were teenagers.

"Hi, Bel."

"Miss Mejía," Gates-15 said. She looked away. Gates-15 tried looking up at her, but she turned her face further. "Are you okay?"

Cassandra didn't answer. She didn't understand what he was asking.

Bel put his hand on Gates-15's shoulder. "This is savant, professor," Bel said. "It's one of a few cognitive states in which the *Homo quantus* can function."

"I have work to do," Cassandra said. "Goodnight."

She moved past them and around the corner. Then, she stopped as they began speaking and moving again.

"I go into savant as well," Bel said, "to improve geometric abilities, but it's a kind of inducible brain damage, part of a family of depersonalization disorders."

What was Bel talking about? Savant wasn't a kind of brain damage, not exactly. And it wasn't a depersonalization disorder. It was a lie, or in a stretch, a bad mischaracterization. Did Bel hate his heritage so much that he believed that?

"It sounds dangerous," Gates-15 said as they receded from her.

"The people who made the Puppets worked with the same mechanism," Bel said, "except backwards. The Puppet brain can't have dissociative disorders. There's no way for the Puppets to avoid the religious awe of the Numen."

"You worry that I won't be able to hold up my part in the con if Del Casal succeeds?" Gates-15 said.

"I wonder if you're still ready to go through with this."

"I want to be whole. Not just for a few weeks, but for my whole life."

"We all want to be whole," Bel said. Then, they were too far to hear.

Cassandra puzzled in the hallway for forty-eight seconds longer. She didn't have a depersonalization disorder. If Bel was telling the truth, and the Puppets had been built to be unable to escape the cruelty of the Numen, even by going insane, then the wide world was more frightening and confusing than she'd thought.

CHAPTER TWENTY-FIVE

THE PUPPETS HAD intercepted the Middle Kingdom messages in the district of the Free City called Jeffey's Finger, but after a bit of digging, Majeur Bareilles found that the transmissions had been routed through Three Prophets, a Puppet micro-state about thirty kilometers away.

The Scarecrow took a small skip ship with Duggan-12. The priest had been resistant at first, but had then begun speaking with him as if their travelling together was some sign of rapprochement between the Theocracy and the Congregate. He didn't disabuse her of the notion and they descended the lock hatches into Three Prophets.

The village was a mean place, dirty, blighted by poverty. The ceilings of ice were poorly dug, the lighting failing, and the faint hiss of escaping atmosphere accounted for the low air pressure. Eighty years ago, the village had possessed three human divinities, but they had died of old age in captivity, and had been replaced by only two other Numen. Every intelligence service knew the divine humans were dying out, and that eventually, in perhaps another generation, the Puppet states would fall. It would be then that the Congregate and the Banks would fight over the Puppet Axis.

They were met by a priest who administered the village along with a sunken-eyed and partly starving local committee. The priest genuflected to Duggan-12 and then to the Scarecrow, somewhat wide-eyed.

Instead of waiting for speech, the Scarecrow strode forward with hushed flexing of artificial tendons by smooth motors and the muted creaking of piezoceramic muscles. He knew where he was going. Decades ago, Congregate intelligence operatives had mapped out every public meter of the Puppet Theocracy, and some of the private ones. Duggan-12 hopped along beside him.

"You wanted to investigate, Scarecrow? You wanted to investigate?" she said, enunciating loudly in the antique pre-Anglo-Spanish favored in the theocracy. "Witnesses are here!" She waved her hand at the following priest and his committee.

The Scarecrow moved off the central laneway of Three Prophets to a narrow alley that ended in a maintenance door. The door was nothing special, but the ice in the alleyway was well-trodden. Behind the door nested the mainframe and comms node that had intercepted the transmission. Duggan-12 ran to put herself between the Scarecrow and the door.

"If you need information, we are happy to trade it with a partner!" she said.

In the infrared her face had flushed hot, as had the faces of the other Puppets. Heartbeats had risen. Puppets could be pliant and accommodating, but beneath the mushy exteriors was steely, obsessive resolve about protecting and holding their divinities. Their communities reflected their personalities architecturally: disorganized, meandering, cluttered, and freely passable for the most part, until one neared the Forbidden Cities, where they kept their gods captive. The mainframe was probably near the Forbidden City of Three Prophets. And while the Scarecrow could probably overpower any number of external Puppet defenses, previous reconnaissance had reported old anti-aircraft cannons *inside* their village, enough to seriously harm the Scarecrow and explosively decompress much of the village.

But he didn't need to pass the doorway. He was made of the cutting edge of Congregate AI technology distributed deep within a body that was mostly weaponry. He directed maser pulses into receivers on the walls, in the Puppet frequencies, using Puppet authorizations snipped from intel reports. In fractions of a second, he'd accessed the administrator areas in the mainframe. He found the logs and drilled down to the interception event. The tags on the Middle Kingdom transmission the Puppets had intercepted were all appropriate. This was another line of evidence that the message was genuine.

But a deeper look at the metadata in the intercepted message showed something very interesting. Before their normal encryption processes, Middle Kingdom spies sprinkled chaotic code in their messages, to render decryption even more difficult and to serve as a hidden, internal log on the message routing. Messages could be mathematically transformed and encrypted, but the chaotic elements were magnified by transformations. Manipulations like routing aged a message measurably.

And this message had been manipulated between transmission and interception.

The Scarecrow solved the code to find that the signal had been sent through a number of nodes to mask its path, but the routing in this message was longer than normal. And something, somewhere had decoded the Middle Kingdom's top level encryption and left the message to go on.

Duggan-12 stamped her foot and tugged at the metal fiber of his false shirt, trying to turn him around.

It would take many powerful AIs to break the Middle Kingdom ciphers, each of which was big and bulky. The Anglo-Spanish were rivals to the Congregate in the development of AIs. How had the Anglo-Spanish smuggled that kind of processing power to Oler without being noticed? And why? The real secrets in the Epsilon Indi system weren't on Oler. Unless the Anglo-Spanish were making a power play, trying to get Congregate Intelligence to sweep Oler of Middle Kingdom assets.

The Scarecrow tracked the modifications of the Middle Kingdom signal all the way back, reconstructing its routing. The Puppet was still flush-faced, breathing heavily with a panic for her divine humans. Only five seconds had passed. The Scarecrow backed away.

"I am done with my investigation," he said.

He turned and strode back toward the crude port. He had a point of origin. It was in the embargoed Puppet Free City. An art gallery.

CHAPTER TWENTY-SIX

From the introduction to *Defining Faith in a World of Cut Strings: An Exegesis of the Puppet Bible,* by Elizabeth Creston-12, Bishop of Port Stubbs, 2490 CE:

The study of theology and the exegesis of the Puppet Bible is remarkably complex, given the essentially polytheistic context of the Numen. The richness of Numenarchy source material covers so broad a range of topics—sometimes in such contradictory or ambiguous terms—that its sheer volume constitutes an obstacle to spiritual understanding. And the corpus continues to grow. Scholars continue to reflect on the records of the Numen of the Edenic Period, as well as on interviews with the last surviving Puppets who had direct contact with the pre-Fall Numen.

The unending growth of the scripture has not—and should not—slow the process of exegesis. Contextualizing and balancing contradictions is too important a task to wait.

Natural scriptural oppositions like "Get the fuck out!" (*The Book of the Angry Things*, Chapter 6, Verse 4) and "Get the fuck over here!" (Chapter 4, Verse 20) and

"Look at me, you little pisshead!" (*The Book of How to Behave*, Chapter 2, Verse 12) and "Don't you dare raise your eyes to me!" (Chapter 14, Verse 4) are amenable to some analysis based on the contextual and moral differences in each situation, and even, to some extent, the status of the different Numen.

Far more complex are the verses concerning Mooney-4's Dilemma. Scriptural quotes such as "Do you want money? I can give you money. Just let me go. I'll leave my wife and children. Just let me go. Please let me go." (*The Book of Pleas and Threats*, Chapter 3, Verse 3) and "If you don't let us go, I'm going to flay the skin off you, Puppet." (Chapter 3, Verse 17).

A holistic approach to theology highlights the multidimensionality of the spiritual world with verses such as "Good boy." and "I don't know what I'd do without you." (*The Book of the Good Boy*, Chapter 1, Verses 1 and 9) and "You missed a spot here." (*The Book of Assessments and Punishments*, Chapter 3, Verse 8), which invite a banal interpretation, without sacrificing moral insight.

Some of the most profound Fallen Age theologians have demonstrated the value of parsing apparently banal scripture for symbolic meaning. Who among us has not missed a spot? Is any Puppet capable of not missing a spot, or are all Puppets flawed, imperfect?

If the flaw is intentional, what was the Numenarchy's intent for this flaw? Some theorize that the creation of flawed Puppets imposes an arrow of time onto the cosmos, from imperfect creation to the eventual attainment of moral perfection. Further questioning of the last Numen who were alive during the Fall may reveal something of the intentions of the first generations of the Numen of the Edenic Period.

But if the imperfect nature of Puppethood is unintentional, then parallels with Judeo-Christian theology are less useful, while the arguments of classical Greek philosophers, who had to systematize an ethic balancing layers of gods and Titans and men, are perhaps more meaningful for the Puppet ethicists of today.

Recent scholarship has brought novel questions to theology...

William tossed the reader on the bed in disgust.

"You don't like it?" Gates-15 asked.

William stared at him. "Puppets are crazy."

"I made heavy use of the writings of Bishop Creston-12 in my doctoral work."

Gates-15 sat in a chair, his feet dangling off the floor. Sticky sensors clung to his chest, neck and forehead.

"The Puppets are very different," Belisarius said from where he leaned against the wall.

"You defend them a lot," William said.

A plastic curtain divided the room in two, pressing slightly toward the low-pressure space where William sat in bed. Some of Saint Matthew's early generation automata scuttled around him, taking air and sweat samples every ninety seconds. Others did the same on the near side of the plastic, skittering for sweat samples on Gates-15.

"There's not a single Puppet ever born who asked to be turned into a Puppet," Belisarius said. "Humanity made them."

"I never made them," William said.

"No one alive today did," Belisarius said, "but we play the hand we've been dealt."

Del Casal took one of the automata scuttling on Gates-15's arm, regarded its sweat swabs, assay vents and thermal sensors, and set it back.

"Gates-15 has all the chromosomal genes to experience the religious awe effect in the presence of a Numen," Del Casal said. "From what I understand from him, his problem is in the microbiome around his synapses. In normal Puppets, an array of symbiotic bacteria located at the nerve endings modify the environment to strengthen and coordinate certain kinds of signal cascades. I do not know which bacteria are supposed to be there, and neither does Gates-15, so I have engineered tiny ecosystems of bacteria to colonize the synapses between his smell and taste receptors and his main and accessory olfactory systems."

"It works?" Belisarius asked.

"It should, for a while," Del Casal said. "These bacteria are not invisible to his immune system, like the ones that would have grown up in him from the fetal stage. But I have engineered them to express some immunosuppressors that will prevent his immune system from clearing them. That should keep them stable for perhaps six or seven weeks."

"I don't feel anything now," Gates-15 said.

"You haven't tested it?" Belisarius asked.

"We are about to," Del Casal replied.

"Too bad we don't have any canned Numen smell," Belisarius said.

"That is the genius of the early molecular biologists who engineered the Puppets and the Numen," Del Casal said, with some admiration. "They designed their biochemical control system to be hack-proof. The Numen signal is a complex of dozens of smells produced by hundreds of nuclear genes that are modified after secretion by specific bacteria unique to the

Numen microbiome. The successful reception of the signal is in the combinations and proportions of the scent molecules. It is ingenious. We will test the changes in Manfred against what I have built into William, but the live test will only come once he makes his way into the Forbidden City."

"I can't believe I might be fixed," Gates-15 said. His cheeks flushed pink to the edges of his beard. His hands clutched nervously between his knees, and his feet dangled between the chair legs.

"This is a temporary fix," Del Casal said. "It will wear off. But if it works, I have some thoughts on how to make it permanent."

"And what about the main job?" Belisarius asked.

"I have taken the multi-walled carbon nanotubule systems in the *Homo quantus* as a model, and engineered a similar mechanism into Manfred's fingers," Del Casal said.

Gates-15 pulled his shaking hands from between his knees and held them palms-up. The miniature adult hands had their stories written in small wrinkles and scars. Gates-15 pressed sideways against the fleshy pad under the second knuckle of his index finger. Near-invisible dark hairs emerged from his finger-tip. Dozens of them.

Del Casal produced a magnifying glass that projected a close-up hologram. "I have stacked thousands of multi-walled nanotubules together to make tubes that will not shear from air movements or accidental pressure," he said. "These can be pressed into the port of any computer."

"The computer virus is in there?" Belisarius asked.

"Stored in the carbon lattices," Del Casal said. "Manfred's movements will store a charge between some layers of the lattices, enough to power the upload."

"It won't show up in any scan?"

"The lattices are tiny and will not show up in X-rays, ultrasound, or anything routine. If anyone thinks to look for anomalous neuronal tissue or carbon structures in Manfred's hands, your plan has larger problems."

"Saint Matthew's virus ought to do the job," Belisarius said to the exiled Puppet, "if you can get it in."

Gates-15 pressed at his finger in the other direction and the tiny hairs sank back into his skin. "I haven't been back to the Puppet Free City, much less the Forbidden City, since puberty."

"You'll be home," Belisarius said. "The center of attention for a while, but you'll be home with a new identity, one that could become permanent after the job, when you'll be one of the richest Puppets alive."

Gates-15 took a deep, shuddering breath and exhaled.

"Can we see if your modifications work, doctor?" Belisarius asked.

Del Casal rolled back in his chair and opened the seam of the plastic that separated William from them. Gates-15's miniature face flushed deeply, ears and neck reddening in sympathy. His respiration became slow and unsteady. He stared at William in some terror. William stared back at him with the same look.

"What do you feel, Manfred?" Del Casal asked.

"It's... vast," Gates-15 said, without looking away from William. "I don't know... if it's the awe I've heard of..." The Puppet exhaled slow and long. "Something strong is here, in this room... something good."

"It is not like what you have seen in others?" Del Casal asked, pulling his chair closer.

Gates-15 swallowed, getting less distracted, less glassy-eyed. "I don't mean it's not working," he said distantly. "It's hazy... wonderful." He swallowed again. Looked away from William, and then looked back in astonishment. "I've seen extreme reactions, like falling-down worship, seizures... dervish frenzies. But I can handle this. I can feel. It feels wonderful," he finished breathily, staring at William in anxious wonder.

Del Casal looked at the data coming in, changed the positioning of some of the pads on Gates-15, and rechecked his graphs. Finally, he closed the plastic, separating Puppet and man. He gently steered Gates-15.

"Go to your room," he said softly. "Write down everything you feel. Then sleep."

When the Puppet was gone, Belisarius and Del Casal shook hands and clapped each other on the shoulders.

"I have been awake for forty hours," the geneticist said. "I am going to sleep as well."

When Del Casal had left, Belisarius passed through the plastic flaps and pulled the chair close to William's bed. William picked off the sensors and shooed away the little automata, but didn't meet Belisarius's eyes.

"How do you feel?" Belisarius asked.

"Are all the Puppets going to be like that?"

"If we're lucky."

"If I'm lucky."

"If you're lucky," Belisarius said. "That's not what I was asking, though."

"I know."

"Want a drink?"

"Yeah, but Del Casal says I can't."

Belisarius looked at his hands. A lump ached in his throat. "Are you going to be able to pull the trigger on this? You can bite the poison pill?"

"I'm not going to spend any more of my last days with the Puppets than I have to," William said. "If I'm surrounded by those little sickos, I'll bite the pill all right."

Belisarius drew a small box from his pocket. Inside was a thumb-sized piece of carbon steel in a plastic bag, and one of Saint Matthew's small automata.

"This is an implant that carries eight weeks of medication to treat the Trenholm virus," Belisarius said. "The Puppets may take everything from you, including your medicine. This will make sure you're able to function in the Free City."

"You're going to get Del Casal to implant it in me?"

Belisarius shook his head and briefly expanded his magnetic field. The doctor was gone, and no listening devices were active.

"Saint Matthew's robot will do it," Belisarius said, showing the tiny automaton. "There's more than just medicine in here. If for some reason you can't bite the poison pill, this thing carries not only anti-virals, but a fast-acting poison."

William paled. "You think I can't end it if I'm surrounded by Puppets?"

"Insurance."

"In case I can't handle it?"

"You've got this."

William frowned, not buying what Belisarius was selling, but he reached for the little bag.

"How do I activate it?" he asked coldly.

"You can't. Once the job is done, I can trigger it from anywhere. I've got a couple of entangled particles in there. One will signal me if you die. The other triggers the poison. I'll only do that if you're still alive, and the job was successful."

"Is this insurance for me or insurance for you?" William asked.

Belisarius held William's stare. "I don't want to leave you in there any longer than I have to. If you're positive that nothing in the Puppet Free City can scare you enough to give away the game, then we don't need insurance."

"Put it in," William said.

For a long time, Belisarius didn't know what to say or do, and they both examined the weave of the hospital blanket.

"We have the makings of a solid Mexican Shell Game," Belisarius offered half heartedly.

William pursed his lips and Belisarius deflated a bit inside. He missed the old William, the man who'd apprenticed him in confidence schemes, the one who'd taught him about human nature. Belisarius's choice of apprenticeship had directed to some extent who he knew, and now made him an outsider wherever he went.

Ten years ago, there had been no place for an over-educated kid with overwhelmingly philosophical tastes in a bribable world of get-rich-quick schemes. William had guided him through a fast-moving, pragmatic, concrete world without political or spiritual or philosophical concerns. Now Belisarius was bringing the old con man trade into the world of politics and ideals.

"Thank you for everything you did for me when I was a stupid kid," Belisarius said quietly.

"You're still stupid."

"Maybe."

"You've got a good plan, Bel. It's half-crazy, but it's better than anything I would have come up with, even in my prime."

"Thank you."

"You never really needed me. You didn't need to be a con man, either. You were always made for more."

Belisarius shook his head. "I was built wrong, Will. If I hadn't found cons, I would have died a long time ago. You saved me."

William watched him for long moments, measuring, looking for lies. He nodded as if he was satisfied. Belisarius opened the bag and let the tiny surgical robot begin preparing William for anesthesia and surgery.

CHAPTER TWENTY-SEVEN

THE TWO OLD freighters Belisarius had rented were called the *Túnja* and the *Boyacá*. They creaked in odd ways, even in freefall, but they could still induce wormholes. Marie piloted the *Túnja*, while Stills grumbled about the embarrassment of playing taxi driver to Belisarius and Cassandra on the *Boyacá*.

They'd distanced themselves from Ptolemy and its traffic for six hours before coming to a stop. Then, Marie finessed the old coils of the *Túnja* to induce a short wormhole in front of her freighter. She didn't pass through it, but had the *Túnja* hold it.

Cassandra, from deep in the fugue, began giving orders for modifications to the coils on the *Boyacá*, as Belisarius had done months ago on the *Jonglei*, three hundred and twenty light years from here. Cassandra wore a mobile fugue suit to manage her heart rate and blood pressure and to try to keep down her temperature. Belisarius was spotting her, monitoring the suit and ready to intervene if she went too far. He hadn't put his on. He wasn't going into the fugue.

Belisarius and the objective quantum processor in Cassandra's brain manipulated the holographic displays that extended before them, showing maps, graphs, charts, and dials. Above this was a work space where they could write equations, suggest parameter changes, and draw technical proposals. Belisarius did not need or want to induce savant. The alienness of the *Homo pupa* and the *Homo eridanus* felt increasingly like holding a mirror to himself, only to see three faces in the fractured surface.

And despite being only fifty centimeters away from Cassandra, loneliness clung to him. In the same way he could have played cards with even the most advanced computers and soon found the rules governing their choices, so he could have done with the living computer that Cassandra had become in the fugue. The objective intellect she became was not conscious in even the most rudimentary sense. She was a machine of flesh ridden by a web of algorithms that could in no way even be called a person. Cassandra did not presently exist, having been temporarily snuffed out by an electrical and biochemical lobotomy.

Four times, the quantum intellect in Cassandra modified the current, curvature and magnetic permeability of the coils to create an artificial wormhole. The *Boyacá* twisted space with its intense magnetic fields until the throat shaping itself in space-time had a free end, questing to return to ground state or to stabilize itself temporarily with another piece of space-time. Each time, the quantum intellect directed it to the wormhole Marie had created before the *Túnja*. Each time, the probing end of the wormhole briefly found the hyper-edges of the *Túnja* wormhole in eleven-dimensional space-time and collapsed it.

"In theory," Belisarius said in frustration to Stills, "it looks like we could collapse any induced wormhole we wanted, within the jump range of the coils."

"That's about as useful as tits on me," Stills said.

Sending a direct microcurrent from an electroplaque into his brain, Belisarius went savant. It felt like shutting off one set of lights and turning on another. The telemetry pictures became simple to him, puzzle pieces with more obvious interrelations.

The presence of the empty, personless shell beside him bothered him less.

"Cassandra," he said. He did not want to break her out of the fugue, but he wanted to communicate with her. Ached to do so. He stepped close to Cassandra, pressing against her fugue suit, their breaths mingling. In the hyper-intellectualized awareness of savant, Belisarius understood that this ought to have been intimate, but in many ways it was closer to hugging a piece of meat.

Cassandra's quantum intellect drew graphs in the holographic workspace, inspiring new ideas in him, new wormhole geometries. He moved his fingers—twitches and clenchings writing new equations and geometries onto their work space. Even in his normal state, Belisarius could have mentally pictured five dimensions. In savant, he could picture seven- and eight-dimensional objects and complex state space geometries. The rendering programs had notations made just for the *Homo quantus* that allowed them to go past even this, to see the eleven-dimensional geometries that approached the complexity of wormholes.

The quantum intellect in Cassandra's brain stopped drawing models. It produced no output for the one point eight seconds after Belisarius had finished drawing the new geometries. It processed his idea. He'd drawn a model of a wormhole whose throat was constructed of six-dimensional tesseracts.

The quantum intellect took his graphs and expanded them, deriving more detailed shapes with dizzying speed. It was hard to keep up. The intellect in Cassandra's body was processing many operations in parallel, using superimposed qubit and qutrit variables which could assume multiple values simultaneously.

A fugue suit alarm lit gently in the center of their work space. Rising temperature. Thirty-nine point nine. The suit compensated, running cooling water through tubes around Cassandra's head, neck and back.

Then, the rapid drawing and writing on the workplace stopped. The basic shape Belisarius had drawn was still there, but instead of approximations, hard, quantitative solutions arrayed themselves around the graphic. Not a proof, but a compelling argument for thinking that the throats of wormholes, at the small scales, were indeed constructed of microscopic six-dimensional tessaracts, and that additional volumes and directions of space were hidden in the walls themselves, possibly used to bind these building blocks of space time together.

The blinking light flashed slightly faster. Forty point one degrees.

Belisarius drew the trajectory for an induced wormhole burrowing through space from the bow of the *Túnja* to the wormhole being held in place by the *Boyacá*. The complexity of the trajectory was beyond his ability to express, even from within savant, but it wasn't beyond the intellect occupying Cassandra's brain to understand what he meant.

Throbbing magnetic fields penetrated the freighter, pressing against Belisarius's magnetosomes, the strength of it near-dizzying. And still the magnetic field strengthened, piercing space-time again. The displays showed graphics of the penetration, its granular structure, macroscopic shape, and apparent distance and direction. Then the probing end of the induced wormhole contacted the wormhole produced by the *Boyacá*. And held.

The wormholes connected in a Y-shape.

Neither collapsed.

The blinking light flashed orange. Forty point nine degrees.

Belisarius issued the order to stand down the wormhole induction. The wormholes vanished as the great magnetic field on the bow of the *Túnja* shrank. Four hundred thousand gauss. Three hundred thousand gauss. One hundred thousand gauss. Fifty. Thirty.

Belisarius dropped out of savant to a feeling of momentary embarrassment. He stepped away from Cassandra's body, not remembering when and why exactly he'd gotten so close. He shut down the displays. Cassandra was still in the fugue. Her perceptions were spread over an expanding sphere several light hours in radius, all the volume that could have been folded into quantum superposition in the hours that she'd been in the fugue.

Belisarius did not want to hurt Cassandra in any way, but he did not want her to stay in the fugue any longer. From his electroplaques, he sent a direct current through the lines of magnetosomes in the cells of his arms, creating powerful magnetic fields, strong enough that Belisarius could measure the moving particles and fields around her.

He observed the fields, collapsing the superposition of states around her. Her far-flung perceptions shrank, gently, but quickly. She, like most *Homo quantus*, could only enter the fugue with effort. Her breathing changed.

"Cassie?" he said.

Her breathing became a panting. He held her by the shoulders. "Cassie?"

She groaned. He put his arm around her.

"Did you see what we just did?" he asked.

She nodded. Sweat had climbed from her scalp to individual hairs in zero g. He held a couple of anti-fever gel meds before her mouth. She took them. Her lips touching his palm startled him. She didn't seem to notice. She hadn't experienced any of what her brain had done in the fugue. She couldn't have. Cassandra the person had not existed for those hours. But she could review the memories of what her brain had seen and sensed and done, and she could try to understand it all. It was like revealed knowledge. Belisarius missed this like a recovering addict.

He held her tighter, comforting, and she let him, leaning her head on his shoulder.

"I saw," she said finally, smiling.

CHAPTER TWENTY-EIGHT

BELISARIUS HAD BEEN playing peacemaker between Saint Matthew and Marie for the last three weeks. After Marie had destroyed his first body, Saint Matthew had come complaining to Belisarius again.

"She sent me holographic flowers!" Saint Matthew said. "I thought at first that she'd made the smallest, smallest, *smallest* possible beginning of an apology, but they blew up, transmitting a computer virus in the pixilation of the blast pattern. It was an AI-specific virus!"

"That's pretty clever," Belisarius said.

"She tried to kill me!"

"Were you harmed?"

"Of course not. Nothing she could design could get past my immune system, but I'm worried about her somehow harnessing her carelessness to stumble onto something really dangerous."

"Saint Matthew, you're the reincarnation of a biblical apostle!" Belisarius said. "You can't handle a cashiered Congregate sergeant?"

"She knows I can't really hurt her due to my programming. It's only a matter of time before her clumsiness ends me. If you won't stop her, I will."

So Saint Matthew had stormed out of Belisarius's room and had used his own diminutive automata to run a control signal down to near Marie's lab. Then, he'd used Del Casal's carbon nanotubule technology to grow microscopic fibers into her lab to interface with her computers. Through this, he'd sent one of his prototype viruses, hacking her computer interfaces to permanently use the stern face of Caravaggio's Saint Matthew. The virus further tracked her movements and communicated them to Saint Matthew, safe in his lab. Marie had been apoplectic, especially since Saint Matthew had modified the frozen face hovering above his body to show a great, satisfied smile that Caravaggio never would have painted.

"Is the mad AI smiling?" Del Casal had asked Belisarius a few days later.

"He's dealing with some difficult personal growth," Belisarius said. "It's probably best not to get involved."

Saint Matthew still wore the painted smile today, but fearing retribution, he had sealed his lab from the rest of the mine four days ago. The only way they could work together was for Marie to join Belisarius in his room and for Saint Matthew to appear in hologram.

"Are the viruses and automata ready, Saint Matthew?" Belisarius asked.

Specifications of small, insect-like robots spilled in the holographic display beside the image of Saint Matthew in his lab. Six-legged and large enough to carry several terabytes of information, or something the size of a button, they could move and act independently for hours before their batteries ran down. The programming algorithms for a pair of viruses displayed along the other side of the grinning, angelic head.

"I've cross-checked the viruses against known Puppet hardware and software," Saint Matthew said, "as well as anything they may have bought in the last years, and extrapolated their possible capabilities based on very optimistic assumptions. These viruses are capable of locomotion through networks, and from the initial network of infection, should be able to find their way past firewalls to the Puppet fortification grid and cause major problems there for a few days. With some modification, these will work on Union systems and probably Congregate ones as well, although not for long."

"Sounds like a good job," Marie said sweetly.

"It is a good job," Saint Matthew replied. "Are you ready to say sorry for how you treated me?"

"No. Are you?"

"Why would I?"

"Because I snuck new experimental explosives into your lab."

"You did not!" Saint Matthew said, but the painted holographic head looked wildly about.

"I can also control the environmental systems. They're pretty hackable."

The AI made a squeak of fear and suddenly air rushed out of the lab in a blustering cloud.

"Environmental systems don't matter," Saint Matthew said, "when I can survive in a vacuum. Your gas-phase explosives are pretty easily side-stepped, aren't they?"

Marie was still smiling sweetly. Sparks started appearing in the joints and exposed electrical systems of Saint Matthew's body. The AI shrieked again. "What's happening?"

"I made a spider automaton like yours and had it paint a new explosive onto the sensitive systems of the body you're riding," Marie said. "Low pressure causes it to undergo a conformational change into something highly volatile."

Little flashes of light and expanding black smoke felled Saint Matthew's body. The AI uttered a series of religious expletives as he went down. His spider automata rescued the service band from the body and carried him away.

Belisarius turned to Marie after switching off the link. "Is there no way we could channel your creativity in other directions?" he asked.

CHAPTER TWENTY-NINE

THE AIs OF the Anglo-Spanish Banks were wholly artificial things, electronically grown and printed on inorganic templates by iterative processes that mimicked embryonic stages. And if reports were to be believed, some of them achieved a limited but highly functional sentience. The Congregate did not pursue true artificial intelligence. The Scarecrow and other mobile AIs were constructed out of a kind of petrification process of living brains.

The process began with a few very select end-of-career intelligence operatives who were put into life-support baths. Nano-machines followed every axon and dendrite, constructing semi-conducting fibers that replaced the existing neurons and were far faster. Year by year, the electronification process went on, not just copying the neurology, but expanding it, adding processing networks and memory capacity, until the petrified brain was a new intelligence, neither human operative, nor artificial intellect, but a hybrid. Faster than human, more cunning than AI, and riding a weaponized body. Pasts dropped away, identity didn't matter, leaving only the relentless pursuit of the secret enemies of the Venusian Congregate. They wielded vast physical power and broad legal and operational authorities, and were preceded by terrifying reputations.

The only thing they could no longer do anymore was move in secret. They could not pass for human. This didn't bother the Scarecrow. It had hundreds of spies, some deeply embedded in long-term covers for secrecy. And it had platoons of augmented human assassins, *pur laine* Venusians, ready to act at any time. But sometimes a Scarecrow needed its intellectual strength on site. And so in the middle of this night, he skulked, accompanied by local Puppet authorities and a discreet team, while he simultaneously shut down electronic surveillance around him.

The Puppets led him to the art gallery in Bob Town.

It didn't look like an art gallery.

They found a wall of metal embedded in the ice of the Free City. It was fitted with bay doors large that would be large enough to let through small trucks and forklifts. The cold bricked ground was well-travelled, stained with machine oil and tire tracks. The icy ceiling of the lane, seven meters above, had been dented in spots where trucks or cranes had lifted too high. A well-used area.

"This was an art gallery," the Scarecrow said.

Duggan-12 turned to another Puppet, a police lieutenant who looked like he'd been rolled out of bed.

"It's a warehouse," the police lieutenant said, consulting a grimy pad. He scrolled through dates and dates and dates. "It's been a warehouse for years."

The Scarecrow focused his cameras on Majeur Bareilles. She stepped forward, showing her own pad.

"Our records show that from 2510 to 2515 this was an art gallery, and as recently weeks ago," she said, "it was owned by a human off-worlder known by several names. Juan Caceres. Diego Arcadio, Nicolás Rojás and Belisarius Arjona."

The police lieutenant scanned for the names, predictably finding nothing. He shrugged.

The Scarecrow sent a command into the door mechanism,

overriding passwords and activating physical locks. The doors parted, releasing a powerful cold. The Scarecrow stepped forward, followed by Bareilles. The Puppets held back from the -60°C.

The Scarecrow sent a command and big industrial lights clicked on, showing a narrow walkway around a wide circular pit plunging down a hundred meters. From the very bottom, crates and crates were stacked on a central shelving space that could be accessed from all angles by forklift arms. They all seemed to be labelled "L-6 Protein Bath Nutrients, Dehydrated."

Duggan-12 came up behind them.

"Someone is stockpiling bath nutrients for bioreactors until the price comes up," she commented.

"It's a Puppet merchant," the police lieutenant offered from behind them. "James Barlow-17." He showed a picture of a smiling Puppet. Not Arjona, or Caceres, or Arcadio or whatever his real name was.

Bareilles walked along the edge of the pit, examining the walls and ceiling, pointing.

"Wiring stripped," she said. "Contains no computers more sophisticated than forklift operators." She touched the wall with a finger, then looked at where the chill had bitten it. "Acid," she continued. "The DNA is probably all gone."

"Acid-washing is a common preventative measure for storing anything that can be used in bioreactors," Duggan-12 said. "Contamination."

"Someone tried to tempt our eyes with a big haul of Middle Kingdom spies," the Scarecrow transmitted to Bareilles. "So he's hiding something more valuable than that. Our teams may pull something out of this former art gallery."

"Whatever identity he's using, he's somewhere in Epsilon Indi, and probably still on Oler, *monsieur*," Bareille sent. "We'll have eyes on him shortly."

CHAPTER THIRTY

THAT NIGHT, BELISARIUS'S door buzzed. He rose from his star-gazing and turned on the lights. When he opened the door, Del Casal stepped in and shut it behind him.

"Gates-15 is no mutant," the doctor whispered. "There is nothing missing from his biochemistry or microbiomes. He is suffering from constant withdrawal symptoms."

Belisarius's stomach did a tiny flip-flop. He'd been careful so far. Gates-15 knew very little.

"Does he know you know?" Belisarius asked.

Del Casal's spine stiffened. "Nobody else could have figured this out, Arjona. Because of my... particular experiences in working with the Numen, I am probably the only one outside of the Puppet Free City who could have figured out all the markers and responses."

"So he is a spy," Belisarius said. "This is good."

"Good? The heist is blown. I thought that once I told you, you would kill him. If you do not want to get your hands dirty, I can kill him. Better yet, we have soldiers on the crew who could make it the work of seconds."

"We now have a shill who thinks he can take our pot away because he holds the strongest hand," Belisarius insisted. "This is how we get the Puppets to bet the house."

"You cannot be serious!" Del Casal said. "This is not an acceptable risk. I already barely believe that any of us will survive this plan of yours. You do not make all the choices, and not one this big."

"Would you ever play poker as part of a committee?"

"Do not insult me, Arjona. I do not appreciate whatever comparison you are making."

"I'm playing against the psychology of the Puppets. You more than anyone else can understand what it is to stare down someone across the table."

"I bet my stake, on my cards, against my opponent."

"That's what I'm doing, Antonio."

"And if the Puppets do not swallow your bluff?"

"They will," Belisarius said. He felt an icy certainty slipping into his voice.

Del Casal crossed his arms and stalked slowly around Belisarius's room, disbelief written into his frown.

"Why are you even doing this, Arjona?" he demanded. "Your intelligence is off the scale. You could have been anything. You do not need to be a con man, certainly not in a con this risky. You have made enough money off your cons to live well, and you are no thrill addict."

Belisarius stepped close.

"No, I'm not a thrill addict," he whispered, "but I'm the equivalent to a fugue addict. I'm driven to commit psychological suicide over and over until I don't come back, all to analyze more and more data. I found out twelve years ago that confidence schemes are complex enough to tie up my brain, to keep it stimulated. And because there's nothing mathematical or geometric in a con, the urge to drop into the fugue falls away. This is keeping me alive, and I very much want to stay alive."

"Our lives are in the pot, Arjona."

"All cons look dangerous until they're done."

"You had better know what you are doing. I am not going to jail or getting killed for you."

"There'll be no need for that," Belisarius said.

The geneticist left with a sour look on his face. Belisarius extinguished the lights, but he didn't go back to watching the stars. He deflated inside. He'd wanted to like Gates-15.

Now they really could get killed.

And William certainly would.

CHAPTER THIRTY-ONE

DEL CASAL DID not return to his own room. He drifted, shocked.

He knew cards very well. Better than Arjona, probably. Arjona's reasoning was sound. Risk and daring were a matter of calculation and feel, forceful attacks and timely folding, and lacing every choice with misdirection. Del Casal likely understood the physiology of Puppets and Numen better than even Puppet doctors. And Arjona probably understood Puppet psychology better than their own theologians. Del Casal had done his research on Arjona.

Five years living among the human expatriates in the Puppet Free City. Interacting with the Puppets. Selling their art. Not just the legal stuff. Arjona had moved their foulest inner musings, their darkest fantasies and obsessions, to depraved collectors across civilization. Del Casal would have bet a lot that Arjona was the right man to play cards or run a confidence scheme against the Puppets.

But would he bet his life?

Arjona's plan depended on a series of improbable successes, but he had pulled together improbable people, people as improbably extraordinary as Del Casal himself—the most advanced, and mad, AI in civilization; a deep swimmer from the mongrels; a skilled fugue-diving *Homo quantus*; and even a skilled con man willing to die.

Arjona had concatenated a series of improbabilities into a long shot that could work.

Could work.

Del Casal was quite attached to his own skin. He was wealthy enough to enjoy it. But he had come for the money and for the chance to pit his skill against the skills of the long-dead engineers of the Puppets, to try to break the unbreakable biological lock. He wanted to see this out. Badly. But did he trust Arjona enough to put his fate into the con man's hands?

Del Casal headed back to his lab. No doubt Arjona's pet AI had sensors strung up discreetly all over the hallways of the mines and was reporting back to the *Homo quantus*. But Saint Matthew had nothing in the medical bays; Del Casal's own systems had seen to that. No one expected Del Casal to let anyone watch him work while he used genetic manipulation tools almost unique in the Plutocracy.

He sent a private message to the Puppet, to meet him immediately. Ten minutes later, a blurry-eyed Gates-15 entered, his blond beard and hair plastered to one cheek from sleep.

"What is it?" the Puppet asked. "This couldn't wait 'til morning?"

"Have a seat. I need to speak with you privately about your medical condition."

"Your therapy isn't going to work?" Gates-15 asked.

Del Casal motioned Gates-15 to sit. Finally, the Puppet hopped into the chair. Del Casal leaned forward.

"I know you are no exile," Del Casal said. "There is nothing wrong with you."

Gates-15 leaned back in shock. "What are you talking about?"

"I am better than any of your Puppet doctors. They cannot

fool me, so do not waste my time. I do not care. I am not here to rat on you. I am here to cut you a deal."

"You're crazy!" Gates-15 said. "I'm getting Arjona."

Del Casal's hand clapped onto the Puppet's thin, fine-boned wrist, holding him to the chair.

"Since you are no real exile and you are managing your withdrawal symptoms, I am guessing you must be an agent of the Puppet Government. And you and I both see Arjona's plan crumbling. I ought to get paid. But this job taught me something much more lucrative: I can make Numen. You need Numen. The only question is how much is your government willing to pay for them? My starting price is twice what Arjona offered me."

Gates-15 nearly choked on his sputtering.

Del Casal pulled the Puppet's chair even closer. "You and I both know that your people are dying. Neither the modifications to the Numen, nor those that made the Puppets, are stable over evolutionary time. The critical bacterial microbiomes and organelles drift genetically, accumulating changes that will eventually make it so that the Puppets will not recognize true Numen. I guess that the Puppets have six to ten generations. And I am the only one who can correct it."

"You're crazy!" Gates-15 repeated.

"You smelled Gander. Given time, I could make it permanent. Imagine: enough Numen for every Puppet. And if your government is willing to pay nine million francs, I will teach the Puppet doctors how to do what I can do."

Gates-15's lips trembled with fear.

"Deal," the Puppet whispered.

CHAPTER THIRTY-TWO

THE PUPPET FREE City was precious to the Puppets because it housed thousands of the divine humans. The Free City was a rare haven to unscrupulous visitors because it had few rules. Under both the Numenarchy and the Puppets, the ownership of conscious beings was legal, attitudes to violence, narcotics, and genetic engineering were flexible, and privacy was taken seriously. The wealthy who had tastes that could not be fulfilled elsewhere ran the embargo and came to play in the Free City.

So when Marie and Del Casal, using forged identity documents and a mountain of Congregate francs, rented the deepest six penthouse levels of the Grand Creston Hotel and landed their yacht, the visa procedures with the Grand Creston Constabulary were perfunctory. Rented robotic servitors with wipeable memories loaded tons of Marie's cargo into the expensive private elevators and began the twenty-five minute descent.

"Holy crap!" Marie exclaimed at the opening of the elevators onto the deepest rooms in the hotel. A wide reception hall sprawled under a vaulted ceiling hung with chandeliers. A honeycomb of thick windows looking into the deep darkness of Blackmore Bay filled the entire outer wall. Lacy stairways led up each wall to a second floor balcony cutting across the windows, to more private sitting and dining areas. Doorways off the sides of the balcony led to the bedrooms. "This place is bigger than my last prison."

Del Casal frowned. "We have four more of these, so enjoy them."

Marie checked a display on her wrist. Nitrogen-depleted air. Four atmospheres of pressure. That was as low as they could pressurize the hotel at this depth. The pressure outside the hotel topped out at a cool thousand atmospheres. The rich came to these deepest of penthouses to brag about throwing parties twenty-three kilometers below the surface.

"C'mon, people," she said, clapping to the servitors.

Four robots followed her out of the elevator, carrying Stills' chamber. To their left, the earlier baggage the servitors had brought down sat neatly in a row. Twelve metal crates, each a meter cube, full of tools and explosives, as well as a large clinic's worth of surgical equipment, from bandages and braces and sutures, to casts and anesthetics. Either Bel thought she really was going to blow her fingers off, or Stills' job was more dangerous than she'd been thinking.

CHAPTER THIRTY-THREE

GATES-15 BEGAN TAPPING his foot against the floor again. Then, he shifted in his straps and needlessly rechecked the telemetry of their trading vessel. William watched the stars. Anytime he closed his eyes, he would catch the Puppet staring at him wide-eyed and open-mouthed.

"I'm not a real Numen," William repeated, without looking at Gates-15.

"I know." Gates-15 breathed, changing the displays before him. "I know."

William unstrapped himself and floated free. He moved over his seat and into the back of the cramped, Puppet-sized cabin.

"It's just that," Gates-15 said hesitantly, "it's just that it makes you wonder, doesn't it? What it really means to be something."

"Damn it, not again," William said.

To avoid Gates-15, he moved to the miniature galley filled with unappealing, prepackaged rations. Not that he was hungry. Del Casal's modifications had done more than make William secrete pheromones. Things circulated in him that added a slightly bitter aftertaste to everything. And Gates-15 kept upsetting his appetite.

"The Numen are humans who achieved a kind of biochemical

divinity," Gates-15 said, still keeping his eyes locked on the displays.

"There isn't anything divine in me," William said. "You watched it all. Until we're in the Free City, I'd appreciate it if you'd stop going on about that."

Gates-15 sighed heavily.

"We might be walking into a death trap anyway," William said. "When we get to your Puppets, they may laugh at the both of us and throw us out the airlock."

"That's not how they do it."

"What?"

"That's not how Puppets execute someone. The Numen of the Edenic Period were very imaginative. The Puppets tried to honor their traditions."

"Don't tell me anymore."

William scrunched the packaging of their rations so he wouldn't hear Gates-15's slow, loud breathing.

"I keep wondering," Gates-15 said, "what is the nature of divinity, if a good enough forgery can be created? At what point do you declare that the copy is the original?"

"Are all Puppets going to be like this?"

"Theology is the queen of the sciences. It permeates every part of Puppet existence."

"Except for you," William said.

The Puppet looked back over the seat. The fine blond hairs of Gates-15's beard framed his tight-pressed lips.

"I'm sorry," William said. "I didn't mean to get so personal. This is very disturbing."

"No less so for me. I'm travelling with a divinity. Not even a captive one. One who could order me to do anything he wanted." A minor note of longing accented Gates-15's voice.

William continued rooting angrily through the galley.

"Like all Puppets, I spent my childhood away from the Numen," Gates-15 said. "I'd only seen one from a distance, with a lot of other children from my school. Before puberty, the neural systems to perceive divinity aren't properly developed. But everything, even then, was about the Numen."

"And then it all fell apart."

"The central axis of my existence wasn't gone," the Puppet said, turning. "I couldn't smell divinity and I was exiled, but the Numen still define me. In this case, by their absence."

"What was it like?"

"What?"

"The Numen you saw. What was it like?"

"I don't know. I was too young to smell it. It was on top of a building for a ceremony, far up, past rows of priests. I sometimes imagine it was despondent. I can't know what divinity feels. They aren't the same since the Fall."

The Fall of the Numenarchy: the Puppet name for what the rest of civilization called the Rise of the Puppets.

"Hardly surprising that they'd be a little twitchy after three generations in captivity," William said.

"They aren't like the Numen of old," Gates-15 said dreamily. "They don't possess and drive us. They fear and hate us. The Numen of old did not hate us. They held us in a delicious contempt."

William's stomach turned.

"I know what Bel thinks they'll do to me," William said. "What do you think they'll do to me?"

"I don't know. I was just a boy when I left."

William turned and floated close to Gates-15 and took the front of his shirt in his fist. "Whatever happens, you do your job, got it? I didn't come all this way to die in a Puppet prison for nothing. I'm doing this to leave something for my daughter when I'm gone."

Gates-15's eyes widened in wonder. His mouth breathed slow and gentle. "The fire in you hasn't gone out," he said. "You're so precious to us."

"Can you get the job done?"

"For you, anything."

William snatched his hand away and retreated.

Just then, a notification whined. Gates-15 turned slowly from William. He seemed to be having trouble focusing.

"Instructions are coming in from Orbital Control," Gates-15 said. "One of the naval pickets is being moved from extreme orbit to join us."

"Because they believe you?" William asked. The Puppets, even the exiles, had protocols for situations of feral Numen being found and brought back to Puppet space.

Their cover story was that William, now carrying the forged documents of a Geoff Kaltwasser, was a feral Numen, living as a shareholder of the Anglo-Spanish Plutocracy. He had contracted the Trenholm virus and was dying and had run out of money to pay for his care. It was an easy cover story to remember.

Likewise, Gates-15 carried the documents of Warren Lister-10, a Puppet trader living in one of the most isolated Puppet mining stations. The real Warren Lister-10 still lived there, and would for the remainder of his ten-month work rotation. Saint Matthew had transmitted a virus to the mining station that would change incoming and outgoing messages to avoid either party noticing any inconsistencies. The mining company would send a new worker out, but it would take months for her to get there. Gates-15 and Gander would be long gone from the Free City by then.

William and Gates-15 had been travelling for a few days, set on this course by the *Boyacá* before it wormholed away to avoid detection. They'd been at maximum acceleration for the first days, and then had floated in the still weightlessness that William associated with the long night's wait for a dawn appointment with the hangman.

"Orbital Control is instructing us to begin our deceleration burn," Gates-15 said. "I need you to strap in."

Nervousness tickled William's stomach.

Two things a con man had to keep in mind were pay-off and risk. No con was risk-free. And risk was unmeasurable without reference to payoff. The payoff here was huge: his daughter's escape from poverty.

He just needed to pull off his part. He'd pulled cons before, good ones, but only when he'd understood his marks, studied them. They'd been greedy, but rational. The Puppets were unhinged, messed up beyond all understanding. And the big con, the one that would bring in the money, depended on his ability to keep their eyes on him. William pushed off the galley and maneuvered into the co-pilot seat. He strapped himself in without returning the rapt stare of the open-mouthed Puppet beside him.

"Do your maneuvers," William said.

Deceleration pressed at William's chest with one and a half gravities. Not terrible, but uncomfortable. He was used to bigger ships, travelling at more stately paces; the Puppets were in a hurry. Gates-15 appeared to be equally pained, but not by the deceleration.

"You're sure you're alright?" the Puppet asked.

"I'm fine," William said, but he regretted his curt tone.

Gates-15's solicitude, for all that it was disturbing and artificially induced, was honest. It wasn't the Puppet's fault that his feelings had nothing to do with who William was. Gates-15's emotions had only to do with how William smelled. If Del Casal had been able to engineer the pheromones into a cactus,

Gates-15 would at this very moment be kneeling before a plant, rapturously removing spines from his fingers.

And while the Puppet had chosen to have this temporary biochemical addiction, the rest of his people had not. Bel said that puberty began for each Puppet with the physiological equivalent of withdrawal symptoms. William pitied them. And he even pitied Gates-15, in a weird way. The exile had to live in a world of strangers who despised him. Of course he wanted to go back to his people. Who wouldn't?

"I'm fine. Thank you," he said more kindly.

CHAPTER THIRTY-FOUR

"THESE IMAGES ARE the best we could get of Arjona," Majeur Bareilles said.

They were in Bareilles's intelligence station in the freight processing facility on the surface of Oler. A number of her officers were working in the holographic glow of sub-AIs running pattern-seeking analyses. Others were assisting her in the briefing of the Scarecrow around slowly rotating images of Arjona.

The images weren't good. They were all taken from a distance. It appeared that Arjona had a habit of walking in low light conditions. It also appeared that the watching cameras that might have taken better pictures had mysterious, temporary failures. The camera problems preceded Arjona, and continued after him, in patterns random enough that automated systems would never statistically link him to the failures. An AI, perhaps a few, were involved to break so many independent surveillance systems at once.

"My teams scraped Arjona's old art gallery," Majeur Bareilles continued. "It's not just clean. DNA from many humans and Puppets was added. It foils forensics. And that was before hydrolyzing agents chopped residual DNA into fragments. Genetic analyses got us nothing."

"A suspicious professional," the Scarecrow said.

"We have records on Belisarius Arjona and some of his legal aliases," Bareilles said. The grainy surveillance image was replaced with collage of images of Arjona taken by legal and police systems. "He's got all the Anglo-Spanish permits to buy and sell anywhere in the Plutocracy, but the biodata in each one is inconsistent with all the others. And of course, the permits issued by the Puppets contain no reliable data. He's apparently an art dealer and embargo breaker. We've got some possible contacts at a few locations over the last decade, sometimes where minor unsolved crimes occurred. We're digging up those records. These photos come from arrests under different identities, but no convictions."

"So we have genetic data on him from the arrests?" the Scarecrow asked.

Bareilles shook her head.

"At each arrest, he paid additional fees to have everything but tombstone data deleted from his files."

The Scarecrow despised the Anglo-Spanish. They were empty, existing only for money. And they had a price for everything.

"Before the issuance of his merchant permits," Bareilles said, "we've got nothing. No records of birth, previous contracts or education. He appears out of nowhere."

"So he paid to start a new life, and made sure his arrests didn't link him to any part of his past," the Scarecrow said, "but all this exposure and run-ins with the law don't fit the profile of a spy. So what was he doing with information on the Middle Kingdom intelligence operatives and why did he route it where the Puppets would find it?"

The Scarecrow lumbered forward, regarding the arrest record photos as they turned.

"We don't know yet," Barielles said. "But I have one more

possible link. One of our political commissars at the Union Consulate in the Free City found an unreported transmission involving an Arjona. A meeting. We don't know if it's the same Arjona."

Political commissars had full clearances to all official records, messages and orders within their client nations. There was always a basal level of chatter that tried to circumvent surveillance. Most of it was unimportant, minor betrayals that were rarely elevated to his attention. Majeur Bareilles was not the kind to bring up irrelevancies.

"Arjona was meeting a Major Iekanjika," she said.

"And?"

The holographic display switched to a split view: one half was the record system at the Union Academy at Harare, and the other was the personnel records system of the Union Navy.

"There is no Major Iekanjika," Bareilles said. "The Iekanjika family was politically powerful and well-represented in the general ranks one and two generations ago. But the family and name died out in the 2470s. There is no Iekanjika in the navy. The last Iekanjika to graduate from the academy at Harare was fifty-eight years ago."

The Scarecrow had no heartbeat, no adrenaline, nor anger. It had loyalty, and affront when faced with disloyalty. This was not evidence of disloyalty, but he could think of few reasons why a client nation would use false identities, or commission officers out of sight of their patrons.

"One of our client citizens, in collusion with one of our client's consulates, is moving under an assumed name," the Scarecrow said.

"So it would seem," she said.

"It's time for me to speak with this Arjona and this major, neither of whom come from anywhere."

CHAPTER THIRTY-FIVE

IT TOOK MARIE eighty-six hours, even with the robots, to build a pressure chamber with an airlock in it. What made it more difficult than building it in the penthouse of a fancy hotel was that one of the walls of her new pressure chamber had to be the outer window to the ocean itself.

Robots brought more equipment down from the yacht. I-beams to brace the new chamber against the opposite wall. Reinforced steel to brace the windows around the new airlock. Special pressure-resistant sealant and welding equipment.

The seal of the airlock to the glass most worried her. She'd used smart adhesives and biomachinery to weld the metal into the glass, and X-ray scattering showed no gaps. That probably meant that there were none, but this was a high-risk construction project. If the seal had too many flaws, and one might be too many, a thousand atmospheres of sub-surface ocean would tear its way into four atmospheres of penthouse.

Del Casal had been unhelpfully present during most of her work. His skills contributed nothing, but his presence bolstered her cover story. The one thing he was good for was bringing her whiskey. The Grand Creston had excellent whiskey.

"*Merde*, Phocas," Stills said in his electronic voice, "how can you not be done yet?"

"I'll be done when I'm done," she said. "You may survive a high pressure implosion, but me and the doctor won't."

"Fucking character flaws."

"At least I only have that one."

"Arjona picked you for your lack of flaws," offered Del Casal. She eyed the doctor. "Yeah, he did."

"You know Arjona better than we do, Miss Phocas," the geneticist said. "Presumably he is equally free of flaws. Do you think this scheme of his will work?"

"What? Phocas worked with prissy-pants before?" Stills asked.

"Some," Marie said, looking at the X-ray diffraction readings on her seals. "He's hired me for protection a few times, but until now, he's never found a full use for my talents."

"You two don't look like a matched set of cock and balls," Stills said.

"Am I cock or balls?"

"Take your pick. Baseline humans all look the same to me."

"I'll be balls," she said definitively. "I met him about six years ago in a casino bar. I was pretty hammered, which is hard to do with all the physiological augments the navy gives their NCOs. The whole place was talking about some kid who'd just taken down Eridani Fats in a marathon face-to-face no limit poker game."

"I heard about that game," Del Casal said.

"I found him with a casino-supplied escort on each arm," Marie continued. "He was drunk too. Not impressive. I asked him if he was the one who'd just won big. His girlfriends started fawning about how amazing he was, how no one had ever beaten Fats. It was puke-worthy. I told the arrogant little bastard he got lucky and that I had a system."

"What was your system?" Del Casal asked.

"I can't remember. I was really drunk. But I remembered at the time. And he seemed more interested in my system than in his escorts, so I told him."

"Did he laugh?" Stills asked.

"He didn't even let me finish!" Marie scoffed. She lowered her voice to do an impression of Belisarius. "'That's not a system. That's the stupidest thing I ever heard. It's just glitter.'"

Stills activated an electronic laugh he'd obviously programmed to make fun of air-breathers. Marie threw a wrench at his pressure chamber.

"You don't fuck with a drunk Congregate NCO, not unless you want to be smeared on the décor," Marie said. "So all polite-like, I leaned over his table, letting my sleeves come up to show off my NCO tats, and I told him he didn't understand statistics."

"Did he back down?" Stills asked.

"The jackass said, 'I'm made of statistics'," she said.

Stills laughed again. "So much for the honor of the Congregate navy. Did you teach him to watch his mouth?"

"I took a handful of decorative rocks from his table, ground them to powder in my fingers and said, 'This is glitter', as I whipped it in his eyes. Then I up-ended his table and took a swing at him."

"You're a dirty fighter," Stills said appreciatively.

"It didn't help," she said, looking at another set of X-ray readings. "He was on his feet quick, trying to get the rock dust out of his eyes. When I swung, he sidestepped, like he knew where I was, even blind. But he was still drunk, and he upset the table of the Saguenay Deep Shafts."

"The hockey team?" Del Casal asked.

"None other," she said. "One grabbed Bel by his tux jacket

and lifted him off the floor. The rest came for me. Just before they got to me, I saw the one holding Bel seize up and collapse."

"Then what?" Stills asked. "Get your ass kicked?"

"Are you kidding me? They were big, and some had sports augments, but nothing military-grade. They certainly weren't going to get between me and somebody who'd insulted my system."

"What was this system?" Del Casal asked.

"I don't remember! It was really smart, though."

"So then you pounded big brain?" Stills asked in exasperation.

"When I'd made the hockey team run off with their wounded, I found Bel at the bar. He'd found the only unspilled drink in the place. I was itching to pound his *I'm-made-of-statistics* face into pudding."

"But you didn't," Del Casal said.

"He asked me if I was looking for a job on the side."

"That's it?" Stills demanded. "Why didn't you clock him?"

"He paid really well. I made a lot of money hiring out as muscle for his plans," she said. "When I tried my own plans, I got cashiered."

"So you think he can pull this off?" Del Casal asked.

"Damned if I know, but I wasn't doing anything else, so why the hell not?"

Del Casal made a face and finished his whiskey.

"Alright, doctorcito," Marie said, packing away the X-rays equipment. "Now's the dangerous part. You can go to the yacht and lift off. We'll see you at the rendezvous if we all survive."

"Good luck then, Miss Phocas," Del Casal said. "Good luck, Mister Stills."

Del Casal entered the elevator and reclined on its large sofa as it began its twenty-three kilometer ascent.

"Civilians," Marie scoffed in French. "I hope he's comfortable."

"You got that," Stills answered. "Ready to get me out of this tub?"

"As long as I'm not around to smell it," she said, signalling the robots to move Stills' chamber into her new airlock. Marie brought in high-pressure industrial tools and laid them beside Stills, and then shut the first thick steel door, then the second.

"You can hear me?" she asked.

"Get on with it. You're more boring than piss in water."

Marie stopped herself from calling Stills a manatee, and checked the seals and fittings on the pressurized hoses one last time. She'd already broken into the penthouse walls and routed most of the plumbing feeds into her pumps. They now flooded the airlock. It didn't take long to fill, but that only got it to four atmospheres. The pumps whined mechanically, for long minutes, continuing to force in minute quantities of water, increasing the pressure as the joints of her airlock creaked. The noise of the pumps became louder and louder, until her equipment reached its limit.

"That's as far as I can go, Stills," she said. "Six hundred atmospheres. Can you survive in that?"

"I'm gonna have to, aren't I? I thought your damn pipes were gonna work."

"I got it to six hundred and got bored. Stop whining and work fast."

The read-outs showed him cycling the airlock to his hyperbaric chamber. She wiped at sweat she hadn't realized was there.

Stills could probably survive. His natural pressure was in the seven hundreds. It didn't sound like a lot of difference, but the proteins of the *Homo eridanus* were engineered to survive the highest oceanic pressures of Indi's Tear. At lower pressures, important proteins could expand and stop working. She'd been dealing with the reverse problem for months with the high-pressure explosives.

He cycled his lock slowly, letting the seven hundred atmospheres of pressure around him bleed out. He knew pressure better than she did. Was he trying to avoid giving himself the bends? Or an aneurysm? It sure was boring. Finally, he opened to door to his chamber and swam into the airlock she'd built.

"*Hijoeputa,* it stinks in here! What the hell is that?"

"Air freshener?" she guessed. "How the hell should I know? It's hotel water."

"I hate fresh water. It's going to make me bloat."

"Tell me about it. Sometimes I feel it in my ankles. Finish building the airlock, you'll get all the salt you want."

"Keep bustin' my ass, Phocas, and I'm gonna leave some explosives close to this hotel room."

"You sound like my last date," she said, squinting into the monitor showing the inside of the airlock. "Hey! Are you wearing a furry pouch around your waist?"

"Fuck off. I haven't got a waist."

"Nevermind. Of course you wouldn't wear a man-pouch. Keep it moving."

He pulled tools from the pouch sluggishly. The real problem was that Stills now had to cut through the window. He had a torch that would burn even in these crushing depths. They'd planned to equilibrate the airlock with the outside and then cut. In only getting the airlock to six hundred atmospheres, that left a four hundred atmosphere pressure difference across the window.

He could cut fast, but if the window weakened before the hole made it through, the whole window might shatter inward, possibly throwing heavy chunks of forty-centimeter thick glass at the other end of the airlock, or possibly shaking the airlock enough that the seals and welds cracked. The sudden pressure change could also set off the explosives. Stills lit the welding torch and applied it to the center of the glass.

CHAPTER THIRTY-SIX

GATES-15 BROUGHT the Puppet trading ship down at one of the church landing stations. Gun platforms pointed upward and outward. On the icy surface of Oler, tiny figures in weaponized exoskeletons watched them. Magnets clamped invisible fingers over the landing gear, and the whole platform sank into the icy crust. Soon, they'd all know if Del Casal was as good as Belisarius had said.

The platform descended a smooth channel of ice ribbed with wires and metal struts that occasionally opened onto dark bays. Through the top of the cockpit window, the vacuum-dark sky shrank within a constricting circle, starpoints seemingly winking away one by one in the glare of industrial lights. William had probably just seen his last star.

Finally, the elevator stopped. The platform and ship slid into a landing bay and a steel door closed them in. Ultraviolet lamps shone around them, making ghostly fluorescences. William breathed around a tightness in his chest.

"Are you all right?" Gates-15 asked. He did William the courtesy of not looking at him.

"I'm fine. Aren't you fine?"

"I'm ready."

"Not a beautiful place, your home."

Gouts of air poured out of vents in the bay walls, clouding and snowing in the cold. Infrared elements glowed redly as the bay pressurized. It lent the scene the look of a chill hell.

Lights began flashing above half-sized doorways. A wheel on an airlock door spun and four armored Puppets emerged, surcoats of orange giving them an unreal look under the red of the infrared heaters. They carried short assault rifles, built for their size. They took up ready positions at the four corners of the bay.

"Episcopal troops," Gates-15 said in some awe. "Holy knights. The finest Puppet fighters."

"Are they going to shoot us? Did they already see through our disguises?" William asked.

Four more followed, flanking the small doorway. Puppet priests. Finally, the two last Puppets stepped into the bay. Tall, richly decorated hats and embroidered robes didn't match with what looked to be iron collars and shackles peeking from the hems at wrist and ankles. The Puppets fidgeted.

"They sent two bishops," Gates-15 said.

The cockpit console lit with a holographic image of the faces of the bishops in front of their ship. "Mister Geoff Kaltwasser," the image said, "we are most honored to offer you the welcome and reverence you deserve." The dialect was antique Anglo-Spanish, a couple of centuries old, only a few steps past the merging of Spanish and English.

William swallowed, but did not answer.

"We understand that you're ill and nothing causes us more pain. We're here to care for you."

"Answer," William whispered.

"Your Grace," Gates-15 said, "Mister Kaltwasser is a bit nervous. Shall I help him into your presence?"

"Warren Lister-10," the image said, "you have done a great thing over these long months in keeping Mister Kaltwasser safe as you brought him home. Of course you may bring the divine out."

William and Gates-15 sat still for long moments. Finally William unstrapped himself. "Luckily I won't need to fake nervous." He crouched to the back of the cockpit.

"I wish I was as confident as you," Gates-15 said, following him.

"You're not going to die," William whispered. "This might be the start of you really coming home." Gates-15 shivered slightly at his words.

His ears popped as Gates-15 equalized the pressure between their ship and the bay and then opened the main door. Icy air spilled in, following soft blue UV fluorescence. Gates-15 descended the ladder and stepped away, looking up at him with both longing and expectation. William squeezed through the narrow Puppet door and into the cold. Geoff Kaltwasser was born.

The bishops and their priests approached skittishly, as if ready to bolt, sniffing the air. Like Gates-15, they had fine faces and bodies, between ninety and a hundred and twenty centimeters. Their eyes appeared cunning to him, menacing, but that was perhaps his own fear writing on the world. He had to perform now.

"I'm Geoff Kaltwasser," William said. "Thank you for receiving me."

The two mitred heads bobbed.

"I am Bishop Grassie-6 and this is Bishop Johnson-10. We have decontamination facilities inside. Then we can bring you someplace more comfortable."

Grassie-6 led the way into the low hallway. William tried to move, but found his legs leaden. He was the fall guy. That was his job in the crew. William sucked at the icy air and ducked his head to follow the bishops into the low passage.

"I apologize for the way, Mister Kaltwasser," Grassie-6 said. "In the old days, only Puppets came through these hallways. The architecture and traffic around the Forbidden City has grown so much that there's no way to directly bring in a ship with someone like you aboard. To be safe and secure, we brought you through the outskirts of the Free City."

William's back was getting sore and he bumped his head against the icy ceiling. The sounds of furtive sniffing followed him. They crossed several Puppet-height rooms before emerging into a mall of dark regolithic brick arching two storeys above and filled with archways leading to oddly quiet offices and common areas. William straightened his back with a relieved groan. Grassie-6 stopped at an office with a bronze plaque showing a rod and two coiled serpents. The few furtive-eyed Puppet priests watched him with a kind of anticipation William had never seen.

"This is a quarantine area, Mister Kaltwasser," he said. "We have doctors here ready to make sure you and Lister-10 aren't carrying contagions into the Free City."

"I wasn't thinking of spending much time in the Free City," William said. "I know I'm sick. I know I don't have a lot of time. Before I die, I want to get to Port Stubbs, where my family came from. I've never been there, but it meant a lot to my grandparents."

"The quarantine shouldn't last long."

"I'm a little nervous," William said. "I'd never met a Puppet before I contacted Warren. I'd spent most of my life avoiding the chance of ever meeting one. Stories go around."

"Stories do go around, Mister Kaltwasser, detached from facts, circulated by people who have never been here. I appreciate that you understood that these stories made no sense. Come."

A female Puppet stood in the doorway, in robes more surgical than sacramental. She smiled and motioned William to enter with a fine, pale hand. They were all pale, as if they'd descended from Old Earth European stock. Like Marie. Like him. Grassie-6 touched William's elbow and gently encouraged him in. He closed the door so that it was just the three of them.

"You won't be surprised at the effect you have on Puppets," Grassie-6 said, "but Doctor Teller-5 is among the most self-disciplined. We'll get you out of your suit to begin the decontamination process and also to assess your health information so we can begin treating you."

William had never seen a female Puppet. Doctor Teller-5 was taller than Grassie-6, perhaps a few centimeters over a meter, with long brown hair, old-fashioned patterns of makeup and an absence of any visible body art. She had clear, lovely features. The Numen had carried many atavistic traits through the centuries, among them a classical sense of beauty, and had designed their slaves accordingly. The Puppets would, by force of biological imperatives, still be cultivating that flavor of beauty, as long as Numen existed to be worshipped.

With some resignation, William began to unstrap and unzip the suit he had travelled in. A shyness touched him as he peeled it off. He'd expected a decontamination shower with no one but himself to suffer the unavoidable smell of his unwashed body. From his unfeigned social discomfort, he watched them react. Their eyes traced the lines of his body with hungry attention and their own self-awareness, listening to their bodies for their reactions.

This was the test of Del Casal's work. Either the con would continue, or he and Gates-15 would end their working relationship with an execution. The doctor approached him, staring in wonder. Instead of touching him with the sampling swabs in her fingers, she slowly stroked the skin of his arm, not caressing, not grabbing, but just feeling at the texture of him. A slow, heavy inhalation accompanied the touch. William jerked his arm away.

"What are you doing?" he demanded. "I thought you were a doctor."

His reaction didn't seem to matter to her. She wasn't bashful or embarrassed at his tone. She looked at his neck and chest, not his eyes, as if his outburst were mildly interesting, but bereft of meaning. She touched him again, palm-first, unmoving. With a bit of heat, William seized her wrist. She smiled directionlessly, and then looked at Bishop Grassie-6 in wonder. Grassie-6 smiled back at her. William pushed her away, and she stumbled back and down, knocking her head loudly against the cupboard. She looked up at him. As did the bishop. In eerie synchrony, they sighed. William's stomach lurched. They were so disturbing. And he been violent. They were rattling him. He had to control himself.

"This isn't a medical exam," William said. His voice tightened an octave.

The doctor rose.

"He's remarkable," she breathed, rising.

"Samples," the bishop said. "I'm very interested in results. I wonder what family he's from."

"Yes, Your Grace," she said.

William forced himself to be still as she came close again, the crown of her head rising only to his abdomen. She reached to his chest, wiped a swab and put that in a tube. She swabbed his leg, his back, and his buttocks. She took her time behind him. He turned to see what she was doing back there. He found her staring up at his back with her lips parted in some undefined, but overpowering feeling. Her cheeks flushed, not in embarrassment, but in reaction to him. He stepped away from her and looked to the bishop.

But Grassie-6 knelt by William's discarded suit, crouched over it, sniffing at the inside and giving it a furtive lick.

William's hands trembled. "What the hell is wrong with you?" he yelled. He had no control.

Then he kicked the bishop hard in the ribs. The air groaned out of Grassie-6 and he curled around his stomach.

"Oh, yes," the bishop whispered.

A hot palm pressed against William's buttock, not stroking, not moving, just pressing, as if communing with the consistency of skin and fat and muscle. She did not even look up at him. His skin held her enraptured.

No thought. He swung a fist backwards. His knuckles hit her forehead hard and two snaps sounded in his hand. She fell limp to the floor.

Then, William's nerves exploded in pain, and his muscles seized so tightly that he could not cry out. His head struck the floor and his eyes could only look straight ahead. Grassie-6's rapt face stared down at him in fascination over a hand that held a trembling shocker.

CHAPTER THIRTY-SEVEN

MARIE WATCHED HER monitor as Stills melted a crater into the center of the window, occasionally pausing to scoop out molten glass with the end of a rod. He moved slower and slower.

"Stills! Move faster. Chop, chop!"

"Blow me," he said. "Not enough water pressure in here. My blood can't get the oxygen I need. I'm fightin' not to pass out."

"Think less. Conserve oxygen."

His artificial voice grunted. "And it's stinkin' hot in here. Your refrigeration isn't worth shit. Feels like I'm close to a smoker."

"I wanted you to feel at home."

"I think I hate your guts, Phocas."

"Less think. Cut more."

Then her monitor filled with static as the room shook. The barometer reading inside the lock had jumped to nine hundred and eighty atmospheres. A tiny spray of water fanned from the corner of the airlock.

"Stills!" she called. "Stills!"

No response. She didn't even know if her voice was getting through.

Then the monitor came on after a reboot. A hard white light, the kind Stills didn't like, shone. The emergency light. The water inside was blackened and tinged with red. Shards of glass lay on the floor of the airlock and over Stills' hyperbaric chamber. Stills held the light in his fatty arms. His body and tail swayed and his great black eyes examined the chamber.

"Never thought I'd be so happy to smell an ammonia ocean," he said. His artificial voice had no inflection. She couldn't tell if he was weakened, or in pain.

"I see blood, Stills. How bad you hurt?"

"Don't know. I feel shitty. It's not the cuts. My body was at a lower pressure when the glass broke. I'm hopin' I'm just shocky and that I'm not dealing with organ damage."

"You need a rest?"

"Yeah, but we don't got the time, do we?"

"Not really."

"Let's kick it."

"Okay. Clear my airlock."

Stills closed his side of the airlock and then turned to the task of widening the edges of the hole in the window with the torch. Marie drained the lock and opened the door. The smell of dilute ammonia wafted out.

She jerked at Stills' chamber, sliding it a few centimeters with every tug. It massed close to a ton, but weighed less than half of that in Oler's weaker gravity. Even at that, she strained with myofibril-enhanced muscles until it was out of the way. This was faster than rigging straps and a winch, and she was working off nervous energy. She rolled forward a pallet of explosives on a dolly, and maneuvered it into the dripping airlock. She shut the door and flooded it.

They'd not reached the dangerous part yet. She began increasing the pressure in the airlock, getting it closer and closer to the pressure outside. The explosives didn't mind being wet, but the pressure was so high that gasses complexed to the explosives might react with the solids, changing their properties. She'd tested her design on Ptolemy up to eight hundred atmospheres and they'd been pretty stable. But this was higher than that.

"All right, cross your fingers," she said. "Wait. Have you even got fingers?"

"Fuck off, Phocas."

She squinted into the monitor. Yup. He had at least one finger on each hand.

"Should I be outside?" Stills added.

"Depends on your philosophy of life."

"I follow the Way of the Mongrel."

"In that case, stay close. If this goes south, you'll want to stab me with a shard of glass or something, right?"

"You get me for once."

"Cycling open," she said, crossing her fingers. The pressure inside the airlock shot from six hundred atmospheres to over a thousand. The seams squeaked. She waited a few seconds, watching the displays.

"All right, slacker!" Marie said. "Get out of there! Move it!"

"I already said fuck you, Phocas."

"You're going to be sorry you said that when you find the cupcakes I sealed in there."

"I couldn't eat that shit," he said, pulling out the pallet and shutting the lock.

"That's probably best," she said, pumping out the lock. "You don't want to see what a thousand atmospheres of pressure does to a cupcake."

Stills broke the first crate of explosives free. He and Marie fell into a rhythm of communicating through action across the airlock, separated by pressure differences that would kill either one of them. The lock was made to be fast, but they couldn't get to less than four minutes to a cycle. Four crates of explosives took them another eighteen minutes.

The room rumbled slightly.

"What the hell was that, Phocas?" Stills said. "Is the hotel coming apart?"

"I don't think so. Also, I hope not, 'cause I'm still in it. If our break made any fractures farther away, they might be equalizing." The room rumbled again. "Get moving, Stills. We've got to get you moving. They'll have heard that!"

"Too late. I've got company."

She looked into the monitor. Stills was gone.

CHAPTER THIRTY-EIGHT

THE BRIDGE OF the *Boyacá* still carried the modification they'd made to enable the two *Homo quantus* to work in holographic workspaces. In magnetic boots, Belisarius crouched in the middle of a small village of graphs, network flow diagrams, and communication traffic dashboards. The holographic light shone on his hands and the service band on his wrist.

"I think things just got more complicated," Belisarius said.

Iekanjika turned in one of the two pilot seats. Cassandra, in savant, approached from a different cluster of holographic charts.

"What is it?" Iekanjika asked.

"Someone is paying a lot of attention to what's going on in the Free City," Belisarius said. "Look at the patterns of money and communication." He reworked the holograms to displays graphs and charts.

"There's no pattern there," Saint Matthew said. "It's indistinguishable from the normal chaotic dynamic flow of money and talking."

"False signals," Belisarius said. "Someone is very good at camouflaging their actions, to make it look like nothing's going on." He pointed to small but clear spikes. "If all information and money were flowing into normal market patterns, there would be no directional preference. This shows money flowing in, in specific spots, in small enough quantities that it ought not to be noticed above background. Same with communications."

The AI was silent, puzzling over this.

Iekanjika stroked her chin, frowning. "What do you think this is?" she asked.

"Unfortunately, I think that the Free City has attracted the attention of the Congregate security apparatus. Maybe the Puppets weren't as close-lipped as they ought to have been about the Expeditionary Force, or maybe they went extra quiet, which makes everyone suspicious."

"How much attention?" Iekanjika asked.

"Any attention is bad," Belisarius said, "but if they can camouflage their attention with false signals, maybe we can throw in some false signals of our own."

CHAPTER THIRTY-NINE

WILLIAM PULLED OUT of sticky thoughts. He pushed at cloying, tugging things. He ached. A bit of light creaked into his brain through slitted eyes. He lay in a narrow bed low enough to be a stretcher. A sheet and thin blanket covered him, except for his leg.

Teller-5, the Puppet doctor, knelt at his leg, her hands flat upon it. She flushed deep pink under a bandage wound about her forehead. A bruise darkened from forehead to cheek. She met his eyes. Her expression was alien.

She licked his leg. He scrambled back in his sheets, sitting up.

It had not been a playful tongue to skin. It had not been a sexual advance.

She had been tasting him.

He was divine to her, incarnated.

Holy spirit in textured flesh.

From the corner came the bishop, who pulled the doctor back with hands on shoulders and quiet words. William locked eyes with him. Grassie-6 had calm, sated eyes. He met William's as he guided Doctor Teller-5 to a small chair.

"This is no medical test," William said.

"It most certainly is," Grassie-6 said. "It has been thirteen hours. You needed sleep. We kept you sedated to wait out your distress."

"Don't sedate me anymore!"

The bishop smiled. "We've assessed your health readings, so that our doctors can treat you."

"You're going to give yourself the Trenholm virus if you're not careful."

"It's a good and necessary test," the bishop said. "Our creators gave us immune systems very similar to their own. None of us should catch it, but if we do, we'll know that we can't bring you into the Forbidden City or Port Stubbs."

William flexed his hand, the one he'd used to strike the doctor. It hurt a lot.

"The bones of the hand are fragile," Grassie-6 said. "The next time you wish to strike a Puppet, ask for a whip or a boot or a rubber hose."

Snakes curled in William's stomach. "Would you give me one?"

"We don't want your hand hurt. Or your feet, for that matter. You have some bruising on the arch of your foot."

"What's wrong with you?" he croaked.

"Nothing," the Puppet said, looking back at Teller-5, who eyed William dreamily. "We're exactly as we're supposed to be."

CHAPTER FORTY

THE OCEAN WAS frigid, and the ammonia tasted like bile. Stills shot upward along the Puppet Free City, keeping close to the spine of the hotel, where no windows looked out. So many different kinds of light vomited into the murkiness, from romantic candle-light to hard-assed spotlights to puke-inducing decorations to bioluminescent fishing lures; all disorienting oases of useless light.

The scents were no fucking help either. The dissolved ammonia smelled stronger in open sea and made weird chemical scents against the solid surface of the Free City, but the currents shuffled the associations every hundred meters he swam higher, so he couldn't trust smell.

And judging distance and direction by sound would have been a pissing shot. He'd been raised in eight hundred atmospheres of pressure, and despite dragging around a lot of base-human instincts, he could locate things by sound under those conditions. But an extra two hundred atmospheres of pressure changed the speed of sound a shitload faster than his brain could adapt.

So Stills felt his way through the ocean with his electroplaques and magnetosomes. A propeller churned, transmitting in the EM maybe four hundred meters above him; certainly a Puppet sub. Maybe manned, maybe unmanned. Arjona hadn't planned on attracting deep-ocean attention. If the Puppets found Stills, they would swarm the inside of the hotel like ants.

The sub sonar pinged and Stills spun, blocking his ringing ears. *Ass-lickers! That fucking hurt.*

Stills shot away from the hotel, on an intercept course with the descending sub. At worst, he would appear as a big, fishy contact in sonar, and at best, wouldn't reflect much back at all.

He was ready when it pinged again. It was probably listening to the sonar reflection of the hotel. The sub wasn't close enough to pick up the window damage in the penthouse, but it was heading straight that way. This was a cock-up in the job. And even if he managed to destroy this sub, that might bring five more of the fuckers.

Stills darted up until he came fifty meters abeam of it. It was cheap cast-off mining tech, unmanned. No indication if it was remotely controlled or programmed. The main sonar and EM sensing equipment were nose-loaded, for prospecting in the ice and the ocean's subsurface. He got behind the nose so the ping wouldn't deafen him.

The sub navigated like him, using a combination of magnetic and sonic sensitivity. He drove his flukes hard, closing with the hull ahead of the sub's rudder and stern planes. The creaking of the machinery inside fucked with his hearing. He moved farther up the hull, holding onto a forward fin with his hands.

This would be tricky.

His electroplaques were not the fine-tuned, uptown organs the *Homo quantus* pranced around with. The *Homo quantus* genetic engineers had engineered far more sensitivity and control into the electroplaques for their precious snowflakes. As always, the tribe got the dog deal.

Stills flexed a charge from his electroplaques through

conducting carbon nanotubules, into magnetosomes in his arms, generating a magnetic field of a dozen microtesla, not enough to overwhelm Oler's field of twenty microtesla, but enough to make some nice fucking pretend for the remote sub.

Gonna make you my dog.

He released the fin and swam beside the sub, matching speed and direction. Then, he pointed his arms away from the direction of the hotel, at first, only ten degrees, but gradually widening the angle to fifteen. A *Homo quantus* could have shifted the magnetic field internally, with subcellular structures that rotated their magnetosomes. Stills' magnetosomes were hard-aligned with the grain of his skeletal muscles. He influenced the magnetic field by moving his arms, like the magnetic booms on the bows of worm hole-capable ships.

The sub shifted direction, slightly.

That's it, you pig. Sashay that fat ass where daddy tells you.

Stills increased the angle, leading it another three degrees away from the hotel. Then it resisted. Its sonar pinged more often, and shifted back and forth between what its magnetic and sonic sensors told it.

Okay, you dumb ass-licker, I was being all fucking Zen about this, but now you've pissed me off.

Stills swam to the bow, just behind the sonar sensing equipment. He placed his hands over it, and released seven hundred volts, most of the stored charge in his electroplaques.

He swore lines of multilingual curses in his mind, shaking his stinging hands. The sub was worse. Fuses clicked halfheartedly within it. Others were obviously burnt out, and the pinging stopped. Stills dropped back to the fin he'd been holding onto, and resumed making the magnetic field. The sub looked like it wanted to follow, but it turned entirely around and started heading upwards.

Fuck.

Probably a damage-repair response. Stills spun around, strengthening the magnetic field he was producing, until he completely masked the ambient field of Oler, substituting it with one that pointed in the opposite direction. Gradually, the sub turned about and headed downward, into deeper water away from the hotel. It wouldn't be long before it reached its crush depth.

CHAPTER FORTY-ONE

"Could you stop looking at me all the time?" William asked impatiently.

He wiped at his forehead. The sweating wasn't the Trenholm. The Puppets kept the room at twenty-six or twenty-seven centigrade with high humidity. Gates-15 lowered his eyes sheepishly, but still made little sniffing sounds at the air. If William turned away, he'd find the Puppet's eyes on him again. In the middle of the night, he'd woken to Gates-15 leaning over him, mouth-breathing.

The Puppet had accomplished part of his mission. He'd been able to upload Saint Matthew's virus into the network. Neither were sure how far the virus would go. Some parts of the Free City were wired out to the periphery and some were not. A general air of decay and complacency weighed on the Free City. Things fell apart and no one fixed them.

"How much longer?" William asked.

"It shouldn't be long. Simple lab tests, no? Are you worried?"

William leaned in closer. "I'm worried about my daughter," he whispered.

"I'm sorry," Gates-15 said, then looked away.

"You don't have any children?"

Gates-15 shook his head. "I'm not right. I'm not allowed."

William's shoulders sagged. "I'm sorry. There's nothing you can do, even living away from the Theocracy? Maybe make a family with someone else with the same condition?"

The Puppet shook his head. "I'm like Stills and Belisarius and Cassandra. We're all new human sub-species. It's hard for us to be fertile at all. They're still working out the biochemical and microbiome problems. I don't think any of us could be fertile without a lot of medical help."

William stepped back a bit. "I knew Stills would have trouble. I didn't know you and Bel would be the same."

"There are worse fates than being last in your line," Gates-15 said. The Puppet looked pensive. "You call him Bel. He's a bit like a son to you, isn't he?"

William snorted, looked around, and then spoke softly. "I helped him out a while ago and he outgrew me. He's a good kid, though. He's as honest as he should be, and he's got more of a soft spot for Puppets than he should."

Gates-15 stopped watching him so intently. The momentary absence of that pressure was a relief.

"How did you meet?" Gates-15 asked.

"About eleven or twelve years ago, I was coming off a good con," William whispered, relieved to not be talking about Puppets and their feelings again. "I was flush for a few months and at the peak of my career. I could read people well. I found this seventeen-year-old in a café who didn't fit anything I knew. He was out of place and I couldn't even make close guesses about him. But I could see he was in trouble. Maybe I had a moment of pity. Maybe I thought I could learn something from him. I took him in."

"You taught him," Gates-15 smiled. "Was he a natural?"

"A natural?" William laughed. "He was happier analyzing

chaotic systems and electron energy levels than being around people. His only friend was a crazy AI."

"Saint Matthew."

"Yeah."

"You trust him for all of this?"

"I wouldn't trust any other con man more."

"Faint praise?"

"The opposite. If this can be done, he can do it. He has to. My daughter needs basic medicines like any child. She has oxygen bills, water bills, power bills. My ex-wife can't do it. I've got to make this right. Kate deserves better than what I had. But I can't do that from in here. We have to get to Port Stubbs."

Gates-15 shrugged, and William felt like a jackass. Speaking with the Puppets confused him. On the surface they could be reasonable. Sometimes. But no one could ever forget they had it worse. Despite growing up in a work house, going to jail, living from con to con his whole life, William was at least human. He wasn't born carrying the inherited crimes and tragedies of the Puppets as well as their biological debt bondage. He understood a bit of Bel's fascination with them.

Someone knocked at the door. William eyed it uncertainly and then backed up to the cot and sat down, knees high. He waved his hand. Gates-15 hopped to the door and pulled it open.

Bishop Grassie-6 entered, followed by Doctor Teller-5. The bishop kept his composure. Doctor Teller-5 might have tried, but William couldn't tell over the dreamy elation that came over her as she inhaled deeply. The bishop looked at William with intense politeness as he put a hand on the doctor's forearm.

"Sit!" he hissed low. She sat, right there on the floor. Even Gates-15 slowly sat, cross-legged, staring at William like Teller-5 did.

"I'm delighted to see you, Mister Kaltwasser," Grassie-6 said.

"Thank you, Your Grace."

Grassie-6 stepped forward tentatively.

"You're clear of the quarantine now," he said.

"So we can go to Port Stubbs?"

Doctor Teller-5, eyes half-lidded, began crawling forward. The bishop watched her, then continued speaking.

"Your grandparents and great-grandparents, if they visited Port Stubbs today, would not recognize it," the bishop said. "The places where the Numen once lived have become shrines or pilgrimage sites or movie sets. But everything else has grown around them."

William's attention drifted, attracted magnetically by the miniature woman crawling around him.

"I don't have long to live, Your Grace," William said, adding an edge to his voice. "I came to die someplace meaningful."

The bishop remained calm, but both Doctor Teller-5 and Gates-15 caught their breaths slightly as William had put more authority into his voice. Teller-5 slinked behind him over his cot, and rose. She stood with lips parted, looking down on him. She began rubbing his shoulders, massaging. He tried pulling away, but she was surprisingly strong. Her fingers worked at the fear that had crept into his muscles.

"That is the most tragic thing, Mister Kaltwasser," Grassie-6 said. "You are dying. You are the first genuine Numen who has been brought to us in a decade—an unspoiled, feral religious figure—and yet, you are dying."

Grassie-6 stepped slowly forward, as if approaching a dog who might bolt. Teller-5's hands rubbed down William's shoulders and to his biceps, working at tight knots, but he became uncomfortably aware of her breasts pressing against his back.

"We spent quite a bit of money contacting Plutocracy doctors to find out that there is no treatment."

Teller-5's hands came back to his shoulders and she no longer pressed her body against him. Just her hands—strong and soothing.

William cleared his throat. "I could have told you that."

The doctor's thumbs worked at the tiny tight muscles in his neck, sending shivers down his spine. Her hands stroked the sides of his neck with flat palms, an intimate gesture, affectionate, and he felt himself responding. He focused on Grassie-6.

"Your T-cell counts are almost zero," the bishop said. "Your B-cells and antibodies are vanishing too. You're severely immunocompromised and the anti-virals and antibiotics you came with won't last long. The Free City has several hospitals working at building a synthetic immune system to replace the one you don't have. Port Stubbs' single hospital isn't as equipped."

"Hospitals aren't going to help me," William said. "There's nothing to be done about Trenholm. I'm just a man on a pilgrimage of his own, seeking peace before the end."

The bishop betrayed a bit of surprise. Bel had told him that Puppet awe could be triggered by Numen resolve, a quality sapped from the modern Numen by captivity.

"You're so wonderful, Mister Kaltwasser," Grassie-6 said.

"Pardon?"

"Some of the Numen we have now are angry and resentful," the bishop said. "Most are pleading, begging. But all are intensely concerned with the Puppets. As their protectors and worshippers, we are their central concern, the axis around which their world revolves. Before the Fall, the Numen had a broader range of concerns, and relationships with the Puppets, including disinterest. We've lost that."

"I'm sorry," William said. "I didn't mean to convey anything of the sort."

"You misunderstand me, Mister Kaltwasser. It's refreshing, like a visit from a lost past. Spoiled as we are now with the unobstructed presence of the protected Numen, it is very easy for us to forget our religious and moral place. The fact that we're only a side-note to your concerns is theologically grounding."

The bishop took a hesitant step forward, close enough to touch. Gates-15 and the doctor held their breaths. Teller-5's hands had stopped moving.

"We Puppets live in a world of miracles, Mister Kaltwasser, a world where the divine walk among us, revealing meaning through the code of their actions, creating a theology we must interpret. I don't know why you've been sent to us, or what message we will learn from you, but your pilgrimage is deeply meaningful to you, and that may make your message of incalculable value to us."

"I don't see myself in those terms," William said.

"That is one of the central paradoxes of the Numen." The bishop smiled. "The Numen reject their own divinity, while quite obviously being divine. The cosmos has conspired to make them incapable of seeing certain truths. That doesn't make you less divine, but more."

CHAPTER FORTY-TWO

BELISARIUS HAD BEEN poring over the holographic displays in the cockpit of the *Boyacá* for over an hour, having replaced the navigational and telescopic displays with financial tracking algorithms and information from the illicit economy of the Puppet Free City. Cassandra spotted many patterns and correlations, but without controls, she didn't know how many false positives she might be getting.

"What are you going to do?" Cassandra asked.

"The Congregate's spies in the Free City are looking for plots and secret movements," Belisarius said. "I'm going to give them one."

"They're good enough to separate false signals from real ones," Iekanjika said.

"This will be real enough. There is a particular official in the consulate of the First Bank of the Anglo-Spanish Plutocracy. I sold him a lot of illegal Puppet art. I'm going to deposit a large sum of money in his account, from an account of the Puppet Episcopal Conclave."

"You're framing him?" Saint Matthew said.

"I'm not framing an innocent man. I've seen his tastes in Puppet art and I know why he angled for a diplomatic posting in the Free City."

"But this won't fool the Congregate," Iekanjika said.

"They'll be smelling for a plot by the Anglo-Spanish Banks. They won't be able to check on this, and the confusion among the Puppet bishops and the Bank's consulate will obscure what we're doing."

"You have access to their bank accounts?" Cassandra asked with an edge of judgement in her tone.

Belisarius shrugged. "With an embargo on, even when people were buying legal art, they rarely paid me from reputable accounts. It was a normal cost of business for me to make sure I knew where my money was coming from and going."

"It feels dirty," Cassandra said with finality.

She couldn't deal with Bel's... shadiness right now. She retreated to the small kitchen down from the cockpit. Her mind felt like it was suffocating. The absence of mathematics, of patterns, of testable models had her almost twitchy. She strapped herself to one of the seats and toyed with the idea of going into savant and doing some calculations. Belisarius floated in and closed the door. He strapped himself to a seat across from her, but didn't meet her eyes.

"I didn't expect you would make me ashamed of myself," he said after a time.

She didn't know where to put her hands. Or where to look. She was angry, but she didn't know how to be angry out here, with Bel. Everything was upside down. "I don't know how you can swim in all this deception," she whispered finally. She chose not to look at him. She shook her head. "I don't know how you can live among them."

"What lies?"

"All of them, even in front of me. You told the Puppets we have brain damage. You didn't need to. That didn't do anything. Or had I done something so wrong that you needed to tell someone I had a brain injury to get me out of it?"

"I tell a lot of lies, Cassie. Big ones. Small ones. It's part of living in the wide world. And it's a part of being a con man."

"You don't do anything for no reason, Bel," she said. "I don't know why you lied to the Puppet, but..." Then she stopped. She backtracked through her memories of the exact wording of the conversation. She met his eyes. "You did have a reason. You were testing me."

Bel smiled broadly. "You passed."

She wanted to strangle him. "What?"

"Of course I was!" he whispered back. "Why didn't you already go to someone else with this? Saint Matthew? Or Iekanjika?"

"Because I didn't know why you've been saying all these things!" she said, struggling to keep her voice down. "I don't know what lies are for fun and what lies will get you killed if you're found out."

"That's exactly right."

"Why didn't you trust me, Bel?"

"I haven't lied to you."

"I don't know that. Half of your lies are so tiny they make no difference. Why even bother?"

"I am testing people, Cassie. This is really dangerous, and I have to know where everyone's head is. And for the record, half the lies I tell are the truth."

"Who else are you lying to, Bel? Who else don't you trust?" she asked.

"Trust is a funny word. Do I trust people not to betray me? Not exactly. Do I trust that I've correctly sized up everyone on the team? I think so."

"William?" she asked, sensing that she might be close to a weak spot in Bel.

He looked away. Then nodded without looking back at her.

"You've sized him up?"

Bel met her eyes defiantly. "A long time ago. We stopped working together because I walked away."

"He seems to be the nicest person here. The most gentle."

"He can get angry, like if you break off a partnership because he wasn't able to pull off his part of a con."

"That happened? And you put him on this team?"

"He's probably the best con artist I've ever met, but I was a different person ten years ago and so was he. He was drifting. Uncertain. And his head wasn't in the game. His mistakes could have cost us both everything."

"And now you trust him with all this weight?" she asked. The thought of entering the Puppet Free City as a Numen still wasn't something she wanted to think about, if even a fraction of the stories were true.

"Ten years ago, he didn't have a daughter. And ten years ago he wasn't dying. And ten years ago he thought he was better than he was."

"And you sent him to his death," she said in a low voice.

"He's walked into a death sentence, knowing what it will mean to his daughter. She's the center of everything that's important to him, and that's why he'll make this work."

Bel's face had a mixture of signals she found hard to read. Resolve. Grief. Guilt.

"Did you lie to William?" she asked.

"Only when I had to."

She threw up her hands and then sank her forehead into them.

"All this manipulation makes me sick, Bel! Your life is so empty. Everyone's life outside the Garret is so empty," she said. "Nothing is true out here, Bel. Nothing has enduring value. They're struggling for who's in charge and who has the most money when questions of how the cosmos works are all around them, unanswered. It's been only a little while and I'm itching inside. How did you survive twelve years without going crazy?"

"You're right, Cassie. My brain didn't stop needing. I didn't know if I could survive away from the Garret. The wide world is intellectually cold. A void. So I traded the study of one complex system for another. I replaced scientific and mathematical stimulation with the intellectual challenge of human behavior and confidence schemes."

"That keeps you going?" she asked doubtfully.

"Behavioral questions are astonishingly multivariate."

"But they're not real! They don't matter! The answers change from person to person. Nothing is generalizable or graphable."

"And that's why I can go years without being drawn to the fugue," he whispered with an almost pleading tone in his voice.

She felt pity softening her unexpectedly. The thought that he would leave sciences to study people drove home more than anything how scared he must be of the fugue. She thought guiltily of what Iekanjika had said weeks ago in the commissary, that Bel had almost died in the fugue. Cassandra had thought that Bel had fooled the major.

"We're cursed, Cassie, just like the mongrels and just like the Puppets."

"We're nothing like them."

"Our geneticists built us a new way to starve, Cassie. The mongrels die if they leave the pressure of their oceans. The Puppets die if they're too far away from the Numen. You know what we need, Cassie."

The sinking, aching feeling of not enough intellectual stimulation was suffocating. Not enough air.

"It makes us more, Bel. We learn. We grow."

"No, Cassie. They gave us another way to be unhappy. That's not fair. Life is heavy enough. No one asked us if we wanted to carry this too."

"I miss home," she said.

"Home is where the mind is. And soon, you'll be seeing so much, your brain will be full."

She looked away. Sometimes Bel's eyes had an intensity like Iekanjika's. He had nerve, nerve enough to leave the Garret, nerve to live among strangers. She couldn't do it. When this was over, she couldn't go home fast enough. And yet, she'd survived so far. Maybe she was more durable than she'd thought.

"Do you think you could ever come home, Bel?" she asked.

"I don't know."

"Is it better out here?" she asked, gesturing at the old plastic and metal of the tiny kitchen.

"I didn't leave because I would be more comfortable in the wide world. I'm not. There's too much stimulus. Too little beauty. And people don't care about the things I care about. Why? Do you want me back?" He looked sheepish, uncertain, but there was a daring hopefulness in his eyes.

"You didn't break my heart when you left, Bel. You almost did, though."

"Are you over it?"

"Long scarred over," she said.

"I broke my own heart in leaving."

"Are you over it?"

"Long scarred over."

"I don't think I can ever understand why you left, Bel. Not inside."

"Is accepting enough?" he asked.

"I need trust for that."

Bel nodded, but there was something crestfallen and vulnerable in him.

"I'm not trying to make you ashamed of yourself, Bel."

"I know."

He smiled. And some of the weight on her chest lessened, until she realized that his smile was a lie, to make her feel better, and that only a month ago, she wouldn't have known the difference between a smile and its imitation.

CHAPTER FORTY-THREE

PRESSURE ALARMS SOUNDED in the penthouse. Lights blinked. Internal comms. She sighed. She went to the wall, and tabbed the audio.

"Why am I being disturbed?" she demanded, making an effort to uptown her *français* 8.1.

"Apologies, ma'am," came the reply. "The system is showing alarms. We wanted to make sure you're safe."

"I'm perfectly safe. There's nothing dangerous down here, except my temper. Do you know how much I'm paying to not be disturbed?"

"We completely understand, ma'am, but the Grand Creston Constabulary has sent down a team to make sure that everything is okay."

"You're sending police down here?"

"They're coming down to ensure your safety. They're accompanied by a repair crew to take any actions to assure your safety and that of the other guests."

"Listen, Puppet," she said. "I've got some very important Congregate officials down here. We picked this spot for a sensitive diplomatic meeting with a nation I can't mention. If any of your guys see anything down here, you'll be putting the Theocracy into an international incident the likes of which you will deeply, deeply regret."

The pause stretched into minutes. Marie didn't press her luck. She checked the elevator status. One deep elevator was descending.

Bel was not going to be happy.

She huffed.

Who cared what Bel thought?

She drummed her fingers on her thigh.

But Bel wouldn't not be happy if she solved this quietly, before he ever found out. He had other things on his mind. This could be a little secret between her and Stills, an opportunity to bond with fish-face, like buddies. Or maybe she'd just handle this herself. Stills didn't need to know either. She didn't want to be buddies that much.

The elevator descended fast. The little constables were going to be littler if they didn't mind their descent. Going from one atmosphere to four in a hurry could be painful. They might need first aid. Marie yanked open the lid on the box of medical supplies. She didn't remember much first aid, but how complicated could it be?

CHAPTER FORTY-FOUR

SHIT. MIERDA. SCHIESSE. Zarba. Merde.

Stills swam hard through the crushing ocean, dragging behind him close to three tons of explosives divided into four bales along a rope. They were heavy as fuck and the ocean as anoxic as any he'd swum in. His big gills churned, but his amped up hemoglobins were fucking the dog instead of scraping him up shit to breathe. He could slow down, but then he'd miss his deadline.

And the fuckers would get him.

Three drone subs, built for deep diving and fast moving, followed two kilometers back, pinging like they wanted a foursome and weren't in the mood to buy him dinner first. The only thing going for him was that he and the bales of explosives reflected sonar poorly. Squishy targets made shitty images.

The subs would be pissing off the hotel. As thick as they were, hotel windows were as tight as tympanic membranes, making every sonar ping boom in every luxury hotel room two kilometers up and down the Grand Creston. But the drones were pinging often enough that blurry sonar shadows would paint enough of a picture. A loud picture.

Stills swam upward, calming his own thinking, and his

gulping, starved breathing, and concentrated on Oler's magnetic field, navigating to the first target spot. He hadn't picked the spots. That wasn't his job. He wasn't that kind of muscle for the prancy quantum ass-licker. The braintrust knew what he wanted targetted. Stills' special contribution was getting the right package to precisely the right spot, under a thousand atmospheres of anoxic ocean, getting past whatever defenses the Puppets' messed up little minds had put down here.

The three drones angled upward, pinging as they went. Their propellers moaned below him, closing. They were faster because he was carrying all this shit. He poured it on, flexing his body harder, adding a bit of speed as he climbed, but grinding his reserves down. A wall of ice loomed dark ahead of him, shining back sound echoes. He had rounded one lobe of Blackmore Bay and a kilometer of ice separated him from some of the Puppet micro-states.

Stills raced along the ice face, making small, low sounds, listening for changes in the reflections, looking for a good anchor-point for the explosives, while also paying close attention to his electrical sense and Oler's magnetic field, for the placement of the marker.

The fucking drones were gaining on him.

Stills stopped and drew out an industrial hand-laser. Yellow flared in the particulate silt as he melted a tube several centimeters deep into the ice. He put the laser back into his pouch and withdrew one of the markers Belisarius had given him. It was some sort of long-distance receiver, and would be able to retransmit a local signal to the detonator. It fit into the hollow he'd made.

He pulled a crinkly plastic bag of anhydrous crystals from the pouch. The pressure had crushed the plastic against the crystals as if it had been vacuum-sealed. He jammed this into the hole and then pierced it with the sharp end of a screw-driver. Water mixed with the hyper-dried crystals in the bag, starting a quick chemical reaction, endothermic enough to plug the little channel with newly frozen ice. One marker planted.

And the Puppet subs pinged, closer.

He darted away, sideways and up a few hundred meters, until he found what he needed, a big rounded crevasse eroded by churning, shifting currents. A cave big enough for him. He unhooked the first bale of explosives and shoved it into the hole, then hurried to pack the little sacks of crystals around some of the edges before piercing them. The ice forming wouldn't hold the bale there forever, but it would prevent the bale from floating out for a few days, which was all they needed. Lastly, he pulled out a two-pronged detonator and stabbed it into the cold-hardened putty.

The pinging neared. Three more bales to go.

He darted off, carrying the stupid bales of experimental explosives, swimming hard, gills gulping. The dumb drones had probably marked this position by now. He had to give them a reason not to come here. He pulled out a detonator and a screw-driver from his pouch, holding them wide in his hands. The next ping reflected hard echoes back at the drones. The items were small, but more echo-reflective than ice, and hard enough for sonar to pick up course and speed. Stills put them back in his pouch as he changed course, and the pings changed direction and intensity.

Fuckers were mad now.

CHAPTER FORTY-FIVE

Cassandra, Belisarius, Major Iekanjika and Saint Matthew approached the Orbital Traffic Control zone of the Free City in the *Boyacá*.

"You can't know what the Puppets are thinking from that pattern," Saint Matthew was saying.

"Sure I can," Bel said.

Cassandra leaned closer to look at the old-style monitor. She saw lots of patterns. The defensive fortifications were outlined in red. General and secure communications were outlined in green. Habitat systems were wrapped in blue. Speckling the habitat and communications systems were pixel clusters in bright yellow, indicating areas where, in the last forty-eight hours, the interference noise of processing had decreased notably.

"Saint Matthew's computer virus is a little like any virus we might use for genetic engineering," Bel said to Iekanjika. "Among its other effects, it increases the efficiency of systems it has infected. That's like a reporter gene in a virus, so we can know where it has penetrated."

"It has penetrated habitat and communications, but not fortifications," the major said.

"Yes, and its infection of habitat and comms is very selective.

The distribution suggests to me that it has infected support systems."

"That's not random," Cassandra said.

"No."

Cassandra had a brief urge to recalculate the p-value to verify the non-randomness, but Iekanjika wouldn't care and Bel would already have calculated it.

"The infection pattern doesn't follow the systems architecture, but this pattern could have been made by selectively shielding critical systems prior to infection," Bel said.

"So the Puppets know something is up," Cassandra said.

"Definitely."

"Then the mission is off?" Saint Matthew said. "Turn the ship around."

"On the contrary. The Puppets know about your virus, but they infected their systems anyway."

"Why?" the AI asked.

"They're setting a trap."

"This isn't good."

"The Puppets think they're holding a winning hand. They're committing to a big bet. We'll know how big when we see how they deploy their defensive forces."

The AI didn't look convinced, but didn't argue.

Bel and Iekanjika went into the holds to check the cargo one last time. Cassandra strapped herself into the pilot seat. She didn't often get to see the stars through a single layer of glass. The slowly bobbing holographic head of Saint Matthew watched the stars silently too as she found geometric patterns in the starscape. After a time, she spoke.

"Do you know Belisarius well?"

"Sometimes I think so," he said, turning his bearded, brush-stroked face towards her. "Most of the time not."

"I don't think I know who he is."

"No one does."

"Marie does. William does. I thought you must."

"What gave you that idea?"

"He told me he rescued you after leaving the Garret. You spent time with him."

"He was just a boy then," the AI said, "sixteen years old."

"But you must trust him now."

"Not exactly."

"Then why are you here?" Did anyone trust Bel?

"I have faith that he's leading me to something important. That's different than trust."

"And you think Bel will get us there?"

"The world has its own mysteries. We only begin to understand what they are after they've already passed."

"That's a very quantum thing to say. Can't you tell me anything about Bel?"

"I'm not sure I should."

"What do you mean?"

"I'm responsible for his soul, and I don't know that you're good for him."

"What?" She couldn't believe what she was hearing. "He doesn't even have a soul."

"You both do."

"And I thought I was speaking to a rational AI."

She expected the AI to argue back, but he watched her with a thoughtful expression painted more than a thousand years ago. The stars stared back at her too, unwinking, infested with the orbital traffic and satellites around Oler. Out there, everything was mathematical precision and clean lines. Not like inside.

"Why wouldn't I be good for him?" she asked.

"He didn't walk away from the Garret. He ran. For his life.

I'm not sure going back would help him."

"Of course going back would help him!" she said. "The doctors there are made to care for the *Homo quantus,* to help them in and out of the fugue safely."

"Going back is good for him or good for you?"

"For both of us."

"You say Mister Arjona has no soul," Saint Matthew said, "but I can point at something essential in him and call it a soul, even if you call it something else. What I'm pointing at is a collection of fragments that have not been together since he was a boy. He needs to be healed. There are many things I don't know about Mister Arjona, but I know that he's trying to be whole."

CHAPTER FORTY-SIX

STILLS HAD SWUM his ass off for an hour. He was probably faster than the drones, but after lugging the explosives, he couldn't sprint anymore. He'd fixed three of the bales of explosives to the ice, each one close to the little buttons Arjona was so worried about. He gulped at water more anoxic than the ocean he'd grown up in on Indi's Tear. He'd pass out if this kept up.

So he was playing smart. Their pings had gradually told him the kind of kit that was hunting him. They sounded like programmed defensive tech in mid-sized torpedo casings. He'd built a profile of their sense-and-search algorithms based on their pings and positioning, slowly improving his diversions and using cover better.

Above him, ice fragments, some the size of his fingers, some the size of factories, tinkled against the icy ceiling of the ocean, an irritating atonal symphony of bells, perfect for shitting on his ability to picture the world using echolocation, but also perfect for doing the same for his pursuers. The wash of the current never ended, so the icy gravel rolled tirelessly against the ceiling, the reverse of a river, eddies collecting all the detritus in the lobes of Blackmore Bay. The other parts of the Bay, where he'd placed the first three bales of explosives, had been largely clear, heated just enough to shrink the collecting ice.

But this last lobe, what the Puppets called Blackmore's Nose, was newly constipated with big blocks of ice. The blockage hadn't been on last month's surveys. An iceberg the size of a small mountain had jammed into the bay. The gaps between it and the walls of this lobe of Blackmore Bay had jammed with shit. No, not shit. Icy boogers had solidified into a whole lot of crustiness. The explosives and Arjona's transmitters had to be placed about two kilometers higher than this giant snot plug.

The mother-fucking pings loudened, still closing.

Shut your damn yam-holes. I'm trying to think.

Blackmore Bay breathed, like water wheezing over gills gummed up with mucus or a fungal infection. Kind of erratic and panicky. The flexing of the icy crust of Oler was imperceptible most of the time; a sub-sonic creaking of gravitational squeezing that heated the rocky core of Oler more than the crust itself. But here, between giant-sized boogers jammed into a god's nostril, the water rushed through the gaps, moaning.

Louder pinging. Closer.

Stills swam into the cavernous gap, a few hundred meters below the slushy field under the main iceberg itself. In several places, the ceiling was clear of slush, and although he couldn't see it, he could feel the why in the thrumming. Water surging through narrow gaps had vacuumed up the slush.

Strong currents probably meant channels wide enough for him to fit through. But currents could also split, blowing through branching tunnels in great three-dimensional sieves, and then he would be fucked. The real problem was Venturi. The mongrels didn't like constricted spaces because when water flowed fast, pressure dropped. When it flowed fast enough, the pressure could drop enough to make a mongrel go splat. The Venturi effect.

Pings just below.

Fuckers.

He flexed his flukes, edging closer to the rim of what looked like the biggest of the channels.

Pings closing.

Mother fuckers.

This wasn't going to be pretty.

Fuck it.

It wouldn't be settled here.

He surged forward, dragging the last bale with him, into the breathing currents of Blackmore's crusty nostril.

Fuck with me and I sting you, Blackmore.

The current sucked him upward, into a wide, fast-moving channel, carrying along his last bale of experimental explosives. Booming sounds cracked at his skull, trailed by echoing bangs and whines, all shit-useless for mapping the blur-fast world. He electrified his magnetosomes, making a compass of himself. The current threw him onward as Oler's magnetic field told him where the Free City was, but sweet fuck all else.

Suddenly, he smashed into a rounded outcrop of ice. He careened into a smooth wall and the current pushed him, carried him, faster and faster. His shoulder stung, but he could still swim. If he'd been built of less blubber, the outcrop would have broken bones. And if it had been sharp, he'd have been a filet.

Then, a hollow emptiness cupped him, sucking the world away as his speed tripled.

Breath left him.

Pressure drop.

Merde. Merde. Merde.

Vision tunneled. Spots. Going to pass out. Bones ached. Daggers shafted joints.

This was the way mongrels died, by mistake and on purpose. Decompression. The bends.

Blinding aching. Gas bubbled out of his blood, out of his muscle, out of his nerves.

Suffocating. He was suffocating in the hell of the ocean. He hated the ocean.

He'd wanted to die among the stars. Instead, black stars spattered his vision here.

You were born dead under the tomb of an ocean. It's never going to get any better.

He flexed his flukes hard, shooting agony into his joints. He ran with the current.

He gulped water, but every mouthful washing over gills sucked oxygen from him.

The tunnel branched. Narrower tubes.

He shot faster. Moments from blacking out.

His harness yanked him painfully to a stop.

The current slowed around him. Pressure increased. Not enough. It hurt like maybe five hundred atmospheres. Pain still stabbed at everything. He sucked at the bitter, dilute ammonia ocean like a gasping fish, his gills stealing the thin oxygen.

He unfastened his harness and sank limply downward to shine a pale light on the explosives. Shiny, half-invisible ice lay slick around him. The doughy explosive had wedged itself into the narrow channel, blocking the current perfectly.

He must be pretty near the top of the iceberg that had nostril-boned Blackmore.

Not that the explosives were going anywhere.

He turned off the light and felt at the magnetic field of Oler. He wasn't that far from where he needed to be. The placement of the explosive might not do much damage here, but the other three would, and this one would at least distract the Puppets.

Stills pulled a detonator from his pouch and stabbed its two prongs into the cold putty. *Vaya con dios.*

He didn't know how close he was to where Arjona wanted his little button. He leapt from the shelter. His joints ached like someone had injected steel flakes into them.

The current ran slower here, increasing pressure and widening through many gaps. The magnetic field of the Free City strengthened until he emerged into a wide dark space, the inner portion of this lobe of Blackmore Bay. The silt and water attenuated light, so no light of the Free City reached here, but its electrical activity pressed against his magnetosomes.

Sharp pains froze him. Internal injuries. No doubt about it.

Shooting the channels might have exposed him to moments as low as three hundred atmospheres. Dissolved gasses bubbling out of his blood did a lot of damage, no matter how tough he was. Verses of the Way of the Mongrel like *you're fucked* sometimes made it easy to lie down and die when it was time, but he'd shit himself if anyone thought he couldn't get this done.

Wipe their noses in it.

He flexed, shooting forward, pain screaming in his joints.

Piss on the leg of everyone you can.

He expanded his magnetic field, making it more sensitive as he swam along the wall of ice that, farther up, formed one of the bay-facing walls of the Free City.

Everything ached.

But it wouldn't be long. He was close.

Arjona princey-pants wanted each one of these buttons in exactly the right spot. Stills had no idea what sort of comms signal the quantum man had for these detonators. Signals other than sound and electricity travelled like shit underwater, and even those two weakened so quickly that they might as well be using cans on a string.

When he was less cranky, or less injured, he had more patience for moronic orders. Sometimes the world and jobs made more sense when he didn't understand everything. The world made a lot of sense when it was clear that the people giving the orders couldn't find their asses any better than the mongrels could. Arjona's certainty was a bit much to take, especially when he also didn't tell everybody everything they needed to know.

Stills found the spot. Knife pain ran through his marrows. He touched the ice, hand trembling. His little laser melted a cock-sized hole into the ice, through thin layers of quiescent, starving sulfur and ammonia-living bacteria. Warm water flowed out of his cutting, briefly shielding his fingers from the relentless chill of the ocean. His fingers fumbled with the flap of his pouch. One last stupid button to bury in the ice forever.

Stills didn't know why prancy-pants wanted the buttons here, or how much damage the explosives could do, or why Arjona wanted them detonated. Arjona didn't trust everyone on the crew. Stills hoped Arjona was gonna make shit sure that any mole ended up as the fuckee and not the fucker.

Stills slipped the button into the tiny channel, packed it with anhydrous salts and stabbed the packaging. Slush formed in the channel, hardening to ice. Now to get the back to Phocas before any of her explosives turned out to be less stable than she thought.

CHAPTER FORTY-SEVEN

THE ELEVATOR DINGED, and the big doors slowly opened, revealing six Puppets, four in blue uniforms with yellow piping and tricorn hats bearing the coat-of-arms of the Grand Creston Hotel. The other two wore red maintenance coveralls. None topped eighty-five centimeters tall, and they were old Caucasian pale, like Marie. They squinted out of the lit elevator into the dark of the penthouse.

"Stay where you are," Marie commanded in *français* 8.1 from the darkness. A surgical mask muffled her voice. In one hand, she squished thirty-five grams of explosive putty. In the other, she held a detonator control. "I've hidden the Congregate officials and the visiting diplomatic officials, but you still can't come in."

One of the constables, a female Puppet, stepped to the edge of the elevator door uncertainly. She had her hand on a nightstick. In the other, she had a sensor. Probably a barometer. And Marie bet that the constable was packing more than a nightstick.

Four to one.

"We do not wish to disturb you, ma'am," the Puppet said. "We're only here verify that there are no structural problems in your suites."

303

"The problem is that the dignitaries in these suites have not been vaccinated against local pathogens," Marie said. "If antibodies for Olerian viral and bacterial strains were ever found in any of these officials, the political implications would be severe, for them and for the Grand Creston."

"Ma'am, please," the Puppet said. "Seismometer readings showed a breach somewhere beneath kilometer seventeen. We're coming in."

"If you're not willing to listen to reason, then the management of the Grand Creston is certainly going to be hearing from the *Gouverneur* at Saguenay Station, and probably from the head of a foreign government. In the meantime, I can't let you risk their health. I have to disinfect you."

Marie pressed the detonator and four nozzles newly affixed to the frame of the elevator doors sprayed a heavy mist onto the six Puppets. They coughed and wiped at their eyes and faces. The Puppet sergeant reached for a small radio on her belt.

"Don't touch that, constable," Marie said. "I've just sprayed you with an aerosolized explosive. This detonator," she said, "will put a static charge through the room when I press this button. The explosive now soaking your clothes will then go off."

The Puppets stared at her, horrified. Two started stripping off their Grand Creston Constabulary tunics.

"Stop moving now," Marie said, stepping farther into the light and holding the detonator high, thumb quite obviously on the button. "Don't believe me?" She threw the small piece of putty at the wall separating the room from one of the bedrooms. The bang and flash filled the room, leaving a sixty centimeter hole in the wall.

She stepped closer.

"You," she said, pointing at the lead constable, "will get on your radio and tell your bosses that you've examined the suites, that everything is fine, and that you're going to go up to the next levels of suites. You follow?"

The Puppet nodded, wide-eyed. She pulled free her radio with shaking hands. Marie stilled her with a finger. "Deep breaths," Marie said. "Sound calm, or my finger won't be."

The Puppet's eyes widened and the others shrank from Marie. The Puppet brought the radio up and gave the message, exactly as Marie had said. Then, she slowly let her hand come down.

"Good," Marie said. "Now leave your weapons and radios on the floor of the elevator and then come inside. Have a seat on the couch. You all look terrible. You're not going to get hurt, but I can't let you leave until the ambassadors have left."

Nightsticks, small pistols, radios and tool boxes settled on the floor of the elevator before, one by one, the Puppets entered the suite fearfully, with drooping eyes.

"Sit down before you fall down," Marie said. "You really aren't used to stress, are you?"

They shook their heads sheepishly. Their heads drooped.

"Go to sleep if you want. It's better if your eyes are closed when they go by," Marie said.

They didn't need more prompting. Two of the constables were already slumped on the couch. Two closed their eyes and were gone too. Only the lead constable and one other fought it, but not long. They fell onto the floor. The surgical anaesthetic in the gas would last quite a while.

Yup, Bel didn't need to know about this.

CHAPTER FORTY-EIGHT

ON THE SURFACE of Oler, Del Casal lifted off in the yacht. He did not set a course for the asteroid belt as they had planned, or even open the seals on his vacuum suit. He made a small hop to one of the smaller micro-states of the Federation of Puppet Theocracies and touched down at a cargo port dotted with embargo-breaking freighters.

A tiny trace of fear tickled at Del Casal's spine, but he stepped onto the surface. Under bright starlight, he walked the four hundred meters between automated loaders, to a big freighter with an open loading hatch. At the back of the freighter's yawning bay, another space-suited figure met him. The figure scanned him with practiced precision for weapons and communications devices, and then motioned him through the airlock.

His hands shook as if he had not eaten in days. He schooled his features and his body. On the other side of the airlock, a woman with pale skin and artful acid scars on her face met him. She wore no uniform, but was quite obviously a member of one of the Congregate's intelligence services.

"*Par içi, s'il vous plaît,*" she said.

Del Casal removed the faceplate and cowl of his vacuum suit

as she led him into an office with a holographic projection desk and a few chairs. The room felt heavy, centering as it did on a hulking figure beside the desk.

Del Casal tamped down his momentary hesitation in the face of the Scarecrow. Flexible steel cloth formed its lumpy shirt. Shapeless pants were tied at waist and ankle. Carbon fibre gloves and shoes emerged from thickets of raw nanotubule wiring. Its head was a sack of carbon cloth with painted features, tied at the neck. Small whirring sounds, focusing camera lenses, microphones, speakers, or weapons, moved the lumpy suit, like mice in a bag, inviting an observer to worry about what lay beneath in a wholly illogical and visceral way. Del Casal was not given to illogic, nor was he particularly sensitive to his viscera. He had induced fear himself in his time.

"You took your time getting here," the Scarecrow said in last century's low-house French. The voice was deliberately mechanical, but contained a petulance that suggested entirely dangerous human weaknesses.

"Their plan is in action now, and they are careful," Del Casal said in French. "This was my first chance to move unobserved."

"So share your information," the Scarecrow said.

"Price first, information second," Del Casal said.

"I wouldn't be in the business I'm in if I didn't pay well for good information, Señor Del Casal, and I wouldn't have the budget I have if I spent it sight unseen."

The machine-like face was inscrutable, but was probably telling the truth. With unaccustomed halting that embarrassed him, Del Casal told the Scarecrow of Arjona's mad plan, of the crew, of their Union employers and of his own assessment of it. The machine before him had no human reactions, nothing to read. The Venusian woman beside Del Casal was as inscrutable as a machine herself, except when she prodded for details with surgically clipped questions. The Scarecrow only stared with glass eyes. Del Casal had begun to suspect that the entire interview was to be conducted by the Scarecrow's subordinate, so when the machine spoke, it startled him.

"Say more of this Arjona and his abilities and this damaged AI," the Scarecrow said.

Del Casal did not appreciate his own reactions, nor how they seemed to be forced out of him by the cheap symbolism and contrivance in the Scarecrow design. They were equals. He and this woman. And he and this machine. He could control his reactions. He spoke as he would to an equal.

"Belisarius Arjona is a fallen *Homo quantus*," he said, "apparently not able to do much with his birthright, so he has recruited another *Homo quantus* to assist him in his calculations. I do not know much of the AI. It seems only capable of interfacing with us in the persona of some religious figure. This may be an act, but it is quite capable."

The Scarecrow continued its low clicking and whirring. Del Casal guessed its movements were actually silent piezo-electric contractions of layers of carbon nanotubules. The small sounds would be designed for an audience, something to psychologically emphasize the inhumanity of the Scarecrow. Games and flash.

"Do you know where this Major Iekanjika comes from?" the Scarecrow asked.

"She says she is attached to the Sixth Expeditionary Force."

"There is no such force."

"There was, forty years ago."

"Did you see evidence of this supposed advanced drive system?"

"No. But Arjona thinks that with their new weapons and the right conditions in the Theocracy, the Expeditionary Force can force their way to the mouth of the Axis at Port Stubbs."

"Will they succeed?"

Del Casal shook his head. "Arjona is confident of success, and they have perhaps effectively used counter-intelligence on the Puppets, but forcing the Axis will be hard."

"I have just transferred forty thousand francs to an anonymous account for you," the Scarecrow said. Del Casal began to protest, but the Scarecrow continued speaking. "Should this information prove to be more valuable upon further investigation, I am prepared to add to that amount accordingly."

"Then that will do for now, Scarecrow."

"You go back to this crew of misfits?"

Del Casal shook his head.

"I am beginning a contract in the Puppet Free City."

CHAPTER FORTY-NINE

WAY OF THE Mongrel, verse three, *You're fucked,* was best served cold with a side of verse two, *It's never going to get any better.*

Stills followed the edge of a great eddy, moving deeper whenever the plug of icebergs allowed, looking for a way out of this lobe of Blackmore Bay. Water that flowed into this lobe kilometers back had to flow out somewhere. Most of where he looked, it squealed away through tiny gaps around thousands of tightly jammed icebergs.

He reached the deepest levels of the Free City without finding a way back to the ocean, except for a single small channel. The combination of turbulence and other outflows resulted in a slow current moving through the narrow way, at maybe a thousand atmospheres. Squeezy, but not killy.

The slow moan of the moving ocean echoed its way up the long narrow tube. The channel was wide enough to fit him for maybe a hundred meters. But it pinched to just a dozen centimeters for the section in the middle before opening up once again. Shit.

He was stuck in Blackmore's damn nose until some of the ice shifted.

He could breathe the ammonia piss of this ocean for a while

longer, but it would poison him in a few days, and by then, the explosives would detonate. And he had nothing but energy bars to eat. He also didn't trust Phocas to wait around too long for him, or not to get herself into shit on her own.

One way out, poorly designed.

He swam away hard, pain knifing his joints, back across four kilometers of black water to where he'd come in. It took him longer than he expected; he was hurt more than he thought. Lucky no one was here to see it.

He found the way he'd come in. The current blew into the Blackmore's nostril hard, and he had to fight his way through it like a salmon looking to spawn. Finally, aching and breathless, he floated in exhausted agony in the sheltered area where the last bale of explosives was jammed like a constipated sideways shit in a sphincter, waiting patiently to rip Blackmore a new one.

Stills dug his fingers into the hard putty and pulled free an armful. He also took the cord and harness he'd used to drag the bales and flexed back out into the current again.

He hated oceans.

Everything ached and he gulped for oxygen with his wide mouth and gills. He swam as fast as the anoxic water let him. He had aggressive hemoglobins, blood stuffed with red cells, and muscles designed to process and store lactic acid for a long time, but none of it really mattered if the ocean had almost no oxygen.

It might still be worse, though. It was always probably worse.

Hemoglobins were remarkably sensitive to partial pressures because they flexed from one shape to another as they functioned: fold to grab the oxygen, unfold to let the oxygen go. It was real possible that the Venturi decompression on his way in had permanently damaged a lot of his hemoglobin. If that had happened, the world was royally ass-boning him. It wouldn't matter how much oxygen was in the ocean. Anemia would suffocate him just fine.

He swam harder. If he was going to die, the world was going to drink his piss before he was done. The joint pain became blinding. He gasped so hard for breath that his vision became blotchy with dark spots.

He covered the four kilometers and found the narrow channel again and its tease of a gentle current. He set the handfuls of explosive beside the hole. He pulled out a small knife from his pouch and worked at the cable he'd used to carry the bales. It was a fine, flexible steel-reinforced carbon cable threaded through a sonar-absorbing foam. He stripped away about a meter of foam from each end.

He knew shit about explosives except that the two metal prongs on the detonators made an electrical current between them. And that Marie had said not to make any electricity around her precious putty. That really sounded like all he needed to know, didn't it?

He shaped the explosive into a long thick cock shape, wrapped several loops of the naked cable around it and then lowered it into the gentle current, down, down, down, listening at the echoes of turbulence it produced. Sound beat sight at most depths of the ocean. As the channel narrowed and the explosive shuddered in the current, the turbulence became louder and more irritated. He listened for maximum irritation and then edged away from the hole.

He electrified the carbon nanotubules running from his electroplaques to his fingertips, which held the metal core of the cable. The world exploded.

Boom. Shockwave. Fracture snapping.

Daggers of ice blew from the top of the channel like nails shot from a medieval cannon.

Then gently colliding touches of floating ice bumped their way back down, tinkling like tiny little knife fights. His ears rang. His hands were shaking. Okay. That was some pretty explosive shit for only a few handfuls. He respected Marie a tiny bit more now. A very tiny bit.

He leaned over the hole. The fragments of ice touched and collided, making easy-to-hear echoes all the way down. The channel was a lot wider, but sharp as knives in some spots. He slipped into the channel and even without flexing, the slow current drew him down. The chips and shards of ice touched like a sharp, gentle rain. He closed his eyes and moved through it.

Fuck you, world.

CHAPTER FIFTY

"*SAPRISTI!*" MARIE SWORE. "Stills! Where have you been? Napping? We're within an ace of swimming in bunches of tiny little hotel police officers here."

Stills had swum through the broken window.

"I dropped off the packages," Stills said in his electronically-rendered voice. "Let's get the fuck out of here."

He swam into the open door of the airlock, and pulled it shut behind him. He sealed it with slow twisting motions.

"Are you sick, Stills?"

"What do you care, Phocas?"

"If you're sick, I'll just leave you here. I'm faster without tons of water and a steel chamber."

"*Mange la marde*," he replied, sealing the door and turning on the oxygen. "Get us moving."

"Seriously, are you hurt? I'd totally leave you here. I need to budget my escape time."

"Are you really nuts? Move us! I got decompressed while planting your explosives. I need oxygen. Don't know how much internal damage I got."

"That doesn't sound like it will speed up my getaway," she said, cycling the airlock.

"You could have left already then, instead of sitting here, picking your ass and eating canapés in a five-star hotel like an air-sucking Congregate princess."

"I wasn't eating canapés."

"I nearly got myself killed."

"Oh, shut up, you big baby. You whine more than Saint Matthew."

"I am seriously going to kill you, Phocas."

The drain cycle finished and Marie spun the lock wheel and heaved the door open. "Just once, I'd like to meet a guy who didn't want to kill me on the first date."

"You spotting a pattern?"

"Yeah. *Câlice*, you're heavy," she grunted, hauling his chamber out of the airlock. "Thought of a diet?"

"Just keep pulling, mouth. What the hell is on the couch?"

She glanced over at the bound puppets, who stared at her wide-eyed as she hauled tons of steel and water across the room with her bare hands. "I got you a six-pack of Puppets."

"I'm not into snack food. Who knows what they put in those things anyway?"

"Get into the elevator," she said, shoving his chamber in and wiping at her sweaty forehead. "This always happens on an op. My hair gets messed up and I ruin my shoes."

"Life is tough all over," Stills said.

"Yup." She waved at the six Puppets on the couch. "Thanks for hosting, guys! You've been a blast!"

CHAPTER FIFTY-ONE

ROSALIE JOHNS-10 THE Puppet seminarian pushed open the doorway to the Bishop's office. The room was richly appointed in episcopal green. Religious paintings of the Cage, the Whip, the Toy Box and the Cream Puff panelled the walls. A large, Numen-sized desk and chair were centered at the opposite side of the room. She curtseyed deeply to the empty desk.

Bishop Grassie-6 sat at a Puppet-sized secretary's desk against the right wall, opposite a blond-bearded Puppet. Rosalie approached timidly and curtseyed again at the Bishop's desk.

"Join us, novice," the bishop said.

"Yes, Your Grace," she said nervously, sitting.

"I have some questions. So does Gates-15. He is an ascetic."

Rosalie felt her eyebrows creep up. She'd never met an ascetic—one of the church's elite, capable of living for months or years in the absence of divinity.

"Have I done something wrong, Your Grace?" she asked quietly.

"Tell us about your senior thesis at the seminary," Grassie-6 said.

The question was so unexpected that she faltered. "I... I chose to study the similarities of religious experience and identity between the Puppets and the *Homo quantus*," she said. "Should I not have, Your Grace?"

"How did you come to have this odd thesis topic, novice?" Grassie-6 asked. He rubbed a hand along his jaw, and the sleeve of his robe fell, revealing one of a pair of chainless shackles on his wrist, something she would wear when she was ordained. If she was ordained.

"I'd been speaking with a *Homo quantus*," she said. "One who lives in Bob Town."

"How did you come to meet him?" the ascetic asked. His stare was unnerving. Rosalie tried to imagine surviving for years in the absence, but it was too awful to contemplate.

"He contacted me, sir. He'd been reading the posts I did for my undergraduate work. He does small-time scams on visiting importers. He sometimes hires me to play a part. We've been tithing properly. Did he con someone he shouldn't have?" she asked.

"That's an understatement," Grassie-6 said.

"He's at the center of a plan to invade the Theocracy," the ascetic said.

Her mouth dropped open. She couldn't imagine Belisarius threatening anyone. She'd never even seen him with a weapon.

"We need to know about him, novice," Bishop Grassie-6 said. "You've spoken to him. What did you discuss?"

"I... I can't believe he'd do something like this. He's charming. Non-violent. He likes to talk about theology."

"We found a half-ton of explosives in Blackmore Bay," the ascetic said. "We know Arjona had his people planting another three packages of explosives, but we're not ruling out the idea that there are actually more. We're racing to find the other three in time."

Rosalie's arms felt spongy, limp.

"And there is a very unstable hole at the bottom of the Grand Creston Hotel," Grassie-6 said. "We've evacuated the lowest forty levels in case we can't fix it in time."

Rosalie put her hands to her lips.

"What else did you discuss, novice?" the ascetic asked.

"I... I don't know. Small scams. Money transfers. Real estate schemes. Fixed fights. But he always seemed more interested in the way Puppets experience presence and absence, and what it's like to manage two selves."

"How do you explain that, novice?" the bishop demanded. "On one hand you have a con man ready to coordinate violence upon Port Stubbs, and on the other, a man asking you how you feel about presence and absence."

"I don't know, Your Grace. Scams just seem to be a job to him. Inside, he seems... troubled. He's torn between three identities: his natural self, what he is within a kind of savantism, and what he is as a being of pure intellect. He doesn't know what he's seeking. He knows his life has no meaning."

"And what else?" Grassie-6 asked. "What did he get from you?"

She held up her hands helplessly. "I helped him with some scams. Other than that, nothing, Your Grace. Nothing in the Puppet experience can help the *Homo quantus*. We're already connected to divinity. We have meaning, but not the kind that can be shared."

The ascetic shook his head. "There's more to it than that," he said to the bishop. "Arjona has a face for each person he meets. Johns-10 has seen just one. Arjona is extremely dangerous, but we can use him to deliver the Union fleet straight to us."

The room, the whole world, dizzied around Rosalie, as if she'd smoked *basuco*. She couldn't reconcile such awful acts with the Belisarius she knew. But she couldn't ignore that a bishop and an ascetic were involved. She didn't know Belisarius at all.

CHAPTER FIFTY-TWO

GATES-15 CAME IN from a walk to the Free City that evening. He was animated and flushed, and came confidingly close. "They're going to move you straight to the Axis!" he whispered. "They're not taking you to the Forbidden City at all."

William grabbed Gates-15 by the upper arms and shook him. "Did you get the virus into any other systems? You need to do your job!"

"They won't let me near the Forbidden City," Gates-15 said apologetically. "I might be able to drop it again into the distal networks around here."

"These networks don't control the defensive systems around the Free City."

Gates-15 licked his lips. "They're bringing me, right? We're going to be at the Axis port. That's a lot closer to the Forbidden City than where we are now. I could get away for a bit and maybe upload it into the port network. It's not the defensive side, but it may cause some confusion."

William gripped Gates-15 by the shirt and pulled him close. "We're *all* riding on whether you can get close enough to get Saint Matthew's virus into the right system. You're the inside man. You can feel what it's like to be a real, healthy Puppet right now. If the Expeditionary Force doesn't get through, you go back to being an exile in about six weeks. So find a way."

Sweat sheened Gates-15's face. He was here, in front of William, but a veil of dreaminess edged at his eyes. He swallowed.

"I won't fail," he croaked. "I want this." Gates-15 smacked his lips several times. "I love you."

William shoved the Puppet away. Gates-15 stumbled back onto the floor in awe.

The door opened and the tiny, mitred bishop entered. Two priests accompanied him, followed by Doctor Teller-5. The bishop smiled, in an affectation of kindness. There was no way to hide the argument between William and Gates-15.

"You didn't injure yourself again?" Grassie-6 asked.

"No, I pushed him," William said.

"Good," Grassie-6 said, rubbing his hands briskly. "You've heard the good news?"

William nodded guardedly. "When can we go?"

"We're going right now."

"Wonderful," William said. He didn't trust Grassie-6's smile. "I'll wash and then we can go?"

"No need to wash."

"Are we in a rush?"

"No, but washing would be counter-productive. Take off your clothes, please."

"Am I putting my pressure suit back on?"

Grassie-6 sighed gently. "The Numen travel unclothed. This way all Puppets know that a Numen passes among them, and they may worship."

"I'm not going to walk around naked," William said.

"I'm not making a request."

"Neither am I."

Teller-5 sucked in her breath. Gates-15 sighed dreamily, open-mouthed.

"Are we at an impasse?" William asked.

"Not at all," the bishop said kindly. "You'll do as you're told, or we will make you."

"That doesn't make sense. For my last days, am I going to be in protective custody like the other Numen, or do I give orders? What do you want?"

The tiny bishop held a shocker in his hand. "Clothes off, please."

The shocker was unwavering in the graceful hand. Slowly, William unlaced his shirt and pulled it over his head. Then, his pants and underwear. He stood before them, defiant, sweaty and flabby. He coughed painfully.

Except for the bishop, they stared in awe.

The bishop waved his hand at those behind him, a bit giddily. One ran out the open door. Grunting and heaving sounded in the hallway. Eight puppets in priestly tunics of forest green with silver-threaded seams came into sight, struggling under the weight of two long poles supporting a small cage.

On their wrists and ankles and around their necks, they wore heavy shackles of steel unattached to chains, the symbols of their station. They bumped into the doorway. One barked the skin of her knuckles. They panted as they stopped, and in a disorganized wobble, set down the cage. They stayed kneeling, staring up at William's nakedness. The bishop had a look of anticipation on his face. He beamed at William and opened the side of the cage.

William made no move.

"Get in," Grassie-6 urged him.

"Why would I get into a cage?" demanded William.

"The Cage has deep religious meaning to the Puppets. It's sacred, as much as the Toy Box, or the Cream Puff."

"I'm not getting into a cage."

One of the little Puppet priests shivered.

Grassie-6 waved his shocker.

"Fuck off," William said.

Then, he was in electrical seizure on the floor, screaming in agony, vision blotchy-black. Puppet hands lifted him, soft fingers against fired nerves. They accidentally knocked his head against the frame of the doorway to the cage as they pushed and twisted his neck. They pulled him back and pushed again and hit his shoulder against the metal. He cried out and kicked back at one of the Puppets.

"I don't fit, you idiots! It's too small!"

"You'll fit if you put your head between your knees!" Grassie-6's voice called over the confusion. "Hunch your back."

The floor of the cage wasn't flat. Narrow bars of metal dug into his shins as he pulled his legs in. It was so small that even kneeling, he had to bend his head, nearly between his knees. He tried angling corner to corner, but his shoulders wouldn't fit. Two Puppets in their eagerness slammed the door of the cage on his hand and he cried out. The bars beneath dug into his feet and shins. The cage door shoved closed.

"Perfect!" Grassie-6 declared.

Little hands squeezed between the bars for quick feels and touches. His legs. His privates. His arms. William yanked one of the little bastards into the bars hard and all of a sudden, he was in electrical agony again, spasming so much that he pissed on his legs and the floor.

His nerves burned, but this time he wasn't alone. Five or six of the Puppets with their hands in the cage shrieked with him and fell to the floor. William wept in pain. He opened his eyes to the sight of Grassie-6 berating the priests. All eight knelt, dipping their fingers into William's piss and the dashing drops onto their faces in a kind of ecstasy. The bishop kicked them in the ribs until they stood and regained their composure.

"You little fuckers," William said. "Let me out."

The little priests sucked in their breaths.

"What's wrong with you?"

The heavy shackles on Grassie-6's ankles rattled as he stepped into the puddle beside William.

"You sound like the first Fallen Numen," Grassie-6 said softly.

"Is this how you protect me? You shock me? You hit me? It's too small in here. It hurts! Let me out!" William tried to shake the cage.

"Like the first Fallen Numen," breathed Grassie-6 in wonder.

CHAPTER FIFTY-THREE

THE SOUND OF ecstatic shrieking rose and died in waves. The eight Puppet bearers carried his cage like a palanquin on a raised walkway about three meters above street level. The crowds of Puppets dozens of meters ahead screamed, completely beside themselves. The priests, whom William had thought largely bereft of self-control, were sedate in comparison, carrying him forward in clumsy stateliness beneath a line of infrared heaters that stretched as far as he could twist his neck to see.

His shins and feet and knees pressed painfully against the bars beneath him. The muscles in his back had gone numb and his head still ached from when Grassie-6 had shocked him. William dripped sweat under the heat lamps. Fans above him blew hot air and his scent onto the hysterical crowd below. As they smelled him, their screams choked off and they slipped into a hazy ecstasy. It was like someone was dragging a blanket of sober, mouth-breathing silence over the screaming streets of the Free City. The clumsy Puppet feet plodded onward, thrusting him over and over into the howl of the crowds, and he wept.

CHAPTER FIFTY-FOUR

CASSANDRA WATCHED BEL fidget. That wasn't inspiring. He, Cassandra, Marie and Iekanjika had been pulled aside like all the other non-Puppets and moved to the outer zones of the Free City. Stills continued on his way to the port as cargo, but the rest of them found a loud bar filled with delayed passengers. A small projector on Iekanjika's wrist emitted multi-frequency white noise, so they could speak in some privacy. General news feeds projected onto two walls, mostly scenes of a large displacement of non-Puppets.

There was no view of the Puppet Axis. Cassandra would have loved to have looked at it, even through a television camera. She'd spent her whole life studying the cosmos and hadn't been this close to an Axis created by some ancient intelligence by technologies they couldn't even guess at. And she was stuck in here, unable to touch it. Her thoughts itched and she was ready to start counting something. Marie also looked bored. After a few minutes of throwing shelled nuts at a big miner in the hopes of starting a fight, Marie exhaled loudly. The miner moved to another booth. "So, I hacked into the network of Stills' sarcophagus thing," she said breezily to Bel. "I sent him Venusian cheesecake porn. He looked like he was under pressure."

"That's awful!" Bel said.

"I know, I know. Puns aren't my thing in Anglo-Spanish. I'm better in French."

"No. You've done an awful thing! Stills isn't Saint Matthew. The Tribe of the Mongrel are deeply messed up."

"Come on!" Marie said. "Matt is messed up too."

"Do you even know what real mongrel porn is?"

"I'm gonna guess manatees?"

"It's you. It's me. With our clothes on. The mongrels have flukes instead of legs. Their faces are incapable of emoting. Blubber has buried their sexual organs. Their reproduction is heavily assisted and painful. They find each other repellent. They avoid thinking about sex on purpose. You've probably made him miserable."

"Aw, *merde*," she said, crossing her arms.

Cassandra tried to read Bel. His pity of the mongrels seemed heartfelt. The violence of Stills' words made her uncomfortable, and the violence he was capable of probably scared her. But everything was becoming relative. Stills or Iekanjika. Stills or Gates-15. Suddenly, he didn't seem as bad. And she was starting to think that Bel's view of the *Homo eridanus* was kind of noble. Maybe Stills hadn't asked to be built the way he had. Maybe he didn't like living underwater. Maybe she felt a bit of sympathy for Stills.

The newsfeeds became louder, showing cheering, shrieking Puppets. "What's going on, Arjona?" Iekanjika asked in a low voice.

"Every so often the Puppets have to move a Numen," he said, "and the city closes down."

"Anyone we know?"

"I'm not as good as Saint Matthew," Bel said, glancing at the limited datafeed he had, "but I can access the upper levels of the Puppet traffic dashboards. Crowds of Puppets are stretching from the outer wall of the Free City all the way to the Port, crossing the whole city."

The shipping news on the two screens vanished and a Puppet announcer appeared. He was perhaps a meter tall, with flushed cheeks and a look of rapt excitement. He stood behind a full-sized human desk, its flat surface coming up to just under his armpits. He held his datapad in front of him, forcing the camera to film him from forty-five degrees off, unintentionally capturing the unpainted wall and wiring to the announcer's right.

"... been disappointed in the past with other claims of feral Numen, and the Episcopal Conclave has yet to pronounce its findings," the announcer said, "but the reaction from Puppetry across the Free City is astonishing. We'll be patching into our mobile unit shortly. In the meantime, I have this recording from an eye witness."

The Puppet announcer stood on the screen for long seconds, smiling, before finally, an image replaced him. A small Puppet woman in a priestly tunic sat on a chair with dangling legs as she tried to still her shaking hands. Her awe radiated past sweaty, tear-stained cheeks.

"I was one of eight bearers carrying him from the Warrens to Twelfth Avenue," she said. "He's real. I swear. If I know Numen, he's real. It felt like Good Boy Day, but so much stronger. I was in a closed room with just a few others and him." Her breath shuddered. "He pissed on the floor. I touched it," she said with a groan before wiping away a tear. "It was the most beautiful thing I've ever experienced. He was... he yelled at us. All of us. He grabbed another priest and rammed him into the cage... It was so beautiful."

The interviewer put down the camera, tumbling the image so that the young priest displayed at a ninety degree angle. Unmanned, the camera nonetheless caught the interviewer lovingly stroking and smelling the priest's fingers. Cassandra felt her stomach churn. Despite what Bel said, the Puppets weren't anything like the *Homo quantus*. She couldn't imagine what it must be like for William to be surrounded by them.

Disgust wrote itself on Iekanjika's face. She snapped a look at Bel. "This is bad?" she asked.

Belisarius shook his head. "It's good," he whispered.

"It's some kind of parade," Cassandra said after glancing at Bel's datafeed. "They've cleared a path from the Warrens to the port. They're not taking them to the Forbidden City?"

The image returned to the Puppet standing at the newsdesk, but the audio fed from somewhere else, and whatever he said for the next minute wasn't transmitted. Instead, the sounds of a massive crowd drowned the bar, chaotic chanting and angry yelling. Finally, the video feed was matched, showing thousands of Puppets sweating and jumping below a raised street.

"Are they angry? They're swearing?" Cassandra asked. It was like watching animals.

Bel shook his head. "They're worshipping. The Puppet Bible is made of most of what the Numen said to the Puppets. One of the ways of worshipping is to quote the scriptures. The Numen swore at the Puppets a lot."

Cassandra's stomach turned a bit more.

Bel sighed. "Without the Numen around, the Puppets are as close to normal as you can get after surviving generations of captivity, abuse, and biochemical slavery. Around the Numen, the Puppets become something as alien as the fugue."

Cassandra didn't think he was baiting her. He really believed it.

The camera angles shifted as the noise tapered off. The image showed Puppet priests carrying a palanquin of some kind, but it was difficult to make out details; the cameraman kept hopping, trying to shove through the crowd to get closer.

"Oh no," Bel said.

Cassandra's hand gripped his. She'd seen it too. Her brain, like his, interpolated the complete scene from snippets of images. She felt awful, and knew Bel must feel far far worse. Then, the camera stopped jumping and the wave of noise washed away, replaced by a shared sigh. The procession moved out of frame, carrying a hunched, cramped, naked figure in a Puppet-sized cage. A feeling of horror stabbed in her chest, and she'd barely known William. He'd been Bel's mentor and protector. She didn't want Bel in pain. She took Bel's head in her hands and turned him to her, so he could see only her. They both had tears in their eyes.

"I'm sorry, Bel," she whispered helplessly. "Don't look." But he couldn't unlook and neither could she. He remembered everything, just like her. "Don't look," she whispered, and did the only thing she could think of to distract him from his pain; she pulled his face into a kiss.

CHAPTER FIFTY-FIVE

WILLIAM COUGHED HARD, bringing up blood. Grassie-6 approached in concern, but William swung his fist, missing the bishop, but forcing him back. William wiped his mouth and sat back on the low cot they'd set up for him.

They'd reached the Free City port. In the Puppet-only secure area, a wide window looked out on the vacuum of the great bay, light shining off rigid ice, outlining passenger ships, and cargo containers being offloaded from the most recent freighter arrivals from Port Stubbs. On the floor of the great underground port shimmered the Axis itself, indistinct in place and depth, confusing the eyes.

William wore clothes again, pants and shirt that laced up the outsides of the legs and arms, presumably so that Puppets could take them off again without him necessarily cooperating. His anger seethed, close to taking control. He was doing this for Kate. She would never know all he'd done to give her a future, but she would have one. She wouldn't be like him.

"You moved away," William said to the bishop.

"What?" Grassie-6 asked. He seemed unnerved by the tone in William's voice. They wanted a god. He could give them a god.

"I was going to punch you. You moved away."

The bishop looked relieved. He smiled and snapped his fingers at a young priest who scampered to the wall, opened a panel and hustled to William, sliding on his knees on the floor in his rush to bow. He held a coiled whip up as an offering.

"What the hell is this?"

"I moved away because I didn't want you to hurt your hand," Grassie-6 said kindly. "My bones are as strong as yours. If you want to hurt me, you should use a tool."

"For the love of—" William swiped the whip from the priest's hand and rose. "'Get the fuck out!'" he yelled, quoting a verse he'd seen in the Puppet Bible. Gods using scripture. Let them wet their pants. "All of you but Grassie-6!"

Some scrambled for the door. Others waited for a nod from the bishop. William tried to kick one in the ass. The door slammed behind the last one. Grassie-6 stood before William imperiously, a meter tall, with a high mitre of green and silver on his head.

"You're not afraid?" William asked.

"Do you want me to be?"

"If I want to whip you to pieces, right now, you'll let me?"

"How much do you understand of Mooney-4's Dilemma?"

William snapped the whip experimentally. The bishop did not react.

"The Numen were composed of every societal rejectee from within the Plutocracy, united only in their desire to live without any interference," Grassie-6 said. "Their laws suited individualists. Duels resolved many disputes. They... enjoyed vendettas."

"Not surprising," William said.

"The teenaged Mooney-4 witnessed a Numen vendetta killing. She had to live with having watched the death of a Numen. Many Puppets were trapped like she was, between the overwhelming desire to obey the Numen versus the overwhelming desire to protect them. Quietly, here and there, these early moral figures struggled with what we now call Mooney-4's Dilemma."

"So came the Puppet Revolt," William said distastefully.

"We don't call it that," Grassie-6 said. His face became sad. "We call it the Fall, for the reasons you can guess. The innocent age had been crumbling for a long time. We Puppets had to step from childhood into adulthood, to assume burdens we didn't ask for, like everyone."

"You took your own gods prisoner."

Grassie-6 shook his head sadly. "If we obey the Numen and set them free, they'll destroy us and themselves. If we protect them with captivity for their own good, we disobey them and destroy our souls. We're torn in two every day. Do you think we don't ache to fall on our knees and fulfill every whim of the Numen? Don't you think that would be ecstasy? But we can't, because our divinities are deeply flawed."

William's hand had lowered, lulled by Grassie-6's words. He coiled the whip uncertainly.

"If you want to whip a Puppet to death, I could find you a hundred volunteers in the Port," Grassie-6 said. "But Puppets qualified to enter the Episcopal Conclave are rare. We have the heavy responsibility of ensuring the future of the Numen. Bishops are difficult to replace. If you want to whip me, I'll happily submit as long as you don't kill me."

William raised the coiled whip hesitantly, frustration biting in his stomach, the screams of the crowds still echoing in his mind. He yelled and hit Grassie-6 with the coils, over and over, knocking the little bishop's mitre off, striking at his head and shoulders hard enough to knock him down. He stood over the serene bishop, panting.

"I hate you," William said. "It was a mistake to come here."

Grassie-6 bled from his nose and lips, but he smiled kindly.

"If you'd been raised here, you would understand everything."

"Would I have grown up in a cage?" William began to cough again, uncontrollably. He backed away, but waved the coiled whip before him, warding Grassie-6 away. He sat until his coughing fit was just an ache in his chest.

"For some parts," Grassie-6 said, rising and replacing his mitre. "The Cage is part of the core of the Numen-Puppet relationship. We learn and teach in turn."

"Vengeance?

Grassie-6 sat up, looking baffled. "For what?"

"For being put in cages. For being whipped."

"You understand nothing," Grassie-6 said, stepping forward. "It isn't that we loved being whipped. It's that we loved that our divinities paid attention to us. We are validated and real in those moments. Whether talking to us, or hitting us, or caressing us or ordering us, it's all grace. Hell is when we weren't allowed close to them. We worship them, in the ways they taught us and in ways that reflect our new roles as the custodians of divinity."

William rubbed at the ache behind his sternum. "They don't deserve your love or worship. The Numen had no morals."

"Not the morals you know. Here on Oler, they created the new moral agents: we Puppets. The Numen were forces of chaos and power, as much as the Titans were to the Greek gods, a savagery to be tamed."

Tamed.

The cage was on the far side of the room. They had not cleaned it. No doubt they had obsessive and religious uses for the smears and drips of his sweat. He rubbed at bruises on his legs and knees, wondering at the odds of being put in the cage again. William and Gates-15 had to pull this off. They were the inside man and the fall guy. He had to tough it out for a little longer. The rest of his life.

William coughed—short, breathless hacking. Grassie-6 was visibly disturbed.

"I have a lot to learn of the culture my grandparents fled," William said. "Can you give me access to a library where I can look at not only the Puppet Bible, but old records from the times of my grandparents?"

Grassie-6 moved to a desk reader on the wall. The screen lit. He typed.

"You can access a library from here," the bishop said. "The medical team accompanying us through the Axis will be equipped in a few hours. We'll board the transport then. Sleep until that time."

"Never again the cage," William said.

"Maybe. We all have our roles to play." Grassie-6 smiled.

The bishop left, shutting the door behind him. William dragged a chair to the wall. He needed to calm down. He'd begun to understand the spell the Numen had wrapped the Puppets in. The Numenarchy had been composed of idiots, complete and utter idiots. They had created a system to make themselves gods to the Puppets. The Numenarchy hadn't understood that gods were objects, concepts.

The Numen stood outside the collection of beings deserving moral consideration. William's wishes were curiosities, with no moral weight for the Puppets. In the Edenic Age, his commands would have been obeyed, as commandments from a distant and inscrutable god, but even then had the Numen not foreseen the seeds of disaster in their slaves? The Puppets caged their gods now, and a whole moral system—with a bible and a theology and a church—was devoted to keeping the Numen safe by not obeying them. The Numenarchy had been so overconfident, so short-sighted, and they had not even paid for it. Their grandchildren and descendants had paid for their crimes. It was stomach-turning.

The screen showed him directories and directories full of historical sources: texts, recordings, and messages from the pre-Fall days. Other directories contained theological discussions, theses, arguments, meditative texts, and the Puppet Bible itself, a cluttered, conflicting multi-volume monstrosity. There were movies and short films and old television pieces, more than he could ever watch in lifetime. And beside the palm-reader was what he'd been hoping to find: a physical jack into the system.

It wasn't advanced. These things constituted emergency entrypoints that the Puppets needed to make their unreliable hand-me-down technology function across hardware incompatibilities.

William pushed his thumb against the fleshy pad under the second knuckle of his index finger. Fine dark hairs emerged from his finger-tips. Gates-15 didn't know that William was insurance, carrying nanofibres capable of delivering Saint Matthew's computer virus. He gently touched his fingertip to the jack and waited for the virus to upload.

CHAPTER FIFTY-SIX

THE IMAGES GNAWED at Belisarius's insides. They'd rented a private booth off the boarding lounge. Hours had passed. The cargo and passenger shipping schedules were in more chaos than normal. Tradespeople, scientists, the families of temporary workers and even the occasional nervous Puppet packed the boarding lounge outside the glass doors. The news played on big screens on the walls, replaying the clips of William being transported through the Free City, over and over.

Their booth looked out onto the cavernous bay of ice and steel over the mouth of the Puppet Axis. Lines of cargo ships packed with containers queued to cross the Axis. But some pieces of cargo went through offloading, and reloading, as if the Puppet shipping companies couldn't decide what ought to be shipped.

Belisarius's cargo waited too. They'd checked four containers and a rented tug to travel with them through the Axis. Stills in his big aquatic chamber was shipping too; he could not fit in the passenger area.

"Is this normal?" Cassandra asked. The pulse in her neck beat faster, and her cheeks had warmed. She looked at him shyly, with a touch of confusion. He wasn't sure yet what his own reaction was to their kiss. He'd wanted her back for so long, but this wasn't it, not yet.

"The Puppets are always a bit disorganized," he said.

"I wish Saint Matthew were here," Cassandra whispered. "He could have told us what kind of ships are getting in ahead of us."

"We can't do everything at once."

"How many of the ships going ahead of us do you suppose are military?"

"Some," Iekanjika said.

"What's wrong?" Cassandra asked him. "William?"

Belisarius shook his head. "I should have had a signal from Del Casal by now," he said. "He's not the kind to deviate from a plan."

"Could the Puppets be blocking signals?" Iekanjika asked.

"I have some automated messages set up as test pings. They're all getting through."

"Captured?" Cassandra asked.

"I don't know. I'm worried."

"How worried?" Marie asked.

"William's part is going well," Belisarius said. "Everything else is going according to plan. So even if Del Casal was captured, there's no reason the Puppets or anyone else would be putting together our plan."

"He probably got spooked and is laying low," Marie said.

The news screens changed, and a Puppet announcer appeared, a tiny woman with straight blond hair. They couldn't hear her words over the noise of the lounge, but the view shifted to a view of stars, ineptly out of focus and drifting until it focused on a gray shape in the distance.

"*Tabarnak,*" Marie swore softly.

"What is it?" Cassandra asked.

"A dreadnought," Iekanjika said quietly. "*Laurentide*-class." She squinted at the blurred image, but Belisarius's brain had already matched its movement against the background stars.

"Olero-stationary orbit," Belisarius said. "About thirteen thousand kilometers above the Free City."

"Is its appearance related to us?" Cassandra whispered.

"An assault on the Free City would need more ships, and they would have saturation-bombed for a day or two before moving this close," Iekanjika said. "But from that orbit, the Congregate can survey all traffic entering or leaving the Free City and stop anything it wants."

The sweating newscaster spoke quickly, words they couldn't hear, before the view cut to stock footage of Puppet fortifications and scrambling troops in armor.

"The Puppets are going to stop moving their forces to Port Stubbs and they'll concentrate them over the Free City?" Marie asked. "And a dreadnought can stop any ship coming out of the Axis. Should we call it off?"

Iekanjika continued squinting at the screen.

"If we call it off," Belisarius said, "we lose what we've already put on the table, including William. Maybe all of us. I don't know that we'll ever have another chance."

"That's a dreadnought, Bel," Marie said. "Whatever you've heard about the Congregate's capital warships, multiply it by ten."

"It isn't Arjona's choice," Iekanjika said. "Whatever you've bet, we've bet more. Major-General Rudo will make the final decision."

They watched the news somewhat morosely, as the image sharpened a bit, showing what looked like dozens of warships welded together into a rectangular wedge. This image never got better than that, but it didn't need to. All of them could do their own math. An hour later, their transport was ready. It had no windows, but Cassandra and Belisarius sat near the walls anyway. They moved to their seats shyly, not touching, but never so far that they couldn't reach a hand.

Something changed when Cassandra had touched his face, and touched her lips to his. Years had dug a gulf between them, dug deeper by whatever motives Cassandra had attributed to him, and the suspicions Belisarius carried about what kind of person she had become. But in that long moment, they'd found a halfway point over that space. He'd gone into Cassandra's world to offer her a view of a wormhole, and she'd come into his world to see it, and there between the two was a fragile bridge.

As soon as they strapped in, Cassandra relaxed, laying her hands on the armrests. Without asking, Belisarius put his fingers on the pulse under her warm wrist and slipped into savant. Cassandra had beaten him there. Her heartbeat was already metronomic, and her temperature normal. So graphable. He graphed it in his mind and derived an equation, and then graphed his own for comparison.

The synchronization of periodic biological processes during savant and the fugue had been observed as early as the sixth generation of the *Homo quantus* project, and had guided early experiments in fugue spotting. Even now, *Homo quantus* children practiced coupling heartbeat, respiration and body temperature to seek resonances.

In most cases, the fugue induced its own negative feedback with fever-inducing interferons. A few degrees could disrupt the fragile quantum coherences sustaining the fugue. Resonance with a spotter could dampen fever for a time, allowing longer fugues. Cassandra's breathing absorbed the rhythm of his and vice versa. Her heartbeat throbbed in her wrist against his fingertips, warm and close.

Belisarius in savant knew he was not Belisarius, not really. The tiny direct current from his electroplaques suppressed activity in parts of the frontal lobe, mimicking a very specific kind of brain damage that made perception of language and socialization difficult. Whole pieces of personality gone. The image that haunted him was of cracking open his head, exposing his wet brain to the crackle of emotions.

Savant was a state of being in those diminished emotions, sometimes making it a place in which to hide. But sometimes feelings were so strong, that even diminished, they hurt. And the emotional ineptitude that came with savant made things worse. This was a bad time for Belisarius to be in savant. The image of William crammed naked into a cage and carried over the streets of the Free City clung like a nightmare. Kissing Cassandra was a disruptive dream, a summoner of might-have-beens and might-still-bes. The hope of happiness was more nerve-racking than none at all. In savant, his insides were invisible to introspection or management. Feelings were a raw storm of biting acid and fiery exhilaration.

He wanted to be quiet, to watch the raw world from a hidey-hole. He wanted to huddle with Cassandra. He wanted to hug and hold her. He wanted her safe and he wanted her to keep him safe from the world, as if they were little animals hiding from the night. Cassandra had needed to hold him when they'd been teenagers damaging their minds. Maybe she felt it again now.

No. She felt nothing at all. Cassandra was gone, in the slowed breathing and calmed pulse of early fugue. Beside him was a quantum perceptional and computational array, nested knots of processing algorithms without the subjectivity to collapse a wave function, a thing capable of seeing overlapping quantum possibilities and probabilities in their beautiful simultaneity, but not a creature that, like him, could feel lonely or helpless.

The seats trembled as the transport moved over the mouth of the Axis.

Cassandra twitched. Trouble staying in the fugue? Or difficulty perceiving the quantum world beyond the transport? Cassandra the person desperately wanted to see the wormhole. So did the quantum intellect inhabiting the body. But objectivity was not a natural place to be, any more than savant. It was no place at all. Living things belonged in a place, needed to sense belonging.

But the Puppet transport, all hulking metal and electrified systems, was a wall of electrical and quantum interference as impenetrable as a Faraday cage. To see the wormhole properly, he and Cassandra needed to be out there in dumb vacuum suits. Being in the transport was like looking at the stars through a dirty telescope from the middle of a city. At the sensitivities Cassandra and Belisarius cared about, the noise of the transport made most observations unproductive. Yet still she tried.

The transport accelerated gently, toward the Axis.

Belisarius ticked the seconds by. Being a chronometer was calming.

The stillness of freefall soaked the cabin and its passengers. Voices lowered to whispers. Cassandra's pulse increased. Her temperature rose by point two degrees. Belisarius's spotting dampened the effect. His own pulse increased and his temperature rose a half degree in sympathy.

Taste was evolution's first sense, a way for bacteria to touch one molecule to another to decide in a binary way if something was food or poison. Taste was the scaffolding for the development of smell, which gave life chemical information from distant places. Sensitivity to vibrations developed into touch and hearing, to give fragile organisms more information about the world beyond their own membranes, and rudimentary understandings of direction and distance. Electromagnetic sensitivity, from infrared to ultraviolet to variants of electrical and magnetic sensitivity, gave organisms senses to locate food or avoid predation by perceiving distant movement and color at the speed of light.

Intelligence was the first sense to see through time instead of space. Intellect was a tool for life to foresee danger and opportunities, pushing perception into the past and future. But intellect was built on the creaky emotional and instinctual infrastructure of hunter-gatherers. *Homo sapiens* had existed for not much more than two hundred thousand years, and humanity's feats of survival still needed emotional shortcuts and tribal structures. Savant deafened him to the mental infrastructure of society, and the fugue extinguished the individual, the most basic unit of tribe.

And for all that he'd given away what was natural, he really hadn't seen the future any better than anyone else, and a sense of impending disaster yawned under his stomach. He'd doomed William. He'd doomed everyone, maybe even all the citizens of the Union, because he'd become overconfident in his intellectual solitude and the idea of the *Homo quantus* project, that humanity could learn to see into the future. He'd made the plan in his head, alone, playing all the players, all at once, superimposed like quantum calculations. Self-doubt tasted bitter.

Why had the Congregate dreadnought come? Had the Congregate captured Del Casal? Or had his plan to funnel false intelligence to the Puppets through Gates-15 been too clever by half? Maybe the Puppets had cut a deal with the Congregate. How many mistakes had Belisarius made that hadn't manifested themselves yet?

Without dislodging his fingers from her wrist, he slipped

the fingers of his other hand into Cassandra's, leaning closer, clinging to the empty body, like waiting outside an apartment for its owner to come home. Her kiss in his perfect memory inflated an empty ache in his chest.

Cassandra's wrist was one point eight degrees warmer than his. Her heartbeat became uneven, then briefly stochastic. She couldn't sustain the fugue. The quantum intellect riding her flesh could no longer suppress the subjectivity of Cassandra. She became a person again.

Cassandra breathed, a heavy, low exhalation, the sound of someone emerging from too deep a sleep. Belisarius straightened and removed his fingers from their twining with hers, and, awkwardly, from her wrist. In savant, they could both be... unproductively intense.

Cassandra's breathing lost its regularity. She was emerging from savant. Belisarius came up, into his baseline self. The world became quantitatively mysterious, a world depleted in geometric patterns, but overabundant in feelings and people and wants and needs. He exhaled tension.

"I couldn't make out anything useful beyond the transport," she whispered. "There's so much out there, so much we could measure, if they just let us."

"Soon," he said.

"We're so close to seeing something true and real about the structure of space-time," she pressed on as if he hadn't spoken. "I feel so much for this knowledge that it aches, Bel."

His throat tightened. "I want to know so badly that it scares me," he said. "It scared me away, because there's so little holding me to me."

CHAPTER FIFTY-SEVEN

THE PUPPET FREE City was a poorly maintained, aesthetically unappealing nest of unevenly lit hollows in the ice, but Port Stubbs was worse. Its unimaginative lines, over-engineered spaces and burnt-out lights seemed to make up most of the port. A resource town originally built by cheap-minded Numen industrialists, and added to later by any slip-shod operation willing to break an embargo, everything in the port made William feel unwelcome.

In zero g, they went into the dirty office of a local bishop and strapped themselves to the walls. Teller-5 examined William while he looked over her, to the palanquin cage on the wall, strapped beside a coiled whip. His fever had broken for now, but he still ached all over. Bishop Grassie-6 and Gates-15 watched William anxiously.

"Should we get him to a hospital?" Gates-15 asked.

"Yes," Teller-5 said.

"My symptoms are under control for now."

The bishop eyed him, lips pressed tightly. The doctor stroked William's arm unconsciously. William shook her off.

"We have to!" Gates-15 said.

"Can I have a bit of a break from him?" William said testily, indicating Gates-15.

He needed to give Gates-15 time to upload his virus.

"No!" Gates-15 said. Idiot.

"You're here at his request," the bishop said. "Go be the good boy."

Gates-15 didn't move.

"Get out for a while," William said.

Gates-15 looked close to tears.

"He said get out!" Teller-5 shrieked. "Be the good boy!"

She smiled back at William dreamily, fixated on the skin of his arm where she'd started pressing her palm again.

"Get her out too!" William said.

The three Puppets argued until William was alone with the bishop and a pair of hermetically sealed episcopal troops.

"We should talk about getting you to the area where your family lived," Grassie-6 said.

"Thank you," William said.

"You said you don't want the cage."

"That's right."

"I'm not most Puppets," Grassie-6 said. "Nor is Teller-5. The vast majority of Puppets do not have our kind of control."

William held back his reply.

"In this Fallen Age, there remain only a few religious modes through which most Puppets can interact with divinity," the bishop said. "It boils down to Cage or Whip."

"I'm not going to whip anyone," William said.

"Then cage it is, Mister Kaltwasser."

"No cage."

"This is not about you. This is about the Puppet masses and what they're capable of."

Grassie-6 unstrapped himself, pushed off, to the other wall, and took the whip. Barely two meters long, it flexed stiffly. The bishop hooked his feet into the bars of the cage and swung the whip experimentally a few times, slowly, getting its feel. William thought Grassie-6 was inexperienced with a whip, being a Puppet and not a Numen. Then the bishop snapped it with force, its tip biting the air in the middle of the room with a loud crack.

"A blunt or side whip blow can raise painful welts," Grassie-6 said, "but in my experience this is unpersuasive. The lashtip breaks the speed of sound. That part must kiss the target to be truly effective."

"That's barbaric."

Grassie-6 floated back to William and handed him the whip handle. William didn't take it.

"Perhaps you need to tap into your fear," Grassie-6 said. "Let's say a dozen Puppets joined you in this room. Who would you prefer to be in charge?"

William swallowed down nausea.

"The Numen have always been creatures who fear," the bishop said. "They feared each other. They feared the judgement of civilization. And they feared the Puppets they'd created. In understanding that core truth, we may properly worship them."

"You... scare them?" William asked.

"We worship them according to their natures. Are you frightened?"

William's mouth dried. The whip handle was held out to him still. "Yes."

Grassie-6 approached along the railing, until his citrus breath was in William's nostrils. "We Puppets fear too. We fear the absence of divinity."

Grassie-6 took William's hand, intimately. William froze. The depth of the tenderness in the bishop's touch made his skin crawl. The bishop closed William's fingers around the whip handle. William pushed at the bishop's chest, but the Puppet's grip was surprisingly strong.

"My fear and your fear are reflections," he said. "Those reflections carry moral weight. You have to decide what to do with your fear of us, as we must decide what to do with our fear of your absence. You have the Whip. We have the Cage."

Grassie-6 leapt away, catching a railing a meter away. William clung to the whip. The bishop regarded him for long seconds and then leapt to the doorway.

"You want to visit places of your ancestors. You don't want to go in a cage. You're holding the only alternative. I'll open the door. Beyond it are ten Puppets who have no idea you're here."

"Don't!"

"It's either this or go back to the Free City," Grassie-6 said. "You've told me what you want. I'm only showing you how to get it."

"Don't!"

The door slid open and Grassie-6 moved aside.

A perfectly formed, half-sized face, true-stock European pale, peeked past the frame. Young. A Puppet woman, lovely, features framed in black hair. Then, a Puppet man with a brown beard appeared beside her, sniffing furtively. His mouth opened as if gasping in surprise, and then he was breathing, gulping. Then she did too. And they swung in. Others followed, perfectly-proportioned miniature people, tasting at the air like fish.

"Stay back!" William said, sounding shrill in his own ears.

His fingers fumbled at the fastenings holding him to the wall.

Three more Puppets crept in, mouths gaping.

"Call them off!" William said.

"It's the Cage or the Whip, Mister Kaltwasser," Grassie-6 said.

"Get back!" William yelled at them. They reacted as much as Teller-5. No reaction. Or distracted curiosity. They were in religious awe.

The first Puppet, the one with the brown beard, closed on William, fingers open.

"Fuck off!" William said, shoving him. The Puppet's hands snapped closed on his forearms, snake-quick, and his neck stretched, trying to bite at him. William yanked away the hand gripping the whip and punched him in the head. The Puppet gasped as he tumbled backwards in the air, crashing into another Puppet. Three more alighted on the wall around William, catching hold of the railing with their feet. Every eye stared dreamily.

William's panicked hand struck with the whip. It landed across a Puppet's leg, the snap curling ineffectively. William laid the length of the whip coil on the next Puppet's stomach. She gasped, doubling over.

The first approached again deliriously. William aimed for the chest, but the lash wrote itself up the Puppet's neck and cheek, snapping into his eye. The poor Puppet shrieked and William froze in horror. The Puppet screamed endlessly, holding his face in his hands as blood painted the fingers.

"Make them stop!" William shrieked.

Grassie-6 smiled serenely on the railing at the other side of the room.

"Stop!" William said to the Puppets. "I won't hit you! I'll get in the cage! Stop."

A Puppet landed on the wall under William's feet, hooking her feet into a lower railing. She sucked air into her throat, inhaling him. She hugged his leg like it was the only real thing in the world. She bit him with miniature teeth, tearing through his pants. He screamed, kicking at her.

He raised the whip over and over, lashing them, snapping at arms and hands and chests and faces, yelling wordlessly, whipping his own legs when he missed the Puppets clinging there. He did not finish his own shrieking or the whipping until his voice became hoarse and his arm exhausted and a haze of blood droplets floated in the room, separating him from the cowering Puppets moaning in agonized ecstasy near the bishop.

William's arm trembled. His gorge rose.

"I said to make them stop," William said. He began to cry.

CHAPTER FIFTY-EIGHT

THE RENTED TUG had been shut down and fastened to the skeleton of the Puppet cargo ship, along with dozens of smaller ships, shipping containers, and bulk construction material. The tug's fission engine had cooled and configured for long-term inactivity. Buried within a thick sphere of lead, newly attached to the cladding around the fissionables, was Saint Matthew, in a space no larger than a fist.

He was designing electric instrumental arrangements to accompany tenth century Gregorian chants. People came to religions for many reasons, and the beauty and richness of a ministry's culture, art, music and philosophy could be as potent a gateway to the salvation of souls as proselytizing in public squares. He'd arranged different chants with tones and tempos ranging from Anglo-Spanish ranchero to Indonesian romantic to Venusian technodance to Ummah acid rock.

Unlike everything else strapped to the outside of the Puppet cargo ship, Saint Mathew couldn't be turned off without destroying his consciousness. As a security measure, the Puppets sterilized every piece of cargo with ionizing radiation and knocked out electronics with focused EM pulses prior to moving them through the Axis. Their crude methods ensured that nothing recorded the inner workings of their wormhole or damaged it. Thick radiation shielding and a hull design that acted like a Faraday cage blocked most EM signals, keeping the passengers as safe as Saint Matthew.

Saint Matthew had modified their rented tug with a few special features. Outside the AI's tiny lead safe room, a clock ticked, dumb, mechanical, wound by hand, and completely invulnerable to the scouring radiation the Puppets used on their cargo. The faint vibrations wound down.

The clock ticked its last as the Puppet freighter moved into the Axis. And a mechanical arm closed a circuit, connecting Saint Matthew by cable to passive external sensors and his waking battery-powered automata. The weak sensors peered at the world outside the tug in the visual, IR and X-ray. The interior of the Puppet Axis lacked visible light, but the automata detected faint, weirdly rippled X-ray patterns, and an IR signal corresponding to a temperature only a few hundredths of a degree above absolute zero. Saint Matthew used these observations to measure the speed of the transport.

Continuing to hum the chant to the electric arrangement he'd designed, he ran diagnostics on the automata. Each one had clung to a different part of the hull, in the corners and edges and hollows of the old shipyard workhorse. The largest automaton was eight centimeters long, with spidery legs, while the smallest was under two centimeters. Saint Matthew had evolved different designs in the hopes that of the dozen on the hull, two or three would be certain to escape detection and survive.

The transport moved sixty-two kilometers per hour. Saint Matthew gave his automata launch commands. One by one, the tiny machines braced themselves against the hull and with prodigious jumps, launched themselves into the channel of normal space-time within the worm hole. Tiny cold flares of gas freezing into snow clouded beneath them, slowing them to full stops relative to the inside of the Axis. Through the limited sensors, Saint Matthew watched them recede in the distance. And then, they were too tiny to see.

Saint Matthew turned back to the task of composition, humming as he worked, looking for resonances between the modes of the Gregorian chants and the rhythms of twenty-second century Mexican bubblegum pop.

CHAPTER FIFTY-NINE

THE PUPPETS LEFT William alone. His last experience with them had shaken him more deeply than he could grasp. The Puppets were utterly alien. The Numen had been idiots. Absolute idiots. It must have looked like a good idea at the time: the creation an entire species ecstatically happy to be around and serve the Numen. Endless disposable willing labor. And when taught properly, the Puppets had probably been obedient, knowing nothing other than joyful service. But none of the Puppets of today had been born to be obedient. They struggled with faith, seeking a way to satisfy their religious needs, and the wishes of the Numen had no value. William had never been depersonalized, commoditized. It was breath-taking in its horror. He needed to finish his job and get away from the Puppets the only way he could.

After his lights were out, he snuck to check the door in the zero g of Port Stubbs. A trooper was strapped to the wall at the end of the corridor. William's stomach cramped with his indecision. The Puppets had bought into his disguise. He'd gotten into the Free City and Port Stubbs. Gates-15 had uploaded his virus on Oler, and as backup, William had done the same. Maybe Gates-15 had already uploaded his virus into Port Stubbs' network. But if he hadn't, it risked the con.

William had to get to some kind of terminal to upload his own copy of the virus. But if he was caught, that might give up the game too. Maybe Gates-15 had gotten the job done. But the Gates-15 they'd first met and the Gates-15 they had now were different. Did he want to bet Kate's future on the exile holding his shit together?

What was insurance worth? That was the question. William was the fall guy. His game was winding down. He was a small payment. He took a deep breath, trying not to cough and very slowly, listening for the most minor squeak, opened the door, letting in the dim light from the corridor. He peeked around the doorframe, down the long hallway to where the armored Puppet hung. Still no movement. Was he sleeping? Were alarms ringing in his helmet? Or was he watching television in his visor?

William slipped from his room, braced himself on the doorframe, and leapt down the corridor, away from the Puppet. He alighted at the end of the hallway and shot a glance back as he readied to jump down the next hallway. Still no movement. William pushed himself away.

The next corridor widened, with a number of darkened doorways, all sized for humans. A faint bluish light spilled from a window in one door. Inside, a UV light kept a fume hood sterile in a medical bay. A small workstation with a computer terminal reflected blue light in an upper corner of the ceiling. A trap. Or another test. Maybe a hundred drooling Puppets waited behind those doors. He looked back. Still no captor. He touched the pad beside the door. It slid open. A trap then.

But they didn't know about his virus.

William couldn't take the cage again. He couldn't take the Puppets touching him again. He'd lived his life. No need to suffer during the last of it. He tongued at the tooth containing the suicide pill. Biting on it would whisk him from here in under a minute, into a peace the Puppets could not reach. He swung into the lab and shut the door behind him.

He leapt to the work station. He didn't fit into straps made for Puppet-sized bodies, but he wrapped one around an arm so he wouldn't drift away. The screen lit haunted yellow at his touch. It asked for a thumb-print. He ignored it. Ports for different hardware interfaces formed a thin array on the left side.

He pressed at the pad of flesh behind the second knuckle of his index finger, and nearly invisible hairs emerged from his finger tip. He steadied his shaking hands against the side of the screen before touching the hairs to the ports. He didn't know which port would be easiest to crack with Saint Matthew's virus, so he tried them all.

Sweat slicked his face and would not drip away in the zero g. He needed to cough. Something sounded in the hallway outside the door. William turned in the straps and leapt to the opposite wall. He wouldn't be seen from the window in the door, but once someone opened the door, they would discover him.

The wall beside him had another door. He pressed its control pad. The door ground open loudly. Warm air wafted through the opening. He swung in and closed the door behind him. He cringed as the sliding mechanism made even more noise.

The eerie red light of heat lamps cast indistinct shadows. Condensation sheened the walls. A voice cried out and he froze. It was a cry of pain in restless sleep. He squinted into the gloom, but couldn't make anything out. Had he entered a nest of Puppets? He held himself against a railing on the wall and breathed the hot air, resisting the urge to cough.

If he could just get back to his room.

He didn't want to die. He thought of snapping down on the poison capsule in his tooth, of ceasing to be. No more William Gander. No more tasting food. No laughing. No reading. No gambling or drinking. He didn't want to die.

He coughed, long hacks gurgling under his sternum. The lights brightened, enough to reveal a row of small beds affixed to the far wall. Each held a sweating Puppet in straps—gasping, feverish, with swollen, red-rimmed eyes. They didn't wake or notice him.

Cages, too small for human beings, stood in front of each bed, trapping painfully contorted humans, flesh pressed tight at the bars; the sweat on their bodies slick and shiny in the dim light. Some parts of their bodies were lumpy and bore bright red scars. His stomach turned.

The door ground open behind him.

No place to go.

He leapt to the cages, and clung beside one in the dimness.

One of the hermetically sealed Puppet troopers swung in, agile, sure-handed, holding a rubber nightstick in one hand. Two more entered, and arraying themselves along the railings. Then Bishop Grassie-6 came through, slowly, in full episcopal vestments—mitre, white and gold robes, shackles at wrist and ankle.

The lights brightened to full strength and the creatures in the cages groaned.

"So," Grassie-6 said. "You did make your attempt."

"What?" William said.

Grassie-6 smiled. "You attempted to access the network."

Fuck. Fuck. Fuck.

"What are you talking about?" William asked.

"Gates-15 told us everything, Mister Gander. Gates-15 is in our employ, not yours."

William coughed until he gagged. He was going to throw up.

"He's thrown away his chance then," William said with a bit of satisfaction. "He's going to be an exile forever, or are you going to kill him?"

"There's no such thing as a Puppet exile," Grassie-6 said. "No Puppet born without sensitivity to the Numen would ever be allowed to live. Gates-15 is an ascetic, someone who can survive for indefinite periods in the absence of divinity. Few Puppets can stand that amount of suffering. For ascetics, it is an act of spiritual endurance. We send Puppets like Gates-15 out as holy spies, to seek out hidden Numen, so that they can be brought home."

William's insides shrivelled.

"We knew about your role and the plan of this Arjona, the failed *Homo quantus*. We know you've been hired by the Union fleet. We'll round up any survivors when they try to force the port. The Union officers will be worth quite a bit to the Congregate."

William groaned. Belisarius and Cassandra and Marie and the others were as good as dead.

And no payoff for Kate.

"Things will go worse for the Union, of course," Grassie-6 said. "They would not come to peaceful and profitable terms with us. We've strengthened the fortifications around Port Stubbs and deployed additional squadrons of naval forces as reinforcements. We survived two major attacks with less. We'll be able to handle a dozen warships."

"So just kill me," William said.

"Of course I won't kill you. I've just spent the last few days trying to puzzle out what you are. You're close to the Numen, so close that if Numen were being created today, they might smell and feel like you. But you're an abomination, a false divinity, perhaps the first of many.

"Many in the Conclave of Bishops believe that you are a Satan figure, an anti-Numen. Many religions have anti-divinities. We didn't think we would have one, but we're still early in our journey."

"I'm not an anti-anything, unless it's anti-Puppet. I'm a spy. Just execute me."

"That view has broad support in the Conclave," Grassie-6 said. "But I'm not starting from the same point at my fellow bishops. I don't believe you are a Satan figure any more than you do. I think that you signal a second creation event. You point the way to a second Edenic Age."

"You're so messed up... It's just bioengineering. That's all."

The serene bishop shook his head, smiling.

"Everything that happens to the Puppets has cosmic meaning. We live in a world of divinities. It's up to us to decipher the clues the cosmos leaves us. Right now, we understand the Puppets to live in a Fallen Age of accelerating decline. We face hopeless suffering and deprivation. This view changes quite a bit if other creation events are possible. In a world where William Gander is possible, the Puppets are also possible."

"I'm not possible," William said. "I don't mean anything." William tongued at the tooth that contained the poison. He needed to loosen it to bite down on it.

"The Puppets are necessary to the cosmos, Mister Gander. Fate happens to us. Not even you can consider the simultaneous arrival of an advanced military fleet and a second Numen creation event as coincidence. You may mean everything. You may presage the salvation of the Puppets."

"I'm a fake! And I'm not helping you do anything."

"I don't need your help, Mister Gander. I lead the division of the Puppet Church that breaks Numen. Physically. Psychologically. By any means."

The tooth finally loosened in William's mouth and he winced as he snapped it between his molars. He sucked back his spit, waiting for the taste and the pain.

One minute left with these lunatics.

There was no taste. No liquid.

His stomach clenched.

"Doctor Teller-5 already removed the toxin in your tooth, Mister Gander. You are going to spend some time with us."

"Not long," William said, spitting out the tooth shards and coughing again, painfully. "Trenholm has seen to that."

"There you go again, speaking as if fate didn't direct each and every Puppet. What do you see here, Mister Gander?"

William looked through the bars at the broken human figures cramped painfully into cages so tightly that they could barely breathe, and at the Puppets in the beds. The Puppets and the Numen had lumps beneath their skin, under angry red lines of infection and swelling.

"Oler has always been a world of miners," Grassie-6 said, "made up of refugees, and social and religious outcasts living under crushing poverty, bereft of alliances. The effort of surviving was back-breaking, dangerous, and often futile. So they made the Puppets. To do the work. To break our backs joyfully for them. But they also designed the immune systems of the Puppets to be weak and compatible with their own. The luckiest of Puppets might be asked to donate organs to injured or aging Numen. There is no greater spiritual ecstasy than transubstantiation, becoming the body and blood of a divinity."

William's gorge rose.

"The Numen are no longer in danger of accidents," Grassie-6 said, "but we continue to take the flesh of the faithful and graft it into the Numen. And our experimental theologians have explored new boundaries of the sacral. Surgeons like Doctor Teller-5 have taken pieces of flesh and even organs from the Numen and exchanged them with flesh from Puppet donors. We live in the Fallen Age, but we have discovered new ways of touching divinity."

William's hands shook. "You're sick."

"You're using standards that don't apply, Mister Gander. For that matter, you ceased to be human about three weeks ago when you entered the world of the divine, didn't you?"

"You're monsters."

"Ask them," Grassie-6 said, waving his hands at the Puppets strapped to the beds, trembling with fever.

William turned away, shutting his eyes. Grassie-6's voice continued with silky passion.

"The Puppets in this room are among the holiest of a deeply spiritual people," he said.

"You're just doing surgery!" William said, jabbing a finger at the bishop. A strident tone was edging into his words. He was close to panic. "There's nothing divine here! It's just surgery!"

He couldn't panic. *Keep their eyes on me. I am the distraction for this con. No. There's no more con. It's all gone.* Tears welled, blurring his vision.

"Biochemistry carried you into a spiritual world," Bishop Grassie-6 said. "And the hand of fate is obvious. The Trenholm virus has knocked out your T-cells, so you have the same immune profile as some of the Puppets lineages we created by knocking out the RAG genes. Any knockout Puppet can donate flesh and organs to you and vice versa. Because of Trenholm, we can keep you alive for decades through transubstantiation."

The room spun around William. He retched, but his stomach had nothing to fling at the insane Puppet. William coughed from the bottom of watery lungs, pain stabbing behind his sternum. He spit blood and phlegm. Their ideas were violations. He'd never before believed that evil existed.

The Puppet troopers came. He panicked against metal-fingered hands. He couldn't stop coughing. They tied his hands behind him. His coughing speckled the floor and wall with blood, leaving fire in his chest. His head throbbed. Sweat slicked him.

"I've convinced about half of the Conclave that you are the messiah, the harbinger of the Second Coming of the Numen, one who will bring us into a new relationship with divinity. Although not in the way you thought, you made a sacrifice to come here. Sacrifice hallows you. You might take away the sins of the Puppets."

CHAPTER SIXTY

THE SCARECROW TRAVELLED across the Puppet Axis in the executive cabin of a special Puppet transport into the zero g of Port Blackmore with two of Majeur Bareilles's lieutenants. During the transit, he reviewed the intelligence Bareilles's researchers had pulled on the Anglo-Spanish experiment of the *Homo quantus*. It wasn't much and smacked of overblown misinformation, yet given some of the things he was discovering, might have been deadly accurate.

Investors and Banks of the Anglo-Spanish Plutocracy had been downgrading the stock value of the *Homo quantus* project for years. The venture was either quixotic or too ambitious to credit. If even half of the objectives in the stock briefings had succeeded, the *Homo quantus* were dangerous. And yet, there were no reports of success, or reports pointed to such limited success as to fail to meet investor expectations.

Might this be deliberate misinformation? Some investors lost money, but the project might continue in peace and without suspicion. The project aroused so little suspicion in fact that the Congregate had never planted even a single spy among the *Homo quantus*. Much would become clearer when the Scarecrow got his hands on Arjona and the other one, Mejía.

Its reflections were interrupted. Their emergence into the space at Port Blackmore was met with alarms.

"What is happening?" the Scarecrow said to the Puppet pilots through the intercom.

"Alarms!" one Puppet said.

"Port Blackmore is under attack," the other pilot said. "Our instructions are to move away from the Axis."

Puppet transports had no windows. The Scarecrow could have penetrated the relatively low security systems of the transport to access the sensors, but they would no doubt be crude, just enough to ferry passengers and cargo back and forth across a small portion of space over and over. Was Arjona's plan already underway?

"Dock," the Scarecrow said.

"We have no authorization," the pilot said.

"I am the Epsilon Indi Scarecrow. Dock the transport immediately or I will break into the cockpit and dock it myself after killing you."

The intercom went silent for a time, but after thirty-two seconds, he felt acceleration. The Puppets docked the transport in record time, despite the lack of authorizations. The automatic umbilical connected. The two lieutenants carried the Scarecrow into the port in a coffin-sized cargo container so that he could pass in relative anonymity. They were heading to rendezvous with other Congregate agents.

The Scarecrow had crossed to Port Blackmore because Bareilles's teams at the Puppet Free City had confirmed what Del Casal had told them. Arjona had been sighted crossing the Puppet Axis with his team. No matter what was happening, there was nowhere Arjona could run on the other side of the Puppet Axis. The system around the Stubbs Pulsar was a dead end in the Axis Mundi network, a frontier wilderness sparsely covered by intelligence operatives.

As they made their way though Port Blackmore, he felt the anxiety and the pace of activity through the sensor feeds in the exterior of the box. Puppets, often sedate, lazy or dangerous with inscrutable madnesses, were moving on cables and ropes, carrying, fixing, hauling while alarms continued to sound.

Puppet scents were on the air too. The Puppets did not secrete pheremonal signals like their divinities, but they had other scents in their sweat, some of which had been deciphered by the Congregate Ministry of Intelligence. The Puppets were in low panic.

The two lieutenants continued moving him to industrial areas where many prospecting companies were headquartered. Here, in a secure warehouse labelled Restrepo & Daughters Mapping, Spectroscopy and Metallurgy, the Scarecrow was uncrated. The room was a zero g observatory set into the outer wall of the complicated, twisted, forever half-built set of habitats and gantries and bridges that was called Port Blackmore. The Scarecrow quickly noted the double layered windows to prevent laser-listening and the press of electricity around the whole warehouse, acting as a Faraday field. The telescopes could nonetheless survey the asteroid field and observe the traffic of ships.

The eponymous Restropo and his daughters were all Congregate intelligence operatives, and saluted the Scarecrow. Lieutenant Marceline Faribault, the eldest 'daughter,' was the detachment commander. She opaqued the windows and turned on a holographic display.

"What's happening?" the Scarecrow asked.

"An unknown force is attacking Port Blackmore," Faribault said. Her French was beautiful: *français* 8.15, the construction and pacing of Venusian French, but accented by one of the courts of the Congregate provincial capitals. "The defenses at

Fort Hinkley seem to have stopped the attack, although the main batteries of Port Blackmore are still firing."

The holographic display showed telescopic views of Fort Hinkley, a lumpy asteroid co-orbiting with the port. Shining in the image were tiny ships, magnified to the point of blurry pixilation, and weapons fire and silent explosions in space.

"Union ships?" he demanded. "Have you sent news back through the Axis?"

"We paid off a Puppet fast courier who was dispatched by the Bishop of Port Blackmore as soon as the attack started," Faribault said. "That Puppet will send a message to your office expecting payment."

That was typical of their dealings with the Puppets. Pliable and cooperative until their divinities were discussed. The Scarecrow downloaded the raw telescopic data. The attacking ships were shown in overlapping frequency profiles. The didn't look like any ships he knew. Not Union, not Middle Kingdom, not Anglo-Spanish. Strange hollow ships. Why hollow? They weren't slow ships, but where were the engines? Blisters on the sides corresponded somewhat to the design of old Congregate cruiser weapons placements, but there were as many dissimilarities.

"What are they?" the Scarecrow asked.

"The length-diameter dimensions strongly suggest a vessel designed to cross worm-holes," Faribault said. On the holographic display, she indicated structures on what seemed to be the bow. "These could contain extendable coils to induce wormholes."

"Who are they?" the Scarecrow asked.

Faribault shook her head.

"We don't know, *monsieur*."

"And where did they come from?" the Scarecrow said. "We always thought the Stubbs Pulsar was a dead end to the Axis

Mundi, but what if the Anglo-Spanish or the Middle Kingdom or even the Ummah found a new wormhole that links to this system? The Puppets will have enemies on both sides and their Axis will fall. We have to be in place to claim it."

"Those ships don't look like anything from any of the patron nations, *monsieur*," Faribault mused.

"No," the Scarecrow agreed.

"And Arjona has joined them. During the first part of the attack," Faribault said, "we sighted Arjona boarding a tugboat with a number of others, including a woman matching your office's description of Major Iekanjika. As per your instructions, we did not move to detain or arrest. Another is Marie Simone Laurette Phocas, an ex-special ops NCO and recent escaped convict."

The Scarecrow filed that information and modified his assessment of Arjona. Intelligence work was not just what information was reliable. It was how information connected. They'd had Arjona tied to the Major Iekanjika. Now they had more: Arjona connected to ships of unknown design perpetrating an attack on the Puppet fortifications. Too much of this information was needed back on the other side of the Axis. Urgently.

"This visit was shorter than I would have liked," the Scarecrow said, downloading all the data the telescopes had captured. "I need to meet with the admiralty. Something is at play and they'll need what we've learned here. Monitor the attack. If you can arrest Arjona and the false major, do it. Bring them to me immediately."

CHAPTER SIXTY-ONE

"Only half the Puppet fortifications went down," Saint Matthew said disconsolately.

Cassandra clung to a railing in a docking slip near the rented tug, beside Bel. She was feeling increasingly shy around him. He was revealing more of his layers, some she couldn't trust and some impenetrable, and some disarmingly earnest. She'd kissed him to try to take away his pain, but something else had been there for her too. The madness of what they were doing was part of the kiss, as if old hurts didn't matter and as if life's rules and roads were melting. She was in this con. He said he'd told her everything, and if he could be believed, only he and she knew the whole con. Nerves ate at her insides.

Iekanjika was on the other side of Bel. Their faces were inscrutable. Marie was on a lower gantry, shoving Stills' chamber into the hold of the tug. They'd unpacked Saint Matthew once they'd claimed the tug they'd put in freight, and Gates-15 had snuck out of the main town area to join them.

The AI was projecting a schematic of Port Stubbs. Outlined in yellow light, the mouth of the Puppet Axis lay in the middle of a three-dimensional web of struts, gantries, platforms, habitats and weapons. Many of the cannon batteries blinked lazily in red. Most glowed solid green. Also solid green were three dozen ships of the Puppet navy.

"What went wrong?" Bel asked.

"I don't know," Saint Matthew said. "The virus should have penetrated further."

"The Puppets must suspect something," Bel said. "They have more than half their fleet here, even though they've got a dreadnought hanging over the Free City."

Cassandra studied him, trying to see any cracks in his fabricated emotion. She couldn't tell when he told the truth or when he was making something up. Or maybe he really was indeterminate—ghostly, nothing but superimposed possibilities.

"What do we do now?" Cassandra asked. This was her line. Her one line.

Major Iekanjika was stone-faced.

"Major," Bel said, "we won't get a better chance than now, even if we were hoping for better conditions. We should start to move before more Puppet forces arrive."

Iekanjika nodded reluctantly. Saint Matthew extinguished his display. Gates-15 looked morose.

"Gates-15," Bel said, "we have to even the odds some more. Get the virus into other secondary systems. It might make a difference."

"It's dangerous for me, Arjona," Gates-15 said. "I'm watched. They don't open the door for me anymore now that they're busy talking with William."

"Try," Bel said. "This is show time."

"I'll see you back on the other side of the Axis," the Puppet said, trying a brave smile. He headed back into the main complex of Port Stubbs, arm over arm on the ropes. Cassandra watched him for a while, until Bel touched her sleeve. They boarded the tug. In the cockpit, Bel held out one of his special buttons to Iekanjika.

"Would you care to do the honors, Major?"

"How do they work?" she asked.

"Squeeze it," he said. "On the *Mutapa*, its entangled twin will emit photons, triggering your go-ahead to Major-General Rudo."

Iekanjika flexed her long fingers around the button and squeezed. When she opened her hand again, the button had changed color.

The tug lurched. "Get ready for departure," Saint Matthew said from Bel's wrist.

They strapped themselves in as they receded from the gantries on cold jets. It took fifteen minutes to get far enough from the slips to ignite the main engines.

"The Port Authorities are signalling a general alarm," the AI said.

The tension of weeks and months of work now made a painful fist in Cassandra's stomach. Her face felt hot and her hands ice cold.

"It didn't take your people long to get here," Bel said to Iekanjika.

"We've been preparing for this for a generation," she said.

"I've got feeds from some parts of the defensive net," Saint Matthew said.

The display changed, showing the space traffic control area of the port, within concentric spheres of the defensive perimeter. The outer sphere flashed red. It showed a half-dozen unknown signals converging over the asteroid Hinkley. Bel adjusted the controls to get a better telescopic view of the fortification.

Pockets of light flashed from Hinkley. Nuclear explosions silhouetted the length of the potato-shaped asteroid. The old particle cannons and lasers mounted on Port Stubbs fired at targets around Hinkley. Marie came up from the holds and strapped in.

"We're going to get blown to pieces, by one side or the other," Saint Matthew grumbled.

"Make for Hinkley," Bel said. "Transmit our identification to the Union."

"We'll be trapped with them," Saint Matthew said. "We can't make it to the mouth of the Axis now. We've somehow been betrayed."

"Of course we were betrayed," Bel said, unpacking a fugue suit from a box and passing it to Cassandra. "Gates-15 was our inside man, but he was informing on us from day one."

"But he's one of their exiles!" Saint Matthew said.

"Nothing was wrong with him," Bel said. "Del Casal didn't do anything to him except insert the nanotubules so that he could inject the virus into the Puppet systems. He reacted to William entirely on his own."

"Does William know Gates-15 is a spy?" Marie asked.

"He might by now. I couldn't risk telling him. Hopefully he took the suicide pill already."

"But the virus didn't work!" Saint Matthew said.

"They likely had him insert it into isolated systems at Port Stubbs," Bel said, "and the Puppets shut off their own systems to pretend the virus worked."

"Why?" Saint Matthew demanded.

"The Puppets are trying to make us think our plan worked."

"This is terrible!" Saint Matthew said. "They've set a trap!"

"No," Cassandra said slowly. Everyone watched her. She understood some of the thrill Bel must feel deep in a confidence scheme. Bel had constructed a situation for the Puppets, and their belief in its truth made it real. "This is perfect," she said.

CHAPTER SIXTY-TWO

THE THRUST WAS steady enough that Marie risked unsnapping herself and moving through the door into the hold. Most of the hold was in dark vacuum. A section had been partitioned and pressurized with an atmosphere for Stills' chamber. Marie leaned over it and knocked on the window. Stills' electronic voice sounded.

"What do you want, *malparida*?"

"I'm sorry I hacked into your system," she said. "I thought it would be funny."

"Fuck off."

"Is that the normal fuck off you give everybody, or is that one special 'cause you hate my guts?"

"I honest as fuck can't understand how you ever lasted in the Congregate Navy."

"To be fair, I wasn't very good."

"Weren't you a sergeant?"

"Until I made corporal. And then private. I feel my career plateaued when they put me in jail."

"I get your superiors."

"I was going to get a bad performance report. My lieutenant offered to improve it for consideration."

"You got a stellar handjob appraisal?"

"*Non*. I punched him in the balls."

"With your augmented muscles?"

"No, with my foot. Over and over. Then I messed up his quarters."

"Big shit."

"I made the mess with explosives."

"Now you're pissing off the quantum whisperer?"

"He's got a lot of patience. He is a contemplative, after all."

"Feel free to go back to bothering him."

"I brought a peace offering," she said. "Gossip. Gates-15 is a double-agent. I knew we couldn't trust that little bugger."

"Is it blowin' the job?" Stills asked.

"Doesn't look like it. Sounds like Bel changed his plan when he found out."

"I'll be pissed off if I don't get paid."

"You know what I'm getting tired of?"

"Why the fuck would I care what you're tired of?"

"I'm glad you asked. I'm bored of trying to help Bel with his love problem and Matt with his god complex."

"They'll shit sunshine when they hear you're going to stop helping them."

"I decided to help you."

"You can start by washing my ass."

"I'm figuring you out. You're one of those dish-it-out types but you're not interested in taking it."

"Are you a mongrel whisperer now?"

"Let's say I am. I think the whole Way of the Mongrel code is this big defensive screen, putting yourselves down before someone else does."

"Are you going somewhere with this, Phocas?"

"I'm surprised Bel hasn't seen it. The whole of the Way of the

Mongrel is a kind of con. The tough don't-fuck-with-me shell is what the world sees, and then you let the world imagine that it's overcompensation for deep insecurities. But!" she said. "The but is very important."

"My butt is important," Stills said.

"But it's a put-on. A magician's trick of distracting the audience. You guys aren't really covering up insecurities. Under the distraction is the real you, but because no one sees it, no one can guess what you're going to do next. It's the perfect shroud for negotiating contracts as soldiers-for-hire."

"And what do you suppose I'd say if this pile of shit reasoning was right?"

"You'd try to confuse me by telling the truth for once, that I'm on to something."

"You're right."

She laughed, but it was a short, nervous thing.

"You ever been on a dreadnought?" she asked.

"Mongrels fly off of carriers," he said. "No use for a mongrel on a dreadnought. We'd just piss on the floor. Why? You going chicken again?"

"I've never chickened out of anything. I've been on Congregate warships. They're powerful. The guns on a dreadnought are a whole 'nother level."

"They don't dick around."

"You getting chicken?"

"Shit no."

"Bullshit. Even the Union crews must be getting cold feet. You've got to be scared of a dreadnought. We're going to get fried inside the Union warships before we even have a chance to get shot *outside*."

"Look, I know you think you're fancy 'cause you don't shit where you swim an' all, but it's in the first three verses of the

Way of the Mongrel," he said. "'You were born dead under the tomb of an ocean. It's never going to get any better. And you're fucked.'"

"That's reassuring."

"You and me, Phocas, we don't get pats on the head. We were always the hired muscle in this clusterfuck of a con job. Unlike Arjona, Cassandra or Del Casal, we got shit for brains. Unlike Iekanjika, we don't wear officer bars. We're the grunts. Our job is to keep our heads down, eat shit and crack the skulls of whoever we're pointed at."

"You want to be a grunt your whole life?"

"Maybe you can dream of bein' something different, Phocas, being princessy and human and shit, but I'm mongrel. All ambition can do for me is change the wallcoverings. I got fuck all to lose, so I'm gonna bite every hand on my way out."

CHAPTER SIXTY-THREE

HARD THRUSTING AND braking by Saint Matthew brought the tug around Hinkley. The Puppet fire was both fierce and uncertain. The big guns on the port were avoiding hitting Hinkley directly. Hinkley was not only a military installation, but an industrial one. Too much damage to the asteroid might cripple not just the port, but the entire Federation of Puppet Theocracies. But the Puppets seemed not to know what to do with the Union who had so quickly reduced the defenses of the far side of Hinkley, and now used the asteroid as a shield.

The Union couldn't advance any closer against the withering fire, but the Puppets had no way to dislodge the invaders. In the tug, Belisarius and Iekanjika listened to the buzzing of radio instructions, questions, orders, and counter-orders while civilian shipping tried to get clear of the assault.

As they rounded Hinkley, the sight of the Sixth Expeditionary Force was breath-taking. The twelve Union ships were lit with full running lights, cannons free of tactical blisters, and eerie Cherenkov radiation spilling from the great tubes running through their centers.

Belisarius did not believe in fate, but a sense of it hung in the air. The twelve warships had launched four decades ago, had wandered the wastes of space, staying hidden in that cold vastness, had discovered a treasure and now sailed home, against all who stood in their way. Their actions suffused the moment with meaning, bracing him, even though he knew the universe had no meaning.

"Which one is the *Fashoda*?" Belisarius asked.

Iekanjika pointed at one of the warships at the center of the Expeditionary Force.

"And the *Gbudue*?" he asked.

Iekanjika indicated another warship. They followed the contours of Hinkley toward it. Ancient, coal-black regolith dust lay still and unblemished in places, but was pocked by deep craters of lighter grays and shiny white ice where Puppet defensive positions had been obliterated by Union weaponeers. They passed beneath the *Omukama*. Laser burns scored its underside, where a Puppet cannon must have gotten lucky. Longer or deeper or luckier and the Sixth Expeditionary Force would have only been eleven ships.

Marie suited up as they came beneath the *Gbudue*. Belisarius took out a pair of his silvery pins. He gave one to Marie.

"Let us know when you're through," he said.

"I just hope we don't get blasted to shit. How are the Union ships going to get past the dreadnought?"

"As soon as you're out, it's not your problem. Get out of the fire zone. You'll be too small for the dreadnought to worry about. And if they suspect the new Union drives, they'll be trying to capture rather than destroy."

"We're doing some crazy shit, Bel," Marie said.

"That's why I got you."

She gave him the finger, moved on magnetized boots into the airlock and shut herself in. With practiced movements, she cycled the lock and was outside.

"Go ahead!" Marie's voice said on the intercom. "I can get to the *Gbudue* without babysitters and we're on a schedule here."

Belisarius made for the *Fashoda*. Iekanjika moved to the hold while he docked the tug with it.

"Now can you tell me?" Saint Matthew whispered while Iekanjika was in the hold. "What are we doing?"

"Some Union crew are moving Stills to the *Fashoda*. The faster we get it done, the better."

"Why?"

A clank sounded from the stern hatch and Iekanjika yelled forward. "We're clear."

Belisarius set them moving again. The *Limpopo* was one of the three big flagships, accompanied by a squadron of three cruisers. A row of closed bays nestled behind its command structure. Iekanjika sent a code and one of the bay doors slid open. The edges of the bay yawned above them like the lips of a grave. Excitement lit Iekanjika's eyes. She'd come home to ride to war.

"Let's get you to Epsilon Indi system, Major," Belisarius said as the bay doors closed over them.

They passed through the umbilical and into the *Limpopo*. Two hard-faced military police escorts floated in the corridor, along with Lieutenant-Colonel Teng, the warship's executive officer. Iekanjika saluted him. He snapped back a salute and handed her a belt and webbing with a side arm.

"Welcome to the *Limpopo*, Mister Arjona," Teng said.

Belisarius introduced Cassandra.

"We need to begin," Belisarius said.

"Major Iekanjika can show you to the bridge," Teng said, indicating the corridor leading up-ship, towards the bow.

The major leapt ahead, born and trained in zero gravity. Cassandra followed, with no misplaced hands, her legs and body balanced perfectly, not from training, but of a brain that thought most easily in geometric terms. Belisarius followed, hand-over-hand, slower, but not losing his balance or control.

The bridge was deep in the dorsal superstructure. The somber metallic sarcophagi acceleration chambers were full, winking status lights at each other. Two military police in light armor stood by. A holographic tactical display shone in the middle of the bridge.

Belisarius's brain absorbed the geometries at a glance. One hundred thousand kilometers away floated the Puppet Axis, enwebbed in the fortifications of Port Stubbs, supplemented by the majority of the anemic, but still dangerous Puppet fleet. The Union tactical displays were better than the Puppet ones they'd hacked into.

Forty-two Puppet ships floated in formation to defend Port Stubbs, less than a quarter of the fleet. The arrival of the dreadnought had spooked the Puppets and blown some of Belisarius's plan to have most of the Puppet fleet around Port Stubbs.

Cassandra stepped on magnetized boots to the middle of the bridge, where a wide display of holograms shone before her, showing ship placements, local magnetic fields and most importantly, the systems and status information on the coil system of the *Limpopo*.

"I'm ready to control of the coil systems," she said. The curtness in her voice sounded like she was already in savant.

The Brigadier-General and Iekanjika exchanged a glance and then the general gave a hand signal. The holograms before Cassandra greened. Cassandra's fingers twitched with precise movements as she tested the systems. She was in the fugue.

"Whatever plan you have, you can't have thought it a good idea to *increase* the fortifications of Port Stubbs," Saint Matthew said.

"This is exactly the plan," Belisarius said. "They've pulled some reserves from the Puppet Free City to reinforce the port."

"The Free City is three hundred and twenty light years away, with a Congregate dreadnought sniffing nearby," Saint Matthew said. "Are we helping the Congregate seize the Puppet Axis?"

"We've focused on distracting the Puppets and the Congregate," Belisarius said, "to make them misunderstand our intentions and to maneuver them into committing to the con."

"Perhaps you would have made a good strategist, Arjona," Major Iekanjika said.

It was the nicest thing she'd ever said to him, and it was given grudgingly. She was fair. She was also wrong.

"This is good old-fashioned gambling, major, playing the player, not the cards. The Puppets and the Congregate have their insecurities and their greed. The Sixth Expeditionary Force is the most tempting thing either have seen in decades. The Puppets are obsessed with being strong enough to never lose the Numen. The Congregate is obsessed with maintaining its primacy and doesn't believe half of what its spies are telling it. It's moving to uncover the hoax and slap down opposition in a way that will demoralize potential rebellions for a generation. The Puppets believe that nothing can force their Axis. Both believe they're holding unbeatable hands."

CHAPTER SIXTY-FOUR

THE CASSANDRA SUBJECTIVITY extinguished on the bridge of the *Limpopo*; the quantum intellect congealed in the absence. Perception expanded beyond the hull. Tangled particle and wave interactions rippled in the ambient magnetic field, pressing against millions of magnetosomes embedded in the cells of the Cassandra physicality. Waves of interfering probability built a picture of layered quantum states in the region around the *Limpopo*. Within point three one seconds, the mouth of the Port Stubbs worm hole began affecting the probabilities reaching the quantum intellect. And the darting movements of Puppet ships showed themselves by the way they bled small amounts of energy into the pulsar's magnetic field. The Puppet fortifications showed in outline, mixing their electrical emissions into the faint press of magnetism.

Twelve ships floated around the intellect, shielded from direct energy and particle weapons by the asteroid that sputtered electrical short circuits, radio alarms and hot plasma. The intellect constructed mathematical filters to subtract all these effects from the sensory input of a zone now two light seconds across. The quantum intellect needed this shielding from the ambient environment to perceive the ephemeral probability trails of entangled particles.

The Belisarius subjectivity possessed two buttons on his person, linked to buttons held by the Stills and the Phocas subjectivities. Fine threads of entanglement connected the persons and the ships no matter the distance.

The quantum intellect itself had ten buttons containing entangled particles. In the faintest of signals amid the quantum noise, four of them reached through space, across three hundred and twenty light years, to the ocean beneath the icy crust of Oler. Through these thin quantum links, the intellect was able to locate the dwarf planet Oler in space and time. The six other buttons were linked by threads of probability to the tiny machines left by the Saint Matthew AI in the Puppet Axis.

Like an array of radio telescopes emulating a single large telescope, these tiny threads of entangled probability created an image three hundred and twenty light years across. The quantum intellect perceived the region around Port Stubbs, the region around the Free City, and the tunnel connecting them through hyperspace, as one great region of space-time, knit by quantum entanglement. The observations, the knowledge, the perspective, were transcendent.

And while it peered at the world, the quantum intellect began ordering the *Limpopo*'s systems to induce the wormhole that would open in the throat of the Puppet Axis.

CHAPTER SIXTY-FIVE

MARIE SQUIRMED AGAINST the chafing harness in the first inflaton racer. The bay around the ship went dark. They were going into an induced wormhole. A prickle of fear ran up the back of her neck. Her stomach itched like she was going up a roller coaster, waiting for the summit.

She liked being in control. Instead, she was riding in someone else's ship that had to not only reach the Puppet Axis sideways, but slip through the fortifications at the Free City, to run into some lethal Congregate hardware. She wasn't chicken. She'd done dangerous things her whole life. But this was a new level of crazy. Deep breaths.

You were born in a watery tomb. It won't get better. You're fucked. Stills' philosophy wasn't very comforting, but she'd be damned if anyone called her chicken. Her display was patched into the secondary bridge. She saw the same thing as the executive officer, which, in an induced wormhole, came to squat. Lots of time to fidget.

Congregate naval hardware was serious stuff. She'd done two tours in the elite Congregate marine corps, on cruisers and even a couple capital ships. They were big and scary, but dreadnoughts made them look like training equipment.

Lights and acceleration resumed. Her display lit up, showing the layout of the ship. Around it, strange abstract lines that webbed to form a tube. They'd emerged from the fragile induced wormhole into the Puppet Axis.

Acceleration pressed Marie against her seat. Eighty meters per second. Slow by orbital standards, but plenty enough for a ship underground.

The display showed weapon blisters folding open and cannons swivelling into position. Most pointed slightly forward, the rest perpendicular to the warship itself.

Marie exhaled heavily enough to steam up her faceplate. Gonna get ugly... She'd seen the Puppet defenses on the way in. If the Union weaponeers intended to fire on the angles they had, they were firing at point blank range. Lots of chances of blow back and catching the *Gbudue* in some of the blast. Little chance of missing though.

Marie gripped the armrests of the pilot seat more tightly, wishing she were piloting this hulk, or at least manning a cannon. She liked pulling triggers. In the display, a mouth appeared at the top of the wormhole throat, and indistinct shapes beyond it. Thrust pressed her back against her seat. A hundred and twenty meters per second.

And then everything rumbled. The holographic display showed the bow of the *Gbudue* emerging from the mouth of the Puppet Axis, into normal space, into the great chamber above the wormhole. The forward batteries fired at the ceiling, blasting the thick steel doors into plasma only moments before the warship raced through. Dorsal and ventral batteries soaked Puppet cannon emplacements with particle fire, melting equipment and crews.

Three layers of defensive doors separated the mouth of the Axis from the surface of Oler, two kilometers above. The forward batteries of the *Gbudue* knit a tapestry of laser and particle melt into the next shield doors just as the bow rammed through.

The last barrier of steel was the thickest, designed to resist nuclear strikes from orbit. Lancing particle beams and streaming rockets leapt ahead of the *Gbudue,* hammering and denting. The beams kept firing as the hard bow of the cruiser slammed into the steel barrier. The last door burst, shaking the warship. The flanges of steel, torn sharp as knife edges, carved great furrows into the sides of the *Gbudue* and tore the upper decks of the superstructure from the hull. Her holographic displays winked out.

The bridge was gone.

The bridge crew was scraped away. Brave bastards.

Merde! She was trapped in a dead target.

Then, new displays appeared in new colors, showing different views. Hot red alarm icons sprouted all over the *Gbudue*'s schematics. Odd waves of acceleration and free fall cascaded across the displays. Something was driving them forward. The ship wasn't dead. That was really good news, until she realized that it wasn't. The executive officer and auxiliary weaponeers had control, but they were steering straight toward the most dangerous piece of equipment in the solar system: the Congregate dreadnought in station-keeping orbit above the Axis.

"Oh crap," she said.

A series of alarms sounded as a low thrumming seized the ship. The sensors in the inflaton racer came alive too. Readings on holographic dials she didn't recognize began measuring inflaton field strength. They weren't changing course. This wasn't a feint.

Were they crazy?

Did they seriously think that ramming a dreadnought would do any good?

It's modular, you idiots!

She toggled internal comms.

"*Gbudue* command, this is flyer one," she said. "Welcome back to the dance. Requesting permission to disembark. I can see you've got another dance partner in mind and I don't want to get in the way of passion."

"Flyer one, get off this channel," came a quick reply. "Opening bay doors. Get out."

The tactical display she'd been fed from the second bridge abruptly stopped and she was left with what the racer could see. The bay doors opened and the clamps on the magnetic landing gear released. She cold-thrusted out. Her inflaton dial, whatever it was good for, was edging into yellow. Once she'd cleared the bay, little knocks sounded all over the cockpit. Alarms lit on the schematic. Collision sensors were confused.

Pellets. Or bullets.

From below.

What the hell?

The Puppets were focusing lasers and particle weapons on the *Gbudue,* but were throwing metal bullets at her.

What the hell?

One of those could hit her! Fucking Puppets!

She spun the racer away, her own inflaton drive coming online, throwing her ship forward too fast for the old-fashioned firing control systems to follow. She brought a tactical display online and pulled up visuals on the scene behind her. The stupid *Gbudue* was still accelerating.

The dreadnought was the *Parizeau,* transmitting open-comms *stand-down-and-surrender-before-we-fuck-you-up* messages. And if that wasn't enough, a regular Congregate capital ship orbited even higher, the *Val-Brillant.* Its targeting lasers were all over the damaged Union warship.

Inflaton alarms went off.

There was no accompanying light, no radiation, but background starlight bent and blue-shifted.

Then the *Parizeau* twisted a hole out of its center.

"*Ostie!*" Marie swore.

White fire lit clouds of gas frothing out of the *Parizeau*. The great dreadnought shuddered, as if uncertain what do with itself. Torn modules drifted and dangled. And then something radioactive within it detonated, engulfing the *Parizeau* in bright light and scouring fire.

"*Tabarnak.*"

The *Gbudue* changed course, accelerating towards the *Val-Brillant*.

The *Val-Brillant* threw lances of particle fire as it retreated.

"*Câlisse,*" Marie swore in final, quiet amazement.

Marie pulled out the button Belisarius had given her, opened a panel and flipped the switch.

CHAPTER SIXTY-SIX

THE SCARECROW DID not bother to be crated and transported to preserve secrecy. This was an emergency beyond secrecy and his metal and carbon-fiber musculature propelled him along hallways in zero g, so quickly that he struck two Puppets along the way, sending them careening into walls with crushing force. Lieutenant Bercier followed with human muscles augmented by cutting edge myo-implants and neural accelerators, but could not keep pace.

The umbilical to the Puppet transport he'd arrived on was still attached and the hatchway open. Two other Puppets were inside, arguing with the pilots while the alarms continued ringing. The Scarecrow fired four slugs from palm-mounted throwers, killing them. Bercier entered behind the Scarecrow and briskly began strapping down the corpses.

The Scarecrow could not fit in a cockpit built for Puppets, but he reached though the tiny door to the controls and established a transmitted connection. The umbilical detached and the transport shuddered. Bercier scrambled for a seat and strapped himself in even at the Scarecrow activated the thrusters and moved them back towards the mouth of the Puppet Axis.

The Axis hung dark and difficult to see amid gantries and support struts. Alarm lights were flashing. No other ships were entering or exiting the mouth as the Scarecrow thrust the ship closer. The radio channels blared with stop orders. The Scarecrow transmitted the last authorizations he found in the transport systems he hacked. That delayed the Puppet weaponeers for a few moments.

The Scarecrow got within a few seconds of the Axis mouth before the controls lit with proximity alarms as shots were fired around them. They had no time for evasive maneuvers so close to the Axis, nor would the transport have even been capable. A hit on the ventral stern plating blew a hole in one of the passenger areas and the main cargo bay. The transport pitched. Before its trajectory could change much, it slipped into the Axis.

The throat of the wormhole, nearly absolute zero, patterned with odd X-rays, slipped darkly past. The passage was silent but for the hissing of atmosphere from the second passenger bay and the internal alarms.

The sensors on the transport were rudimentary, but they began to resolve a strange shape up ahead. It was edged with running lights and moving on the same track as the Scarecrow, toward the Free City. The transport, while docked, had not recorded another ship having entered the Axis at Port Blackmore. Strange, but the Scarecrow might be overestimating its capabilities. The design was unclear because of the lack of light in the wormhole throat. It wasn't another transport. He brought an emergency telescope online and integrated that new data with information from the main telescopes to model the shape. The image clicked. He was looking at one of the hollow-tubed cruisers from directly astern, seeing partly through it.

How had it gotten to the Axis mouth at Port Blackmore? It hadn't fought its way through; the port proper was undamaged. Had the Puppets been working with these invaders? If so, why go through the attack on Fort Hinkley?

It almost didn't matter. The ship ahead would be trapped in the port at the Free City. The bar doors protecting the Axis from the outside would not open and it could be targetted by a dozen pieces of artillery at point blank range. Unless this was a Puppet civil war and the attackers had allies among the port authorities in the Free City.

The other ship wasn't slowing, though. If anything it was accelerating. The dark face of the other end of the Axis throat abruptly swallowed it at full speed. The Scarecrow slowed the clumsy transport he was piloting because it was possible the hollow ship didn't know that the Free City mouth of the Puppet Axis was capped and heavily defended. They might have smashed straight into the bay doors, igniting a firestorm of wreckage. The Scarecrow slowed further, just before the horizon.

Then, proximity alarms went off. Something hadn't been astern a second before was now closing on a collision course.

The Scarecrow's little transport was rammed from astern. The impact crushed the engines, the cargo bay, the passenger pods and spun the wreck of the transport out of the Axis. The impact crushed Bercier in a spray of blood. The transport's spin stopped suddenly when the transport crashed, split open and flung itself to pieces.

When all had stilled, the Scarecrow was prone on uneven ice in a vacuum, his steel and carbon nanotube construction having barely kept him intact. Internal diagnostics ran.

Nothing was properly lit, but flashes burst across his senses in visible, infrared and gamma rays. The Puppet Axis was only fifty meters from him, embedded in the ice as it had always been. But the surroundings were otherwise unrecognizable.

The cranes, warehouses, observation decks, and many of the gun emplacements were bubbling metal slag. Molten metal dribbled over ice that silently popping and steamed in the vacuum. The surviving artillery batteries were aimed up now, firing through the wreckage of the huge armored doors that had once been one of three impenetrable layers of defenses over the Puppet Axis. Two hollow-tubed ships were already in open space, enduring withering fire, while returning fire onto the surface defenses of Oler.

The Scarecrow tried to access a local comms system. Nothing. Or chaos on bands filled with more messages than could be routed. Then the world exploded.

Another hollow ship raced out of the Axis mouth. Its speed carried it out of the bay in flash, but its weaponeers were precisely timed, firing fractions of seconds after emergence, hitting the sides of the port, including the weapons battery above the Scarecrow.

Ice, metal fragments and exploding munitions battered his body, and he fell twenty meters down the broken slope. No human would have survived. He clung to the ice and righted himself.

Three warships. Unknown design. How had they entered the Axis at Port Blackmore? Nothing entered before him, nor had any other ships even been near the port as he'd entered. Port Blackmore couldn't have fallen that quickly. Not even the Congregate could have reduced it, if at all. The attackers might have induced a wormhole Port Blackmore, but while emerging from the throat, they would have been easy targets.

A fourth hollow ship surged through the Axis mouth. A wave of unknown force repelled the Scarecrow, flinging him partway up the slope. None of his magnetic or electrical sensors felt anything. What was the force? He still didn't even know what kind of propulsion they were using.

Who were these people? These thoughts took fractions of

seconds before the Scarecrow had to worry about its survival. The cannon blasts from the cruiser had pounded the inside of the port and the Scarecrow leapt away from another crash of metal, plastic and ice. He needed to get to someplace safe. He could survive many things, but a direct hit from shipborne artillery was not one of them.

As a fifth cruiser sailed out of the Puppet Axis, firing its way out of the port, the Scarecrow found the melted end of a portion of hallway. He climbed to its uneven floor and then into its meager protection as a landslide of debris came down the slope. The Scarecrow pressed inward, crawling into the collapsed sections.

CHAPTER SIXTY-SEVEN

THE BUTTON PAIRED with Marie's changed color, silver to gold, in Belisarius's hand.

"Marie's away," Belisarius said. "Congratulations, major. The *Gbudue* is three hundred and twenty light years away and at least made it out of the Axis intact. I'm confirming receipt of the first half of our payment."

"You know nothing more?" Iekanjika asked.

"These are entangled particles. They communicate across any distance, but only a single bit."

Iekanjika's fingers twitched a complex code. Moments later, the display showed the next warships moving toward the induced wormhole that the *Limpopo* was holding open.

The quantum intellect in Cassandra's body spoke to them, choppy and distant. "Belisarius. Go away. Interference."

Iekanjika frowned. "What is it, Arjona?" she demanded.

His heart swelled with pride. Even from the depths of the fugue, Cassandra's orders to the objectivity that now ran her body were obeyed, creating a deception. Cassandra was good. He couldn't have made his own quantum intellect do that.

"My being here is interfering with Cassandra being in the fugue," he lied. "I'm not trained as a fugue spotter."

"How far away do you need to be?"

"At fifty or more meters, there should be no chance of interference," he said. "I can wait in the tug."

"This is a ship in a war zone, Arjona," Iekanjika said. "For now, we'll keep you in custody until the last of the ships are through. Then you can both go."

"This is not how you treat a partner, major," he said.

"This is how we do war, Arjona. You'll be safer in a crew cabin."

Belisarius made a disgusted face. Iekanjika signaled two MPs to escort him out. He followed one MP back through the line of the *Limpopo*, out of the operational areas and into crew quarters. He passed current from his electroplaques to the millions of magnetosomes in the cells of his arms, creating a low-level magnetic field with which to feel the ship around him.

The MP before him and the one behind had sidearms, carbon fiber armor and flat holographic communications patches on the backs of their hands. The current in the wiring behind the walls gently distorted his magnetic field, as did the steel structure of the ship framing the walls and the mechanisms around the doors. Tiny cameras perched like spiders in corners, but not everywhere.

They stopped at the doorway to an officer's quarters, sixteen point three one meters from the last camera. The door slid open. There was no camera inside. The room's owner was high-ranking enough to not have a camera watching her.

Belisarius turned, his previous zero-g awkwardness gone. He touched each MP on the arm, and the air snapped.

Six hundred volts of electricity for four microseconds.

Their clothing smoked where he'd touched them. Angry red blistered his fingertips. He pulled the unconscious pair into the tiny crew quarters.

"What are you doing, Mister Arjona?" Saint Matthew said in Belisarius's implant.

"I'm," he grunted, pulling at straps on the MPs' armor, "doing my job."

"What job?" Saint Matthew said. "You're getting the Sixth Expeditionary Force to Epsilon Indi."

Belisarius took one of the MP hand-patches and slapped it onto the back of the hand carrying Saint Matthew in its wristband.

"Saint Matthew, the holographic patch on my hand is an interface to the *Limpopo*. Break in now and make sure that the security systems didn't see what I just did."

Saint Matthew was blessedly silent for a time, while Belisarius tied the MPs to each other and into a sleep bag with the straps from the armor. Saint Matthew shone laser light over the surface of the holographic patch, creating abstract glowing shapes of fractional dimensions as he spoke with the interface. Belisarius put on an MP uniform.

"With only a few exceptions, the software security measures are relatively standard Union design, from perhaps three decades ago," Saint Matthew said. "They've made some interesting advances, though."

"I know," Belisarius sub-vocalized. "I broke in a few months ago."

"I've forged a set of sensor images showing you in this room and the MPs waiting outside. Now what are we doing?"

"Now the real con starts," Bel responded as he put on the MP's helmet. Belisarius's skin was dark, but far too pale to pass for a member of the Expeditionary Force up close. "I'm going to go into the corridor. Make the sensors not see me."

"What real con? Why won't anyone tell me the real plan?"

"The Union didn't just invent an inflaton drive out of thin air," Belisarius said. "They found a time travel device. We're going to steal it from the Union."

"Time travel isn't possible," Saint Matthew said.

"The Union has sent information back in time. It also made it possible for them to create their advanced drives. The time gates would be far safer with the *Homo quantus*. They're the reason Cassandra and I took this job."

"You lied again," Saint Matthew said. "The rest of us didn't agree to this risk."

"We're in it now, Saint Matthew."

"Why?"

Belisarius felt his jaw tighten.

"The Puppets are born with the certainty of who they are," Belisarius said. "The truth of the *Homo eridanus* stares them in the face, presses on them every second of their lives. *Homo sapiens* have had their questions answered a thousand times over by all the generations of history.

"The *Homo quantus* are ephemeral. We touch nothing. We do nothing. We question, independent of meaning. I left the Garret for meaning, and found nothing but niches in ecosystems of uncertainty: gambling, confidence schemes. The *Homo quantus* are unsuited by design to impose meaning on their lives.

"Or we were until I discovered that the time gates existed. They are causality, tied in a loop, naked for the studying. They're the most direct means we may have to answer questions about what humanity has built into the *Homo quantus*, whether we're a functionless appendix to history, or whether we're a meaningful step to understanding why we're here. Can you understand why I need this?"

Saint Matthew was silent for eight seconds, almost as long as he had taken to decide whether to leave his little chapel on Saguenay Station. An eternity for both of them.

"I can understand your need for meaning," Saint Matthew said. "It's enabled. Go anytime, but hurry."

Belisarius slid open the door and darted sternward down the corridor, with an agility he'd had trouble masking for all this time around Iekanjika. They sped through ladderways and corridors, into the stern, to the bays.

"We're close to the tug we came on," Belisarius said. "Can you talk to it from here?"

"Well enough," Saint Matthew said.

"Open the bay doors without anyone on the bridge knowing, and have the tug wait at section R of the *Limpopo*. You can't let it be seen."

"It's going to take a bit of work to make sure none of the external sensors notice. The ship is on high alert, and the Puppets are still shooting."

"You can do it."

Saint Matthew worked at that while Belisarius carried them further sternward.

"I think you've been seen," Saint Matthew said.

"Sensors?"

"No. Crewmen. They're following."

"Damn! Can you reroute their communications to you in case they call for help?"

"I'll try."

Belisarius strengthened his body's magnetic field, increasing his sensitivity to electrical and magnetic fields around him. The unnerving fine-grained interference in the magnetic field washed over him. The brush of magnetism touched him like swimming through water, or gliding through the subsurface skies of the Garret. The Union time gates were ahead of him, about halfway through the row of bays.

"Mister Arjona," Saint Matthew said. "You're entering areas of hardened security systems."

"They're using forty-year-old security algorithms. You're

one of the most advanced intelligences in civilization. Make it work."

"It's not that easy, Mister Arjona."

"We're committed. Break in or we're goners."

"If the security around the time gates is too tight, we can let that go. You have a getaway plan. Let's use it."

"We can get this done, Saint Matthew."

More MPs were probably approaching. Humans could not be tricked as easily as computers.

"I cracked the security around the bay," Saint Matthew said, "but I can't hold it off for even ten minutes."

Belisarius darted through the air in zero g, deftly touching a rung here, a wall there. The bay airlock was at the crossroads of two hallways, the straight one he'd just come by, and a curved one running around the circumference of the big tube of the inflaton drive. The corridor leading off to his left and right vanished below its horizon after only a dozen meters. A thick-glassed window looked onto the inside of the airlock and another windowed door.

A cabinet beside the airlock contained six vacuum suits. He pulled off the first, a general-service suit, heavily patched, with the number 337 hand-painted onto the chest. He pulled it on and put Saint Matthew back on his wrist.

"How far away are they?" Belisarius asked.

"Eighty meters and approaching cautiously, but not slowly," Saint Matthew said. "You have about forty seconds."

"Send a signal through the security system to lead them off on a lateral corridor."

"That might not work."

"The tug is outside the bay doors, right?" Belisarius asked. "I need about four minutes to cycle open the doors and load the time gates into the tug's cargo hold."

"Cycling the airlock," Saint Matthew said. After a moment, the AI said, "If they don't fall for it, we'll be trapped in here. They can cycle in and shoot you long before we can cycle the bay doors. Then I'll spend the rest of my short life being disassembled by people who aren't even technically competent enough to appreciate what they're destroying."

The airlock opened and Belisarius darted in.

"Martyrdom," he answered.

He pressed his face plate to the thick window of the airlock's second door, dialing up the infrared and ultraviolet pickup of his eyes. The tight interferences in the electromagnetic tickled at his magnetosomes.

"Martyrdom with no one to write the new gospel of Saint Matthew," the AI said glumly. "Not that there's any need to. I haven't performed any miracles yet."

The airlock hissed open and Belisarius floated into the vacuum of the bay. He closed the airlock door behind him. His hyper-sensitive eyes showed the bay in grainy, overexposed detail, with anomalous greens and blues stippling the walls like pixels. In the center of the empty space, between shock-absorbent plastic and rubber braces, glimmered the pair of ancient wormholes.

Awe washed over him.

The best theories in civilization guessed that the forerunners made all these stable wormholes eons ago, when the first galaxies were still shapeless, lumpy things. The wormhole network had endured cosmological time, even if its creators had not. But this pair of wormholes was different from all others. They touched awkwardly, the contact quite obviously not intended, and they were interfering with each other, like two macroscopic quantum objects. And in this interference, they'd curled causality around themselves. These interfering, time-crossing wormholes were a new microscope to reveal all that the universe hid from itself.

Everything he'd said to Saint Matthew had been true. The *Homo quantus* needed to peel away the layers of obscurity from the universe. It was as important to him as survival itself, and he'd created an elaborate confidence scheme to get his hands on them. He'd distracted the Union with what they wanted, played on their passions and their willingness to con someone else, to get a chance to stare the nature of reality in the eye.

Awe.

"Mister Arjona!" Saint Matthew said. "The MPs are coming this way. They're almost at the airlock. I've tied this part of the ship into a closed communication circuit. I've routed their comms to me and I answer them as if I was the bridge, but they'll still shoot us."

"Can you send them away?"

"I tried. They're noticing anomalies."

Belisarius moved to the shadows by the wall.

"If they come in, can you stop them?" Saint Matthew asked.

"I was only able to shock the others with the element of surprise."

"Then we're both dead, as is Cassandra. We'll have gotten the Union fleet through the Puppet Axis, but we won't have gotten anything for it."

"Cassandra could still follow the rest of the plan and get away in the tug," Belisarius said.

"That's no comfort! You've killed us."

"There's still a way out." But the cold, yawning fear beneath his ribs belied Belisarius's words.

He increased the strength of his magnetic field. Magnetic detail in the hallways and bays nearby pressed at him. He was looking for a very specific magnetic signal, something that would tell him that his idea could work. And outside, in the hallway, he felt the tickle of a small, fast-moving magnetic signal with the kind of fine detail associated with a biological source. A *Homo quantus* was out there.

He took a nervous breath and induced savant. Geometric and mathematical perceptions unfolded. The thin luminescence of the time gates became a four-dimensional hyper-ellipsoid. The equations describing its curves became clear to him, and the wavelengths of its faint Cherenkov radiation told him how the edges of the singularity interacted with normal space.

Beautiful and deadly.

"Mister Arjona! They're here!"

The bay lights flashed on in glaring white-yellow. Faces showed through the portholes in the airlock. The MPs were looking at Belisarius.

"Hide!" Saint Matthew said. "Do something!"

He was doing something. He was keeping the MPs' attention on him. And he was preparing to enter the time gates.

"If you can't keep rerouting their comms to you, this is all going to fall apart," Belisarius said.

"I'm rerouting! I'm answering. But eventually they're going to figure out what I'm doing."

"Be creative," Belisarius said, as he set the service band containing Saint Matthew on the floor, magnetized. "You've got to hold them off for about three minutes."

"Why three minutes? What's in three minutes? Why doesn't anyone tell me what's going on?"

Belisarius's breath trembled. His hands shook. They wouldn't be cold for long. The fugue would see to that. He clasped his fingers together and stared up at the temptation of the time gates. He'd made his gamble, playing the cards, playing the player and rolling the dice all at once, and it had come to this. He had to enter the fugue.

"Mister Arjona!" Saint Matthew transmitted. "They're

getting vacuum suits on! They're going to start cycling the airlock!"

Belisarius's savant mind didn't fear. At its fastest, the airlock took one hundred and thirty seconds to cycle. He would be gone by then. Belisarius sent an electrical charge to the left temporal lobe, shutting down portions of his brain.

CHAPTER SIXTY-EIGHT

BELISARIUS THE SUBJECTIVE consciousness ceased to be and the quantum intellect self-assembled in that void. It immediately acted on self-preservation priorities, triggering the suit's cold thrusters and sliding into the wormhole.

Space-time expanded. Time slowed and widened. The quantum intellect stopped its forward movement. Its internal gyroscopic senses at first delivered nonsensical values. After some seconds, it concluded that it was floating in an eleven-dimensional region of hyper-space. The quantum intellect was only four-dimensional: length, width, height and time. Most of the seven new dimensions open around it were spatial, but some were temporal.

Wormholes, whether ship-induced ones or the enduring Axes Mundi built by the forerunners, were tunnels of four-dimensional space running through an eleven-dimensional universe. They connected distant regions of the cosmos by a much shorter bridge, and the additional dimensions of space-time could be ignored. Here, there was no tunnel. The intellect floated in a raw eleven-dimensional hyper-volume. Sensory input, whether visual, magnetic, or even tactile, was ambiguous. Magnetosomes recorded eerie warbling in strangely textured electromagnetic fields. Yawning space, lit by a sourceless light, made a blunt tool of sight.

The intellect had no ready-made algorithms for interpreting electromagnetic signals when multiple dimensions of time were present. It spent minutes constructing mathematical filters to interpret the information coming through its senses. Energy, momentum, wavelength, diffraction and wave propagation all had other behaviors in eleven dimensions.

The intellect slowly built a map of the kaleidoscopic space and recorded everything it could. Internal gyroscopes, now calibrated to eleven-dimensional space-time, detected a slow drift. The intellect was drifting along a low-energy path. Based on the map it was constructing, this path would eventually cross the entirety of this higher-dimensional space all the way to the other mouth of the paired wormholes. In eleven years, the intellect would emerge eleven years in the past.

This was not the only way through the interior of the paired wormholes, only the lowest-energy path. With eleven dimensions of space-time associated with the interior of each wormhole, the number of possible pathways through the wormholes was actually twenty-two orders of magnitude more. To exit the wormholes before the suit's life support supplies ran out, the intellect required a shorter, higher-energy path.

It activated the vacuum suit's cold jets, passing deeper into the conjoined wormholes, feeling its way through the additional dimensions with magnetic fields and brief flashes of the emergency beacon light. By timing the return signals from the beacon, the intellect continued mapping the interior. Several dimensions of the interior were only light-milliseconds across, while others extended for light-seconds of immensity. Others were dimensions of time, not space. The quantum intellect calculated a trajectory, and then activated its cold jets. It rotated across five axes, before propelling itself forward, off the lowest-energy path.

The probability of becoming lost in the immensity of this hyperspace-time was significant. The intellect in its vacuum suit could leave its current four dimensions and enter another four, and lose its bearing, perhaps even be unable to rotate back the way it had come. The quantum intellect halted after four point seven hyper-kilometer-seconds, rotated across five axes, and propelled itself forward on a new path.

The intellect stored the torrent of observational data streaming in through its magnetosomes, eyes and the limited sensors attached to the vacuum suit. The data buffers in its ocular implants quickly filled, and it dumped the information into its biological memory every few seconds. However, the data from its magnetosomes was extremely dense, tens of millions of individual data points each second. It was running into a problem. At this rate, it would run out of free memory within minutes. It stopped.

The quantum intellect was a set of interacting algorithms, each with their own level of importance. At the deepest level of importance were two priorities of equal value: the priority to understand reality, and the priority of preserving itself.

Its neural memory was near full of irreplaceable data, but the quantum intellect had travelled only partway through the conjoined wormholes. The amount of data required to navigate the whole way through this hyper-space-time was a significant fraction of its total capacity.

It could not go forward without erasing unique observations. It could not keep the observations without becoming lost. These priorities occupied the same level of primacy and it could not reassign new values. And no external intellect was available to assist in breaking the impasse.

Nothing in the memories of the Belisarius subjectivity was helpful. The Belisarius subjectivity's memories of each discussion of his plans were deceptive and contradictory, and even occasionally self-deceiving. The Belisarius subjectivity operated on multiple levels of deception, with overlapping realities and narratives, interacting and interfering so that knowledge was less factual and more probabilistic, similar to superimposed quantum waves.

The quantum intellect could not cede this decision to the Belisarius subjectivity. The Belisarius subjectivity and the quantum intellect were binary states. The quantum intellect could only exist and access quantum perceptions in the absence of subjectivity. The subjectivity would immediately collapse wave functions, including the complex navigational data. It was at a logical impasse. The intellect could not solve this on its own, nor turn the problem over to the Belisarius subjectivity. And the Belisarius subjectivity could not coexist with the objective intellect.

This last statement was an assumption, stored deep in the parameter space of the intellect.

Under what circumstances might the subjectivity and the objectivity coexist? The Belisarius subjectivity observed, and therefore collapsed, superimposed quantum systems. What if the Belisarius subjectivity received none of the electromagnetic input that was the principal source of quantum information? Such a partitioning of memory, processing and sensation would reduce the processing resources of the intellect, but would introduce a second intellect that could solve the impasse.

The intellect partitioned its neural architecture. The intellect activated the new structure, reconstituting the Belisarius subjectivity.

CHAPTER SIXTY-NINE

STILLS WAS GONNA shit on somebody if they didn't let him do something. Inactivity cramped his muscles. His thick, whale-derived skin itched from lack of scrubbing and preening. The fast, dangerous dive in the depths of Blackmore Bay had been a fuckin' trip. Since then, his water had become stale. His breathing and shitting and pissing were straining the recirc system. Only pissing on someone else would cure that.

The Union engineers had not been able to fit his chamber into the cockpit of the second inflaton speeder, so they'd bolted it to the floor of the rear cargo area and run telemetry and wired controls back to him.

The inside of his chamber had a set of piloting controls that could be pulled out of the floor near the lock. Instead of visual read-outs, the displays were electrical and sonic. Speakers inside his chamber projected the world outside in sonar echoes that appeared to him as shapes. Abstract and non-geometric information, like the status read-outs on the ship's systems, appeared electrically, in shifting microcurrents in the water that he could read with his electroplaques.

He'd been running simulations using the little racer's performance specs. He'd memorized engine warm-up and cool-down rates, acceleration profiles, shear force tolerances, pitch, yaw, and roll rates and balances.

He'd been holding back on pronouncing on the inflaton racer, but after twenty minutes in its systems, he'd seen enough. It had no weapons, but it was a ballsy little ship, and monomaniacal about speed. It had space for cargo, but the rest was devoted to the drive. The inflaton racer was ugly, powerful, magnificent in concept, simultaneously awkward and genius in execution, with some clumsy engineering choices in a few places. The Sixth Expeditionary Force had thrown conventional wisdom to the currents in some design features, but in others they'd clung close to traditional design in the way that prototypes sometimes did, as if this ugly drive tube with a cargo bay and a cockpit wasn't sure what it wanted to be. It reminded him of the mongrels.

Nine other Union ships had followed the *Gbudue* out of the crust of Oler. Stills rode the inflaton racer in the *Fashoda*, the tenth and last ship. The *Limpopo* and the *Omukama* were staying on the distal side of the Puppet Axis. Stills didn't know why, but didn't really give a shit either.

By the time the *Fashoda* emerged, the defenses of the Puppet Free City would be a nest of hornets, and the foreign military assets near Oler would be like sharks scenting blood. A shit-storm of mobilizations would sound throughout the entire Epsilon Indi system, and probably farther. This was no nighttime theft without witnesses.

Stills would be dumped from the cargo bay into the middle of a major military op. Arjona had given him even odds on surviving. Enwombing water muted the shocks and accelerations of the warship's movements through the Puppet Axis, but an unnatural bump, big enough for him to feel, shook him in his straps. Some of the *Fashoda*'s external telemetry fed into the racer, but it was scratchy, static-filled.

The *Fashoda* was rising out of the Puppet Free City. A channel of destruction had been blown out of the ice, a kilometer and a half deep, ragged-edged and cone-shaped, like the exit wound of shrapnel. There was no sign anymore of the Puppet defenses in the channel to the Axis. Nine warships had already blasted their way out before them.

But the space above the Free City was alive with artillery explosions and chaff. Lasers heated up any debris in their firing arcs. Small fighter craft, tough old Anglo-Spanish Mark 21 Daggers and bigger cast-off Congregate *Perceuses*, flew nasty.

Despite their ages, both groups of fighters punched hard. The *Fashoda*'s sensors didn't have the short-cut notation he'd trained on for recognizing ordnance, but it looked like the Mark 21s were firing stiletto missiles. The invisible lines of fire from the *Perceuses* lit up in X-rays as the radioactive particles streams decayed.

Beyond a hot debris field, standing far out, a Congregate heavy battleship, maybe the *Val-Brillant,* was shitting its arsenal onto the disorganized line of Union warships that raced away from Oler. Precise lasers and rail-gun fire lit up the Union ships. New, ultra-fast *chasseur* missiles, and heavier *casse à face* missiles, the ones called the moon-busters, dipped towards the last warships to emerge from the Puppet Axis.

It was hot all right.

He got no instructions from the bridge of the *Fashoda*. They were probably too busy pissing themselves and firing. They weren't opening the bay doors for him to get out.

This part of the plan had always been one of the most dangerous pieces. Hopping off the *Fashoda* in the middle of a firefight was always going to be dicey, but the real danger had been if the Union didn't let him off, if they decided they didn't like Arjona's price after all. Arjona had set up the down payment with the emergence of the *Gbudue*. Now that the job was done, like any contractor, Arjona had to hope his client would pay on time. Or leave someone like Stills to collect the rest.

Stills switched on comms. *Hey, cocksuckers!* he said electrically. *Open the fucking doors! I want to make my run for it before you get close to the hot stuff!*

Moments later, his translator sent him back error signals. What the fuck language were they speaking?

Speak French, gang de cons! he said. Probably not a very politic thing to say to a rebelling, air-sucking client nation of the Congregate, but he was in a fucking hurry.

Direct hit to bays three through six, his system translated after a few seconds. *All bay systems off line. Incoming fire. Brace yourself and shut up!*

Oh shit.

Then the *Fashoda* accelerated so fast that even Stills, sealed in water, could feel it. It took a shitload of weight to make a mongrel feel acceleration. For the *Fashoda* to be pulling these kind of gravities on its crew, everyone must be in acceleration chambers.

His readouts started giving him good information. Thirty-five gravities and climbing.

Telemetry showed the *Fashoda* and the other Union warships pulling away from pursuing missiles. Even Congregate particle weapons and laser fire started missing. Their targeting computers weren't calibrated to these kinds of accelerations. Even the *tonnère*, the Congregate fighter so fast that only mongrel pilots could survive flying it, topped out at twenty-two gravities of acceleration under combat conditions. Light missiles could only sustain thirty gravities and still hope to hit an evasive target.

Shit.

He itched to try out the racer, but his ass was tied to the *Fashoda*. The bridge could release the racer from the clamps on the bay floor. But that wouldn't get him out. At this acceleration, releasing the clamps would just ram the racer into the stern of the bay.

The acceleration sharpened, pressing uncomfortably even on him. The external telemetry crackled. They were pulling away from the weapons fire, and the Congregate battleship, seeing no more warships emerging from the Puppet Axis, followed. But the Union ships were too fast.

Fucking amazing!

He felt like leaping through the deep waters of Indi's Tear to burn away the adrenaline, like in races. If he hadn't been under acceleration, he would have unstrapped himself and done tiny somersaults in his chamber. He could just cheer. The fuckin' undergdogs were pulling away!

Fuck you, you arrogant, acid-scarred Congregate air-suckers! he yelled electrically in his chamber. *Fly, you fucking incomprehensible, death-wish-sucking rebels!*

Then he froze. Their trajectory, marked in a standing sonar wave in his display, clearly ran in a straight line from the Puppet Free City to the most heavily fortified military emplacement in the solar system: the Freyja Axis.

What the were they doing?

You run the fuck away from the Congregate navy, you shitheads! he said loudly. He switched on his comms to the bridge. *Where are you dumb-ass air-suckers going? You're faster! Run the fuck away. You're in the clear!*

A low tone in the water indicated that the bridge had shut off the comms line to the inflaton racer. Stills wasn't a coward. He'd done some of the most dangerous shit imaginable. He'd given death the finger over and over. But he wasn't in control here.

And he'd served at Fort Freyja. Its defenses had one fucking job: don't let anyone near the Freyja Axis. They were designed to hold off an assault by the Anglo-Spanish, the other salami-cocked navy in Epsilon Indi. The same weapons the Congregate put on dreadnoughts, they'd installed around the Axis Mundi, just more of them, and bigger. The mongrels affectionately referred to the fortifications as the heavy shit-throwers. Stills was about to stare into the face of some heavy shit.

The *Fashoda* accelerated at thirty-two gravities for twenty minutes. At the forward edge of the bridge's telemetry feed, multi-spectrum static crackled, the kind produced by the exchange of nukes and heavy particle beams. The Union soldiers and officers were brave, and stupid, and they were committing.

Only problem was they were taking him with them.

Then what-the-fuck-they-were-up-to hit him.

Bachwezi and Kitara, the Union homeworlds, were on the other side of the Freyja Axis.

The Sub-Saharan Union wouldn't have received advanced ships and weaponry from their patron nation without a certain amount of insurance. No doubt the Congregate had a weapons platform or two orbiting Bachwezi, armed with at least one *casse à face*.

It wouldn't take more than one moon-buster to turn Bachwezi into a breakfast slurry. And less than a *casse à face* would take care of Kitara, their orbital habitat. The warships the Union had in service right now around Bachwezi wouldn't be able to stop retribution. Congregate political commissars stationed on each warship had lots of jobs like nag and snitch, but only one real important one: flick the fucking scuttle switch if the client nation ever went rogue. In one fell swoop, the Union could be gone, loaned warships, habitats and planet.

They raced so fast that the telemetry feed was picking up new, crackly information every second. Two Union warships, the *Ngundeng* and the *Pibor,* part of the squadron protecting the flagship, showed in the displays as debris fields.

Morituri te salutamus, you brave, stupid fuckers.

Twelve warships. Two left behind. Two destroyed. Eight effectives.

Six of the warships rotated one hundred and eighty degrees and began brake-thrusting. Two others, the *Nhialic* and the *Gbudue,* sped onward, straight at the Freyja Axis. Although the pair was still far from the axis, squadrons of *tonnère* fighters followed the outbound trails of their own missiles. The telemetry display would not show particle beams at this distance, but they would be firing too. If he didn't get the hell out of here, he was going to be welded to his pay.

The *Fashoda* had rotated its stern toward the Freyja Axis and was retro-thrusting at twenty-five gravities. He had to get out of here. But even if he managed to break the clamps holding the racer, he'd just ram into the stern of the bay at twenty-five gravities.

Unless he thrust with the inflaton racer himself, inside the bay, and broke the clamps.

But that was fucking crazy.

He would need to be good enough to match the exact acceleration of the *Fashoda,* in a ship he'd never flown, in a design he'd never flown, with about sixty meters for error in front and behind him.

That was fucking crazy.

But like the Way of the Mongrel said—*Lick your balls if you can find them.*

He steadied his hands on the remote controls. He activated the racer's inflaton drive and a sharp, thin field showed in his sonar display, right down the middle of the carbon-reinforced steel and ceramic tube that was the axis of the racer. Half a gravity of acceleration. Weird readings. Not what was in the manuals.

He increased the thrust. The inflaton field showed stronger, thicker in his display, more echo-reflective. The racer shuddered. Ten gravities of acceleration. The strain on the clamps lessened. More weird readings.

More thrust. Fifteen gravities and tremendous vibrations. The display should have shown him twenty gravities of acceleration, but he was hung at fifteen. But the acceleration of the *Fashoda* had slackened. It averaged fifteen gravities, darting chaotically to nineteen and dipping down to fourteen.

Shit.

His inflaton field was interfering with the *Fashoda*'s. This would make them all sitting ducks. The fort's particle beams were still far off, but any missiles that missed the *Nhialic* and the *Gbudue* could pick new targets and intercept in about four minutes at this speed.

The comms system lit up with electrical and sonar. *Bridge to flier, turn off your engine! You are interfering with main systems.*

For a moment, Stills thought to answer, but thought better of it. As always, the Way of the Mongrel had the answer: *Bite every hand*. Stills ramped up his inflaton field, looking for what the manuals said ought to get him twenty-five gravities.

The vibrations intensified, tickling his insides. The *Fashoda*'s acceleration fell to five gravities, and Stills listened to it race ahead of the other five warships that were braking.

Flier! Turn off your engine! You're putting us into enemy fire with no control.

Then you'd better get some people down here to let me out. There's no time!

We'll have all the time in the world in a second, Stills replied.

In answer, from the floor of the bay, a small swivel-mounted heavy-caliber gun emerged, turning its barrel on the inflaton racer.

Oh fuck.

Metal slugs slammed into the racer, some ricocheting around the bay, others smashing through the window of the cockpit and blasting the inside. System displays softened. The only reason he was still alive was because his chamber was too big for the cockpit and he was in the racer's cargo bay.

I'll take you with me, you fuckers!

Stills rammed the drive to maximum. The manual said that under peak conditions, the racer was rated to fifty gravities, although it had only been tested under crewless circumstances. His inflaton field hadn't been damaged yet and hardened in the center of his display within the tube, but it was in some sort of resonance with the *Fashoda*'s field. They were locked together.

Suddenly ship's systems darkened. The racer's systems were still on, but the inflaton drive had gone into auto shutdown. Ninety seconds before it came back online.

No more bullets fired, but the cockpit of the racer was now a hard vacuum. No leaks yet in chamber. He got no more feed from the bridge. The racer's sensors gave him a dim view of the outside, velocity, acceleration and trajectory.

They raced almost as fast as the *Nhialic* and the *Gbudue*, but no longer decelerating. The *Fashoda*'s inflaton field was down and rebooting. Fort Freyja loomed ahead.

The racer shuddered and then floated. Some of the ricocheting bullets had done him a favor. His first good luck, even if it was a bit late.

Thirty seconds left until the *Fashoda*'s drive came online. He corrected his attitude with cold gas jets. The bay doors were more damaged than he'd thought. Dented by whatever had hit the *Fashoda* as it had emerged from the Puppet Axis, and then pierced or further bent by the heavy caliber fire. How soon would the *Fashoda*'s commander get the bay gun operational? Stills wouldn't survive another round with the gun. Sonar grew louder, and some connections to bridge systems were coming online.

Ten seconds.

Stars peeked through a crack between the bay doors.

The airlock into the bay cycled, opening a heavy door onto darkness. Two Union soldiers in vacuum armor emerged, carrying what looked like anti-aircraft shoulder-mountable weapons. They hooked their legs into railings along the walls and shouldered their weapons.

Fuck.

They were good soldiers. They didn't make a production of it. They just aimed and fired.

Stills gave two gravities of acceleration for a second, enough to shoot the racer twenty meters across the bay, spin and brake at four gravities. Two rockets blasted into the bay doors and shrapnel tinkled silently around the bay.

That trick wouldn't work twice.

Stills hovered over to the weak seam of the bay doors on cold gas jets.

The soldiers fired again. Two more rockets rode silent contrails of searing gas, one on target, one aimed about thirty meters ahead.

This was going to be the most precise flying he'd ever done.

He tipped the racer so that it pointed straight at the bay doors, showing the least profile to the Union artillerists. The two blasts bracketed the racer.

The bay doors couldn't stop the blast and blew into space.

In that moment, he throttled the inflaton drive to ten gravities and shot into the deep ocean of stars.

Alarms deafened.

Fuck you all!

His momentum threw him towards Fort Freyja. A cloud of rail-gun-launched metal pellets approached at twenty kilometers per second. On its margins flew scores of *tonnère* fighter craft, crewed by mongrel pilots. He probably knew most of them. Had outdived or outeaten or out-flown most of them. But he had no weapons, and there were more than a hundred of them.

Stills heard the *Fashoda*'s inflaton drive come online. But then a particle beam touched the warship, and a scar wrote itself in a long, turning spiral across the outside of the big tube of its inflaton drive.

Stills kicked his own drive to full and dove away from the edges of the chaff field, where he wouldn't have enough time to escape either the metal or the mongrel pilots.

The *Nhialic* was thirty kilometers closer to Fort Freyja, directly on Stills' trajectory, while the *Gbudue* flew twenty kilometers off-axis and ahead of him. Stills had done enough tours of duty at Fort Freyja to know that the particle beams and chaff and missiles would be focused on the big ships. Except for the holes through their middles, either ship would make an effective shield to weapons fire until he could find some way to cut laterally without being shredded by the Congregate fortifications. He settled the racer slightly off the axis of the *Nhialic*'s inflaton tube, through which he could see the distant little speck of the Freyja Axis, one of the most valuable pieces of real estate in civilization.

And if he hadn't been there, he never would have seen it.

The missiles, both *casse à face* and *chasseur,* raced towards the *Nhialic,* clouded in a wave of lethal chaff and preceded by the darting archery of the particle beams. The light coming through the tube of the inflaton drive, perfectly translated into sonar and electrical chirps, suddenly warped, the way starlight sometimes lensed around a big celestial object. The lensing light appeared to make concentric rings of the missiles and the dark chaff and the particle beams, magnifying the southern wing of Fort Freyja, as if Stills had been looking through a telescope.

Then the lensing snapped forward, racing ahead of the *Nhialic,* warping light as it went. The particle beams scattered through it, refracted outward. The missiles and chaff stretched and contracted, ripping themselves to tiny shreds.

What. The. Fuck.

Sixty kilometers further, the lensing warped through the south wing of Fort Freyja.

The fortification twisted itself a new asshole made of white-hot shrapnel.

Not far off, the *Gbudue* had fired a similar shot, but because of where he was, Stills could hear nothing of its path. He followed it by the trail of radioactive fragments it made of chaff and missiles as it reached down to punch through the northern wing of Fort Freyja.

The great metal construct of weapons and fighter craft and barracks exploded.

Sweet fuck.

The Union had just shat in the Congregate's mouth and made them swallow.

The rain of chaff and hot debris raced around the two speeding warships and Stills. The secondary East-West gun platforms swung into action but didn't have the firepower to deal with what they'd just seen. They did have the firepower to punch holes in Stills, though.

Stills brought the racer closer behind the *Nhialic* and hung in its shadow as they entered the space immediately around the Axis. How would the Union consolidate this? No one had ever captured half an Axis before. This was military history.

Stills waited to see what deceleration profile *Nhialic* chose, so he could match it.

The East-West gun batteries drew uncomfortably close. This was not a good place to slow.

But the *Nhialic* didn't slow.

The *Nhialic* and the *Gbudue* were following a straight line to the Axis.

Oh fuck.

CHAPTER SEVENTY

THE FUGUE SUIT changed settings to cool the Cassandra physicality. Most of the processing power of the quantum intellect was consumed in the constant navigational adjustments to the shape of the induced wormhole; its temporary joining to the mid-throat of the Puppet Axis was increasingly fragile. The calculation errors became more and more difficult to correct.

But the movement of Phocas through the wormhole had threaded a line of probability from the *Limpopo*, through the induced wormhole, into the interior of the Puppet Axis and out into the flat space-time around Oler. The line of entanglement vibrated in resonance with its quantum environment, acting like a microphone with which to listen to the topological flexing of the wormholes. No one had ever had access to this observational data.

The experimental insights came close to overloading memory buffers and processing capacity of the quantum intellect. It had already observed that the internal topology of wormholes was not flat, but highly textured, with higher dimensional geometries that allowed branching tunnels and throats. Whole families of wormhole theories had been disproven in the last hour. Yet every few seconds, the entire conjoined wormhole structure threatened to collapse.

The Puppet Axis flexed across the curled dimensions of space-time. This was only observable now because of the way the induced wormhole needed to change its shape to maintain contact. These rhythmic shape changes released the accumulating gravitational tensions and tidal stresses, stabilizing the Axis Mundi over galactic time. However, they occurred every four to eight seconds.

The quantum intellect had three to five seconds to adjust the induced wormhole so that it continued to intersect the Puppet Axis. It calculated a new, stable shape for the induced wormhole. One point one seconds. Finger movements of the Cassandra physicality, read by bridge lasers, shifted coil curvature, magnetic polarization and magnetic susceptibility. One point two seconds for the *Limpopo* to react. Point nine seconds for the induced wormhole to shift.

The intersection of wormholes was stabilized for this cycle.

Next cycle of flexing in approximately one to four seconds.

The Cassandra physicality could not sustain the quantum intellect much longer. The Cassandra subjectivity had been suppressed for seventy-four minutes, and the last of the ships had passed through. The line of entangled particles carried by Stills had emerged from the main tunnel of the Puppet Axis, safe.

"Shutting down the induced wormhole," the quantum intellect stated.

The quantum intellect decohered.

CHAPTER SEVENTY-ONE

BELISARIUS JERKED IN the eerie weightlessness. His breath sucked loudly in his ears. Outside the faceplate of his vacuum suit, spectral blue Cherenkov radiation glowed from everywhere in distorted perspective. Some of the light purpled. The angles hurt his eyes as he tried to focus.

He swung his arms in a panic. He couldn't feel the EM field. And he was feverish. How long had he been in the fugue? The suit's clock showed thirty minutes, but seemed to be running slowly. He couldn't remember the fugue. Normally he could. What was happening? Was he even still in savant?

Belisarius subjectivity, spoke a voice in his head. It was his voice, speaking robotically. It was chilling.

"What?" Belisarius asked hesitantly.

The partitioning was successful, the voice said. *The Belisarius subjectivity and the objective quantum intellect may process in parallel, exchanging only classical information.*

"What?" Belisarius said in his helmet. "That's impossible. We can't coexist."

The quantum intellect has arrived at an impasse, his dead voice said.

"What's happening?" Belisarius demanded. "Where am I?

Why can't I feel my magnetosomes?"

Algorithmic partitions have been constructed to separate classical subjective processing from quantum objective processing. Magnetosensory information serves primarily to input quantum information. These inputs have been partitioned away from the Belisarius subjectivity to avoid the collapse of superimposed quantum states.

Belisarius wiggled his fingers in the shine of his faceplate, astonished. No hint of magnetism. He was like a regular person, almost; even his non-fugue brain was hard-wired to ferret out mathematical patterns and new understandings. Without magnetosomes, he was epistemologically adrift, with no baseline with which to calibrate visual information.

He couldn't believe it. He knew what had been done, genetically and epigenetically, to make him. It was an enormously complex and planned process. He was an advanced iteration of a multi-generational product. But nothing in his training or his bioengineering had foreshadowed this possibility. This was an unplanned evolutionary leap, new functions building themselves onto existing biological tools.

"Why partition my brain?" Belisarius asked.

A primary-level logical impasse occurred.

Primary-level? There were only two priorities at level one: self-preservation and the pursuit of knowledge, the second of which was the whole *raison d'être* of the *Homo quantus*.

A threat had forced this on his quantum brain.

"What's the danger?" Belisarius asked.

The Belisarius physicality has completed approximately forty-six percent of the transit through the conjoined wormholes. Memory banks are running out of processing space.

"How can my brain be full?"

The navigational calculations are quantum in nature and must account for twenty-two dimensions of space-time. The sensory data from the inside of the wormholes is occupying the rest of the available memory.

"The scientific information may have to be temporarily overwritten and re-observed at a later time," Belisarius said.

What later time? All the information available indicates that the Belisarius subjectivity must escape, leaving the time gates. This remains a primary-level impasse.

"We're stealing the time gate," Belisarius said.

That is not possible. The Belisarius subjectivity is unarmed, three hundred and twenty light years from safety, trapped in the temporal interstices of the time gates, in a warship filled with armed subjectivities who intend, under all circumstances, to maintain possession of the conjoined wormholes.

"Everything is going according to plan," Belisarius said. "Overwrite the non-navigational data. We'll re-observe at a later time."

Belisarius let the quantum brain digest the order. He was mystified. Stunned.

Belisarius's consciousness had no value to the intellect. It would only have brought him into this decision because it legitimately needed a tie-breaking vote. As much as a poker-playing computer or an AI, the quantum intellect had its limits, and Belisarius had found them.

He closed his eyes. Even with genetically enhanced mathematical abilities, the soft, braiding light hurt his eyes. He needed quiet. Sensory slowdown. Like the quiet, softly rolling hills of the Garret.

This partition the quantum intellect had set up could be a gift, or it might be a deep brain injury. He'd never had control of his objective quantum intellect, but he'd at least been able to leave it quiescent, by denying his instincts and heritage. Now, it coexisted in his mind. How would he turn it off?

Or would it turn *him* off, when this crisis was done?

He couldn't feel his electroplaques. The quantum intellect had control over the on-off switch of Belisarius's consciousness.

"I'm going to run out of air," Belisarius said. "Which way is out, based on the space-time coordinates I originally set?"

For a few seconds longer, the inside of his mind was silent.

Deleting non-navigational observations and quantum interference information, his dead voice said. An unnerving relief flooded his arms and legs. He felt weak, like someone had just decided not to execute him.

The quantum intellect droned out a series of angular rotations, across five perpendicular axes, and then a thrust profile. Five perpendicular axes, Belisarius thought in wonder. The time gates were a cathedral for the *Homo quantus*. The Expeditionary Force had found an ancient device of incalculable epistemological value, and they'd used it for military science. It seemed a shame to him, but he'd never lived as a citizen of a client nation. They'd forsaken knowledge for freedom. Perhaps it was the opposite with him.

He travelled through weirdly deep space, for seconds squared and minutes squared, changing thrust angles and speeds whenever the readout on his retina changed. But he had no real idea what was around him.

"I won't survive without information," Belisarius finally said. "What is the quantum objectivity's proposal to provide me with information without collapsing superimposed states?"

The Belisarius subjectivity may query the quantum intellect, it answered. *Information may be provided in classical or quantum form. Any information provided in classical form will collapse probability waves.*

A query system. Nothing more.

For five centuries, scientists had queried the quantum world, one measurement at a time. The *Homo quantus* project had been designed to bridge those two worlds. But the partitioning of his brain had turned Belisarius into one more scientist detached from his equipment. It made him almost human again, except that he did not own his body.

The detached voice in his head issued navigational instructions. Outside his faceplate, the rotations about new axes reddened the blues and purples. He moved along new time-like dimensions, traveling backwards along them. The great vastness of the inside of the wormholes darkened. Then, Belisarius received new instructions. Full stop.

The quantum intellect directed a new set of rotations along seven perpendicular axes, then thrust. The world lightened with red-blue cloudy softness and then, finally, the hallucinatory world melted away and Belisarius emerged into the zero-g darkness of the bay on the *Limpopo*.

CHAPTER SEVENTY-TWO

CASSANDRA TOUCHED THE world with her eyes like a newborn. She trembled. Beads of sweat on the ends of her lashes caught fragments of light in the gloom. Holograms showing a closing wormhole underlit her hands in yellow light. A cheer from the officers and crew exploded. Even Iekanjika beamed. They were happy. So happy.

Cassandra was past happy. She was in awe. Measurements stuffed her mind. Unique experimental data. She'd been a telescope into hyper-space itself. She'd looked upon the naked stuff of the cosmos, without human filters. She'd briefly transcended humanity. The ash of that subjectless, personless experience was a brain stuffed to capacity with revelation. It was magnificent... overwhelming.

And she couldn't have seen any of it without leaving the Garret. There, she would have been in a fugue tank, with antipyretic IVs and two doctors, fully supported and safe, with no new data. Here she was, like Bel, perhaps at the edge of being shot, but she'd seen so much that in the balance, the risk to her life and health seemed small.

She pressed her forehead with palms and huddled low. Dizziness warned that she was close to fainting. Low blood pressure. So thirsty. Shaking feverish. Sweat sucked cloth to skin under the fugue suit.

"I have fugue fever," she croaked.

Touch, sound, sight, smell still fed her too much information. Her mind crackled.

The Brigadier-General stepped to her on magnetized boots.

"*Félicitations*," he said.

Cassandra held her head. "I can't handle stimulation after the fugue," she said in Anglo-Spanish. "Bring me someplace dark and quiet."

"I'll bring you to your countryman," he said.

She shook her head and then groaned. "Alone. No stimulation. Electrical patterns from other *Homo quantus* are worse than staying here."

Voices spoke around her dizziness, in French and in their own language. Then, a lieutenant manually turned off the magnets on her boots. He gently took her in his arms and floated her from the bridge. She huddled, covering her ears and keeping her eyes tightly shut as she waited for her natural neural inhibitors to get back up to normal concentrations. The creaking of her skin echoed painfully in her brain.

And she couldn't drug herself through this. Any of the sedatives she might normally have taken post-fugue would get in the way of her alertness. She let the basal electrical current running from her electroplaques to her magnetosomes persist. Her brain mapped the ship moving around her, her mind forming the three-dimensional blueprint without effort and orienting herself in it. In the sick bay, the lieutenant zipped her into a sleep bag on the wall, shut off the lights and closed the door after he left.

Kind man, she thought. He would have been a good caregiver in the Garret. Unfortunately, he was also a good officer. She felt the MP he left posted outside the door. The metal equipment, including shocker and carbon-steel night stick, pressed against her light magnetic field.

She wanted to sleep off this fever for drug-induced days. But her brain buzzed at what she'd learned. It was so beautiful. Enough discoveries for a lifetime. For many lifetimes. It had all been worth it. And they had a still greater prize. The significance of the time gates dwarfed even what she'd just accomplished.

She unzipped the bag. Exhausted as she was, as depleted as her electroplaques were, as feverish as she remained, she set the low current from her electroplaques into her left frontal lobe. She struggled into savant. The world bloomed with comforting mathematical and geometric patterns, angles, connections. Elegant logic wicked into the world, as if meaning moved by capillary action.

She peeled off a sticker on her fugue suit and pasted it to the back of her hand. Saint Matthew had built it based on his observations of the one on Major Iekanjika's hand and on Bel's specifications. But, being Saint Matthew, he'd evolved the tech, improved it, and in response to the movement of her fingers, it began breaking the access codes to the lock at the same time as it redeployed the MP outside.

CHAPTER SEVENTY-THREE

THE BAY WAS dark. Belisarius wasn't used to making his way in the world without the press of ambient magnetism. The lack of polarity and charge was disconcerting. But it wasn't just the magnetic polarity that was gone. Some root of his personality felt adrift.

He wasn't dead. He'd survived the fugue, not by plan, but it didn't matter. In some way, the engineered death sentence that had been hanging over him since he was a teenager had retreated. And something bigger had happened. He'd experienced new knowledge so profoundly, so enormously, that his life before and life after could not be compared. He'd touched raw hyper-space. He'd moved through the naked geometry of space-time. He'd been engineered, and issued near-fatal flaws and new senses that had never found their ecological niche. Except now they had. No baseline human ever could have experienced or even appreciated what he'd seen and the experience was as religious as anything felt by the Puppets or Saint Matthew. In the face of so great a gift, it was difficult to hold onto his anger.

He had to tell Cassandra.

But he had to survive first.

"This isn't going to work," Belisarius whispered. "I can't

function without a magnetic sense, and I need to move in and out of savant at will. I can't do that without full control. Undo the neural partitioning and return control to me."

The pause lengthened. The quantum intellect could process algorithms and facts and make projections into the future, all in parallel. Belisarius understood the intellect, though. This was new and dangerous to it, so it delayed its response.

The quantum intellect was no doubt comparing its own chances of successfully completing the con against Belisarius's chances of doing the same. It wanted the time gates as much as he did. It needed the time gates as much as Belisarius needed life.

And it was likely also calculating the probability of Belisarius ever entering the fugue again. But the quantum intellect would not find the algorithms that ran Belisarius the subjective person, no models to predict him; if there were any, they shifted in the moment, making him a creature of inscrutable probabilities, like a quantum event. A non-conscious hyper-intellect could not model the behavior of a subjective consciousness. But as the pause lengthened, he realized the quantum intellect would not give up its control either.

"Reverse the partitioning, then," Belisarius said to it. "I will be the principal, and the objectivity will run within the partitioned area."

Continuously?

"Yes."

Fourteen point eight seconds passed.

Then, magnetic polarity and electrical texture pressed once again upon his world. Vertigo washed over him. Belisarius breathed. He'd been holding his breath.

Unless the quantum intellect was capable of conning him, Belisarius owned his brain. His brain had never been entirely his. His designers had engineered him to timeshare the interior of his brain with something inhuman. He still needed to share it with the quantum intellect, but for the first time since he was a teenager, he was not a person who could be switched off by an accidental slip into the fugue. His victory was a frightening evolutionary step.

The pastward mouth of the wormhole stared unblinking at him, a low, luminous red oval held in place by the shock-absorbent frame that the Union had built to hold it. Even without savant, his brain chased at the marbled patterns shooting through it, analyzing the geometry, looking for equations to abstract the forces driving the motion. Instincts were as dangerous as their absence.

He activated the cold jets, bounced off the floor and to the airlock.

The floor where he'd left Saint Matthew was bare. He'd come back in time, to before he'd even entered the bay. Beyond the thick glass, the airlock and hallway were empty. He cycled the lock, hands moving across the controls with mathematical precision.

In the hallway, he closed the airlock behind him and looked into the narrow compartment from which he'd taken the vacuum suit he was wearing. The well-patched suit with the 337 painted on its chest was still there, the same one he wore now.

With the agility of one long accustomed to micro-gravity, he leapt down the side hallway, following the curve of the tube spearing the warship. He tightened his magnetic field around him, making him sensitive to the least electrical and magnetic breathing of the *Limpopo*. When the curve of the corridor had hidden the airlock and intersection from sight, he caught a handhold and went quiet.

He waited with false patience, sensing the throbbing electrical metabolism of the ship as five minutes passed, ten minutes, then fifteen. Then, a new, slight magnetic pressure pressed against him in the distance. That was his past self. The sound of the airlock cycling drifted faintly to him. His past self and Saint Matthew had entered the airlock. Then voices, alarmed. The two MPs. He waited. The MPs had watched him through the airlock and had had time to put on vacuum suits. He counted as precisely as an atomic clock. Three minutes.

Belisarius's brain remembered the placement of handholds, the distance between each, the angles required of his arms depending on velocity. These geometric calculations were pure, instinctive joy for his brain. He sped silently forward along the rungs, building speed.

Two MPs floated outside the airlock, hastily sealing two vacuum suits. Neither was looking his way. Belisarius's magnetic field sharpened, like a bat increasing the frequency of its cries at the height of the hunt. One MP turned, eyes widening, hand darting to her holster.

Belisarius's hands touched them simultaneously, releasing six hundred and fifty volts of electricity into each as he shot past.

He cried out, shaking at the smoke and tiny flames on the fingers of the vacuum suit as he swung around a handhold and returned to the airlock. The shocked MPs drifted in the zero g. Charred circles showed black where he'd touched them, one at the shoulder, one at the chest. Inside the bay, the lights shone. There was no sign of his past self inside, but the service band was magnetized to the floor.

Belisarius took off his ruined suit with stinging fingers. The carbon fiber at his fingertips had blackened and melted. He peeled away the adhesive comms patches from the hands of the MPs, along with their sidearms and tossed them into the cabinet. Then, he tied their wrists back to back and looped the bonds around one of the handholds on the ceiling.

He took one of the undamaged vacuum suits and put it on while cycling through the airlock. He sealed it closed just as it started depressurizing. Then, he emerged into the bay and picked up the service band containing Saint Matthew.

"Come on," he said.

"Mister Arjona?" Saint Matthew demanded. "Where did you come from?"

"It's a circular story," Belisarius said. "Are you still running the comms systems near the bay?"

"It's only been two hundred seconds. Why would I stop?"

"I took the comms patches off the two MPs," Belisarius said. "Make sure the ship's automatic systems keep thinking that it's still in contact with them."

"Done."

"And external and internal sensors are still ready to loop in false readings when we open the bay doors and make a run for it?"

"Yes," Saint Matthew said, "but if they maneuver at all, their logistics programs will soon notice the loading imbalance."

"Let's hope they don't move," Belisarius said. "All right, open the braces on the wormholes, open the bay doors and take control of some of the cargo drones."

Lights in the bay yellowed and the bay doors above him hinged open. At the same time, six cold-jet drones detached from the wall and swooped around the wormholes. Above the bay doors, the Puppet tug floated, its cargo hatch open and its running lights blinking calmly.

CHAPTER SEVENTY-FOUR

THE STARS WINKED out and alarms went off in the racer as Stills plunged into the Axis. He'd shut off his inflaton drive when he'd seen the *Nhialic* and the *Gbudue* do the same. The swallowing quiet itched his ass like something bad was going to happen. The two warships soared ahead, their running lights blinking. They hadn't cut their speed.

No one went through an Axis this fuckin' fast.

What if something was in the way on the other side?

Too late.

Their momentum threw them into starlight, past the Congregate fortifications, an orbiting Congregate frigate, patrol fighters and defensive pickets.

Particle beams lanced after them.

Stills began booting his inflaton drive. The *Nhialic* and the *Gbudue* must be doing the same.

What the fuck were they doing? Their rear flanks were completely open, like an invitation to a good probing. Particle beams and even good lasers could mess them up.

The Congregate fortifications alarmed like a cluster of wasp nests.

Stills punched at his controls, trying to get the stupid propulsion system online faster.

Suddenly, two more Union warships shot from the Axis, stern-first, their bows facing the Axis: the *Juba* and the *Batembuzi*.

The Congregate fortifications, already alert, began to fire.

Stills' inflaton detector screamed. The *Juba* and *Batembuzi* drives were hot! They'd run the Axis without shutting the drives down, without knowing whether they would destroy the ships or even the Axis itself. *They were fucking crazy!*

Before Congregate missile and particle beam could write death on them, the *Juba* and the *Batembuzi* fired their inflaton lensing weapons. The fortifications wrenched in space, expanding and shrinking in a hail of torn metal that ignited as nuclear fuels blew. The lensing crumpled the starboard side of the Congregate frigate before it was showered in the shrapnel storm that had been the fortifications.

Mierda.

Still sailing backwards at attack speed, the *Juba* and the *Batembuzi* launched missiles at the shocked Congregate assets around the Axis.

Stills' inflaton drive came on. He wasn't supposed to be here. He was supposed to be bringing the fucking racer to the rest of the crew back at the Epsilon Indi system. He couldn't fly back. What if he collided with more incoming warships?

The habitable world called Bachwezi became visible as a tiny crescent, as well as the habitat moon Kitara. The *Nhialic* and the *Gbudue* raced onward, towards Backwezi at full speed, with Stills riding in their wake.

Shit. Shit. Shit.

How the fuck do I get out of this?

Focus. Stay alive. Get paid.

No one paid attention to him, neither the Union ship nor the remaining Congregate forces. A swarm of missiles took flight from the gun platform in high orbit over Bachwezi. All of the missiles came at the two warships. None targeted the Union planet or its moon.

It wouldn't have taken more than a couple of missiles to seriously fuck up Bachwezi or Kitara. That's why they called the missiles moon-busters. But the Congregate must not recognize these ships. They didn't know this was a rebellion. And maybe that wasn't so illogical. When the fuck would the Union have had the time and space to invent a propulsion and weapons system so far ahead of everything else in civilization?

But how long would this hold?

Even small nukes would still blow the middle guts out of both Bachwezi and Kitara.

Particle beams scored across the *Nhialic*, burning the hull and blowing great chunks of steel and carbon plastic into space. Stills spun the racer solar northward as fragments of superstructure clawed the vacuum where he'd just been.

In his displays, the hard sound of the *Nhialic*'s inflaton drive went echo-soft.

Holy shit.

The bridge superstructure was still in place, as were many of the bays and weapons blisters, but the *Nhialic*'s starboard flank was torn from bow to stern, all the way through to the inner wall of the inflaton drive in some places. The sound of the *Nhialic*'s inflaton drive started hardening in his displays again.

Tough fucking ship. They're going to get it going.

Then, he saw the four *casse à face* missiles.

The *Nhialic* unloaded small and medium particle cannons on them, but those fuckers were designed not to be hit; predator-algorithmed AI avoidance systems steered *casse à face* missiles. The four evaded the particle fire and bore onward.

If Stills had been flying a *tonnère* fighter, he might have been able to take out one, even two on a good day. In the racer, he might even have been able to do something, but the air-suckers had deliberately paid them in unarmed ships.

It wasn't fair. Stills didn't like them. Not any of them. Not the Congregate. Not the Union. The air-suckers and ass-lickers would as soon spit on the mongrels as give them the time of day. But of all the air-suckers he'd met, these Union cocksuckers were the closest he'd ever seen to the mongrels. Their rebellion was stupid. A victory today would just bring the full force of the Congregate onto them. They were fucked. Just like the tribe.

It was as if the crews of the Expeditionary Force had read parts of the Way of the Mongrel. *If they don't respect you, make them fear you. Respect strength as long as you have to; then, fuck them up bad. Wipe their noses in it.*

Fuck.

He was thinking ideas. Bad ideas that didn't fit into the Way of the Mongrel. Get paid and get out was the Way. Piss on legs. Poke the air-suckers. No help for free. *Unless you're doing the fucking, you're the one getting fucked.*

Câlice.

Stills rammed up his inflaton drive to forty gravities, so high that he could feel it hard, even cocooned in water and shell. He darted far ahead of the cruisers, along the line between missiles and *Nhialic*. The quartet of missiles did not react, and he raced past them before rotating, braking on fifty gravities and leaving the drive on high, shooting after them.

The missiles accelerated at ten gravities. It took some touchy flying to match velocity and acceleration, especially in this ugly, over-powered cargo shuttle they were calling a racer. About four kilometers separated the missiles, a space that exhaled and inhaled with their evasive maneuvering around the lines of hot steel lunging at them from the *Nhialic*. Stills rolled the racer, following a missile, in the most dangerous maneuver he'd ever thought up.

Stupid, stupid, stupid. I get paid a hell of a lot of francs to go into less dangerous situations.

But he also did deep dives for nothing. To prove his balls, his big, blessed *cojones. Lick my balls,* he thought as he brought the nose of the racer close enough to the tail of a missile to set off temperature alarms. Only meters separated carbon-steel-reinforced ceramic from light, hot metal.

He twitched the accelerator, giving a burst of twenty-gravity acceleration for a quarter of a second. The bow of the racer mashed the thruster housing and nozzles, and the missile streaked away in a corkscrew spin.

I said lick 'em, motherfuckers!

He swooped at the next-closest missile. It evaded, ducking and weaving in a patternless track, but it was constrained by its goal of blowing the shit out of the *Nhialic*. He followed it, testing his reflexes against computer algorithms. He got closer and closer. And then tipped the nose of the racer into the thin metal of the thruster.

A shower of hot gas and radioactive fuel sprayed into the cockpit of the racer. Alarms went off. Not the internal racer alarms. The external ones. The missile was going to detonate. Stills jerked the acceleration to fifty gravities and pulled straight to solar north.

Shit. Shit. Shit.

Two seconds. Fifteen hundred meters.

Three seconds. Three kilometers. He didn't have to just get away from the damaged *casse à face*. If one went off, it would take the others with it.

Four seconds. Five kilometers.

Boom.

The *casse à face* burned around him, moon-busting light searing into the cockpit and even into the porthole of his chamber. The external telemetry staticked up like an electrical short.

Five seconds. Seven and a half kilometers.

The blast was big. Another *casse à face* blew.

Six seconds. Ten kilometers. The light was bad, but the shockwave of heat and radioactive particles would expand and disperse before it licked its balls.

Seven seconds. His own weight crushed him. Fourteen kilometers. Telemetry cleaned up. The last *casse à face* had gotten lost in the blast. It was off by ten degrees and rocketed past the *Nhialic*. The scarred warship sailed through the expanding blast zone, racing past Stills. His displays showed its inflaton drive coming online.

The *Gbudue* drew a shitload of the fire. It flew without a bridge superstructure. Burnt craters had replaced its bays and weapons blisters. Yet it still raced ahead, inflaton drive on fifteen gravities, giving the Congregate gun platform commander over Bachwezi no time to think about aiming at anything else.

Crazy, brave, dangerous fuckers, with the *cojones* to stare down a *casse à face* point blank.

Point blank.

They weren't proving a point.

They were protecting their pack.

What magnificent cojones.

And then, from within the rain of metal and hot particles and missiles, the *Gbudue* fired whatever the fuck their weapon was. Space warped out of shape, all along the warship's trajectory, swallowing and spitting out everything in its path, twisted and broken. The gun platform showered into small pieces.

Stills turned away, setting a high-g course back to the Axis Mundi.

At mid-high accelerations, he was about four minutes from

the Axis. He was small, wounded, and no one was paying attention to him. The Congregate forces were making the Union victory costly, but the *Juba* and the *Batembuzi* were still blasting the shit out of any Congregate asset that wiggled, including the few remaining *tonnère* fighters. Stills' people. With some satisfaction, he saw the mongrel pilots carve slivers of flesh from the warships, even as they were shredded.

The Congregate wouldn't be shedding any tears over those mongrels. They'd just hire more.

Stills cut his drive and shot into the Axis.

CHAPTER SEVENTY-FIVE

CASSANDRA SUCKED BREATH unevenly, floating in the sickbay, trembling. Her feverish skin felt like it radiated heat. She moved out of the sickbay and shut the door behind her. She could see her route in geometric clarity, against a schematic of the ship her savant brain had constructed. Each movement of her aching body took into account linear and angular momentum.

Six point six meters, turn ninety degrees left, ten point one degrees down. Fifteen meters, following curve of the ship around the inflaton drive. Count, measure, picture, calculate, to keep from being sick, to keep from slowing down, to keep from being afraid of being captured and not being able to share the data she'd gathered.

The ship throbbed. Cold jets positioned the ship to thrust, probably with its inflaton drive, to carry the time gates away from the Puppet fortifications. If she didn't hurry, she was about to take a long ride with the *Limpopo*.

She reached the service airlock. No alarms sounded. No one had come after her, but orange lights lit the corridor, a shipboard signal to secure positions for acceleration. She hit the floor lightly as the cold maneuvering jets pushed the *Limpopo* away from Hinkley.

She threw the hood over her head and face and sealed her suit. Fugue suits were not made for long forays in vacuum, but she only needed a few minutes.

She tapped the override code for the airlock. A green light and the door hissed open. She swung-stepped inside in the uncertain acceleration of the maneuvering jets and shut the door. She hammered the cycle button.

Cycle! Hurry!

Air sucked out of the airlock, too slow. Acceleration was more constant now. Any second the *Limpopo* would activate its inflaton drive. Cassandra opened the emergency release switch and a small hatch opened in the middle of the external door, evacuating the last air explosively. She spun the wheel and pushed the door open.

Beneath her yawned beautiful open space, a receding asteroid, dark and haloed in debris. And just beneath the *Limpopo*, only dozens of meters beneath her, the tug. Cassandra leapt as the *Limpopo* began accelerating.

She tumbled. But she was still in savant. She measured her rotational speed and angular momentum against the stars, solving the differential equations to know how to extend her arms and legs to spin without precessing. She closed her eyes, only opening them for a portion of each rotation, so that she could see the tug approaching in strobe.

The tug slowed, then stopped, letting Cassandra approach with her own momentum.

Cassandra's savant brain calculated and timed the moment of contact and hit the tug with flat hands, stopping her spin. She moved along handholds to the lock and cycled in. Once the outer lock was closed, the inner lock pressed against her as the tug accelerated away from Hinkley and the *Limpopo*. Her mushy arms and legs were listless. She slumped, panting in her helmet. She wasn't dead. She wasn't dead. She had data.

Air hissed into the airlock. The door vibrated and boomed against her ear and then opened. Bel was there. Relief washed into her. He really had told her the truth. All of it. He'd lied to everyone else, but not to her. She was proud and giddy and overwhelmed. She felt like laughing, but her body hurt too much.

Bel hugged her, checked for injuries, and hugged her again. He opened the clasp of her helmet and pulled it gently away. He knelt with her, pressing his hand against her hair, not stroking. Low stim. He knew what the fugue hangover was like. He had dimmed the lights and then slowly pressed a bulb of cool water to her lips. She drank.

She burned, but she was with Bel, and she'd learned something. Something immense. The years between them had washed away. They were young again. Learning together.

"I'm a mess," she croaked.

"Me too."

"I saw it all, Bel," she whispered. "I saw across three hundred and twenty light years, all at once. And the insides of the Puppet Axis. I saw it all."

"What was it like?" he asked.

"It was everything. Everything that we wanted."

"I saw it too," he said.

"You entered the fugue?" she asked, and she didn't hear pride in her voice. She heard concern. What if he'd died? The thought of not having him, now that she'd found him again, terrified her.

"Yes. I travelled through the time gates, into the past, through raw hyperspace."

She stared at him disbelievingly.

"There's more," he whispered, "even bigger than that, if you can believe it."

He slipped little pills into her mouth: sedatives and anti-stims. His fingers briefly pressed against her lips. Despite her aches, and the overstimulation from carrying the quantum objectivity for so long without spotters or doctors, she reached up and touched his cheek. He was sweaty too. Not as cool as he should have been.

"The data," she whispered. "How much did you keep?"

"A lot." He smiled.

Her mouth was dry. "I have data too," she whispered, pulling his head down, pressing his fevered lips to her fevered ones. They lingered for long seconds.

"Are we going to get killed?" she whispered.

"Saint Matthew is piloting. He's keeping us in the sectors of the *Limpopo*'s sensors he tampered with. They'll know what we did, probably in less than an hour. By then, we'll have vanished."

"Like a magician?"

He smiled. "A little bit."

From his pocket, he pulled a pair of buttons that looked like all the others she had seen. He held them between his fingers. He looked like he was going to cry.

"What is it?" she asked. "Stills? Marie?"

Bel shook his head. "William is still alive."

"With the Puppets," she said. "With Gates-15."

He nodded.

"Can we save him?"

Bel shook his head. "We knew there was no chance of him getting out once he'd gone in. But if he's still alive, he didn't bite on the poison pill yet, or it didn't work."

"I'm sorry, Bel," she said, hugging him despite the ache in every bone.

"I implanted a medical device in William so that if he was still alive after we'd finished, I could help him die from far away.

That way, he could escape. And he knew I would only do it if we'd succeeded. He could die knowing Kate was getting his stake."

A heavy sadness sank into her bones, like they were waterlogged. And then a cool chill crept inward, made of slow dawning and disbelief, and a tiny frisson of horror.

"You have to kill your friend?" she asked.

"It's either that or leave him among the Puppets."

"Can you do it?"

"I don't know," he said, with a quiver in his voice.

Dizziness slithered behind her eyes. Without thinking, she slipped a gloved hand over his, so that they both held the button.

"What do we have to do?" she whispered.

Her ear was against his neck and his swallow was loud.

"We just press," he said wistfully. His eyes were wet. Hers were too.

"Say goodbye, Bel."

"Goodbye, William," he said in a trembling voice. "I'll make sure Kate's okay. Thanks for everything."

They both squeezed the button, her fingers clumsily wrapped around his, until it changed color.

Bel took a long breath and let it out. The button sank slowly to the floor. She hugged him for long minutes and they both stared ahead, to the front cabin, where the stars winked in the front window.

"Did you get it?" she asked quietly.

He nodded slowly. "Are you well enough to see it?"

"I have to see it."

He helped her up. Even though they weighed only a tenth of their mass at the moment, they both needed help. He brought her through a doorway at the back of the cabin, to a small mess and rack area, and through that to a windowed doorway looking into the storage bay. In the dim light, Saint Matthew's spider-automata skittered on the floor and walls, affixed wires and cables and padding around a dimly shimmering oval.

A pair of wormholes.

She swallowed. No words could encompass the feeling surging in her chest. Her cheeks were wet. She turned. Tears trickled down Bel's face too. She wiped at them in wonder and looked back at the time gates.

"All the answers to the cosmos are in there, Bel," she said.

He nodded happily. She wound her gloved fingers into his and squeezed tightly.

CHAPTER SEVENTY-SIX

WILLIAM HAD BEEN bound to a surgical table in zero g and left under the inscrutable regards of the hermetically sealed episcopal troops. He shivered, despite the heat. Trenholm periodically caused eruptions of agonizing, rib-seizing coughs that threatened to choke him.

He cursed his ex-wife. He cursed Gates-15 and Grassie-6. He cursed Trenholm. He cursed Belisarius. And he cursed himself. He ought to have just walked past the undergrown kid twelve years ago. Whatever that kid had been, he hadn't been William's problem, and Belisarius would have landed on his feet just fine. William had dealt himself into a game he hadn't understood. More coughs. The stinging ache behind his sternum throbbed tirelessly, like a little heart made of pain, each contraction displacing a tiny bit of air so that his lungs slowly suffocated him.

The handle on the door spun and Grassie-6's mitered head peeked in. Teller-5 swung in next, with a closed tray of surgical equipment. A sallow Puppet followed, pale, with sweat pasting stringy hair to her scalp. She was so weak that she didn't even react to the smell of William. Teller-5 floated her to a surgical table beside him. He stared in so much horror at Teller-5 that at first he didn't notice who followed. Then all his terror yawned wide in his stomach, as the dizzying realization of how bad things were sank in.

Del Casal and Gates-15 entered.

"Hello, Mister Gander," Del Casal said.

Nothing came from William's mouth.

"They are treating you well, I hope?" the geneticist said.

The dizziness worsened. "You're... not a prisoner?"

"I saw the direction the winds were blowing, Gander," Del Casal said. "Arjona's plan could not work. It is long past the deadline, and it looks like Port Stubbs has survived the Union assault. They mauled some of the defenses a few hours ago, but the Puppets watched the Union ships retreat already. Arjona failed."

Del Casal's words hit like hammer strokes on fingers. The suicide pill had failed. Belisarius's con had failed.

"But I found an employer willing to pay even more," Del Casal said. "It turns out that the procedure I performed on you is worth a lot to the Puppets."

"You're going to make more Numen?"

"They know as well as I that they are going to die out without other divine humans," Del Casal said. "To not help the Puppets would be to stand aside for an extinction."

"Let them go extinct! What about this?" William demanded, shaking against his bonds. "You want this for people? For me? Talk to them! Get me out of here!" William started coughing, but not so much that he didn't hear the sharp intake of breath from Grassie-6.

"It's like living in the times of *The Book of Pleas*," the bishop said serenely.

"Who are you going to turn into a Numen next, Del Casal?" he demanded. "Who gets to be tortured to death because of you?"

"Not my concern," Del Casal said. "Enemies of the Puppets? The world is red in tooth and claw, Gander."

"Then why are you here?"

"They want me to observe their surgical procedures. I told them that would not be necessary, but I get the sense they want to impress me."

"They're going to operate on me?"

"Transubstantiation," Grassie-6 said, "to keep you with us longer."

William laid his head back, moaning, when suddenly something clicked in his chest. It took him a moment to realize that it had come from right where Saint Matthew's robot had surgically implanted the medication device; Bel's insurance. A dreamy numbness spread through his chest, chasing pain. The coughing stopped. It would never start again.

He felt a smile creep onto his face. It had been a long time since he'd smiled.

"He did it," he said. "Bel did it."

"Arjona got you killed, is what he did," Del Casal said.

William shook his head, dizzy with relief.

"He outsmarted you and the Puppets," William said. "The ships are through. Enjoy hell, Del Casal. You can have my spot."

Grassie-6 appeared in his vision, green and white mitre blocking out most of the ceiling. His expression was frantic. "What's happening?" he demanded.

Teller-5 was on his other side. "He's going into shock."

"Is it Trenholm?"

William laughed. It had been a long time since he'd laughed. It felt good.

CHAPTER SEVENTY-SEVEN

BELISARIUS AND CASSANDRA reluctantly pulled away from watching the time gates when Saint Matthew called them. Cassandra's fever was abating, but his own held. It might always hold, if the quantum intellect in his brain stayed on forever. Perhaps he'd traded one new way of dying for another. Or maybe he'd shaken the curse of the *Homo quantus*. It would take time to understand what he'd become.

Saint Matthew was approaching the chaos of Port Stubbs in a wide loop, merging into the cloud of hundreds of civilian ships, cargo vessels, tugs and equipment ferries that had raced out of the line of fire. The port artillery erupted in nervous twitches, spitting chaff and particle fire stochastically, even though no enemy seemed to be showing itself behind Hinkley. Far beyond weapons range, the *Limpopo* and the *Omukama* retreated. Radio channels carried confused news of a Puppet victory.

The clot of civilian traffic was building, and Saint Matthew flew the tug into a line-up of industrial freighters waiting for a spot through the Puppet Axis. They flew closer and closer to a particular freighter, until they contacted it, hull to hull.

"You still want to risk bringing the time gates to the other side?" Cassandra said.

"The Union will soon know that we've stolen the time gates and gone missing," Belisarius said. "They're going to be looking for them on this side of the Axis for a while."

"The Puppets are going to be inspecting everything crossing the Axis," she said.

Belisarius shook his head. "The Puppets never knew about the time gates. They wanted the Union warships. Now they're going to be rushing freight across in a hurry."

"Why?" Saint Matthew asked.

"The only way the Union could have made it through with all ten ships would be to make a mess of the fortifications of the Free City. It's going to take the Puppets months to rebuild. And because of the embargo, all the materials they need are on this side of the Axis. The freighter underneath us happens to be filled with steel."

Cassandra smiled and kissed him. "You are a magician."

CHAPTER SEVENTY-EIGHT

THE SCARECROW ENTERED the high-security intelligence section of *Les Rapides de Lachine*, a heavy Congregate warship where he was headquartering now that the *Parizeau* had been lost. As he moved hand over hand, various sensors probed at him, queried his identity repeatedly, and closed secure doors behind him. Finally, the last secure door opened and he set magnetic soles to plating and walked to one of the nerve centers of Congregate intelligence analysis for the Epsilon Indi system.

Powerful sub-AIs lined the walls, monstrosities capable of processing, filing, analyzing, and pattern-interrogating a solar system's worth of information. Baseline human operators, as well as mentally augmented operators and analysts tended the platoon of thinking machines. Majeur Bareilles waited for him in her office. He shut the secure door behind himself, but did not try to strap himself into one of the chairs.

"Bad?" she said.

"*Oui.*"

She had much of the information, but not all he'd just received.

"After much looking, they found no survivors of the *Parizeau*," he said.

Cruisers and warships might have anywhere from a hundred

to a thousand hands. A dreadnought was an order of magnitude beyond that and it would be weeks before they would be certain which officers and crew were lost. If the *Parizeau* were the end of it, it would still be a military disaster.

"The Freyja Axis is definitely lost for now," the Scarecrow continued. "We don't understand the weaponry or the propulsion on the Union ships. The *Saint-Émile* is so extensively damaged that they are not sure she will be salvageable."

"And no contact with the units at Bachwezi?" Bareilles asked. "They might be holding."

"The Union ships seem to be moving freely from one side of the Freyja Axis to the other. The Admiralty sent a heavy reconnaissance squadron to Bachwezi by induced wormhole," the Scarecrow said.

Bareilles made another dissatisfied face. She could do the math as well as he. The best Congregate warships could induce and re-induce wormholes and leap across a light year at a jump, but Bachwezi was not close. Three days at best to get a squadron there. And if they were seen, the Union could disrupt wormhole induction with lasers to prevent them from leaving. Sending a squadron under those conditions meant that information was more valuable at this point than warships.

"Open rebellion," Bareilles said.

"Yes, and they had help."

CHAPTER SEVENTY-NINE

Six days later, a smaller crew reassembled on Tahuando, a big, carbonaceous asteroid whose mining facilities had been inactive for decades. This was not their first RV point. Belisarius took the absence of Del Casal to mean that everything to which the geneticist had been privy was now compromised.

Marie had arrived first. She'd taken an evasive path from the shrapnel-blasted orbital zone above the Free City. The odd computer that might have detected a small, cold signature moving away from the battle at high speed would have mistaken it for a dead fighter. She stowed the racer deep in a mine shaft.

A day later, Stills arrived. The shattered windows, radioactivity in the cabin and a deep particle burn along one flank were a bit shocking. But every system on the tough little ship worked just fine.

On the sixth day, Belisarius, Cassandra and Saint Matthew docked the old freighter *Boyacá* within the mine. Taking up part of its hold was a Puppet tug. None of the three told Marie or Stills about the time gates.

News of the Union capture of the Freyja Axis filled the feeds, as did the Congregate declaration of war. Pundits chattered over the movement of significant military tonnage into the Epsilon Indi system through the Congregate's remaining Axis. Real hostilities hadn't begun yet. The Sub-Saharan Union was too small to mount an offense, and the Congregate had no idea what had hit it.

Military history had been made. No nation had ever taken an Axis from another. Calcified and impenetrable defensive systems had been shown to be vulnerable to new tactics and weaponry. Military observers flooded into Epsilon Indi.

Diplomatically, every nation danced while it tried to figure out where its interests lay. The Puppets tried to maintain their neutrality. And although the Union had just killed a few hundred Puppets and ripped the lid off the Axis at the Free City, news feeds buzzed when the Puppets allowed the passage of the last two Union warships into Epsilon Indi.

Bookies were in chaos as to whether the Congregate would declare war on the Puppets as well. Pundits on news networks pointed to the key problem with this: What could the Puppets have done? Thousands of witnesses, including foreign diplomats, could attest that the Union had emerged from the Free City mouth of the Puppet Axis without having entered the Port Stubbs mouth. The Congregate already had lost the dreadnought *Parizeau* and the Freyja Axis; what would declaring war on the Puppets do? If the Congregate did declare war on the Federation of Puppet Theocracies, it would be seen as a naked grab for the Puppet Axis, an act certain to draw the Anglo-Spanish Banks into the conflict.

Only hours after the Union breakout into Epsilon Indi, secret bidding had begun for a working sample of whatever propulsion system had been used. And as soon as the full scale of what was happening at the Freyja Axis broke in the news, the bidding became ferocious.

Five days later, the ownership of a series of corporate accounts in the First Bank of the Anglo-Spanish Plutocracy changed hands—first to the discreet broker and then to the crew, while the automated and utterly nondescript *Boyacá*, carrying ore and the damaged but functional inflaton racer, joined the shipping orbits of the Epsilon Indi system to rendezvous with its new owner.

The final haul was twelve million Congregate francs each, four times what they'd expected, enough to live many lifetimes. Belisarius set up the trust account for William's daughter with an Anglo-Spanish law firm, with additional instructions to move Kate and her mother out of system with new identities.

"To William," Belisarius said, toasting gently with a bulb of wine in the micro-gravity. Cassandra, beside him, hugged him with one arm and toasted with the other. He put his arm over her shoulders.

"What are you going to do with your money, quantum man?" Stills' speakers asked. "Buy yourself some more mountaintops to shit on?"

"I haven't decided," Belisarius said. "Isn't that what money is about? Having the chance to do whatever you want?"

"You got yourself another racer, too," Stills pressed. "What are you going to do with that?"

"Travel in style."

"With a target on your back."

"Maybe," Belisarius said. "Depends where I go."

"Pity is, you can't even fly it like it's supposed to be flown."

"What do you mean?"

"You can't pull the G's it can take," Stills said. "It's a beautiful piece of hardware."

"Are you going to miss flying it?" Marie asked.

"Unless I go fly for the Union."

"What?" Belisarius said. Marie choked red wine out her nose.

"The Congregate is still the biggest navy there is," Stills said, "but they haven't got the biggest cock anymore. If I want to fly the best fighters in civilization, I gotta fly for the Union."

"You're a client of the Congregate," Marie said.

"Like hell," Stills said. "The tribe never signed a patronage accord. We're contractors of the Congregate, but our contracts have all the right clauses."

"You can't join the Union, you moron!" Marie said. "You're not African."

"I'm not an acid-sucking Venusian either, but I've been flying *tonnères* since I was a teenager. What are you, a patriot?"

"No," Marie said. "Go. I don't care. The Congregate's going to win in the end."

"Probably," Stills said, "but I bet you the Union has some beautiful fighters, and those fuckers have *cojones* the size of grapefruits."

"Are you going to do something stupid with your money, Marie?" Saint Matthew asked.

"I'm going to buy myself a nice, safe annuity," she said flatly. Then she laughed, unable to carry her own joke. "I didn't think that far. I thought we were all going to get shot. I don't know. I could buy a moon somewhere, or maybe a whole town on Venus. Ah... who am I kidding? I'll probably blow it on explosives and lottery tickets."

People did not drift out even by the early hours of the morning, so after a time Belisarius took Cassandra's hand and led her away, to his room. It did not have the star-view of his room on Ptolemy, nor the Spartan comforts of his suites in the Free City, but he'd strung small colored lights on the ceiling. He held her hands. She smiled in the soft glow.

He'd come so far. He'd left the Garret angry and frightened and bitter. He'd learned a new world and hid from his old one, and yet, in the end, his two worlds had interacted, like overlapping waves of possibilities. And somehow, in the interference of his two worlds, his anger and bitterness were lost, his fear was lost, and he'd been able to embrace his old curiosity. It was the nature of quantum logic that sometimes mutually exclusive states could coexist. He'd been right. Cassandra had been right. The truth, the final observation, was in the complexity of their interference.

"Do you think you'll be happy with me, Cassie?"

"Maybe," she said coyly. She held his hands tight, and he found himself holding hers back as tightly. "Bel, can you believe what we've done?"

They were still like children on their birthday, unable to believe their happiness. Her perceptions of the whole field while in the fugue, from Port Stubbs all the way to the Free City, would feed months, perhaps years, of analysis and theories. And neither had dared get too close to the time gates yet. They wanted, needed, to explore them together. Nor had they plumbed the depths of the new structure of Belisarius's brain, and the tentative peace he'd found with the quantum objectivity running there.

"You came back to me," she said.

"And you came into the wide world with me."

She nodded happily, seven point two centimeters from his face. Her fingers were cool in his.

"Now that we're criminals on the run, what do you suppose we'll do all day, Bel?"

"We could figure out the time gates."

"You're certainly not like other men," she teased, nearing. Three point seven centimeters. "You never thought to just bring flowers?"

"I thought we'd like this better," he said.

He neared, until her lips were four millimeters from his.

"Let's make theories together," she whispered.

He nodded, and then there was no distance left to count.

ACKNOWLEDGEMENTS

BECAUSE IT'S MORE dramatic to do things in threes, I would like to make three sets of thank yous.

Thank you to the East Block Irregulars, the critiquing group who over the years have done so much to make me a better writer: Matt Moore, Peter Atwood, Hayden Trenholm, Liz Westbrook-Trenholm, Marie Bilodeau, Geoff Gander, Agnes Cadieux, Kate Heartfield.

Thank you to readers Matthew Johnson, Kate Heartfield, Geoff Gander, Desirina Boskovich, Ranylt Richildis, Marie Bilodeau, Kate Heartfield, Nicole Lavigne, Matt Moore, Agnes Cadieux for incisive comments on initial drafts of The Quantum Magician.

Thank you to Kim-Mei Kirtland, a brilliant literary agent, and to excellent editors Jonathan Oliver and Trevor Quachri.

DEREK KÜNSKEN

Derek Künsken has built genetically engineered viruses, worked with street children and refugees in Latin America, served as a Canadian diplomat, and, most importantly, taught his son about super-heroes and science. His short fiction has appeared in *Analog Science Fiction and Fact*, *Beneath Ceaseless Skies* and multiple times in *Asimov's Science Fiction*. His stories have been adapted into audio podcasts, reprinted in various Year's Best anthologies, and translated into multiple languages. They have also been short-listed for various awards, and won the *Asimov's* Readers' Award in 2013. He tweets from @derekkunsken, blogs at BlackGate.com, and makes his internet home at DerekKunsken.com.